DEAD BECKONING

MIKE COBB

Dead Beckoning by Mike Cobb

ISBN 978-0-578-33988-7 (pbk.)

MG Cobb Books LLC

www.mgcobb.com

First Edition, March 2022

To the memory of
Dorothy Barker.

Map of Atlanta

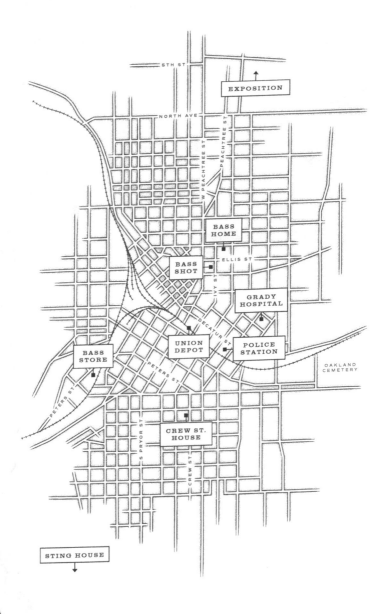

Map of Exposition

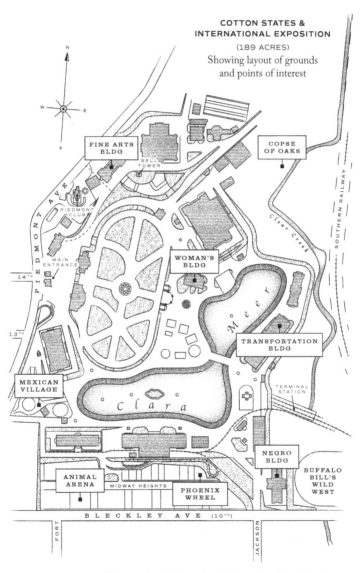

COTTON STATES &
INTERNATIONAL EXPOSITION
(189 ACRES)
Showing layout of grounds
and points of interest

N

W E

S

FINE ARTS
BLDG

BELL
TOWER

COPSE
OF OAKS

PIEDMONT
CLUB

PIEDMONT AVE

WOMAN'S
BLDG

MAIN
ENTRANCE

14TH

13TH

Clear Creek

SOUTHERN RAILWAY

Meer

TRANSPORTATION
BLDG

MEXICAN
VILLAGE

Clara

TERMINAL
STATION

NEGRO
BLDG

BUFFALO
BILL'S
WILD
WEST

ANIMAL
ARENA

MIDWAY HEIGHTS

PHOENIX
WHEEL

BLECKLEY AVE (10TH)

FORT

JACKSON

SOURCE: *Grant Wilkins, C.E. for the Cotton States & International Exposition Co.*

Major Characters

BAKER AUGUSTUS BASS
A prominent Atlanta merchant who moved from Thomasville, Georgia with his wife, Ella, to start a new business.

ELLA MCKINNON BASS
Baker Bass's wife, a socialite from Thomasville.

JOHN BASS
Baker and Ella Bass's eldest child.

COMMISSIONER J.C.A. BRANAN
An Atlanta police commissioner.

DET. ED CASON
An Atlanta detective.

WILL COLEMAN
A young Negro porter at Aragon Hotel.

DET. THOMAS GREENBERRY "GREEN" CONN
An Atlanta detective.

SARAH CONN
Green Conn's sister.

CHIEF ARTHUR CONNOLLY
Atlanta police chief.

DELORES DAMPMAN
A friend of Herbert Jenkins and frequenter of a local brothel.

DR. WILLIAM GILBERT

The Fulton County (Atlanta) medical examiner.

HERBERT THOMAS JENKINS

A traveling tobacco salesman.

CHRISTOPHER JOHNSON

A local Negro. In and out of work farm.

FRANK KEELER

A newspaper reporter.

CAPTAIN W.P. MANLY

Captain of the Atlanta police force.

DET. WILLIAM MEHAFFEY

An Atlanta detective.

THADDEUS MONCRIEF

An Atlanta policeman.

LEMUEL P. "LEM" MUREAU

A traveling tobacco salesman from out of town.

CORONER JACKSON PADEN

The Fulton County (Atlanta) coroner.

CECIL THOMPSON

An Atlanta policeman.

A Word of Caution

IN A WORK OF HISTORICAL FICTION, THERE IS OFTEN tension between fidelity to the time period and the risk of offending the reader. Certain offensive words and cultural norms, which are unacceptable today, are used throughout this work. While the decision to use them was not taken lightly, their presence is important to the historical accuracy and integrity of the story. It is hoped that their incorporation will, at the very least, shed light on a period in our history when attitudes and mores that are taboo today were commonplace. Their use is not intended in any way to disrespect the reader or any group of people.

Introduction

IN MOST STORIES OF IMPORT, OUTCOMES TURN ON A seminal event, without which there would be no story at all. As for the narrative that will unfold on these pages, that event occurred on a rain-soaked Friday. The year was 1895. The place was downtown Atlanta. The cast of characters were perhaps not atypical of those you would have encountered in any small but up-and-coming American city at the turn of the century. On that day, as dawn was breaking, a single gunshot pierced the early morning air. A prominent downtown businessman lay writhing on the wet pavement. He was an ambitious man, a proud husband and father. He worked hard to support his family against what sometimes seemed insurmountable odds. He would die within a few hours. His passing would remain one of a handful of high profile, unresolved deaths in the history of the city. Did he die from his own hand? Or was he murdered? And if so, by whom?

But stories of any meaning or merit turn on much more than just one event. The event is merely the inflection point. The real narrative, the one truly worth telling, runs much deeper and broader. This story is based on a good but dispirited man, his short life and untimely death, and the story of the days and months that preceded, and followed, that ill-fated August morning, when others before us walked the city's streets.

This is a work of historical fiction based on actual events. While conjecture and presumptions of form, character and detail have been added to enhance the story, and liberties have been taken as to the salient, underlying facts of means, motive, opportunity and deed, the principals' names have been retained from the annals of history. Primary events, people and places portrayed in this account are taken from historical sources.

Part One

THE SHOPKEEPER

ONE

BAKER BASS

Spring-Coiled

ON THAT FRIDAY MORNING HE WOKE EARLY, WELL before sunup, as was his custom. To start the day later was unthinkable. He, like most of his friends and fellow merchants, had been raised on a working farm. The life of cultivators and scythes and flails and furrows, of broody hens and cotton mules, didn't have much regard for anything other than backbreaking labor, determination, and perseverance. He may have left that world behind, but not the deep-seated work ethic that made him who he was.

He sat on the edge of the bed vacillating between recalling times past and pondering how this day would unfold. He ran his hand across the bedspread's popcorn stitching, feeling the little knobs run across his calloused skin like tiny perturbances across an otherwise quiescent sea of white.

He reached out to the bedside table for his watch and chain, inserting the fob through the buttonhole in his vest. He twisted the watch stem, turn by turn, careful not to overwind as he felt the crown tighten against his thumb and forefinger. He stood up from the bed, placed the watch in his vest pocket and made his way down the darkened hallway. He savored the earthy aroma emanating from the far rear of the house. Ella, his wife of twenty years, would have risen before him to make the coffee. He could make out the faint glow from the coal embers under the tin pot and could hear the clink of ceramic cups and saucers as she prepared the kitchen table.

Twenty-three years away from Palmyra, from the workaday grind of a North Carolina cotton farm, had changed him in so many ways. What would life have been like if he had stayed behind and eked out a hardscrabble existence with Robert and Jesse and the lot of them? The war that had riven the country, pitting North against South, had destroyed much of what they had worked hard for and had left burned-out homesteads and wiped-out crops. But in some ways life had been more unburdened back then. At times his thoughts would take him back to those days. Fishing for carp on Quankey Creek with crickets, grubs, and week-old dough bait. Sitting in the only room in the house big enough to accommodate the entire family, worn out and dog-tired after a full day in the field, and sharing stories ranging from drudgery to derring-do as the flames lap the sides of the hearth. It seemed an eternity ago. But those were the days of his youth. And perhaps they could never be recaptured. Perhaps if he had stayed behind things would be little different from his life now in the city.

"With whom are we sharing the honors this morning, Ella?" he asked, with a smile, as he passed through the doorway and into the kitchen, "Mr. Arbuckle or Mr. Maxwell?"

She wiped the sweat from her brow with the cotton dish towel that she always kept tucked in her apron pocket. She ran the palms of her hands along the sides of her chignoned hair, greying at the temples, and then breezily down the front of her apron bib, as if to ensure her presentability.

"Mr. Maxwell today," she replied. "Mr. Arbuckle decided to take off for a spell."

"Off to New York, no doubt," he quipped, letting out a half-suppressed laugh.

It was a standing joke. Both he and Ella preferred Arbuckle's Ariosa for its rich flavor and egg-and-sugar glaze, a patented enhancement intended to prolong the freshness of the beans. But since it originated in Brooklyn, it was harder to find than the pre-roasted blend named for the Maxwell House hotel in Nashville. Pre-roasted coffee was a convenience they had grown accustomed to, but they missed the days when the beans would be roasted in a skillet over an open fire, filling the house with the fragrance of toasted nuts.

"Ella, I heard yesterday that Oliver Wendell Holmes died. It happened late last year. I don't know how I missed it. Surely it would have been in the papers."

"How did he die?" she asked, looking up from the coffee pot she held in her hand.

"I don't know. They say he just fell asleep and passed quietly. When my time comes that's the way I want to go."

"Well, let's hope you don't have to worry about that anytime soon," she replied.

"I should hope not."

"What made you think of him?"

"Well, hearing of his passing reminded me of that splendid little book, *Over the Teacups*. Do you remember it?"

Ella nodded. She set the coffee pot in the center of the table.

"A quote from the book lingers, 'The morning cup of coffee has an exhilaration about it which the cheering influence of the afternoon or evening cup of tea cannot be expected to reproduce.' My morning cup, that's what gets me going," he paused, "and, of course, the few minutes I have to spend with you before confronting the day."

"Sit down, Baker," she said. "You seem spring-coiled." Ella seated herself at one end of the kitchen table. "I always enjoy your early morning banter. It's one of the things that first attracted me to you. But it does little to conceal an ever-present restlessness."

"You don't need to be distracted by my concerns," he protested. He sat down across from her. "I'll be OK."

"But I do worry about you. Always."

"Ella, we came here to start a new life. I am an ambitious man. You know that. But I learned a long time ago that things are never as easy as we would like. There are inescapable setbacks along the way. Always. But each of us has to figure out how to deal with them, on his own terms, and press on. You have enough to occupy your day without having to worry about me."

He looked away. Their eighteen-year-old son John sauntered into the room, grabbed a chair and parked himself between them on the long side of the table without saying a word. He reached across the table and poured himself a cup.

"Good morning, John. You could at least grace us with a howdy-do," she said. She swept her hand across the table toward her husband. "Your father's in the room too, you know."

"I'm sorry, Mother, good morning. And to you as well, Father," John said, as Baker looked up. "I don't intend to be disrespectful. It's just that I don't share your fondness for rising hours before daybreak. I guess engaging in conversation at four in the morning is something I just haven't mastered yet."

"Good morning, John. You're forgiven, but you will learn with age that manners and the art of conversation know no time of day. Are you going to the exposition grounds again this morning?" Baker asked.

"I am. I'm still working in the Transportation Hall. The way things are going I doubt we'll be finished until midnight, or later, only hours before the fair opens. It's only two weeks out, you know." John paused. His mouth curved into a smile. "They say they'll bring the *General* down from Tennessee in a few days. That will be a high point of the whole caboodle as far as I'm concerned."

For three decades, Baker had heard stories of Andrews' Raid. He had been a mere eight years old when James Andrews, a civilian spy and contraband merchant, led a Union party behind Confederate lines to Big Shanty, north of Atlanta, and commandeered the train engine. The men headed toward Chattanooga, destroying tracks and telegraph lines along the way. But they ran out of steam north of Ringgold. Confederate soldiers, fast on their trail, caught up with and captured them. Eight men were tried as spies and hanged. Andrews was one of them. The *General* had been retired from service four years ago and stored in a siding in Vinings, just across the Chattahoochee River from Atlanta, before being restored and taken on tour, first to the Columbian Exposition in Chicago. And now it would be on display again, at the Cotton States exposition, scheduled to open in Atlanta in two and a half weeks.

"And why are you so mighty eager to see a locomotive? You can see them all day just a mile or so across town," he needled John.

"Because, Father." John shook his head in apparent disbelief. "The *General* is not just any locomotive. It's the most famous iron horse of the war. You know that better than I. I only wish I could have been there to see the stringing up of that good-for-nothing Andrews and the whole damned lot of them. They got what they deserved."

"Will you be home for supper, Baker?" Ella changed the subject, looking past John.

"I expect so," he said. "I'm meeting with Jenkins later today. I don't believe you've ever met him. He's the man who comes to town and sells me tobacco. But I should be home by seven."

Baker rose from the table and retrieved his coat and hat. Ella followed him into the living room. She reached out and touched his hand. He was not one to show affection, but that morning they embraced as they stood together in the partially lit room.

He pulled the collar of his coat jacket tight around his neck to fend off the wind and rain as he stood just outside the threshold of the front door. The morning was cooler than usual. He could see the water droplets bouncing off the ladder bars on the lamp post halfway up the block as if they were performing a choreographed dance, casting tiny reflections in the dark. A tortoiseshell tomcat scurried across the street. He could make out the faint clip-clop of a dray horse in the distance. "Yet another rainy day," he muttered behind his mustache as he descended the three steps leading from his front porch to the sidewalk's edge. He never carried an umbrella, would never have considered it. In fact, he disdained them. He considered them inherently unmanly, preferring instead to rely on the brim of his Homburg.

Baker wondered whether perhaps there was some credence after all to the prevailing superstition of the day that, due to recently discovered sunspots measuring nine times the Earth's diameter, and invoking an image of truly biblical proportions, a rain on the first dog day meant rain every day for forty days and forty nights thereafter.

That morning, as every morning, he planned to walk the one and a half miles to his store on the edge of town, anticipating the day's events each step of the way. Most days when he arrived, being the creature of habit he was, he would open the store and before the day unfolded have breakfast sent to him from Carrie Mangham's eating house five doors down. He had heard her say more than once that, while she learned the basics clinging to her mother's apron as a child, she honed her cooking skills under the recent tutelage of a freed, illiterate slave named Abby Fisher and her book, *What Mrs. Fisher Knows About Southern Cooking*, the dictation of which had been entrusted to friends. Baker thought, *Miss Mangham learned well from her mother and the mulatto from South Carolina. Even Ella can't come close to matching her talents in the kitchen.* He felt a slight tug on the buttons of his vest. *Perhaps the skinny boy from Palmyra isn't so lean anymore. Surely Miss Mangham is to blame, in part, for that.*

When he first bought the store he had tried different routes to break the routine with an occasional diversion. The most direct one, the one he reckoned he would take this morning, would take him down Ivy Street, through downtown and past the Union Depot. He would choose to endure the congestion and grime and soot from the constant comings and goings of the steam trains rather than take a less direct route. And as he passed most mornings, he would peer up at the station's broad center arch, mansard roof, pilaster-flanked windows and brick cupola, straining to see them through the dark. He would admire the building's majesty with a reverence reserved for such things as he had not been exposed to before moving to the city. Even General Sherman, whose troops had burned its predecessor to the ground as they marched to the sea, would have marveled at its splendor. The route would take him along Lloyd Street across the railroad tracks. At Peters Street he would turn right and walk about eight more blocks to his store near the East Tennessee, Virginia & Georgia freight depot.

Although it had been worse in prior years, the crime rate was still high. Anyone walking the streets before sunup bore a palpable risk of assault. He knew that all too well. But while protecting himself from an unknown assailant was on his mind, there were other preoccupations that took him off his guard that morning.

Am I paranoid, or is the world falling apart?

We're close to sending our boys off to fight again, this time on another man's soil. I don't care what President Cleveland says. How long can we stay out of that damned mess in Cuba? We'll send them down there and they'll come back in palls. The last thing we need is another war. It took years to get over the last one.

And the economy. God knows, we've been through a lot. I bring my family to the city to start anew. To make my fortune. And no sooner do we arrive than the whole country falls into a depression. The Panic of '93. I don't know who named it that, but I can't think of a better word to describe it. I'm no financial expert—never claimed to be. But when the gold reserve plummets almost overnight. When the stock market crashes a month later. When banks are calling in loans and refusing to issue new ones. When money is so scarce you wonder how you can possibly settle the debts that fill page after page of your account book.

When businesses are shutting down all around you, you don't need to be a financial expert to know you could be next. I've gotten by, but I have another two years, at least, before I fully recover.

And as if that weren't enough, something unexpected comes along out of nowhere, something much more personal. Like a stranger coming up behind you, tapping you on the shoulder and then leveling you to the ground before you have a chance to react. And then, just as you're finding your feet, he knocks you down again. That's what it feels like.

There had been accusations. Double-dealing. Even arrests. Charges had been made against him that were unsettling, and he worried about the outcome. What would it all mean for him and, more importantly, for his family?

His thoughts turned to Ella. In his mind he saw her peering through the window that morning as he looked back one last time before making his way down the street. He saw her furrowed brow, the drawn skin around her tired eyes and the lines on her face that bespoke the hard life she had endured since the move. Lines that had been absent not that many years ago. A stark contrast to the delicate, cheery-eyed, carefree young lady he remembered when he first laid eyes on her outside the old store back in Thomasville.

BAKER BASS

Thomasville

TWENTY-THREE YEARS AWAY FROM PALMYRA. HAS IT *really been that long?* Baker thought back to the day he decided to leave.

He was eighteen. His older brother Robert, twenty-six and married at the time, had taken over tending to the farm, with the help of Jesse and the rest of the Bass clan. The clan—hell, it wasn't a clan—it was more like a horde—a throng—a herd. Mama, Papa, and a run of fourteen children. For Christ's sake, they could barely put food on the table. He knew he had to move on.

He remembered it was a Thursday evening in the middle of June as he sat alone on the back stoop of the farmhouse. Or was it a Wednesday? Or a Friday? It didn't really matter. "By damn it's hot," he groused under his breath. The temperature had gotten up to ninety-five in the middle of the day but, mercifully, things were cooling off as the sun began its descent. Every fiber of his tattered, denim dungarees was soaked from a full day in the cotton fields. His joints ached like an old man's. He wiped his forehead with the back of his sun-cracked, boll-scratched hand, sending the beads of sweat flying into the evening air like tiny flickering shards of glass. In his other palm he held a handful of wild blackberries gathered from the bramble bushes on the dirt path back to the house. He could hear the rolling, guttural give-and-take of yellow-billed cuckoos—first close by—*ka ka ka ka kow kow kow*—then farther away—*ka ka ka ka kow kow kow*—then close by again. Back and forth. He tossed the berries into his mouth, savoring the juice as he bit through the skin, the perfect balance of sweet and tart playing on his tongue. He bent forward and spit a mouthful of bitter seeds onto the ground. A tiger swallowtail fluttered across the yard and landed for a moment on a tulip tree leaf. Just then another swallowtail appeared. He watched as they flew away in a courtship dance, disappearing into the distance. "It's time," he blurted out, startling himself in mid-sentence and looking right, left and behind to make sure no one was within earshot. "I think I'd best be moving on."

He gazed into the distance, past the tulip tree, past the brambles, past the cotton barn. The hills beyond were washed with a palette of luminescent pastels as the sun set behind him. "But where?" Up to that point his universe had not extended past the confines of Palmyra. What little he knew of the rest of the world, he knew from the books Miss Pennypacker would loan him. "Knuckle Whacker Pennypacker." That's what the kids called her back in grammar school. His fingers hurt at the mere thought of her approaching from behind and popping them with a ruler. But had *he* called her that? Where she could *hear* him? The singular person in his life who had instilled in him a love of reading? Thanks to Miss Pennypacker, he would soak up whatever he could put his hands on—books, flyers and merchandise catalogs retrieved from Phelps' general store, the occasional out-of-town letter.

"Wait. The letter from Wiley. Where did I put it?" He jumped up, pivoted to face the house, and ran inside, the screen door slamming behind him. He went straight to the bedroom he shared with three others and lit the oil lamp sitting on the nightstand. He found the letter, folded carefully in its original envelope, in the bottom drawer, his drawer. The top drawer was Jesse's. He retrieved the envelope and held it under the lamp. The return address read "Mr. Wiley Bass, Bass Farm, Ochlocknee, Thomasville, Georgia." Baker's second cousin, on his father's side and two years his senior, had written him a year earlier urging him to visit. He removed the letter, unfolded it and read it aloud. The closing passage jumped out:

> Yankees are moving here in droves and they're bringing their money with them. The weather is warm, it never snows, and hunting and fishing are abundant. Oh, and did I tell you about the young ladies in these parts?

Baker rummaged through the cigar box he kept stored in the drawer. He had a little money saved up, not much but enough to get him to Thomasville and tide him over until he found work. Breaking the news to Mama and Papa was not easy. Papa understood but Mama took it hard, so hard that she let out a thunderous yowl and proceeded to cry for days. He tried to console her, knowing how hard it must have been to see one of her own move so far away. "Don't worry, Mama. I'll come home to visit. And I'll write often. At least once a week. You can be sure of that." He held her hand and rested his head on her shoulder.

"Hell, they probably would have done the same thing at your age if they had been in your shoes and had had the opportunity," Jesse had said. Papa gave him a few dollars to help him get by. He packed a single weather-worn valise, purchased second hand from Phelps' store. Jesse drove him twenty-five miles by wagon to the Eagle Tavern in Halifax. There he boarded the first available westbound coach and traveled one hundred fifty more miles to the newly formed town of Greensboro. It took him three days, with horses swapped out along the way. He figured it would have taken two if the second driver hadn't fostered a bit too strong a romance with a bottle of Old Forester whisky at the layover at Casso's Inn in Raleigh. When they reached Greensboro the coach driver let him off right in front of the single-track stop on Elm Street.

"You stand right over yonder," the driver had told him. "They'll be a train come along directly. Just make sure you get on the one to Atlanta, otherwise you may end up in Charleston."

He got on the right train with the help of an officious conductor––OK, perhaps that wasn't the right word––but the man was a bit too authoritarian for his taste. Almost nine hours later, the train pulled into the Union Depot in Atlanta. He descended the steps from the train car, valise in hand, and located the Western Union window. He retrieved his cousin's letter from the side pocket of the valise, where he had placed it for easy access, and read the return address. He composed a telegram to Wiley—"COMING TO VISIT ARRIVE LATE TOMORROW BAKER BASS STOP"—and paid the attendant forty-five cents. He would have sent it earlier, but Western Union offices were hard to come by. Hopefully his cousin would get it in time and would come to greet him. He then purchased a ticket on the next Macon-bound local. The man at the ticket window had warned him that his journey would take him through a circuitous assemblage of towns—to Macon, then on to Savannah and west to Thomasville.

"Ain't always been that way," the ticket man had told him, "but them boys, Sherman's boys, they took them tracks, pulled 'em up, heated 'em til they was red hot, twisted 'em and made hair-pins out of 'em. It'll take years to get 'em back the way they used to be."

After two more train changes, Baker arrived in Thomasville. He leaned out the window as the train pulled into the depot. He saw his cousin standing on the platform awaiting him, a broad grin on his face.

Soon after arriving, he took a single room at the Davis-Hall boarding house. Mrs. Hall—it would be months before he learned her first name—ushered him up the stairway to the second floor. As they climbed the stairs she recited the house rules, one-by-one.

"We're early risers here. Breakfast is at six o'clock sharp. If you're more than twenty minutes late you don't eat."

Baker grinned. Six o'clock wasn't early. Not where he came from.

"Lunch. You're on your own. Supper is served at seven. Family style. That's when you'll get to know your housemates. We're all good people. Down-home people. God-fearing Christians. Have you found a church home yet?"

He shook his head. "No ma'am, I just got here."

"Well, you will. We have plenty to choose from.

"Yours is at the end of the hall. Your room, that is. The last one on the right. No smoking in there. If you want to smoke you can do it in the parlor downstairs. Outside is better.

"And no loud noises after nine. Some of our people go to bed early. And I lock the doors at eleven. If you're not in by then, don't knock on the door askin' me to let you in, cause I won't. You can sleep on the porch."

At the landing halfway up the stairs, she stopped and swung around to face him. "No liquor in the house. Period. And no lady friends upstairs. Ever. That'll get you kicked out faster than anything."

He nodded. When she opened the door to his room, the first thing that jumped out at him was the wallpaper, faded and peeling along the picture rail. Pineapples!! Hideous pineapples of green, brown and yellow. He envisioned waking up to tremors each morning. He scanned the room. The hodgepodge of disparate pieces of furniture, all of which had seen better days, looked as if they had been thrown together by a blind man. A standard size single bed with iron frames that rattled and squeaked when he sat on the bed's edge. A writing table with cabriole legs, one of which had been repaired with an artful contrivance of baling wire. A straight-backed chair with a fiddle splat. A table lamp with a tarnished, filigreed casting at the base. And a small storage chest that could have come from the Newport barracks. It would do. He swung the bed around and pushed it as close to the front wall as he could, with the baseboard facing the window so that when he awoke each morning he would open his eyes to the dawning of a new day…and not the pineapples.

Staying with his cousin was out of the question. It was too far out. He needed to be able to walk to work, wherever work ended up being, but surely it would be in town. He set out to find a job, as his dwindling cash reserves would only cover a month's worth of room and board. He trudged up and down the crisscross of streets in the business section of town…Broad…Jackson…

Monroe…stopping at each commercial house and storefront. Most people he talked to had nothing to offer, but on Crawford Street he landed a chance to prove his mettle as a clerk in a general store owned by Edward Pennington, one of those Yankees his cousin had written about. The store was housed in a two-story frame building. Pennington and his wife lived upstairs.

"Let me make something clear, Bass," Pennington rasped, a half-smoked cigar resting between his right thumb and forefinger, "I don't know you and I don't know where you come from. But I'm willing to give you a try."

Pennington stepped from behind the front counter, stacked shoulder-high with boxes of newly arrived merchandise. The glow from the overhead lamp reflected off his fly-rink head.

"There are rules around here that you need to know. Your job is to dust and stock," he said, pointing to the boxes and pronouncing the words so they came out sounding more like dusht and shtock. "No interacting with my patrons until you've shown yourself to be a worthy underling. And get here on time. I don't take kindly to tardiness. You'll have two fifteen-minute breaks, one in the morning and one in the afternoon. Do you understand? Fifteen minutes. And thirty minutes for lunch. And I'd just as soon you don't take your breaks and lunches inside."

For a moment Baker thought he must be back at the boarding house listening to Mrs. *No First Name* Hall bark out commands like a quartermaster sergeant. Did he really want to end up kowtowing to two overbearing order givers? He took the job anyway. He assumed it wouldn't be easy, seeing as how he had never worked in a store before. But he was up for the task, and surely it would be no harder than farm work. He would put in his time and decide whether clerking was right for him. If not, he would have saved up a little money and could move on.

The task was easier than he had imagined. After all, how hard is it to unpack boxes and barrels and crates and stick their contents on the shelves? To pick up a rag and clear the dust from the countertops or grab a broom and sweep the dirt from one end of the store to the other before you discharge it in a violent haze out the back door? Truth be told, he was downright bored, and each day he yearned for something, anything, to break the monotony.

One afternoon, after just a few weeks on the job, Baker was standing outside the store on one of his "don't-take-'em-inside" breaks. He looked up to see Wiley walking down the street, approaching from the corner of Jackson and Crawford. He was accompanied by two young ladies. Baker recognized one of them as Wiley's future wife, whom he had met when he first got to town. He remembered seeing the other one out and about. The last words in Wiley's letter, right before its closing, popped into his head. *Oh, and did I tell you about the young…*

"Baker Bass," his cousin called out as he walked up.

"Hello Wiley. I haven't seen you almost since the day I got here. And I thought you were my friend, being my cousin and all. What the dickens have you been up to?" Baker nudged Wiley on the shoulder with his closed fist.

"Of course we're friends, Baker. It's just been hard to get off the plow lately," Wiley replied as he glanced over his shoulder. "You remember my fiancée, Miss Rebecca Singletary?"

"I do indeed. Good afternoon Miss Singletary." Baker's hand reflexively touched the brim of his boater.

"And Baker, I'd like you to meet Miss Ella McKinnon. Rebecca and Miss McKinnon went to school together."

"Good afternoon, Miss McKinnon. It's a pleasure to meet you."

"Likewise, Mr. Bass," she smiled, engaging but never making direct eye contact, as a slight blush crept over her face.

Her modesty belies her beauty, Baker thought. He found it endearing and mysterious in an odd sort of way. And he was intrigued by the scent, however faint, of bergamot and lavender. Courtship had not been top of mind, given his preoccupation with proving himself at daily drudgery so Mr. *Dusht and Shtock* Pennington would give him more responsibility, but he decided right then that he wanted to get to know this Miss McKinnon girl.

He finally mustered the courage to ask her to join him for a Saturday visit to Bryan Branch. Leisurely strolls and an occasional rendezvous under the gnarly limbs of the Big Oak, Thomasville's imposing live oak at the corner of Crawford and Monroe, would follow. Word in town was that the Big Oak was almost two centuries old at the time and was the largest oak tree east of the Mississippi. Its massive branches, spreading over fifty feet in every direction and blanketing the ground below it with cool shade, made for a perfect place for afternoon picnics.

Over time, as they would come to sit under that tree almost every weekend, he learned that her given name was Ellinor. He learned that she had attended the Thomasville Female Seminary, a school for girls founded by Miss Cornelia Hansell and touted as one of the finest institutions in the South for the proper education of young ladies. Her father, a prominent farmer and merchant, had vowed to give his only child an upbringing befitting the family's standing. She came from a long line of Thomas County citizens who could trace their American roots all the way back to before the Revolutionary War. Baker dared not tell her, lest she think he was bragging, that his own roots went back even further—to Jamestown. He had heard the stories of the colonists' exploits ever since he was a toddler—of King James and the Virginia Company, of the *Susan Constant's* journey across the Atlantic, of John Rolfe and Pocahontas—stories handed down across generations. As he grew older he wondered whether those tales of adventure were nothing more than an attempt to recapture the family's past glory. But none of that mattered anymore. The scrabble of Palmyra was testament to that.

It was under the Big Oak, on a swelteringly hot July morning less than three years after he had first arrived in Thomasville, that Baker asked Ella to marry him. He thought that towering, centuries-old tree was fitting for the occasion. Four months later, on a blustery evening in the middle of November, they exchanged vows. Each was twenty-one. The wedding took place at McKinnon's Grove, the rambling farm where Ella had been reared. The Methodist church was considered, but only fleetingly. Having been built only a few years earlier, it replaced its twenty-seven year old predecessor, dilapidated from lack of repair and heavy use as a Confederate hospital. But the new church was just a plain, white frame building with nothing to set it apart, save for its only distinguishing feature, a dramatic steeple-like cupola.

So there he was, the boy from hardscrabble Palmyra, plopped smack-dab into a foreign world, one of privilege and polish, of gentlefolk and upper crust. It required some getting used to, but he took to it with relish. Thanks in large part to the largess of Ella's father, they settled into a new home just outside of town, with southern magnolia trees, rolling hardwoods, and an abundant pecan orchard. They named it, fittingly, Magnolia Farm. He stood on the front lawn and looked up the steps to the columned porch, with steep pitched roof and three dormer windows above. To his left was a meadow. In the distance, beyond the grassy field, was a copse of hardwoods. An early-morning dew had formed on the blades of grass. The sun reflected off the water droplets, blanketing the meadow in a patina of white. It reminded him of the cotton fields back home. He let out a loud chortle. *What has it been? Three years? I've gone from picking, drying and cleaning cotton bolls to—what do they call it?—walking in tall cotton,* he thought. *What did she possibly see in me that would have possessed her to invite me into her world? I was like that kid from the side of the tracks where the coal dust settles—and she was this refined young lady from Miss Hansell's finishing school.* He shook his head in disbelief.

From their first stroll down Monroe Street, Baker and Ella had enjoyed a simpatico liaison, *something* between them that neither could quite pinpoint but that they both were thankful for. They were made for each other. She had taught him to shed his back home ways and backward cant. He had taught her grit and perseverance, qualities she had never needed in the bounds of Thomasville. And each was the better for it.

For Baker, the hardest part was adjusting to Miss Lula Boynton and Sukie, the fledgling half-breed. His own family was never fortunate enough to have had servants, let alone ones that insinuated themselves into the household as if they were kin. He knew Miss Lula was fiercely devoted to the only family she had ever known. Why, she had practically raised Ella from infancy. Born on the McKinnon farm as a slave, she had chosen to stay with the family after her deliverance, even as those around her chose to fly away. Baker still had trouble getting used to her and the other one living on the farm.

But he was grateful when, two years into their marriage, Miss Lula was there for the arrival of John. Baker and Ella were overcome with joy. *He has his mother's milk-blue eyes,* Baker thought as he held the baby in his arms for the first time, *and her dimples, ever so faint, playing at the corners of his mouth.*

Miss Lula was by Ella's side not just for the birthing part, but for the rearing part as well. Over the course of five years, two more sons would follow. Then, in 1884, Ella gave birth to Florence, but the baby contracted enteritis and lived only a few days. Florence's death was a painful reminder to Baker of his own sister's death as an infant. For a time they resigned themselves to the fate of having a brood of boys. But then, the following year, she found herself pregnant for the fifth time and gave birth to Mary.

In time, Pennington would give the underling clerk, who had spent his days dusting and stocking under his boss's overbearing eye, more duties. Baker began to interact with customers. In his spare time he scoured catalogs from up north, salvaged from his fellow boarders. He helped the old man bring in new merchandise. Smart things that the town had never seen before. *Afternoonified* products Baker called them. As the business grew he ended up running the store, with two junior clerks under his purview. Pennington's confidence in him grew, and the old man's watchful eye was not so watchful anymore. Pennington had even let him buy into the company. He was a businessman now, not just an employee. While it wasn't much, it was something he could call his own.

He was grateful for the opportunity, but he longed for more. *Here I am in my mid-thirties and still beholden to another man, he thought. I want my own place, with my name over the door.* But when he looked around town, at all the stores that had cropped up from so many Northern merchants settling there, he realized it wasn't the best place to start anew. It was getting harder every day to compete. The last thing the town needed was yet another store. Plus the old man would consider him a turncoat and would do whatever he could to drive his business into the ground.

One evening, at the end of the workday, he stood inside the entrance to the store. As he leaned against the door jamb he looked out at the comings and goings down Broad Street. It was flush with men in their vested suits and derbies, ladies in their petticoat-lined bustles and children riding bicycles and hoop trundling down the middle of the roadbed. He closed the double door, secured the lock and pulled the shades down. *Those damned carpetbaggers. They come down here to get rich on our backs,* he thought before catching himself. *But wait, Pennington is one of them, isn't he? He came here from Philadelphia because he saw an opportunity to better himself. You can't fault a man for that. I'd do the same if I could. I'd strike out for greener pastures in a heartbeat if the opportunity came along.*

He walked over to the oak counter that ran along the side wall, the full length of the front room, and rested his hand on the glass top. He panned the shelves lined with dry goods and tobacco, groceries and medicinals. His eyes fell on a bottle of Hamlin's Wizard Oil. On the label a traveling circus procession rolled into town. An African elephant, crouched on its knees, filled half the frame, its trunk wrapped around a medicine bottle as the tonic, labeled as the BEST PAIN REMEDY ON EARTH, gushed into its gaping mouth. Men and women, boys and girls, even a small dog, frolicked as the caravan proceeded down Main Street. There was something about that label, the heady thrill of adventure, of new faces in a new town, that aroused his wanderlust.

Once upon a time a young man of eighteen had sat on the back stoop of his home in Palmyra and had uttered the words, "I think I'd best be moving on." If ever there was a time to move on again, almost two decades later, it was now. On his ride home that evening his horse's gait was suspended in slow motion. He was oblivious to the normal jostling and jerking as he traveled the rutted road west of the city. His mind raced between thoughts of exploit and urgency. He pondered the possibilities. Going back to North Carolina was not an option, as there was no opportunity there. There was Florida, perhaps Tallahassee or Jacksonville. But Northern opportunists were flocking to the state, and he feared he would be no better off than in Thomasville. New Orleans was a possibility. He and Ella had gone to a trade fair there and had enjoyed the city. But it was four hundred miles away. Staying in Georgia made a lot of sense, but he really didn't know the state outside of the confines of Thomas County.

When he reached the farm, he tied up his horse and went straight to his roll top desk, barely acknowledging Ella standing in the hallway as he swept past her. He retrieved a map of Georgia and unfolded it. In the upper right hand corner was an inset of Savannah. That was a possibility. The town, like Thomasville, had been spared by the war. But he worried about yellow fever—"Yellow Jack" they called it. Just a few years earlier it had wiped out damned near twenty percent of the population. And hurricanes were the last thing he wanted to deal with. Right below the Savannah inset was a small map of Atlanta. A circle designated the city boundary. Inside the circle were Oakland Cemetery to the east, the Colored University to the west, the U.S. Army Barracks just below it, and a dizzying maze of streets and landmarks in between. Near the center were the State Capitol and City Hall. His only visit to the city had been when he changed trains on his trip south. But the map intrigued him. Ever since the war's end, the city had enjoyed a rebirth of sorts and was on a path to becoming a major trading center. With his fingertip he traced a line that coursed its way from Thomasville, through Albany, then Macon and to Atlanta.

In a small cubbyhole next to where the map had been, he found a rumpled copy of *The Sunny South*, Atlanta's weekly literary magazine. He had discovered it left in the store by a customer. When no one had claimed it after a week or so he brought it home, stuffed it into the cubbyhole, and there it had remained for over two years. He thumbed through it. Three pages in, his eyes landed on an article extolling the city's virtues.

> Of all points in the South, not one combines so many of the essentials for an ideal city as Atlanta. It is blessed with pure water and good air. It is healthy. It has never been visited by an epidemic of any kind. It is a progressive city, where everything new in science and art is sure to come. It is a city of churches and is without a peer in the observance of the Sabbath. Its people are cultivated and refined, and its morality is phenomenal. It is convenient, being a railroad center.

That same afternoon, as the spring breeze wafted through the magnolia blossoms, he sat on the front porch swing. He called for Ella to come and sit beside him.

"Here Ella. Please. Take this and read it," he said, turning to page three and handing the magazine to her. Ella took the magazine from his hand. She read aloud.

"What does this mean, Baker?" she asked. "Why are you showing this to me?"

"Ella, we have to leave."

"But why?" she asked, her eyes widening and her eyebrows tightening in a frown.

"Ella, there's no future for us here."

"But why Atlanta? It's so far away. Couldn't we move some place closer?"

"But where?"

"What about Albany? Or Tallahassee?" she replied.

"Those towns are no match for Atlanta. Do you know they say that in just ten years it will be the fourth largest city in the southeast, behind New Orleans, Nashville and Richmond? It's already hosted two international expositions, and another one, the largest ever in the South, is being planned right now. We could be there for it. We could be part of it. Do you remember a few years ago when we went to the one in New Orleans? This one will be even bigger. There's hope for us there, Ella. Not here. Not in Albany. Or Tallahassee. Or Valdosta. Or any other town within two hundred miles of where we're sitting."

"But how can we just pull up stakes? How will we get by?"

"We'll sell the farm. It will bring a pretty penny, I can tell you that. And with the money I've saved up, we'll have what we need to start over."

Ella wept. He had moved before. She never had. But duty to her husband prevailed and she relented. That autumn, having sold the farm, they headed north with all their possessions. They left Miss Lula and Sukie behind, knowing her father would see to their needs. It would take them six days to reach the city.

When they arrived and settled in, Baker opened a store, not unlike Pennington's, on Peters Street on the southwest side of town. He and Ella built a house on Ellis Street, one large enough to accommodate their family. Proud Victorian homes, adorned with elaborate arches, decorative panels, fancy brackets, and filigree, sat back a few feet from the inner edge of the sidewalk. Although the Bass home was modest compared to what they had given up, it was one of the few brick houses in the neighborhood at the time. The street was lined with oak trees, smallish when they moved there but with the promise of becoming majestic in future years, perhaps not as imposing at Thomasville's Big Oak, but majestic nevertheless. The sidewalks were paved with stones arranged in a smart herringbone pattern, although they had already begun to show signs of settling here and there. Unlike most of the streets in the city, the curbstones were crisp, with keen-edged corners and curb cuts, affording easy access for pedestrians, bicyclists and pram-pushers. The street itself was surfaced with rectangular cobblestones.

Unlike Ellis Street, Peters Street was much more commercial, anchored on its east side by railroad tracks and on its west by shops and industrial building facades. And then there was the East Tennessee, Virginia & Georgia freight depot not far from Baker's store. Sometimes, upon arriving at the store, he would stand outside and gaze up at the sign over the front door— DRY GOODS, TOBACCO AND SUNDRIES—and below it the solitary line, set apart in Clarendon font—*BAKER A. BASS, PROPRIETOR.*

He knew he had adjusted to things better than Ella. They were a world away from the small town fineries and social attention she had enjoyed in Thomasville. In the city they were just two out of seventy-five thousand souls struggling to survive. Some were surviving more than others, and he never forgot how fortunate he and Ella were. But it was still hard. One thing changed in contrast to his days in Thomasville. He always carried a handgun for protection. A .38 caliber Smith & Wesson.

THREE

BAKER BASS

A Catching Twinge

BAKER MADE HIS WAY DOWN ELLIS STREET THAT RAINY Friday morning at August's close, sidestepping the pools of water that had formed in the dips and hollows of the sidewalk. He shifted his feet to one side, barely missing the curb's edge. A catching twinge diffused through the muscle behind his right shoulder blade. He flinched. The discomfort was tolerable. He had experienced much worse. But it was a reminder of what had happened almost three months earlier. He rubbed the back of his shoulder and replayed the events of the afternoon in early June when two policemen had shown up at his store.

He had been standing on a ladder with his back to the room, stocking goods along the side wall, when they sauntered in. It was almost two thirty. He had not considered it out of the ordinary when he turned around and saw them standing in front of the merchandise counter, casual and nonchalant. He knew one of them from the regular Peters Street beat. The other he had never seen before.

"Good morning gentlemen," he spoke first, stepping down from the ladder. "On your rounds, I see."

"Mr. Bass?"

"Yes," he replied, knowing the one clearly knew his name without having to ask.

"Mr. Baker Bass, we have a warrant for your arrest. You must come with us."

"What could I possibly be under arrest for? I've done nothing wrong."

"You're under arrest for selling stolen goods," the unfamiliar one replied.

Baker stepped from behind the counter and looked around. The store was full of various and assorted items procured from various and assorted parties. "Stolen goods? What stolen goods? I don't know what you're talking about."

Again, the unfamiliar one spoke up. "Sir, you just need to come with us."

"But I demand to know what evidence you could possibly have against me."

"Mr. Bass, we don't have those details. We just have orders to haul you in. You'll have to take that up at the station house. Now please don't make any trouble."

"You're the ones making trouble. You can't do this to me."

"Like hell we can't," the familiar one replied.

Baker dug in his heels and placed his hands on his hips. The man he didn't know reached up and grabbed his right shoulder, burying his fingers into Baker's muscle and gripping so hard that a sharp pain radiated down his arm.

"Don't touch me. I'm an innocent man," Baker shouted as he jerked his shoulder away. The policeman thrust his right palm into Baker's chest, shoving him against the counter's edge. Baker lost his footing and started to fall, catching himself on the countertop with his right hand. He regained his balance and swung at the officer. That's when the other one, the one he knew, drew his pistol and aimed to the left of Baker's sternum.

"Listen Bass, either you cooperate or we'll drag you away in manacles. We'll parade you down the street for all creation to see. All your neighbors. And your regulars. We'll have a reporter here when you sashay down the street with chains on your ankles. You'll make the front page of tomorrow's paper. Is that what you want?"

"I'll tell you something right now." Baker steeled himself and wagged his finger in the men's faces. "I'll go along with your little charade because I have no choice. But rest assured you'll hear from my attorney. And when we go before the judge and they put YOU on the stand," he pointed his finger at the familiar one, "that's when you'll get exactly what you deserve. You can't just haul a man in for nothing."

Baker was trotted off, but not for long. His attorney, Thomas Glenn, made bail within the hour. Upon leaving the station house, Baker hightailed it straight to Glenn's office. He barged through the door, catching his attorney unawares and demanding to know about the charges against him.

"Don't spare me any details, Glenn," Baker roared as the door slammed behind him. "Tell me everything."

Glenn stood up from behind his desk and walked across the room to where Baker was standing. He made an arc in the air with the back of his hand, pointing to one of a pair of armchairs a few feet away.

"Pull up a chair and simmer down, Bass. I'll tell you what I know. But I warn you, it won't help if you get all in a lather over this."

As the two men sat across from each other, Glenn began to lay out the details behind the accusations.

"Do you know a man named Conn?" Glenn asked.

Baker shook his head.

"How about Mehaffey?"

Again, Baker shook his head.

"They're both detectives. Greenberry Conn. Everyone calls him Green. And William Mehaffey." Glenn leaned forward and peered over his eyeglasses. "Are you sure you've never heard of them?"

"I think I've heard that man Conn's name before," Baker replied, "But I don't know him. Should I?"

Glenn got up out of his chair and walked across the room. He stood at the window with his back to Baker. He retrieved a brier pipe from his coat pocket, tapped a fingerful of tobacco in the bowl and lit it before swinging around and walking back toward him.

"They claim—especially Conn—that at the very least you received stolen goods. And you knew they were stolen. And yet you turned around and sold them." Glenn sat back down. "It gets worse. Conn is telling everyone that you probably purloined the goods yourself."

Baker leapt from his chair. "That's a dratted, bald-faced pack of lies," he shouted.

"Sit down, Bass." Glenn pointed to the empty seat. "Here's what I know from the police. There was a railcar break-in. At the Southern Railway yard. Belt Junction, I believe. A security guard, a man named Avant, was making his rounds. Halfway through, he approached a thirty-foot boxcar sitting alone in the middle of the yard. It had arrived the day before from Virginia with a goodly amount of Wild Turkey tobacco. It was supposed to head out for points west later that afternoon. The side door was open. As Avant neared the car he saw a rusty door latch lying on the ground. He picked it up and examined it. It had been broken off from the door frame. He hoisted himself onto the door runner and peered into an empty boxcar. He looked around but saw no one. Nor did he see any signs of foul play, save for the broken latch and the missing tobacco. His first call was to his boss. Then he called Chief Connolly."

"Have you spoken with Connolly?" Baker asked.

"Yes, that's how I know what I do. I went right to the chief when I learned of your arrest. Much of the detail I'm telling you isn't in the indictment. The one thing you'll learn about Connolly, if you ever meet him, is that he won't stop talking. He likes to ramble on about himself. He'll bore you to death. The man brags a lot. And if you get him talking about a case he'll spill his guts. He'll puff out his chest and go on and on. It makes him feel important. That's what I was aiming for and that's what I got."

"Can I meet with him?" Baker asked. "I'd like to—"

"Let me continue," Glenn interrupted. "Conn and Mehaffey set out to find the tobacco. At first their search turned up nothing. Just dead end after dead end. But the tide turned when, having had no luck in the city, they extended their search to surrounding towns. This past Wednesday morning they boarded the six twenty-two bound for Fairburn. They got off in Monk." Glenn paused briefly and relit his pipe. "That surprised me. I didn't know there was much of anything in that godforsaken town except a forgettable railroad stop with nothing but a car shed and a couple of rickety benches. But they tell me there's a tobacco merchant there, a man named Scarborough."

Baker flinched. He sat up straight and set his chin.

"Bass, did I say something to surprise you? Do you know this chap Scarborough?"

"I do. He is an old textile man. He worked for years at the Manchester Mill. Then he was called to fight with the Nineteenth Georgia Infantry. Fought at Yorktown…Seven Pines…Frazier's Farm. When he came home, the mill had burned to the ground. He set out to find work. That's how he ended up in Monk. He thought it was a good place to settle since it's on the rail line between Atlanta and Fairburn."

"Bass, slow down. You're running on like a jackrabbit. Are you nervous? I don't need to know the man's life story."

"I understand, but based on what you've told me he seems a little like Connolly. When you first meet him he'll prattle so much that yawning tears will come out of your eyes."

"Apparently this man Scarborough's getting up in years. Is that true?"

"He must be in his seventies now," Baker said. "I wouldn't be surprised if he hung up his fiddle soon, given his age."

"That's what I assumed. Well, Conn and Mehaffey paid him a visit—without a warrant, I might add. They rifled and ransacked his store. They upended tables filled with merchandise. They cleared shelves and cabinets. They left all the contents scattered over the floor. I'm told that Scarborough just stood there, helpless and dumbfounded. They finally found a very large supply of tobacco. Wild Turkey. Much more than Scarborough should have had on hand. It was hidden inside and behind a chifforobe, set several feet from the wall in a back room. Apparently they roughed Scarborough up something awful. They threatened to arrest him unless he fingered the man he bought it from. The detectives told him the city jail wasn't a wholesome place for a person his age. That's when he claimed he got it from you, Bass. They confiscated the tobacco and called for a wagon to carry it back to the station house, where they locked it away in a vault. Then Conn swore out the warrant against you." Glenn removed his glasses and stared into Baker's eyes. "Did you sell Scarborough the tobacco?"

"I probably did," Bass said. "I've sold him quite a lot of tobacco over the past couple of years."

"Yes, but did you sell him *this* tobacco?" Glenn paused. "Let me ask it a different way. Did you very recently sell this man Scarborough a large supply of Wild Turkey tobacco?"

Baker nodded. He felt a bead of perspiration form on his upper lip.

"And from whom did you buy it, Bass? I'm assuming you bought it."

"*Of course* I bought it."

"Look Bass, we've known each other a long time. I don't mean to be adversary, but I'm doing you a favor. I know you're innocent, but if these charges were to ever go anywhere—if you ended up in front of a jury, say—you'd better be ready to be peppered with uncomfortable questions."

"I suppose I bought it from the same person I buy much of my tobacco from, a traveling drummer named Jenkins—Herbert Jenkins—but he's just a middleman."

"You *suppose?* You don't know?"

Baker's skin tensed between his brow ridges. He fidgeted, eager to get on. "Yes—yes—I guess I remember now. It must have been Jenkins," Baker replied after a long pause. "He came in and said he had a sizable shipment at a good price. I bought some of it. I turned it quickly. But let me make one thing clear. If that tobacco was stolen, I certainly knew nothing of it."

Baker returned to his store that day assuming that somehow everything would be resolved. But no sooner had he resumed a semblance of normality than the two detectives showed up and arrested him a second time. He was released on bail and, again, he found himself sitting in Glenn's office.

"Who is this no-account Conn, anyway?" Baker asked. "Why is he out to get me? What have I ever done to him?"

"I don't know much about him," Glenn replied. "What I know I learned from Connolly and from some good old fashioned *sticking my nose in places it wasn't meant to be.* The chief despises him. I know that. He calls him an opportunist. Says he wouldn't think twice about bribing witnesses—falsifying evidence—hell, even turning on his mother if that's what it took to get what he wants."

"So why doesn't Connolly fire him?" Baker asked.

"Because, from what I hear, he was handpicked by one of the police commissioners. And he's not the only one. The detective bureau is their little stooge squad, and they dole out favors like licorice sticks and penny candy. They've also had Connolly in their thrall since the day he became chief. His hands are tied."

"Well that's a sorry state of affairs," Baker replied, "when a police chief can't even get rid of one of his own men."

"I can't disagree with you. But do you want to hear something knee slapping funny? I'm convinced the main reason Connolly doesn't trust Conn is because he doesn't wear a mustache," Glenn laughed. It was the first time Baker had ever seen his attorney loosen up.

"And what about this other man—what's his name—McAfee?"

"It's Mehaffey. M-E-H. Rhymes with taffy. I know even less about him. He may be on the up and up. Or he may be cut from the same cloth as Conn. It's hard to say. But he is a detective, after all. If I were to speculate, which is what I suppose I'm doing now—well, you already know how I would weigh in."

"So the two detectives barged into my store. They didn't let on why they were there or what they were looking for. I knew there was little I could do, given what I had already gone through with the police. They were fixated on the remains of a wooden crate out back. A wooden crate, of all things. It was broken into pieces and discarded in a barrel. They had a damned conniption fit over it. Why would they possibly care about an old, broken-up crate, I thought. Well, they put the cuffs on me again and took me away, but they left the barrel and the broken crate behind." Baker looked at Glenn. "So tell me, why in Sam Hill did they arrest me this time?"

"Well," Glenn said, "a large amount of tallow was stolen from a store on Alabama Street." He paused and locked eyes with Baker. "The amount taken was not nearly as substantial as the Wild Turkey, but you know better than I that tallow is even more valuable than tobacco. The police arrested a man named Christopher Johnson. You must know who he is."

"Of course I do. Everybody knows Johnson," Baker said. "He's just a good old mudsill of a Negro. He helps me out from time to time—odd jobs around the store. But he has a problem with the bottle that gets him in trouble. Every time a theft occurs in this town, that poor soak is one of the first people they haul in. He's in and out of the county work farm."

"Well, when Johnson was arrested, he admitted to having stolen the tallow, but he claimed he was on a drunken tear when he did it."

"That doesn't surprise me in the least," Baker said.

"Johnson said he turned around and sold the tallow to you. At least that's what Conn claims. We haven't heard that directly from the Negro. We can go only on what the detective has said."

"I've told you Conn's a damned liar," Baker shouted.

"Calm down, Bass. Let me go on. Johnson was sentenced to four months on the chain gang. And then Conn took out the second warrant. When he and Mehaffey went through your place and found the crate, he claimed it had at one time contained the stolen tallow."

"Listen to me, Glenn." Baker jabbed his finger in the air. "Christopher Johnson *did* come around trying to sell me the tallow. I'll freely admit that to anyone who asks. The truth is the truth. But *I did not*—I repeat, I did not—buy the tallow from him. In fact, I accused him of having stolen it, cursed him and ordered him to leave at once."

Baker left Glenn's office seething with anger.

And now it was late August. Almost three months had passed without the slightest chirrup from the courts, although Conn had continued to dog him. Baker was almost to the Ivy Street corner when his thoughts turned to his mother back on the farm, widowed only a year after he left Palmyra. And Robert. And Jesse and the rest of the clan. And Ella's mother, who had chosen to remain in Thomasville after her husband also passed away. And Wiley and Rebecca. And old man Pennington, with his bald head, barking orders through his cigar-stained teeth. Baker's mind raced as he recounted each step in the journey that had taken him, over the course of two decades, from Palmyra to Thomasville to Atlanta. He never expected the odyssey to be straightforward, painless or without its hitches. But back in the day if any of them had told him he would end up in the mess he was in now, he would have looked at them askance and told them they were not up to dick mentally. The worst part was that, while he tried to shield Ella from it all, she bore the burden of living his angst vicariously and not knowing its source. *What is worse,* he thought, *knowing every detail? Or being in that helpless state of knowing something bad is afoot and not knowing what it is or how to deal with it?* He needed to tell her what was going on. He knew that. But he just had not been able to bring himself to it. *I'll tell her tonight, he thought. I'll sit her down and tell her everything.*

A faint thumping of hoofbeats from afar became louder. He looked up Ellis past Ivy. He could discern the hazy image of a dairyman making his morning rounds. Save for that, the streets were empty. As he neared the intersection, the wind whipped up around him. He pulled his collar tighter around his neck and held it in place with his left hand. With his right he grabbed the crown of his Homburg.

"That man Conn must be off his rocker—or just plain criminal— or both," Baker muttered to himself as he walked down the street. "He's out to do me in. I'm sick and tired of his threats. I have a mind to visit Judge Landrum on Monday and get an indictment against him. Turn the tables on him. I'll have the son-of-a-bitch's hide if it's the last thing I do. I'm not a violent man, but if I meet him on the street I swear I'll bury my bunch of fives in his face."

He stopped briefly at the corner before going left and continuing up Ivy.

FOUR

ELLA BASS

A Gunshot

ELLA HAD WATCHED THAT MORNING AS HER HUSBAND stood in the doorway. As he walked onto the porch. The fresh smell of rain permeated the living room. He closed the door behind him. She wiped the condensation from the glass pane with the ball of her hand and gazed through the window as he descended onto the sidewalk and disappeared down the long street. His diminishing silhouette vanished in the semidarkness.

She stepped back from the window and looked down at her apron. A faint wash of light from the streetlamp nearest the house passed through the spot where she had wiped the glass and landed on her bib. An angular visage of a face, its edges blurred, flickered on the cotton cloth. The practical side of her knew the image was nothing more than the light's undulations along the bib's folds. And the light's fluttering was an indication that the streetlamp was about to burn out. But it struck her as odd, as if there were something more to it. Suddenly the image disappeared. Although she knew the lamp had finally given out, she nevertheless felt a shiver course through her body.

Her husband had been despondent of late. There had been some sort of skirmish with the law—just what it was she didn't know. He wouldn't talk about it. He had always been reserved, reluctant to discuss what bothered him, even with family. Perhaps especially with family. And she knew not to push him. But she worried about him from sunup till dusk. She had come to assume the worst when things didn't feel right. And this was one of those times. She never experienced such angst and helplessness back in Thomasville. And it wasn't just the events of the last few months. Ever since they had moved, things had been different— *he* had been different. He was more aloof—detached—on edge. Would they ever be able to recapture the small town comfort and contentment they had left behind? Or should she just accept the way things were? Ella was reared on the mother's milk of the Methodist church. The Deep South holiness revival church. *Perhaps I'm being called, like Job, to accept God's boundless power and man's limited understanding. The secret things belong to God.*

Baker had been gone only a short time when she was startled by what sounded like a gunshot coming from nearby. She paused for a moment. She thought of her husband. Out of duty to her chores and to avoid pondering the unimaginable, she went on about her business preparing for a full day of housework. The laundry would be washed, boiled and rinsed. The ash box would be emptied. The floors would be swept. Tasks she wasn't accustomed to back in Thomasville. Without Miss Lula and Sukie, and even with part-time help coming in twice a week, her days in the city were long and arduous.

It's probably nothing, she thought. But in a matter of minutes, she heard a knock at the door. She pulled back the white lace curtain ever so slightly and peered out the window. A Negro man stood on the porch. She called for John to come into the room. As John approached, she reached out to the brass box lock. Her husband, as he was more often than not prone to do, had left the door unlocked. She slowly, carefully, turned the key clockwise, her hand trembling.

"Get out of here nigger," John yelled out through the door.

Ella chided her son with a silent, sideways glance. She never abided such language. Perhaps it was her proper upbringing. Or perhaps it was because, as an only child, she had spent her early years playing with the children of her father's slaves. And she would continue to feel a special kinship with them well into her adolescence, long after they had won their freedom.

"I said go away nigger," John snapped, ignoring his mother's silent rebuke. She reached out and touched his forearm.

"Miss Ella—" the man shouted through the closed door.

He knows my name. She examined him through the window. It was dark on the porch, save for a faint ray of light passing through the transom from inside the house. But she could make out enough to see that he had a round, bulldoggish face. His eyes were owlish and deep set. While she visited her husband's store only occasionally, she remembered a black man who sometimes did odd jobs there. He fit the description. She didn't recall his name, probably never knew it. *Is that the man standing in the dark on my porch, his overalls drenched from the rain?* She turned the key counterclockwise and cracked open the door slightly, pressing her left foot against the bottom door rail to prevent a separation of no more than an inch from the sill.

"Miss Ella—"

"Who is it?" she called out.

"Miss Ella, they's a man been shot. He's down on the curb. Down Ivy way. I think it's Mister Bass."

John bolted out the door first, barely missing his mother and the black man as he ran down the porch steps, onto the sidewalk, and toward Ivy Street. Ella threw off her apron and trailed close behind. They arrived as the man was being placed in a horse-drawn ambulance. John stopped the driver, Angus Parker, just as he was about to pull away. John and his mother ran to the back of the wagon. Grady Hospital's resident physician, a man the locals called Doc Shaw, was sitting in the back next to the wounded man. John identified the man, his head crudely wrapped with a makeshift, blood covered bandage, as his father. Ella, who up to that point had been staring into the distance, unable to lay eyes on the person she feared was her husband, lunged toward the open rear door of the ambulance, throwing herself onto his body. She ran her hand across his bandaged head. She placed her cheek against his face. He felt cold to the touch. She reached inside his shirt just below his torn collar and felt the slight rise and fall of his chest. His breathing was shallow and irregular. She spoke his name but he never responded.

"I'm sorry lady," Shaw said. "I know it's hard, but you'll have to move out of the way. We need to get to the hospital as soon as we can."

John pulled his mother away. "No. Please don't leave me," she yelled out.

Ella looked around at the crowd that had gathered as John steadied her with his arm. The faces in the gathering crowd were a mere blur. She wondered if the shooter might be lurking nearby, taking perverse pleasure in what he had wrought. Parker sped off, leaving her standing on the curb frozen in place, her heart racing, her skin cold and sweaty, trying to make sense of what had just happened.

"John, we must go to the hospital now."

Ella and John proceeded on foot to Grady Hospital, nine blocks away on Butler Street.

FIVE

CECIL THOMPSON

Things Can Change in an Instant

CECIL THOMPSON THOUGHT OF HIMSELF AS A SEASONED veteran of the downsized, ragtag assemblage of moilers that passed for a police force. He spent most days resenting the fact that he and his fellow patrolmen were overworked, underpaid, and underappreciated. He bristled when he thought about his wages, a little over two dollars and fifty cents a day. And he had to work extra hours without pay. And he wasn't allowed to work a second job. The force had been shorthanded ever since the commissioners decided to cut back its ranks, and many of the ones that were still around had been called away to the exposition grounds. But he did the best he could with what he had. And he took exception when people referred to the whole damned lot of them as greenhorns. Nobody would call him that to his face and get away with it.

It was in the spirit of doing his best that he made his way down Houston Street on the same August morning when, less than an hour later, John Bass would find himself bounding down the front steps of his house with his mother close behind. Thompson carried himself with a sense of duty and with an intimate knowledge of every cobble on every street, every crack in every sidewalk, and every dark alley that on this or any other morning could provide refuge for an attacker lying in wait. He respected the authority conveyed by the badge he wore on his Prince Albert coat, and his swagger sent a clear message that he would enjoy the challenge of the day, as with any day.

He knew the dangers he faced. Things can change in an instant. Putting himself in the middle of a burglary, rape or murder always brought with it the risk of never making it back home. But most mornings—he always worked the early morning shift—were more mundane: disorderly conduct, public drunkenness, street fights, arresting idle Negroes for loitering. And then there was an assortment of crimes on the books that he and the others had a hard time even keeping track of—things like allowing unhaltered mules to run at large, rock throwing, lunacy, hitching to shade trees, reckless bicycling, spitting on sidewalks, and obstructing the natural flow of water. Vulgar women, sailor's trulls and strumpets were occasionally hauled in at the whim of the police, and the detective bureau was charged—at least in principle—with cracking down on lewd houses. But the brotheled life was by and large tolerated, so long as those living it were confined to a few locations, especially the ones around Jackson Street. There were also common areas set aside for street trade, Negro hangouts, doggeries, dives, dance halls, and other places of bad reputation.

By all accounts, it promised to be a typical day, though it had been raining all month. There was that massive West Indian storm the whole town was talking about. Someone had said the storm was so violent it "forced the Gulf Stream back to its sources, and piled up the water to a height of thirty feet in the Gulf of Mexico." He remembered reading those words, or maybe hearing them, he didn't recall which, but they stuck with him as he walked his beat that morning. He wondered what encountering a thirty-foot-high wall of water would be like.

He stopped at the corner of Houston and Piedmont. He reached into his coat pocket and retrieved his watch, a gold clad No. 10 Mechanical given to him by his now-deceased father. A tiny sliver of light from the waning crescent, that dark, nebulous phase before the pitch black new moon sky, reflected in the glass crystal. He couldn't make out the time. It didn't help that the hands disappeared against the background of the mechanical skeleton. He walked a few feet over to a solitary incandescent streetlamp and held his watch up to the faint light. He still had to strain to read the watch face. It was five past four, halfway through his midnight-to-eight o'clock shift.

He thought back to when, eight years earlier, the city had begun to electrify, as they called it, replacing the gaslights one by one. The new lamps may have been more efficient, but as he struggled to read his watch face, he wondered if they were really much better. While the arc lamps scattered around the city were brighter, the carbon electrodes burned away quickly. And as for the incandescent ones, he had never grown accustomed to their faint yellow-orange glow. And every time a lamp went out, which in his mind was too frequent, it was his job to notify the station house so someone could lug their ladder out and replace it. He found it puzzling, if not downright inconceivable, that a newspaperman a year earlier had praised the electric street lights, claiming that "there is not a better lighted city in America than

Atlanta, and there is not a citizen of Atlanta who will not gladly testify to the excellence of the city's street lighting service."

Thompson continued down the street. His partner, a man named Moncrief, trailed a few feet behind. They were on their regular beat, patrolling along the edge of the black shantytown known as Darktown. He thought that most self-respecting people, if they had any sense at all, would skirt its perimeter—Auburn Avenue … Jackson … Forrest … Piedmont—never venturing into its core. *Who would—unless they had a damned good reason to?* he thought. *It's just a cesspool of a place, what with all the rubbish along Jackson Row—pools of stagnant water everywhere—it's downright unbearable. Rats—and God only knows what else—scurryin' across the road day and night. Niggers huddled around open trash fires in the dead of winter—the middle of summer—it doesn't matter if it's thirty degrees or eighty degrees out—they'll still be out there at night huddled around those damned fires. Shacks, shelters, and shotgun houses with four or five people beddin' down in a single room—full of fleas and bedbugs.* Thompson supposed that every southern city had its own Darktown and that the one he and Moncrief knew was no better—or worse—than any other.

Thompson looked back at Moncrief. "What's wrong Thaddeus, havin' trouble keepin' up? Your hangdog stoop reminds me of some decrepit creature twice your age," Thompson badgered his partner of four years.

"Cecil, you just mind your own business," Moncrief shot back. "I can keep up just fine, with you or anybody else." He scuttled to catch up.

"It's just that you look hopeless sometimes. And what about your mustache? It looks like you haven't trimmed it in weeks?"

"Go to hell, Cecil. Just because I ain't from the same rugged farm stock as you. Just because I ain't some highfalutin gentleman—a dad-blamed nobleman—that's what you think you are—with your pruned whiskers, your pomaded hair, and your manful cheekbones. That don't make you any better than me."

"Alright, Thaddeus, don't get testy. I don't mean any harm by it."

"You just need to keep on struttin' down the street and mind your own dang business, Cecil."

"What a blessed chump," Thompson muttered under his breath but within earshot of Moncrief.

As the men made their way down Houston Street, Thompson's left hand rested on the burl walnut handle of his .41 caliber revolver. Moncrief tapped his oak nightstick against the curbstone as if he were rehearsing the codes he had learned in training. Two light taps for all clear. Three quick, hard raps to summon help. Two. Three. Two. Three.

Thompson stopped and turned to Moncrief.

"Thaddeus, stop your damned thump-thumpin' for a minute. Did you read about that white man from Ohio that was killed down near Bainbridge? I think his name was Keller. They say he was no more than twenty years old—maybe not even that."

Moncrief stopped tapping and looked up. "I believe so," he replied. "The one that went down to River Junction? They found his body in a swamp?"

"That's the one. I read that they arrested a nigger named Ford—or Davis. He's one of them that uses an alias—probably hidin' from the law. But whatever his name is, don't be surprised if you read in the paper tomorrow morning that they sent him to the gibbet today. It all happened mighty fast."

"Do you think he did it, Cecil?"

"I'm sure he did. No reason to think different. I don't care how much he says he didn't. A hit dog'll holler, if you ask me. Justice gotten-on-with is justice done when you're dealin' with his kind. That's what I say. No need to drag it out."

The two men had just passed Piedmont and were almost a block east of Courtland when they were surprised by a quick footfall from behind. Thompson pivoted, his hand still resting on the butt of his revolver, and found himself eye-to-eye with a Negro boy. The boy froze, fear swimming in his eyes. He shifted his weight from one foot to the other as if he were about to take off.

"You'd better think twice before you pull foot, boy," Thompson said.

The boy looked familiar. Thompson had seen him darting down Houston Street on prior mornings. As Moncrief looked on, Thompson questioned him, thrusting his truncheon with his right hand into the boy's chest.

"What's your name, nigger?" Thompson asked.

"Will Coleman, please sir," the boy replied in a near whisper, looking down at the ground as he spoke.

"Where are you in such an all-fired hurry to get to this time of day?"

"I'm a porter, sir."

"You're a *porter?*" Thompson shot back, a generous dose of sarcasm in his voice. "And *where* are you a *porter?*"

"At the Aragon Hotel, sir. I'm on my way to work, please sir," the boy mumbled, avoiding eye contact with the officers.

"Speak up, boy, and look at me when you talk."

"I'm a porter, sir. At the Aragon Hotel," the boy responded, looking up but past Thompson. "I'm late to work."

"What did you say, boy?"

"I'm late to work, please sir."

"Don't sass me, boy."

"Where do you live?" Moncrief interjected.

"Down on the alleyway off Hilliard."

"Which alleyway off Hilliard?" Thompson asked.

"The one between Irwin and Wheat."

Thompson knew the alley well. It was in the heart of Darktown. The corner where the two men and the boy stood was along the most direct route from there to the Aragon. Thompson looked the boy up and down. He was dressed like the porter he claimed he was, what with his weatherworn leather brogans, slightly dingy charcoal plaid knickers, club collar shirt and bow tie. "What do you think, Thaddeus, should we let the little nigger boy go?"

"I don't know, Cecil. He looks mighty suspicious to me." Moncrief looked up at his partner. A slight grin came upon him. "Maybe we need to rough him up a bit. Haul him in. What do you think, boy?"

"Aw, come on, Thaddeus, we may as well let him go. He ain't doin' no harm. You just get on now, but you'd best not let us see you out here again."

As the men proceeded down Houston Street, the boy scurried past them. Thompson stopped midway between Piedmont and Courtland and lit a cigarette. He had rolled it earlier that morning. He preferred Wild Turkey, named not for the animal but, rather, for the Turkish tobacco seed *Nicotiana rustica*. He knew that because it said it in tiny print on the side of the can. If you squinted and looked hard enough you could read it. That particular strain of tobacco was claimed by Virginia as its own even though, Thompson reckoned, the farmers who cultivated the plant he hand rolled and smoked probably knew nothing of the seed's origins or of the country a lifetime away that claimed it. And the turkey on the can's label perpetuated the belief that the tobacco was named for the bird and not the place. He had just extinguished the match and tossed it into the roadbed when he and Moncrief were startled by what sounded like a single discharge from a gun. It had come from close by, from somewhere in the direction of downtown no more than a block or two away. They ran to the corner of Houston and Courtland. Following the most direct path to what they surmised to be the gunfire's rough location, they turned right on Courtland then left on Ellis. As they proceeded up Ellis, and when they neared Ivy Street, Will Coleman came loping back toward them from the middle of the Ivy block. He was shaking and flailing his arms.

"A man's on the sidewalk. Sprawled out. I think he's been shot."

"Where?"

"That way," the boy pointed toward Ivy Street. "Part way down there."

Thompson and Moncrief ran the block from Ellis to Ivy with the boy trailing behind them. They turned left onto Ivy. As they reached the middle of the block they saw the man lying near the curb across the street from where they were. There were two narrow alleyways on the west side of Ivy between Houston and Ellis. One of them, the one Will Coleman would surely have taken every morning, ran to the back of the Aragon. The other ran through to Peachtree Street alongside DeGive's Grand Opera House from the rear. An eight-foot embankment, covered with high weeds from the heavy rains, separated the sidewalk from the hotel and the opera house. The alleyways cut through the embankment. The man was lying on his back, facing away from the street. He had fallen in front of a vacant lot between the two alleys. His feet were hanging off the curb. His head was lying in a pool of fresh blood. The officers looked around. They saw no one. The houses on each side of where the man lay were vacant. It had been no more than five or ten minutes since Thompson and Moncrief had been surprised by the gunshot. It was still dark. Thompson knelt down. He struck a match for light. He looked at the man's face. He didn't recognize him. He was reluctant to search the man's pockets for identification, lest he disturb the body and cause greater harm. The man was middle-aged, white. He was well dressed, with a closely trimmed beard and mustache. Thompson felt the man's pulse. It was weak. As he crouched over the man he placed his handkerchief on the single gunshot wound, a little more than two inches above and to the rear of the man's right ear. He pressed hard in an attempt to stanch the bleeding. Moncrief formed a makeshift bandage by tying together the ends of his own handkerchief and two others he had retrieved from the gathering crowd. He handed it to his partner. Thompson replaced his own blood soaked handkerchief with the makeshift bandage, wrapping it around the man's head and tying the two loose ends together. Thompson noticed the man's white starched collar. It had been torn out at both ends. There was blood on the right collar point. His shirt had been ripped straight down the front from the collar button.

A men's chocolate-brown wool hat lay on the sidewalk several feet away, almost touching the curbstone. It was banded by a light grey moiré silk ribbon. Moncrief picked it up and turned it over.

"What are you doing, Thaddeus?" Thompson asked.

"I'm lookin' for a name. Somethin' that might tell us who he is. See here. There's a label inside." Moncrief held out the hat, its crown facing away from Thompson. The label read JOHN KEELY MILLINERY, WHITEHALL STREET.

"That's who made the damned hat, Thaddeus, not who owns it." Thompson noted that the hat looked powder burned and black along the edge.

The man's watch and chain lay in full view in his vest pocket. Thompson would later learn from witnesses who had gathered at the scene that the grass on the nearby embankment seemed to have been disturbed, but at that moment he was too preoccupied to notice it. His eyes fixed on the pistol in the man's right hand. It was lying in his palm. The man's finger was on the trigger but he didn't have a firm grip on it. In a moment or two, as Thompson watched, the man reflexively released his finger from the trigger and relaxed his hand. Thompson picked up the gun from the man's open hand and examined it. It was a five-cylinder, .38 caliber self-acting revolver. It looked like a Smith & Wesson. He held it up to the streetlamp. There were empty cartridges in three chambers, including the chamber under the hammer. The other two chambers contained unfired cartridges. He removed one of the cartridges and examined it. It looked like a .38 caliber New Colt Police centerfire. He returned it to the chamber and placed the revolver in his coat pocket.

Four years earlier the city had installed a state-of-the-art Gamewell Police Alarm System, consisting of a number of alarm boxes located throughout the city that connected by telegraph directly to the station house. Pundits had predicted it would improve response time and efficiency by as much as thirty percent. As Moncrief made his way to the nearest box to summon the ambulance from Grady Hospital, Thompson hoped they were right.

Several nearby residents, one of whom was a physician, told Thompson they had been awakened by what sounded like a commotion or a scuffle, followed by the gunshot. But they had gone back to sleep thinking it was nothing.

The sun had not yet risen. As Thompson knelt over the wounded man he was interrupted by the darkened image of a stranger approaching from his left.

"Ach, Herr Polizist, I seen it," the stranger called out as he stabbed the morning air with his left index finger, pointing in the direction of the body lying on the curb.

"Excuse me," Thompson responded, struggling to understand the stranger over his heavy German accent and broken English.

"Ach Gott. I seen it happen. I seen dot man put zee gun vorwart to his het. Den he pulled der trigger. Den it jest eggsplode. Dot's what I seen."

Thompson stood up to face the stranger. "Who are you?"

"Offizier, der name ist Smit. John Smit," the man thrust his hand in Thompson's direction then quickly withdrew it.

"Your name is what? Smit?"

"No, Smit. S-M-I-T-H. Smit."

Thompson put his hands on his hips. "Do you really expect me to believe your name is Smith?"

"Ja, it's Smit," the man said, looking down at the ground, "now it's Smit. Vuz Schwerdtfeger. But ven I gommence to move to Box Ankle I change it. Nobody cud pronounce it. And people look at me vit a funny look. So I change der name to Smit."

"And what are you doing here?"

"I drive dot milchwagen ofer dere," the man said, pointing to a driverless dairy wagon a few yards down the street. "I don't live in Box Ankle no more. I live in DeKalb County jetzt."

Thompson had heard of the town of Box Ankle just north of Forsyth. How it got its name from an argument that broke out between two men at a cockfight. One man pushed the other one over a box and broke his ankle. Rumor was that both men had been drinking. Thompson knew the town had been settled by German immigrants.

"Where were you?"

"Vere vuz I?"

"Yes, where were you? When you saw him do it?"

"I was dere. Nicht ganz to dot corner," Smith pointed toward Ellis and Ivy. "At der end of der milch run."

"You stay right here. Don't leave." Thompson's attention turned back to the man lying on the curb. At first, no one milling around in the crowd claimed to recognize him. Perhaps it was because his head was covered in blood and facing away from the street. And it would have been difficult for anyone more than a foot or two away to have recognized him in the predawn darkness. But a Negro approached Thompson. He said he had stayed with his mother on the edge of Darktown the night before and was on his way to work. He believed he knew the victim, not from the man's face, which he couldn't make out in the dark, but from his hat, an open crown Homburg with a distinctive band, lying on the sidewalk a few feet away. He said the hat looked like the one worn by his boss. But before Thompson could ask him his name, the Negro took off running toward Ellis Street.

Thompson watched the Negro run away as Angus Parker approached from the south, maneuvering the ambulance down the city's furrowed streets. Parker brought the wagon to a halt beside where the body lay. Moncrief held the man's back as he helped Parker put him into the ambulance. Moncrief's grip began to slip. Thompson noticed the man's coat was torn. He wondered whether his partner may have accidentally torn it as he struggled not to lose control of the limp body.

The crowd began to dissipate. John and Ella arrived just in time to identify the man. The ambulance pulled away, headed to Grady Hospital. Thompson took the .38 caliber revolver out of his coat pocket, brandishing it for all to see. John walked over and asked if he could hold the gun. Thompson handed it to him. John examined it briefly and handed it back without saying a word.

SIX

ANGUS PARKER

No Hope

ANGUS PARKER CLUTCHED THE LEATHER REINS, WORN thin from too frequent use. He gripped them so hard his knuckles turned white. He preferred the four-ring Wilson snaffles, resting in the bars between his two bay mares' teeth, over other bits he'd tried. They gave him more control as he sped through town. The carriage's rubber wheels, a recent improvement over wood, helped him navigate the rutted downtown cobbles and rocks, pits and furrows with relative ease. Parker glanced back through the opening between him and the rear compartment. Doc Shaw was rummaging through the large wooden box positioned next to him, tossing aside the splints and tourniquets, the stomach pump, the bottles of morphine and persulfate of iron, until he found five bandages in the bottom of the box. He rewrapped Baker's head as best he could. Parker looked back and saw him searching for something else.

"What are you looking for, Doc?" Parker yelled out.

"The bottle of whiskey. It's gone. Somebody's gotten into the booze and gone up the pole again, Angus," Shaw shouted over the hoofbeats. "At least they didn't take the straitjacket, but if I ever find out who did it I think I'll use it on him."

Parker brought the carriage to an abrupt stop beneath the hospital's arched portico. He and Shaw carried the man through the door and into the operating room. They went straight to the center of the room and lifted the body off the wood-and-canvas stretcher and onto a large table covered with a crisp, white linen sheet. Parker reached up to the single incandescent fixture hanging above the table, Grady being one of the few buildings in the city to have electric lights. He struggled in the semidarkness to twist the socket key. Small sconce lamps adjacent to two narrow wooden side tables along the north and south walls provided some additional light, albeit meager. A three-panel bay window would provide ample sunlight later in the day.

Soon, Bass's wife and son arrived. And Officer Thompson.

The pungent smell of iodoform filled the air. Anything that might be needed was in the room. Surgical instruments were carefully arranged on one side table. A bullet probe. Cauterizing tools. A trephine hand drill. Pliers and forceps. Bone saws. Scalpels. Amputation knives. A few jars of cotton, gauze and dressings were within easy reach. And an almost full bottle of Sennine, hailed as the "new American antiseptic." And neurosine and opium. And of course whiskey, even though the hospital was acclaimed as alcohol- and tobacco-free. On the other table, metal trays had been placed to receive any tissue, organs, bone fragments or foreign objects that might be removed. Two blood-stained leather surgical aprons hung from brass coat hooks on the north wall of the room.

Three attending surgeons gathered around the table. Dr. John Westmoreland, founder of the Atlanta Medical College and the senior among them, placed the back of his hand on Baker's forehead just above his eyes. "Cold, clammy and mottled," Parker heard him say. Parker watched as Westmoreland rebandaged the man's head to control the flow of blood. That was about all he could do. No efforts were made to remove the bullet. No trephine. No bullet probe. No forceps. No leather surgical aprons.

Parker looked up at the clock hanging on the north wall. The back-and-forth of its pendulum was slow, methodical, marking the inescapable passing of time. On that particular morning, he thought, its cadence had a doleful monotone. It was ten o'clock. Westmoreland turned to the other doctors and shook his head. The unspoken message was clear. The man could not be saved.

Ella asked that her husband be moved to their home. She said she wanted him to pass in whatever semblance of comfort she and John could provide. Baker was loaded back into the ambulance. Parker carried him the few blocks to the house on Ellis Street. The sense of urgency that had filled the air earlier that morning, when Parker had crossed the same streets, was now gone. Each turning of the wheels marked another advance toward an inevitable end.

John helped Parker carry Baker into the house and place him on the bed. Ella rested his bandaged head on a soft feather pillow. She arranged wool covers over him to prevent chills. Nothing more could be done.

Parker stayed behind to assist. Baker never regained consciousness and at twenty minutes after noon he breathed his last breath. Parker turned to leave. As he neared the front door he looked back and saw Ella standing in the bedroom's darkened threshold, clutching her Bible tightly in both hands. Her four children were at her side.

SEVEN

WILLIAM GILBERT

The Bedroom Was Dark

ON FRIDAY AFTERNOON, THE DAY OF THE SHOOTING, DR. William Gilbert sat in his office at 33-1/2 Whitehall Street. He had just returned from a house call a mile away on North Bell. The unfortunate soul, a woman in her mid-fifties, had a grievous case of dropsy. He had administered a tincture of foxglove and had promised to return later that day. He never did. A full day would pass before he made it back.

Two pictures hung on the wall behind his desk, flanking his Atlanta Medical College diploma. On the left was a portrait of his grandfather, also named William, a dashing man with arched eyebrows and a penetrating gaze, dressed in a cutaway morning coat, starched Hamilton collar and charcoal silk cravat. On the right was his great uncle Joshua, visibly younger but of equally good looks and similarly attired. *Those pictures must have been taken forty-five—maybe fifty—years ago, not long after they started their practice together,* he thought. *They look so dapper. So sophisticated. Hell, they were a couple of old country doctors just like me.* He chuckled.

Gilbert couldn't recall a time when Uncle Joshua hadn't taken every opportunity to regale him with stories of his grandfather, who had died two years before he was born. In the summer of his fourteenth year, Gilbert had convinced his father to let him spend a month in Atlanta with Uncle Joshua. He had never been to the city before, and he remembered the anticipation as his uncle navigated the wagon down the dusty, red clay road that led from the farm just outside Cambellton, the only place he'd ever known. They would travel fifteen miles, roughly following the contours of the Chattahoochee River, before veering eastward and continuing another ten miles or so into the city. The time they spent together that month would pique his interest in medicine and change the arc of his life. One conversation in particular stood out.

"Your grandpa was eight years older than I," Gilbert remembered his uncle telling him as they sat on the old man's front porch. "He would have been proud of you. You're named for him, you know."

Gilbert nodded. Uncle Joshua would remind him every time he saw him that he was his grandfather's namesake.

"I called him Willy, but to most everybody else in the family he was Will. Oh, how I looked up to him. He moved to Georgia from South Carolina in eighteen and twenty-nine to go to medical school—the one over there in Augusta. I recall that it had just opened the year before. I cried when he moved away. When he got out of school he settled around Utoy Creek, not far from your father's place. There weren't many people living there back then. But they sure needed a doctor and they didn't have one. And that's why your grandpa moved there."

His uncle paused and placed a generous plug of chewing tobacco between his gum and lower lip.

"How did Grandpa end up in Atlanta?"

"Well, that's another story. Back when he moved to Utoy there wasn't much to speak of all the way from there to the Tennessee border—just a smattering of farms and whitewashed houses, slave and sharecropper shacks, a tavern and a coach stop here and there. But then, in thirty-seven, they built a railroad from Chattanooga down past the Chattahoochee River. They drove a stake in the ground at the southern end of the railroad and called it Terminus. The whole area began to grow after that, and almost a decade later they changed its name to Atlanta."

Uncle Joshua looked off into the distance.

"Oh, I almost forgot. Somewhere along the way, before it became Atlanta, they changed the name to Marthasville. It was named for the governor's daughter, Martha Atalanta Lumpkin. Anyway, around the time it became Atlanta, I had my medical diploma in hand as well. Your grandpa and I saw an opportunity to serve an even bigger community, one that was growing fast. So we moved to the city and set up a practice together. People tell us we were the first doctors to stick up our shingle here."

Gilbert looked up at his uncle. The man's eyes welled up.

"The only thing your grandpa ever wanted to do was help people. That was his whole life. And he had a lot of years left in him—if they hadn't been cut short. Did anybody ever tell you how your grandpa died?"

Again, Gilbert shook his head, knowing that his uncle would tell him the same story for the hundredth time, but thinking it better to go along with him and act like he'd never heard it before.

"Well, it was in September of sixty-four. We were fleeing Sherman's army along the Decatur-McDonough Road. The whole family. Your grandpa fell way behind the rest of the group. When your papa went back to check on him, he found him lying on the roadside, dead from a heart attack. He was on the ground near his horse. His head was resting on his saddlebag."

Uncle Joshua paused.

"Billy, I don't know if anyone ever told you this, but your grandpa dreamed that one day his son, your father Jeremiah, would pursue a career in medicine. But it just wasn't meant to be. Your father's a good man, but he wasn't cut out for it. He wouldn't be happy if he didn't have dirt on his hands, chickens to feed, and cows to milk."

"Was Grandpa sad, Uncle Joshua—I mean because Papa became a full-time farmer?"

"He resigned himself to it. He knew it wasn't meant to be. But what your grandpa wouldn't have given, God rest his soul, to see his grandson follow in his footsteps."

Billy Gilbert went on to become a doctor just like his grandfather and great uncle. By that time, the little town of Campbellton was already damned near dead, its steady decline having begun when the Atlanta & West Point Railroad decided to route their new tracks through the more terrain-friendly town of Fairburn. So he, too, set up practice in Atlanta. It wasn't long before he distinguished himself as a physician with impeccable skills and a compassionate bedside manner. In 1892, three years after Uncle

Joshua passed away, he was assigned the part-time job of county health officer. One of his duties was to perform postmortem examinations, bedside manner be damned.

He was winding down the week. He planned to revisit the dropsy patient later that evening and, if she had improved enough for him to take a break, albeit a short one, he would spend Saturday with his wife, Minnie. Perhaps they would take a morning trip on the seven thirty Chattanooga-bound Western & Atlantic local to visit one of the open air pavilions at Vinings station. Ever since his first visit there on a warm May afternoon three years prior, for the annual Irishmen's Picnic, he had developed a fondness for the place. And if he and Minnie found themselves in the area they might indulge in a side trip to the nearby Lithia Vapor Baths, the source of the bottled lithium water he drank daily. He had also been planning for some time to take a ride across town to visit the exposition grounds. Hundreds of workers, many from out of town, were busy putting the final touches on the buildings and open air exhibits. The grand opening was just two and a half weeks out. It was a favorable weekend for that as well. But all of this depended on the weather cooperating.

Gilbert's thoughts had wandered far from medicine when, shortly after one o'clock, he was caught off guard by a shadow in his doorway. He looked up to see a familiar face, a messenger from the coroner's office. The boy said a man lay dead in his bedroom at 74 Ellis Street. Jackson Paden, the county coroner, had requested that Gilbert go to the house right away to perform an autopsy. Gilbert knew Paden well enough to know he would waste little time convening a coroner's jury. The dropsy patient and the weekend plans would have to wait.

The bedroom on Ellis Street was dark when Gilbert arrived. He threw open the drapes. He approached the dead man, who lay on the bed where he had died only a few hours earlier. He removed the wool covers and upper bed sheet. The man was supine, his arms stretched across his chest forming an X pattern, with his palms down and his fingers almost touching his collar bones. Gilbert rolled him over onto his left side. The man's arms remained in place. He held the man's right forearm in his hands and gently pulled it away from the man's chest. The forearm momentarily remained suspended in air before it snapped to its original position. The muscles in his arms had begun to stiffen. The skin along the small of his back was mottled with a plum-red discoloration, indicating to Gilbert that lividity had set in. A smattering of magenta splotches, haloed by light grey coronas, appeared on his shoulders and upper arms. Gilbert retrieved a large magnifying glass from his bag. He shifted the body so the light from the window shined on the man's face and head. He lifted the man's left eyelid. Then his right. The corneas had begun to cloud. Gilbert noted a dark, red-brown stripe running horizontally across the man's left eye where his upper and lower lids came together, just above his pupil, suggesting his eye had not been completely closed when he died. As Gilbert removed the bandage from around the man's head he noticed the bullet hole in his skull, about two and a half inches above and to the back of his right ear. He pushed back the man's blood-soaked hair for a closer look. There was a contusion on the opposite side. His skull on that side was crushed. The bullet had lodged opposite where it had entered, stopping just under the cheekbone. He removed the flesh and hair around where the bullet had become fixed. Using a trephine, he bored two small holes through the bone. He retrieved a surgical saw from his bag and with it he cut away a section of bone. He extracted the small steel ball. He examined it, holding it up against the light that passed through the bedroom window. It was covered with torn tissue and blood. He wrapped the ball in a cotton cloth and placed it in his medical bag. He examined the man's hair and scalp. The hair around the wound looked singed. The wound itself looked powder burned. Gilbert had seen enough gunshot wounds to make an educated guess that the gun, when fired, could not have been more than twelve—perhaps eighteen—inches from the man's head. Close range. The evidence was consistent with, but not conclusive of, suicide. Gilbert completed his examination, cleaned up around him, and rebandaged the head. He returned the upper bed sheet and wool covers to the bed and left the house. He walked to the Fulton County Courthouse, at Hunter and Pryor Streets, to brief the coroner.

Paden, upon hearing Gilbert's findings, summoned Chief Connolly from the station house four blocks away. A few minutes later Conn and Mehaffey, not the police chief, showed up at Paden's office.

"What are you doing here? I sent for Connolly, not you," Paden barked, glaring at the two men.

Mehaffey spoke first, staring straight at Paden, his nostrils flared, his cheeks flushed. "The chief's busy. We came instead."

"And did the chief tell you to come in his place?" Paden asked.

"No, the chief doesn't know we're here," Conn replied, looking away from both Paden and Gilbert as he spoke. "The desk clerk at the station house told us you requested Connolly or a detective."

"I didn't ask for Connolly *or* a detective," Paden shot back, his voice rising. "I asked for Connolly. You're not Connolly. And another thing, have you been assigned to the case or are you just here on your own?"

"We haven't yet but we will be. We've spent two months investigating that damned crook Bass. We know more about him than anybody else in the department—maybe anybody else *anywhere*." Conn shifted his attention to Gilbert, who was standing on the other side of the room and up to that point had not said a word. "So, esteemed doctor, what's the verdict?"

Gilbert looked over at Paden.

"Go ahead Dr. Gilbert." Paden nodded. "You may as well tell them what you found." Paden then turned to Conn and Mehaffey. "You're here and the chief's not. I get that. But rest assured he'll hear from me. And I can only hope he has your heads when he does."

"Well," Gilbert spoke, stepping toward Conn and Mehaffey and standing no more than three feet in front of them, shaking his head and waving his right hand, "you should know as well as I that the task before me was not to reach a verdict. That's the job of a coroner's jury. I am not a coroner. And I am not a jury. I'm just a country doctor who happened to do a medical examination. But I can tell you that he died of a single gunshot to the head. From close range. And my findings are consistent with the sentiments I've heard since early this morning."

"What sentiments?" Conn asked.

"That the poor man took his own life," Gilbert responded. "But I must point out that I can't conclude, from my examination alone, that he was the one that pulled the trigger."

"I'm *certain* he did it," Conn shouted.

"Be quiet, Conn," Paden said. "*You* may be certain, but from the rumblings I've heard around the courthouse today—word travels fast, you know—there are other people who are convinced it *wasn't* suicide."

"Name one person," Conn replied, holding his index finger in the air, "just one."

"I'm not going to name anybody, not to *you* anyway. We'll see what the coroner's jury has to say. Now get back over to the station house where you can be of more value than you are here. And Gilbert, drop whatever you're doing and get your written report ready for the jury. I'm convening them in the morning."

Conn and Mehaffey had no sooner left Paden's office than Gilbert looked over at Paden. "Green Conn. What a miserable specimen of a man."

EIGHT

JOHN BASS

It Doesn't Make Sense

THAT FRIDAY EVENING, AS DUSK SETTLED IN, JOHN Bass stood alone in the living room on Ellis Street. Mary and her other two brothers had been sent to a neighbor's house for the night. John could hear his mother sobbing, calling out her husband's name, as she sat at the foot of the bed in the adjacent room, the very room where his father had died just a few hours earlier. The very room where Dr. Gilbert had wielded trephine and bone saw. The very room from which the lifeless body had been taken away by GEORGE R. BOAZ, UNDERTAKER AND LIVERY STABLE PROPRIETOR, soon thereafter. There had been visitors. There had been onlookers. But for now there were none. Perhaps it was the rain. The downpour had continued, as it would likely do throughout the weekend. The wind was pounding hard, blowing the water against the window pane. His eyes fixed on the torrent hitting the glass, filling the room with a dull drubbing.

How could things have changed so quickly? he asked himself. *My father was in reasonably good spirits when he left the house this morning.* Word on the street was that the detectives had concluded Baker had killed himself. John was bewildered. Even with all that had happened the past several months, his father had no reason to take his own life. Yes, he was dealing with challenges, but nothing that would have driven him to that. And there was the issue of the bullet's trajectory. *How in the world,* John thought, *could he have fired the gun?* The bullet entered his father's head above and behind his right ear. It passed to the front left side of his skull, traveling along a downward course. He would have had to fire the pistol from an unlikely position. Standing in the center of the room, facing the mirror that hung beside the oak mantelpiece, John reached behind the back of his head. He stretched his right arm back from his shoulder as far as he could, twisting his hand in the direction of his head, high and to the rear of his ear. He pointed his index finger and flexed it back toward his palm, as if to pull a trigger. It felt awkward. Uncomfortable. Strained. The muscles tensed in his forearm, wrist, and hand. And in his shoulder. John remembered his father complaining about his right shoulder ever since the policeman roughed him up in the store. *Why would anyone, in the throes of suicide, have chosen such an odd way to do it, especially with his shoulder the way it was? And why would he have done it right out there in the open, on the sidewalk? It just doesn't make sense.*

John was still standing before the mirror with his arm extended behind his head when he heard a muted rapping at the door. At first he didn't hear it over the sound of the rain. It became louder. He looked out the window. One of Baker's close friends, a man named Young Gresham, was standing on the front porch. He was holding what appeared to be a basket of funeral biscuits.

John closed the door to the bedroom and opened the front door. Gresham entered the room. He placed one hand on John's upper arm as he handed him the basket with the other. John placed the basket on the table nearest the door. Gresham removed his hat and placed it on the floor just inside the doorway.

"Mr. Gresham, you're soaking wet. Let me get you a towel."

John fetched a large flour sack towel from the rear of the house. Gresham dried himself off. He held the wet towel in his hand and looked around the room.

"Just throw it on the floor there. I'll get it later. Here, have a seat." John pointed to a chair next to the fireplace. Gresham sat down. John took a seat facing him.

"John, is your mother taking visitors?"

"Mr. Gresham, she's not in a good place right now. I think it best that you see her another time."

"I understand. Please tell her I'm thinking of all of you. I am always here for you if you need me."

"I'll tell her. Thank you for thinking of us."

"John, I'm here for another reason as well. You and your mother need to know that I spoke earlier this evening with a newspaper reporter. I told him what Baker had told me yesterday afternoon around four o'clock. He said that sometime earlier in the day—I believe about three hours earlier—a friend had stopped him on the street and told him another man had been going around town saying he'd just as soon see your father dead."

"Who?" John shot out of his chair. "Who's been going around saying that?"

"As implausible as it may seem, your father didn't tell me."

"Well, who was this friend who stopped my father on the street and told him about it?"

"Your father neglected to tell me that as well. John, I know it doesn't make a lot of sense that he wouldn't have told me more, but I'm telling you everything I know. You can rest assured that if your father had told me either man's name I would tell you, of all people."

John sat back down. After a long silence he found his tongue.

"I need some time to make sense of all of this. I need to find out who threatened my father's life."

"John, I have to believe there is some connection between his death and what he's been dealing with the last few months—with the police."

"I have little doubt of that. Listen, I don't deny that my father sold the tobacco to the merchant in Monk, but if it was stolen he didn't know it, and he certainly didn't steal it himself."

"Do you know where he got the tobacco, John?"

"Well, I assumed all along that he had bought it from that tobacco merchant, Herbert Jenkins. But then Jenkins showed up earlier today—just after the undertaker had taken my father away—to pay his respects. I had never met him before. I asked him about it and he said my father had bought the tobacco from a man named Milroy, or something like that."

"Had your father ever mentioned anyone by that name before?"

"No, not that I remember. I rummaged through his paperwork at the store late this afternoon and found no record of the purchase, but I was in such a dither that I may have overlooked it." John paused. "And by the way, as for the tallow, here's what our lawyer told us. He has testimony from a farmer who was standing at the doorway of the store around the time of the theft. A Negro came in offering to sell the tallow for a cheap price. My father refused. The farmer followed the man out of the store and bought the tallow from him."

Gresham stood up to leave. "John, I must go. But I wanted to share with you what I heard. I have little doubt that your father was murdered."

"One more thing before you leave, Mr. Gresham. I will tell you something that I have not yet shared with anyone, not even my mother, but I intend to reveal it to the authorities soon. I never before had seen the pistol that I held in my hand this morning after the police officer flaunted it—the one they claim they found in my father's possession. The gun the police recovered is a cheap copy of his own Smith & Wesson, the kind they make to look just like the real thing but they sell for half the price. I hear they're bringing a lot of them in from Spain. Most people buy them and don't even know the difference." John hesitated for a moment. "And there's another way I can tell my father's gun from any other. Engraved on the side plate, just above the handle, are his initials, B.A.B."

"Do you know where your father's gun is?"

"I've searched the house and the store and I can't find it anywhere."

NINE

JACKSON PADEN

He Summoned a Jury

AS SOON AS GILBERT HAD DEPARTED, PADEN SUMMONED a coroner's jury. They met early Saturday morning. His instructions to them were clear.

"I'm an old, parsimonious Scotch-Irishman. And I'm as prudent with my time as I am with my personal effects. Let's get this done. As quickly as you can. I don't cotton to long, drawn out hearings."

A few minutes after nine o'clock, the six jurors, all white men in their forties and fifties, entered the inquest room adjacent to Paden's office on the second floor of the courthouse at the corner of Hunter and Pryor Streets, a three-story brick building with an imposing Queen Anne clock tower. They selected E.M. Berry as their foreman. The choice of Berry to lead such a serious and austere effort was never in question. After all he was venerated as the man who single-handedly brought Tabler's Vegetable Liver

Powder, a miracle cure for disorders arising from a torpid liver, to the state. If you couldn't trust a citizen of such repute to get things done, then what man could you trust?

A double arched window ran from waist height almost to the ceiling, flooding the room with morning light. The jurors sat on one end of the room behind a four-foot wooden partition that separated them from the row of tables reserved for attorneys, including those representing Bass's family. The witness box was on the other side of the window, across the room. Paden's elevated dais and seat were in front of the window between the jurors and the witness box, revealing him in stark silhouette. An evidence table sat in the center of the room. At the other end of the room, directly across from Paden, were three rows of chairs for witnesses, detectives, reporters, and a handful of onlookers, all of whom crowded into the room. Some latecomers were forced to line the back wall.

Dr. Gilbert took the stand first. As he rose from his seat and approached the front of the room, he carried his black leather medical bag, emblazoned on its front with a silver medallion engraved with WLG. He placed the bag on the evidence table and slowly unlocked its metal jaw hinge. As he reached into the bag, he looked up at the jury, pausing just long enough to ensure the tension in the room was primed. He retrieved the bullet he had extracted from the dead man's head, with a torn, desiccated piece of tissue attached. He held it between his right thumb and index finger and waved it around the room.

"I submit to all witnesses present in this room today the very projectile that entered the unfortunate Mr. Baker Bass's skull and crossed through his cranial cavity, incapacitating him and lodging itself on the other side, just below his zygoma."

Gilbert touched the top ridge of his own cheekbone with his left hand.

"Here, right here," he said.

He then extended his left hand and pulled off a sliver of extracted flesh attached to the bullet.

"And this is a mere tiny sampling of the brain matter that the projectile carried with it as it passed along its journey near the fissure of Sylvius," he said. He then paused for a moment, shook his head, and said, "but never mind that, you don't need to know the medical details."

Gilbert returned the bullet and tissue to his bag, locked the jaw hinge and took his seat in the witness box. He retrieved his handkerchief from his vest pocket, wiped his hands briskly, and looked up at the jury foreman.

"I'm ready now."

Gilbert recounted the autopsy he had performed in the dead man's bedroom that Friday afternoon. The bullet hole. The blood soaked hair. The contusion and crushed skull. The trephine. The bone saw. The section of bone cut away. The singed hair. The small but distinguishable powder burn near the man's temple.

"And is it your professional opinion, Dr. Gilbert, that Mr. Bass could have died by his own hand? Or he could have been murdered?" Paden asked

"It is my firm position," Gilbert replied, "that it would be difficult to reach a conclusion other than suicide."

Paden rose from his seat and approached the witness box. "Dr. Gilbert, is it not true that yesterday, in my office, you stated that your findings were consistent with, *but not conclusive of,* suicide? And if that is the case, why are you changing your position before this jury?"

"I did say that yesterday, but as I thought more about my findings over the evening and this morning, I reached the conclusion that Bass surely must have taken his own life."

"But in reality, Dr. Gilbert, you're just speculating, aren't you? You cannot state with certainty, based on your examination, that Bass committed suicide. Isn't that correct?"

Gilbert looked down at his lap, then back at Paden. "That is correct."

"Is it not true, Dr. Gilbert, that someone could have shot the victim from close range? And in that case the autopsy would have revealed the same findings as you have reported?"

"That is correct."

Paden looked over at the jury box. "Mr. Berry, does the jury have any questions for the witness?"

Berry shook his head.

"Alright then, Dr. Gilbert, you may be excused."

Almost as soon as the medical examiner had stepped down, Dr. Shaw took the stand. Shaw testified that he had examined Bass's head and hair in the back of the ambulance as he replaced the makeshift bandage. He also stood by as an observer in the operating room as Dr. Westmoreland and his colleagues treated Bass. He said there were no powder burns and the hair was not singed around the wound. He also testified that the hole where the bullet entered was round and the skull was not torn. He said the skull would have been torn up by a pistol fired within a foot or two. He believed the shot was fired from some distance behind the man.

Paden called Gilbert back to the witness box. Gilbert continued to maintain that there were powder burns around the wound and that Bass's hair was singed, although he did not rebut

Westmoreland's testimony that the bullet hole was round and smooth around the edges.

Paden wondered how the testimonies of two physicians could be in such direct contradiction. Was it possible that Gilbert had mistaken something else, perhaps dirt from the fall, for singed hair and a powder burn? Or could someone have gotten to the doctor and convinced him to change his story? Or could Shaw have possibly missed those clues in the darkened rear compartment of the ambulance and the poorly lit operating room?

Paden returned to his perch and stood before the crowded room. "Gentlemen of the jury, we have heard testimony from two esteemed doctors. While they are in agreement as to the physical cause of Bass's death, their testimonies are in conflict in so far as some aspects of the wound itself are concerned. For now, short of paying a visit to Boaz's funeral parlor or, God forbid, bringing the man's body, which has surely been embalmed by now, into this very room, we will have to live with this disagreement. Perhaps other witnesses can settle the matter." He looked over at the jury. "Shall we move on?"

Foreman Berry surveyed the other jurors then nodded to Paden.

"Very well then. We shall turn our attention to the events surrounding the discovery of Bass lying on the sidewalk yesterday morning."

John Smith, the German milkman, took the stand. Paden and the jurors leaned in, struggling to make out what he was saying. But while his testimony may have been marginally intelligible, what with his heavy accent and vexing mix of German and English, one thing was clear. He testified that, when he arrived at the scene of the shooting, he saw the gun lying about two inches from Bass's hand. He had not seen Bass pull the trigger. He made an assumption that Bass had shot himself, he claimed, based on common sense—"what else could it be?"—and statements made by the officers as they stood over the body. Paden and the jurors concluded that there was little more they could learn from Smith. After all, he had, in no more than ten minutes on the stand, contradicted what he was purported to have told Thompson and Moncrief at the scene. Smith was excused.

Thompson and Moncrief testified next. They took the jurors through a recounting of events from the time they heard the shooting until the departure of the ambulance down Ivy Street. They contradicted several aspects of Smith's testimony. They insisted that he had told them, at the scene of the shooting, that he saw Bass pull the trigger. Also, Smith testified that he arrived at the scene before Will Coleman and the officers, but Thompson and Moncrief said otherwise. And although Smith testified the pistol was on the sidewalk about two inches from Bass's right hand, the officers said it was lying in the man's palm.

Will Coleman, dressed in his full porter's attire, followed Thompson and Moncrief. He backed up their accounting of events. Upon being excused, he rushed out of the courtroom to his job at the Aragon.

J. M. Wilson, the manager of the Kimball House billiard room, was then called to the stand. He testified that he lived across from where the shooting occurred. He said he had not heard the shot but that his wife had been startled by it and had awakened him. He heard someone running down the street. He dressed and went across the street to where Bass was lying. It was still dark. By the time he got there the officers had arrived along with a black boy, later identified as Will Coleman. He made no mention of the milkman. In addition to describing the position of the body and the actions of the officers, he shared a critical observation. Paden knew the monthlong torrential rains, culminating in the most recent effects of the West Indian storm, had resulted in an overgrowth of high weeds along the Ivy Street embankment. They created an ideal environment for retaining imprints on the soft, wet ground. Wilson said he saw what looked like footprints on the wet bank about halfway from the bottom. It looked as if someone had slid down from above. And at the top of the embankment, immediately above where the footprints were, the weeds had been parted. He said he had brought these observations to the attention of the officers who were there, but they were preoccupied and paid little attention to what he had to say.

Wilson stepped down from the witness box. Paden looked at his watch. "We just may be able to finish this endeavor before the noon hour. The next witness I would like to call is a man whom some of you will know—a man whose testimony we must hear—a man who made it clear to me that he does not want to be here this morning. I had to coax him mightily to show up—even threatening to have him thrown in the jailhouse if he didn't. There are other witnesses, by the way, who could attest to conversations they had with the deceased prior to his death, including one of Bass's close friends, a man by the name of Young Gresham, but none whose testimony would come close to matching what you are about to hear. If you decide you need to hear from the others, then we'll send a boy out to bring them in. But as I have told you before," he looked over at the jurors, "I don't want this to get long and drawn out." Paden scanned the room. His eyes fell on a slight man, with muttonchop whiskers and clad in a white linen shirt and baggy, suspender-held grey cotton trousers, sitting in the back of the room.

"Mr. Hughes, please take the stand."

The man rose, passed by the evidence table, was sworn in, and seated himself in the witness box.

"Please state your name and occupation."

"My name is C.T. Hughes," the man spoke between his teeth. He fidgeted and jiggled his knee. "I own a bakery on Alabama Street."

"Mr. Hughes, please tell us how you knew the deceased and what you know about the events leading to his death." Paden held his arm up with his palm facing toward Hughes and paused for a moment, looking at the jurors. He turned to face the witness. "And Mr. Hughes, I implore you to tell us *everything* you know that is relevant to his death. You may proceed."

"Baker Bass was a friend of mine," Hughes began. "A few minutes before one o'clock this past Thursday afternoon I was standing on Decatur Street taking my last few drags from a Richmond Gem. Mr. Bass came by—if you happened to know him, you would know he didn't take to people smoking cigarettes around him, even though he sold a mighty lot of tobacco—so I put mine out in a hurry. Anyway, we struck up a conversation. As we walked up the street he began telling me of his business troubles. He said he had been bothered a great deal. He said some detectives had been hounding him. He said they were trying to do him in. When we got to the corner of Decatur and Peachtree, he stopped cold in front of Beermann's Place. A goodly number of locals were congregating, as they often do, in front of the cigar display in the shop window. Mr. Bass pulled me a few yards away so we wouldn't be within earshot. It was there that he began to tell me what I am about to relate to you. He described to me how a friend had told him a short time earlier that he had heard a man say he'd just as soon see him dead. The friend told him the man would have no compunction about doing it himself, publicly if he could not do it privately."

"Mr. Hughes, I am always reluctant to allow hearsay testimony, but this is important enough that it needs to be heard." Paden said. "And after all, no one is on trial here. Did Bass tell you who this friend was, the one who conveyed this information to him?"

Hughes shook his head. "No sir, he didn't tell me that."

Paden walked over to the where the jurors were seated. He swung around to face the witness box. "Did Bass tell you the name of the man who allegedly threatened to kill him?"

Hughes looked down at his lap and twisted in his chair.

"Mr. Hughes, as I stated before, you have to tell us everything you know."

"Yes," the witness continued. "He said he was a member of the police force. He mumbled a name that I had never heard before."

The jurors, newspapermen and spectators in the room leaned forward.

"And what name did he tell you?"

"Unfortunately I don't remember," Hughes replied, fiddling with his glasses as he spoke.

Berry leapt from his seat. "Mr. Hughes, this is preposterous. How could you possibly not remember something that important?"

Paden glared at Berry. "Mr. Berry, I will not allow outbursts in my courtroom." He then turned to the witness. "Mr. Hughes, you *must* recall the man's name. How could you forget something so important?"

"I don't know. I wish I could remember. Perhaps I was too stunned to make sense of what I was hearing. Mr. Bass said some policemen, more than one, had made accusations against him that were not true. He said he thought they were afraid they would lose their jobs, or worse, when Mr. Bass fixed his flint by proving his own innocence."

"Listen, Mr. Hughes, I don't believe you appreciate how serious this is. Do you know how much trouble you'll be in if you withhold evidence? Either your memory fails, as you implausibly claim, or you are refusing to tell us what you know to protect your own backside, but we have to know who this man was," Paden bore down, his voice rising. "So here's what we're going to do." He looked across the room. "Detective Cason, could I speak with you for a moment?"

Ed Cason, a senior member of the detective bureau, approached Paden's dais.

"Cason, I want to go to the station house. As quickly as you can. Retrieve a list of every policeman on the force. When you return, I'm going to have you read every name, one-by-one, until Mr. Hughes's memory improves. I don't care how long it takes." Paden looked at his watch.

It took nine minutes for Cason to make his way the four blocks to the police station, retrieve the list of names, and return to the inquest room. Paden had the detective stand in the front of the room, just below his dais and between the jurors and the witness box. Cason pronounced each man's first and last name, including his own. The jurors listened, expecting Hughes to finger someone. But as each name was called Hughes shook his head and said he could not remember. He never came up with the policeman's name. Paden gave up and ordered him off the witness stand.

Hughes was followed to the stand by Sam Green, a black porter at the Big Bonanza Saloon, a gentlemen's barroom owned by the mayor and located in the Kimball House Hotel next door to Beermann's Place. Green said he was on his way to work shortly after four o'clock Friday morning, walking up the north side of Ellis toward Peachtree. As he neared the corner of Ivy and Ellis Streets, he saw a man run from Ivy and continue down Ellis. The man's back was to him. The street light at the corner had gone out but it was still light enough for him to tell that the man was wearing a green jacket with black stripes. He had not heard a pistol shot, but he pointed out that he was hard of hearing—nigh deaf in one ear and not much better in the other without the aid of an ear tube or trumpet. He continued up Peachtree to work. He was unaware that someone had been shot until a woman told him later that morning. Paden noted that, while Green said he hadn't heard the gunshot, he may have been the only person to have witnessed the killer, assuming there was one, running from the scene.

When Sam Green's testimony was over, the jurors said they had heard enough and were ready to reach a verdict. However, a newspaperman who was present told Paden he had heard a rumor that three men knew who the unnamed policeman was, and two of them were in the inquest room that day. Herbert Jenkins, the traveling tobacco salesman, was one of those men. Jenkins had said he and Bass were friends and that Bass confided in him on a regular basis. Jenkins claimed to know of the dogged efforts on the part of some members of the police force to destroy Bass's business. Jenkins had refused to reveal the policemen's identities to a reporter the night before. But he had said he would do so in front of the coroner's jury.

Paden called Jenkins to the stand. A tall man with an aquiline nose and lean cheeks rose from the third row of chairs at far end of the room. Paden noted his dark eyes and olivaceous skin. Jenkins approached the witness box. He was no more than halfway across the room when Charles Camp, the attorney representing Bass's family, rose to his feet.

Camp's sonorous voice resonated throughout the room. "Coroner Paden, sir, having conferred with Mrs. Bass and her eldest son, it is my opinion that further evidence at this time would compromise any case in a criminal trial against an accused killer—or killers. With all due respect, I shall remind you and the jurors that the purpose of this inquest is *only* to determine how Mr. Bass died. Therefore, I request that no further testimony be allowed *unless* it can further these proceedings to that end, and to that end alone."

The jurors said they had heard enough evidence. Jenkins was never allowed to testify. Paden ordered the inquest room cleared. The jury deliberated no more than thirty minutes before they informed Paden they had reached a verdict. The witnesses, attorneys, reporters, and spectators returned and took their places. They listened as Berry stood before the crowded room.

"We, the jury impaneled and sworn to inquire into the cause of the death of Mr. B.A. Bass, who was killed on Ivy Street on the morning of the 30th of August, find from the evidence of witnesses sworn that said deceased came to his death from a gunshot wound on the head, fired by some person unknown to the jury and believe the same was murder."

The inquest ended after three hours of testimony and deliberation. The coroner's jury had spoken. The issue was settled, at least in the eyes of the coroner's court. Paden knew that the jury had chosen to err on the side of caution, lest a guilty man go free. The burden of finding Bass's killer now fell to others.

TEN

ELLA BASS

Wormwood and Melancholy

THAT SAME SATURDAY AFTERNOON, ELLA FELT THE strident drumming of the four o'clock Georgia Central steam train as it pulled out of the Union Depot and made its way through the rail yard, bound for Albany by way of Macon. She and her children sat in the first passenger car. The baggage car, just in front of them and to the rear of the tender, carried her husband's remains.

With John and the others by her side, she opened her well-worn Bible, which she had held firmly clenched in her hands since boarding the train. Her husband had passed by that very same rail yard in the predawn hours of countless mornings as he walked to work. He had known the area well. He would have seen the trains pulling out of the station headed for Washington, or Nashville, or Charleston, or points beyond. Or perhaps Albany. He would have taken in the smells and the sounds of the coal-fired engines. The soot would have darkened his crisp, white shirt. But not on this day.

As the train approached Albany, Ella thought back to the time, a decade earlier, when she and Baker had taken the Number 40 Atlantic Coast Line fast mail train from Thomasville to New Orleans to attend the World's Industrial and Cotton Centennial Exposition. She had been pregnant with Mary at the time. Baker had discouraged her from accompanying him, given her condition, but she insisted. And she was grateful that she had. The memory of that trip was one she would forever cherish. She remembered her husband gazing out the window as the train passed from town to town. A railway clerk would toss the day's mail pouch off the train at the appointed spots. Then he would quickly extend the train car's catcher arm to hook and retrieve the pouch of unprocessed mail from the same station. These trains were designed for speed, and while they were intended for the delivery and retrieval of mail, they often accommodated passengers in express cars. There were no faster trains in service. Baker and Ella would arrive the following morning in the city that, along with Baton Rouge and points between, had been home to the highest concentration of millionaires anywhere in America before the war, thanks in large part to sugar plantations and slaves. They had packed generously for that trip, with two steamer trunks on the verge of coming apart at the hinges. It was the first time they had been out of the state since they had married, save for Baker's solitary trip back to Palmyra to attend the funeral of his father, who had lived for only a year after Baker left home.

Soon after she and Baker had arrived at the fair, they listened to a Mexican band play Norteño music with accordion, tololoche, and bajo sexto, the band members decked out in leather-fringed jackets and straw cowboy hats. "Muy bonita," she recalled them calling out, as Mexican señoritas, with ribbon-braided hair and dressed in vibrant, flowing skirts, danced the conjunto polka, encouraging the crowds of visitors to join in. She remembered yanking the pins from her hair, shaking her long tresses loose, reaching for Baker's reluctant hand, and pulling him toward her. Baker struggled to follow her lead as they performed the hop chasse steps in two/four time. Miss Hansell's polka lessons had paid off.

She remembered buying a postcard for a penny at one of the vending kiosks on the grounds. The glass enclosed Horticultural Hall stood in the postcard's background, the American flag undulating in the wind above the building's central glass tower. Palm trees adorned the grounds surrounding the hall. Splendidly dressed men and women, some on horseback, rounded out the postcard's scene. In the immediate foreground, a young child held her father's hand. They were accompanied by a woman, presumably her mother, riding sidesaddle on a sorrel Arabian. Ella had felt a personal connection to the little girl in the picture. She flipped the postcard to the back side and penned on the right section, with the elaborate flourish she'd learned from Miss Hansell, the words "Mr. and Mrs. John McKinnon, Thomasville, Georgia." She could still remember, ten years later, the gist of what she had written on the left panel, even if she didn't recall it verbatim. She remembered writing in tiny script so as to get everything she had to say in the limited space available.

The city of New Orleans is like nothing I have ever seen. There are so many people decked out in their finest attire. The hustle and bustle just makes our heads spin. We are having a grand time and enjoying the fair. I only wish we could have been here for the official commencement. I am told that President Arthur opened the festivities all the way from Washington by telegraph. Imagine that. Father, yesterday we visited the Cotton Exchange. You would have marveled at the splendid building and all the hurry-skurry there. Mother, please tell the children that Baker and I love and miss them.

Or something to that effect. She signed her name with the exuberant adornment of a furbelow, Yours truly, Ellinor. She affixed a one-cent Benjamin Franklin Banknote Issue stamp in the upper right corner. She found the nearest postal box and dropped it in, knowing her family back home would be delighted to share, at least in a small way, in what she and Baker were experiencing at the Great World's Fair.

Baker had bought a one-inch silver souvenir token, emblazoned on the front with an eagle perched atop an American flag shield and accompanied by two additional shields. One represented the scales of justice. The other showed a bale of cotton. The word Souvenir was inscribed on the back side. From that point on, he carried that medal with him everywhere he went.

The train rolled into the Albany station. Ella's thoughts jolted back to the present. Surely Baker would have been as enthusiastic about the Atlanta exposition, scheduled to open in just two weeks, as he had been about the New Orleans fair. It occurred to her that no one had mentioned the souvenir token being on Baker's person when he was discovered lying on the sidewalk. She wondered if it had been lost or perhaps stolen.

Two carriages awaited her as she descended the steps from the train car. One would transport her and the children the sixty miles to Thomasville. The other would follow behind with the casket. Returning to Thomasville was bittersweet. She had not been back since her father's death three years earlier. At that time she had pleaded with her mother to move to Atlanta, but her mother had chosen instead to remain with extended kin in Thomasville.

As the carriage approached her home town, Ella recalled the time she had served on the welcoming committee when Jefferson Davis paid a visit to Thomasville. She and Baker had been front and center. No event in the town had brought more excitement. Davis had only recently written his book, *The Rise and Fall of the Confederate Government.* The cause was still alive in the hearts of many who vowed never to let it die. At nine o'clock on a crisp May morning, the presidential train had pulled out of the Savannah, Florida & Western Railroad yards and headed southwest toward Thomasville. The merchants closed their stores. The town's cornet band awaited his arrival. When his train pulled in at Jackson Street a little after three o'clock, a throng of two thousand jubilant spectators were there to greet him. The men threw their hats in the air. The women waved their white lace handkerchiefs. As he appeared at the rear platform of the train, the band played "Dixie" to thunderous applause.

On Monday morning, less than two days after she and her children arrived with Baker's remains, Ella stood on a windswept bluff at the McKinnon family cemetery at Laurel Hill, on the northeastern edge of town. She watched as Wiley, Robert, and

Jesse Bass, her cousin George, and two of Baker's Thomasville friends lowered the wooden casket into the red clay earth, next to the graves of her deceased family members. Next to Baby Florence.

She replayed the events of a mere three mornings prior. Things had happened so quickly. Images flew through her mind like fleeting projectiles, each one fading into the next. Baker's diminishing silhouette through the fogged window. The gunshot. The stranger at the door. Running down Ellis Street with John. The back of the ambulance. Her cheek against Baker's cold face. The feather pillow. The wool covers. The clock on the bedroom wall. Twelve twenty. Friday afternoon.

On the following Wednesday, Ella and her children returned home on the morning Georgia Central train to an empty house on Ellis Street and to the bitter redolence of wormwood and melancholy.

ELEVEN

JOHN BASS

To Make His Father Proud

JOHN BASS HAD JUST TURNED FOURTEEN WHEN THE family pulled up stakes and headed north to Atlanta. Baker Jr. was two years younger, Fred was nine, and Mary was five. He could still remember that spring day in ninety-one when his mother sat him down at the foot of the bed and broke the news. "Your father and I have decided it's time to leave Thomasville."

Your father and I? The moment the words passed her lips, John knew the decision had not been hers. Perhaps it was the tear that slowly coursed down her cheek. Perhaps it was that the corners of her mouth pulled down. At the time, he was too preoccupied with his own affairs to pay much attention to those things.

What were the first words out of my mouth? But what about my friends? That's what fourteen-year-olds think about. But he had done a lot of maturing in these past four years. And now, with his father gone, he felt an unaccustomed weight on his shoulders.

His mother had been born into the fineries of Thomasville society, pampered as an only child and given the best education a young girl could expect in the capable hands of Miss Hansell. As an adult, Ella always did what was expected of her. She made a comfortable home for her husband and children. She had never had a paying job. She had never considered it—never needed to.

Now the burden would fall on John to somehow see to it that the lot of them—his mother, Baker Jr., Fred, and Mary—were provided for. Prepared or not, he had become the man of the house. Baker Jr., at sixteen and working as a junior apprentice at C.T. Hughes's bakery, could get by on his own. But the others were too young. Fred was only thirteen, a year younger than he, himself, had been when they moved from Thomasville. And Mary was nine.

Before the move, he had worked on his grandfather's farm, as had his brothers, and he had helped his father out on the occasional weekend at Pennington's store. Upon relocating to Atlanta, he had attended Boys High School for three years. He considered himself fortunate to have continued his education beyond the common age of fourteen. His mother had demanded nothing less. Aside from sometimes assisting at the Peters Street store and, over the past year, working pre-opening construction at the exposition grounds, John didn't have a wealth of experience to fall back on.

The long train ride back from Thomasville, after they had lowered his father into the ground at Laurel Hill and paid their last respects, had given John ample time to ponder the family's future. His mother, Bible at the ready, occupied a window seat in the far rear of the coach. Her head held low, she rocked back and forth, tracking the rhythmic drum-drum-druming of the locomotive. Her tear-stained face was bereft of presence. John needed to give her grieving space. The others sat beside and across the aisle from her in stunned silence. John deemed it best to leave them be. He settled into a seat separated half a car from the rest of the family, and there, for the duration of the trip, he mulled over his options.

There were farms on the edge of Atlanta where he could work, but tilling the soil was the last thing he wanted to do. He had left that life behind with the move north. He was a city boy now—a man actually—with city sensibilities and city aspirations. So what could he do in the city to make enough of a living to feed four, maybe five, mouths? He had enjoyed his time at the exposition and had picked up valuable carpentering skills. Perhaps he could get a job wielding hammer and saw at one of the construction projects around town. Shopkeeping was another option. His father had put four years of sweat into building the business on Peters Street. Did he owe it to the man's legacy to keep the store in business? Had he gained enough experience, scant as it was, to make a go of it?

It was not until the train pulled into the Union Depot, with steam screaming and engines chugging, the tsss of the air brakes, the screech of iron grating against iron, that John made the decision. He would do whatever he could to keep the store going. He would go to Peters Street early the following morning and begin preparing to reopen. While his mother would likely protest his abrogating the traditional mourning period, he felt an urgency to get moving. His father would have understood.

On the afternoon of his father's passing, John himself had tacked the note—handwritten in large block letters—to the front door beneath the black wreath.

CLOSED UNTIL FURTHER NOTICE DUE TO THE DEATH OF MR. BAKER AUGUSTUS BASS. REST HIS SOUL.

That same afternoon, he had rummaged through the paperwork at the store, looking for any record of the tobacco purchase that had heralded the start of his father's troubles. He had also searched for his father's Smith and Wesson. He found neither.

Now he stood on the sidewalk and looked up at the sign over the door, just as he had seen his father do. DRY GOODS, TOBACCO AND SUNDRIES—and below it, in the Clarendon typeface his father was so fond of—*BAKER A. BASS, PROPRIETOR*. He was sure his father, looking up at the sign, had felt a great sense of pride. John, on the other hand, felt little beyond apprehension. He looked past the handwritten note and through the window of the closed door. For a moment he thought he saw his father standing midway down the length of the store, feather duster in hand. If he hadn't known better, he would have sworn his father nodded ever so slightly before continuing to go about his dusting.

Baker Bass had been dead, and the store closed, for six days. John would spend this day cleaning, filling the cash register with enough cash to get through the weekend and into the following week, polishing its cast brass to a lustrous finish, and putting things in order for a reopening the following day.

As he cleaned and dusted the long counter, his thoughts turned to the days in Thomasville when his father had toiled in Pennington's store until the old man—what did his father call him? *Dusht and Shtock*—finally made him a partner. John would toil just as hard, but he had no idea what the future held. He was up for the task, but was he up *to* the task? Only time would tell.

On Friday, the sixth of September, John left the house on Ellis Street two hours before sunrise, as his father had done every morning. Just seven days earlier, he had sat at the kitchen table, sharing Maxwell House and banter with his parents, Baker and Ella sitting at the ends and he between them. What had he said that morning? *I don't share your fondness for rising hours before daybreak...I haven't mastered the art of engaging in conversation at four in the morning.* But things were different now. And, like it or not, he would adapt to starting the day well before cock-crow.

He had just descended the steps and was headed toward Ivy Street when he looked back to see his mother gazing through the window, her face faintly illuminated by the streetlamp. She was crying. This time, it wasn't a single tear, but a stream cascading down both cheeks. "I'll be alright, Mama." He mouthed the words. He had never called her that before. For some reason, on that morning of all mornings, *Mother* just seemed too distant. Too formal.

When he reached the corner, he looked left down Ivy Street. It was as quiet as it must have been around the same time a week earlier when, halfway down the block, someone had apparently slid down the bank and confronted his father, felling him with a single shot. By the time John and his mother had arrived that morning, a crowd had formed—police, doctor and ambulance driver, onlookers—perhaps the killer himself.

But this morning, John decided that, rather than trace his father's path, he would continue up Ellis to Peachtree Street. He walked down Peachtree past the Aragon Hotel and the Opera House on his left, the First Methodist Episcopal Church on his right. He would continue down Pryor Street past the Kimball House, crossing the tracks at the westernmost end of the Union Depot. Another ten blocks, thirteen if you counted the smaller side streets, and he would arrive at his father's store. Along the way, he would stop in at Carrie Mangham's eating house and order breakfast delivered, just as his father would have done. If all went as planned, he would report to Ella that evening that he had suffered no untoward encounters, no interlopers, no coming up against strangers.

He removed the handwritten note from the door, placing the tacks in his pocket and methodically folding the paper into a four-inch square. He could not bring himself to discard the note. He inserted the key into the Yale cylinder lock his father had installed back in June, and passed over the threshold into uncharted territory. The store was cold and dark. John laid a fire in the stove and lit the row of lamps along the side wall behind the counter. He took note of the sweet aroma of tobacco combined with sarsaparilla, linseed oil, and molasses—with pungent overtones of ripe cheese, pickles, and sauerkraut. It was a well-dug-in combination of smells, one that he would never forget. Had he been too preoccupied the prior day to notice? Had the cleaning liquid he had used to mop the floor, or the flour-and-vinegar paste with which he had polished the brass register, somehow masked the aromatic patina? Or perhaps he hadn't wanted to acknowledge it, as it would always remind him of his father.

John thought back to the day his father had first opened the Peters Street store. For the first six months, business had been far from brisk. But as locals got to know the new merchant in town, his name displayed prominently over the door, they began to choose his store over others in the neighborhood. Baker Bass had a knack for getting to know people. He might not have cottoned to everybody he met, and he had a few run-ins along the way, but he never met a stranger.

John hadn't cultivated the affability of his father or the genial ways of his mother. And he didn't share their benevolence. His father had known all the store's customers by their first names, knew what they did for a living, knew their husbands or wives' names, their children. Hell, John was sure he wouldn't know the name of the first person to come into the store, or the second, or the third. If he stood any chance of making it, that would have to change. He positioned a pencil and a memo booklet next to the cash register. His father had preferred the Deering Harvester Company Vest Pocket Memo because of its compact size (2-1/2 by 5 inches) and the fact that the local salesman handed them out in bulk to favored merchants. John would make note of each customer's name, along with a brief physical description. In time, he would get to know them all.

As he dusted the counter around the register one last time before opening the store, he noticed a slip of paper peeking ever so slightly from beneath a Rose Leaf Cut Plug tin. He lifted the tin.

Added strength and skill lie just beyond the bounds of comfortable effort. If you would grow, stretch a little.

Written on the paper, in his father's hand. When had his father put it there? John hoped that, over time, he could acquire the strength and skill to make his father proud.

Two weeks passed. John had filled the memo booklet with names and personal vignettes, even going so far as to add little sketches in the margins—Mr. Fletcher - waxed mustache, lazy eye...Leonard Holloway - longish face, bushy eyebrows, never stops talking...Miss Abby Deakins - brown hair with a shock of blonde, the sweetest trill of a voice, prim and proper...He would put a check mark by each name to denote the number of times that person visited the store. What he had failed to do—an oversight that he now regretted—was keep track of each patron's purchases, for store traffic far outpaced sales.

Late in the day on Friday, the twentieth, a man showed up whom John had never before seen. A bit rotund, with thick jowls and a greying stubble beard. Grey sack coat, a tad tight in the chest, bow tie, and derby. He entered the store with a self-confident stride, tipped his hat, and proceeded to examine the goods throughout the store with an uncustomary attentiveness to detail. John watched as the man looked up and down every shelf, occasionally picking up and examining items that were readily at hand—a tin of Sweet Georgia Brown hair pomade, a bottle of Kendal Black Drop elixir, a silver-plated hair brush.

"Are you looking for anything in particular?"

The man walked over to where John stood. Extended his hand. "I'm Ordinary Calhoun. And you are?"

"I'm John Bass."

"And your mother is Ella McKinnon Bass?"

"Yes."

"And you both live at 74 Ellis Street?"

"That's correct. Will you please tell me what this is about?"

"Mr. Bass, I visited your house this morning but no one came to the door. I'm here about the lawsuits."

"What lawsuits?"

"The ones the creditors have filed to recover monies they claim they are owed for merchandise they sold your father."

John was not aware of any lawsuits. Was it possible they had been sent to the house? Or perhaps to the family's attorney? Had his mother known about them and not told him?

The man retrieved a folded document from his coat pocket and handed it to John. "I'm here to inform you that, in an effort to sort all of this out, I am prepared to appoint a Mr. C.B. Reynolds temporary administrator of your father's estate."

Part Two

THE DETECTIVE

TWELVE

SARAH CONN

Baby Face

"HEY, BABY FACE."

Sarah stared at her brother. His chin and cheekbones were weak. His eyes were wide set and large, like a doe's. His skin was smooth and pallid—bleached out looking—like a hen's egg.

"Shut your bone box, Sarah Jane."

"You're a baby face and you can't help it. You ain't never gonna be able to grow a mustache, you know that?"

"I said shut up, Sarah Jane, or I'll give you a blinker." Green Conn balled his right hand into a fist and shook it in his sister's face.

"I wish Daddy was here. He'd show you a thing or two. You're too big for your britches if you ask me."

"Daddy ain't here. And he may never come back. I'm the man of the house now."

"Thomas Greenberry Conn, you ain't no man of the house,"
Sarah said. "Why, what are you now, twelve?" She let out a cackle.

Green puffed out his chest. "I just turned fourteen, Sarah Jane.
You know that."

"Well, I'm a whole year older than you. Almost a year and a half.
You can't boss me around."

"I'll do as I please. You can't stop me."

"You watch. Daddy's comin' home. I can feel it in my bones.
And when he does—"

"Sarah Jane, I told you to shut your bone box. Daddy's been gone
for two years. Ever since he signed up to fight. Do you remember
that? Or have you forgotten already? I haven't. Eighteen and
sixty-two. Company F. Thirty-sixth Regiment. Georgia Volunteer
Infantry. You probably didn't even know that. But I do. Nobody's
heard from him in over a year. Don't you know anything?"

"I knew that, Thomas. I also know you're a lazy good-for-
nothin'—"

"Why, I have a good mind to just haul off and give you a good
old-fashioned anointing right here and now. Nobody'll ever call
me a lazy good-for-nothin' and get away with it."

Sarah pointed across the field of crabgrass to the shed a hundred
yards away, with its weathered walls of squared hewn white pine
logs. A stand of loblollies, just past the shed, separated the Conn
homestead from the next farm over. An overgrown privet thicket
partially obscured the view through the stand of trees and had
begun to encroach on the shed. A scattering of rock piles and
red clay outcroppings surrounded the side of the shed facing the
farmhouse. The occasional blackhaw bush displayed a smattering
of wilted, two-month-old white blooms.

"You see that shed over there, Thomas?"

"Don't call me that. My name's Green."

"OK, *Green*. Do you see that shed over there?"

"You mean Daddy's blacksmith shed?

"*Of course* that's what I mean."

"*Of course* I see it."

"When's the last time you went in there?"

Green paused for a moment. He rubbed his chin in mocking contemplation. "Well, let's see. Maybe right before Daddy went off to fight?"

"And don't you think you could have found the time to get in there and learn to do what your Daddy tried to teach you before he left? Learn how to support the family—if you're supposed to be the—what did you call yourself—*the man of the house?* Instead of relyin' on Momma and me to feed and put clothes on us?"

"I pull my weight. I work the farm."

"You don't work the farm. The corn'll turn in the fall and you'll just let it sit there. Waitin' for Momma or me. I've seen you out there. You're a joke. Nancy and Irena and I did ten times as much as you—maybe twenty times—before the both of them went off and got hitched."

"Yeah, you're all older than me, too. The whole lot of you. Why shouldn't you do more than me?"

"But I thought you said you were the man of the house. Some man you are. You didn't answer my question. Why don't you try to forge like Daddy?"

"I ain't never gonna be a blacksmith," Green shot back. "I'm better than that. As soon as I'm old enough I'm gonna leave this jerkwater town. Oak Grove ain't big enough for me. Hitch a wagon. Head down Johnston's ferry way. Find me a place in the city. Make a name for myself."

"Better than that, you say. I just wish Daddy could hear those words comin' out of your mouth. He'd have somethin' to tell you about that. You'll get your comeuppance. You'll see."

The year was '64. A month had passed since that day in May when Sarah Jane Conn had provoked her baby-faced brother into admitting his longing to leave the farm at the first opportunity. She had no doubt he would try to do it. It was only a matter of when. Comeuppance or no comeuppance. It didn't make any difference that he was fourteen. If he got it in his mind to do something, he was just ornery and bull-headed enough that nobody could stop him from trying.

He may just end up a guttersnipe.

But before Green could fulfill his promise to take off, tragedy struck. It was a Monday afternoon. Sarah looked up at the western horizon to the most remarkable array of red and yellow and orange that she had ever seen. It looked like something from a painting. Like the ones Mr. McMurtry did in his spare time. Dense smoke and dust clouds filled the sky. It looked like a kaleidoscope. She caught the occasional scent of sulfur wafting through the air. It smelled like the odors that used to come from her father's blacksmith shed. She heard a dull, distant rumble. Thrumming like a drum. *Where's Daddy?* she thought.

She heard a rustling noise. Coming from the stand of loblollies. It was old man Wilson. Running toward her. Smack-dab through the pines and privet thicket. Brushing away the needles and leaves with both hands.

"Where's your Momma, Sarah?"

"She's around back. Washing the soldiers' clothes."

"Go get her. And your brother. Now."

Sarah ran to the far end of the house.

"Momma, Mr. Wilson's here. He needs to talk to you right now. And you too, Thomas."

"Something awful's happened," Levi Wilson said to Sarah's mother as they stood between the crabgrass field and the house. "The Yankees have gone and tried to take Kennesaw Mountain. It's just a matter of time. The river's our only hope. Let's hope they can't cross it."

Martha Conn picked up three-year-old Henry and held him against her hip. Little Martha, only a year older, tugged at her mother's summer dress.

"Mrs. Conn, ma'am, don't hold it against me for saying it, but this is no place for a mother and her young'uns to be by themselves."

"But where will we go? This is all we have. We're barely getting by as it is. We don't have the means to just off and leave."

"Momma, what you meant to say is all we got is a piss pot," Green interjected.

"Thomas Greenberry," Martha Conn shot back, "you don't talk like that. Not to me. Not to Mr. Wilson. Not to anybody."

Green stormed off in a huff.

"Listen Martha, you can all come and stay with us for a while. We'll make room. This'll pass. In no time you'll be back here. That's assuming the damned Yankees don't burn the whole county down."

The Confederates held the Federal forces back at Kennesaw Mountain. But that did little to stop their advance. Levi Wilson's hope that the river would protect the people of Oak Grove was just that—a hope and nothing more. The Union forces breached the Chattahoochee, crossing at Isom's Ferry near the mouths of Sope and Heard's Creeks. By the time the incursion ended, they had placed two pontoon bridges across the river and had taken Oak Grove, one of several staging grounds for the siege of Atlanta. By the autumn of 1864, Sherman's troops had virtually destroyed Atlanta and had marched on to the sea.

Toward the end of '64, Martha and her children returned to their home. Through what Sarah thought had to have been an intercession from the Lord Almighty himself, both Mr. Wilson's place and their own had been spared the ravages that much of Oak Grove had suffered.

One December morning, soon after they had moved back home, Sarah sat on the front porch. The bitter cold penetrated the blanket draped over her arms and shoulders. The skies to the west were a somber grey. No red. No yellow. No orange. No dense clouds of smoke and dust. There was an eerie silence. She felt a ghostly sense of desolation, as if everything around her had been lost—except the farm—what there was of it after months of neglect. She wondered if her family would ever recover. She wondered if she would ever see her father again.

Three months passed before Thomas Greenberry Conn got his comeuppance. Sarah had known it would happen—eventually—but she had no idea just how. It was a Monday, just like the day back in June of '64 when Levi Wilson had come running through the loblollies and privet. She stood on the front porch. But this time the sky was pale blue, save for a scattering of cottony clouds. The summer sun beat down on the crabgrass and red clay. The air was oven-hot. Perspiration soaked the front panel of her cotton dress.

From where Sarah was standing, she could see part way down the dirt lane that continued all the way past the Wilson farmhouse to the main road leading to the Sope Creek Bridge. A wavy haze covered the lane's packed clay surface. It looked as if puddles were scattered across the road bed, although she knew it hadn't rained in days.

Through the shimmering haze, she could barely make out a figure approaching in the distance. Inching along. *Who is it?* she thought. *Mr. Wilson? Maybe a stranger looking for work. Or the man that brings dry goods from town. Or a damned Yankee. Why is he hobbling like that?*

Her first instinct was to run inside and fetch the shotgun Momma kept by the door. But as the figure neared, she realized it was Daddy.

"Momma. Thomas. Martha. Henry. Come quick. Daddy's home."

She ran toward him. As she approached, she saw that his left arm was in a makeshift sling. He supported himself with a long, gnarly walking stick. It looked like he had fashioned it from the limb of an old oak tree. His left leg was contorted to an awful pitch.

"Daddy, what on earth happened?" She hugged him hesitantly.

He was about to respond when Momma approached. "Oh, William," Momma called out. Momma threw her arms around him ever so carefully. She planted a kiss on his cheek. Henry and little Martha gathered at his feet. Green lagged behind.

In the farmhouse, Momma put a cane chair at the head of the kitchen table, the place where Daddy always sat. The place that had remained unoccupied since the day he had left. Momma arranged cushions in the seat and against the back of the chair and helped him to sit. She propped the gnarly stick beside him against the wall. She motioned for Sarah, Green, and the two younger children to gather around the table. She sat at the other end.

Daddy insisted that Momma and the children first share stories of what life had been like for them over the past three years. They told him of the struggles to keep food on the table. The five dollars a week Momma made on the side washing the soldiers' uniforms. The bright red, smoky sky on that Monday afternoon in June. The rumbling in the distance. The smell of sulfur in the air. The evacuation to Levi Wilson's house. The breaching of the Chattahoochee. The invasion of Oak Grove. The sparing of the farm. Coming back after the Yankees had left. Surrounded by ruin. Trying to make do.

Daddy was reluctant at first to talk about what had befallen him since he had enlisted as a private in April of '62. It was Sarah who coaxed it out of him.

"They took us all to Dalton first. But we didn't stay there long before they hauled us off to Chattanooga. I spent almost a year there. Did you get my letters?" Martha nodded. "Then they sent us off to fight in Vicksburg. They put me in with General Taylor's men. We tried our best to hold the city, but we were outnumbered two-to-one. They just kept coming. It was at Milliken's Bend that they got me. Artillery fire. I was laid up in a hospital tent. Then, on the fourth of July, that was in sixty-three, we surrendered. They took us all in as prisoners. The fourth of July of all days. Can you believe that? They paroled us back into the custody of the

Confederate army five days later. Sent us off to Mobile Harbor." He took a deep breath. "They were supposed to send us back from Mobile Harbor to Chattanooga, but that's when I snuck out. Took off with two of my buddies from the thirty-sixth. Been on the run ever since."

"That was almost two years ago, William. Where have you been all this time? We've been worried sick about you."

"Martha, I know you have. I can't tell you how much I wanted to come home sooner. But I knew if they caught me I'd be in deep trouble. I couldn't even bring myself to write, thinking they'd somehow track me down. We kept our heads low. Stayed in Mobile for a while. Then we started making our way through Alabama toward Atlanta. But when we got near the city—that was last year—we were stopped in our tracks by the sight of Union men coming through. We hid out."

"How did you get by all that time?"

"My buddies weren't injured like me. They took odd jobs along the way. They fed me. Took care of me. I knew they would. Then we laid up on this farm in Monroeville for a while. The farmer and his wife, couple by the name of Odom, took us in and made sure we got two good meals a day—three on a good day. One of these days I'll have to repay them all for what they did for me."

William looked across the table. "Thomas, you've been awful quiet. What have you been up to since I left?"

"My name's Green now."

"Tell him, *Green*," Sarah interjected. "Tell Daddy what you've done the past three years."

"Shut up Sarah Jane."

"I'll tell you what he's done, Daddy. Nothin'. Nothin' at all."

"Is that true Thomas—*Green?*"

Green was silent.

"Well, I'll tell you what we're going to do," Daddy said. "Tomorrow morning you're going to follow me into the forging shed. You're going to learn to blacksmith once and for all. You'll do the work. I'll watch."

Sarah lay awake that night worrying about Daddy. *Did he really sneak away like he said? Will the Confederate army come looking for him? Maybe they're already on his trail. Maybe they're swarming over the area like turkey vultures, waiting to pounce when the time is right. Will they capture him and haul him away?* She got out of bed and crept over to the bedroom window. She pulled back the curtains and stared into the dark.

She was sure Thomas—she still couldn't bring herself to call him by his new name—lay awake too. But he was worrying about something else—about what Daddy was going to do to him when he got him out there in the blacksmith shed.

For months on end, under Daddy's imposing eye, Green spent ten hours a day striking red hot iron over an anvil face. He complained almost daily that his nostrils burned from the malodor of molten metal. He swore the heat was so stifling that he was certain he had found the infernal gates of Hell itself.

Sarah would sometimes sneak up to the shed and peak through a crack in the door. An acrid pall of smoke lingered in the air. More often than not, her brother had a scowl on his face and, she was certain, a chip on his shoulder that even the strongest boy in Oak Grove wouldn't be able to knock off.

This went on through the summer and into the fall. At some point the training was over. It was time for her brother to assume the forging duties that Daddy's war infirmities prevented him from doing. Green would split his time between blacksmithing and helping tend to the farm. The scowl that had formed during those ten-hour days in the shed was now permanently attached to his face, like somebody had fixed it with a branding iron. She couldn't look at him without imagining a great big chip of wood resting firmly on his shoulder.

The Confederates never came after Daddy. He succumbed to his injuries in '68, long after the war had ended. It didn't take long after that for Green to leave the farm and move to Roswell, Georgia, to open a blacksmith shop where, as he put it, there were more than two nags to an acre needing shoes. *What did he used to say? He was better than that?* Sarah mused. *He thought he was better than that, but Daddy put him in his place. Now he's doing just what he said he'd never do.*

Momma and Sarah stayed on the farm with the children. They struggled to make a go of it. By '78, Martha and Henry had both grown up, married, and moved on. Sarah and her mother tried for a short while to keep the farm going. But they finally gave up. They moved to Cross Keys, in DeKalb County, where they did domestic work and made extra money washing clothes for neighbors. Nearing thirty, Sarah resigned herself to spending the rest of her life as a spinster. And her Momma as a widow.

Sarah heard from Green only infrequently. He married in 1880, at the age of thirty. Soon thereafter he turned in his hammers and tongs. After fifteen years of blacksmithing, first under his father's demanding eye, and then by himself, he decided to move on. He and his wife relocated down the road to Atlanta, where he joined the police force. Sarah doubted she would hear much from her brother from that point on. *Maybe he was right all along,* she thought. *Maybe he wasn't cut out to follow in Daddy's footsteps. He thought it was beneath him. Maybe, just maybe, it was.*

THIRTEEN

ARTHUR CONNOLLY

Justice Sought

EARLY SUNDAY MORNING—1895—A WEEK AND A DAY after Bass's death. The city was enjoying only scattered traces of rain, a welcome respite from the torrential downpours of late. Arthur Connolly sat at his desk in the station house on Decatur Street. The sweet scent of linseed oil from the freshly painted walls permeated the air. His surroundings were palatial compared to what he had been accustomed to for most of his tenure as police chief. And he had a new mahogany desk chair. Lord, how he had wanted a new chair. Nothing fancy, just something not handed down from his predecessor, and a little more in keeping with his ample physique. He ran his hands up and down its smooth arms. The old arms had been rough, their lacquered finish worn from years of use.

He spit a wad of Redskin cut plug chewing tobacco into the brass spittoon at his feet and leaned back in his chair, interlacing his fingers behind his head. He thought about the earliest efforts to maintain law and order in the city, long before he joined the force. The city had been guarded by a single marshal and a handful of deputies. He had been twelve years old when, in 1863, one of those very deputies, Tim Shivers, was killed in a shootout with a ne'er-do-well named Whit Anderson. As a young boy, hearing about how Shivers took a bullet in the line of duty, and then seeing his father and uncles go off to war, Connolly was captivated by it all. He vowed to carry a gun and fight for justice and the common good one day. He got his opportunity on his twenty-first birthday, when he applied to become a policeman and was accepted the same day. At that time, the department was just beginning to grow from a rabble of frontier vigilantes to a reasonably well-behaved uniformed force. Good, honorable men were in demand—and hard to find. Connolly spent eight years, first walking the downtown beat, then moving up the ranks to captain, before becoming chief.

"I reckon I've done a lot in fifteen years—as much as any man could," he boasted to an otherwise empty room. He thought about the old, three-story station house on South Pryor Street. It had been cramped, cold, and damp. The basement flooded every time there was a heavy rain. He had told the board of commissioners every chance he got that it was unhealthy and disagreeable. Unfit for human habitation. And not what a growing city like Atlanta deserved. For one thing, there were too few holding cells. He decried the fact that his men sometimes had to lock up the more respectable class with the most depraved of criminals, rowdies, and ruffians—bummers and hoe-downers. In 1889 the board had made meager efforts to make things better. Succumbing to the plea for an end, once and for all, to the sin of amalgamation, they replaced seven old cells with fourteen iron cages. But in

Connolly's eyes that was far from good enough. Just thinking about what he had been through made his blood boil.

"Damn those son-of-a-bitch commissioners," he shouted, so loud that a sergeant in the adjacent room came running in to see if something was wrong. "Cantankerous and pigheaded. That's what they are." He looked up at the ceiling, stretching his arms into the air. "Why did it take those jackasses so long to come around?"

But they had, in time, come around. After years of prodding and pleading, Connolly got what he wanted, the building on Decatur Street where he sat this morning. The new station house had opened with great pomp and circumstance. It was hailed as modern and spacious, capable of accommodating one hundred fifty prisoners in forty-three cells and equipped with what an *Atlanta Constitution* writer said was every modern prison convenience. On opening day, Connolly's regulars, all one hundred of them, had paraded down the street to the new building. He had led the way on his prancing stallion, its newly shod hooves letting out a thunderous clap as they made contact with the roadbed. He stopped frequently to jump off his horse and glad-hand the people he recognized in the crowd as if he were running for governor.

The first detainee in the new cellblock had been an eighteen-year-old white boy named Charlie Mason, a despondent young man charged with petty larceny. He became quite a celebrity as sympathetic ladies, feeling compassion for him, all alone in a huge new jail, passed dimes into his cell. It had all started when Bertha and Jo Tindall, Charlie's spinster neighbors two doors down on Juniper Street, decided to pay him a visit with a generously endowed basket of homemade confections—chess pie, gingerbread, and cider cake. Before they knew it, they had created a following of kindhearted friends, and friends of friends—all making their way to the jailhouse—insisting that the desk clerk lead them to young Charlie's cell. "You ladies just need to move on now," Connolly remembered telling them. "Charlie's going to be just fine." In his short time in jail, Charlie had taken a liking to the station house mascot, so much so that, when it was time to release the boy, he didn't want to leave.

That old fice dog was the one occupant of Pryor Street who wishes we'd never moved from that Godforsaken place, Connolly thought. Old Bruff. He was a living terror to the rats scurrying across the floor. Curling his lips. Baring his teeth. Growling and chasing them all through the station house.

Connolly reeled off his accomplishments since taking over, touching his fingers one by one to his palm. *Decatur Street. The Gamewell boxes. The detective bureau. A police wagon. Another wagon four years later, with not one horse but two. That good-for-nothing Chairman English admitted it was the best in the country, and he tried to take all the credit for it.*

A knock at the door interrupted Connolly's ruminations. Through the one-inch gap between the floor and the door's bottom rail, he could see two shoes shuffling—back and forth—back and forth—nervous like. *Who could it be if not Manly?*

"What is it, Manly?" Connolly bellowed.

Captain W.P. Manly, Connolly's second-in-command, entered the room and approached his desk.

"Sir. What are we going to do about the Bass affidavits? The crowds are restless. We can't just sit here and do nothing."

Charles Camp, Ella Bass's attorney, had taken sworn affidavits from a half dozen people. He vowed to do whatever it took, full chisel, to see justice done. And he was telling people to take heed—he was about to reveal the most sensational developments. He was telling everyone who would give him an ear that there had been a conspiracy against Bass. That some members of the police force were involved. He planned to present the affidavits to a grand jury that morning. And word got out that he planned to release them to the newspapers at the same time. Rumors spread throughout the city. Crowds gathered in front of the *Journal* and *Constitution* newspaper buildings.

"Manly." The police chief, absent his usual bravado, spoke softly and deliberately. "I want you to go down to the newspaper building. Be there when the affidavits are announced. Judge the mood of the crowd. And then I want you to get to each and every one of the witnesses. Meet with them. Get their stories. Learn everything you can. And then report back to me. And another thing, we need to keep the detectives, especially Conn and Mehaffey, as far away from this as we can. They've already poked their noses where they don't need to be poking. Do you know they even went so far as to meet with Paden and that doctor, Gilbert, without my knowledge? I'm ordering you to take charge…And Manly, wipe that damned coffee off your mustache."

Manly turned to leave. He had gotten to the threshold of the door when Connolly called him back. "You heard what I said, didn't you? Report back only to me. I don't want to hear anything secondhand."

Connolly considered himself a rare species, one of those by-the-book policemen people hear about but seldom encounter. He derived some satisfaction in knowing that the color grey was a hue that knew no place in his world. He kept, on the corner

of his desk, a framed cardboard sepia of the eight members of
the detective bureau. Their mission was to conduct undercover
work, investigate crimes and apprehend offenders who eluded
the uniformed police. Connolly wanted the picture close at
hand, not so much out of pride as to remind himself daily of the
pitfalls of having a privileged group of entitled men under the
thumb of the board of commissioners. He knew the board was a
bastion of cronyism, power, and patronage. And the policemen,
principally the detectives, became pawns under their influence.
Kickbacks were common, meant to keep them quiet or to bribe
them to close their eyes to illicit activities, like the whoring mills
around Jackson Street. Connolly bristled whenever he thought
about the cozy relationship the commissioners, and some police
for that matter, had with the Jackson Street houses and the
colorful madams who ran them. Rewards and reprisals, through
promotions and demotions or even firings, were common, and
there was little Connolly could do about it. He was as much a
pawn in the commissioners' thrall as anybody. And he knew the
detective bureau was the *ultimate* favor, the destination of those
fortunate officers who chose to kowtow to the bigwigs.

Connolly also knew it didn't help that it took so little to be a
policeman. They had to have lived in the city for a year. They had
to have paid their taxes in full. They had to be between twenty-
one and thirty to join the force. They had to be able to write their
names and read a few lines from the city code manual. And they
had to be white. The chances were good they would have come
from modest means. Short of swearing an oath, little more was
expected—and they took their training as perfunctory. All of this
created the perfect breeding ground for kickbacks and corruption.

Connolly shook his head. *Why do I subject myself to this day in
and day out? I could have been a barber.*

FOURTEEN

WILLIAM MANLY

Six Affidavits

MANLY WENT STRAIGHT TO THE *CONSTITUTION* OFFICE
at the corner of Alabama and Forsyth Streets. The crowds
had gathered under the arched brick façade. One enterprising
merchant had set up a stand and was selling coffee for the
exorbitant price of ten cents a cup. Some in the crowd said they
were convinced Bass had killed himself. Others said he had been
murdered.

At eight fifteen a message boy arrived on a bicycle. He rushed
into the building, carrying a sheaf of papers under his arm. No
more than twenty minutes later, the affidavits were posted side-
by-side on the front window of the newspaper building. They
were prefaced by a letter that began "To The Editor." Given the
heightened interest in Bass's death, and the sensational nature of
the affidavits themselves, the editors of both major dailies, the
Journal and the *Constitution,* had chosen to make them available

to the public right away rather than wait until the papers hit the streets. The affidavits claimed that members of the detective bureau offered several men money to testify that Bass had received stolen goods when, in reality, he was innocent of the charges.

Manly read through the affidavits—every word on every page. He took a pencil and a memorandum book from his pocket and wrote down the names of the people he needed to interview. There were six men. He set out to locate and meet with each of them.

He first tracked down a black man named Hal Harper. Harper was a hauler for J.J. and J.E. Maddox, wholesale grocers. Manly located him with the help of Charles Camp. Harper agreed to meet away from the station house so as not to tip off the detectives.

"One morning a few weeks ago," Harper related, "I was loading goods in the back of a wagon over at the depot, when—"

"Which depot?" Manly interrupted.

"The Central Railroad depot. When this security guard, name's Florence. Mr. Joseph Florence. He comes up behind me. And he says 'Boy, what's your name?' Mr. Manly, I was scared, so I says in a low voice like a mouse, 'My name's Hal Harper, sir.' Then he says to me, 'Didn't I see you down here last week loadin' barrels of sugar onto your dray?' I told him I was down there one day. I loaded some barrels for Mr. Maddox. But I didn't rightly know what they had in 'em. I just do what I'm told. Mr. Manly, I swear I didn't know what was in them barrels." Harper looked up, his face flush. "So he asks me where I took the barrels when I left and I tell him I took them right down to Mr. Maddox's warehouse. On Lloyd Street." Harper looked down at the floor.

"Please go on," Manly urged.

"And then he asks me if I knew some barrels of sugar was stolen from the rail yard. I told him I didn't know that. And I didn't steal no sugar. And then he says, 'Well, we'll just let your boss and the police sort this out.' And he takes me to the guard house and calls for a wagon. They take me to the jail and keep me there for five whole days. And you know what, Mr. Manly?"

"What?"

"Mr. Maddox wouldn't even help get me out."

"How did you finally get out?"

"Well, it's a long story," Harper continued. "Two days after I was arrested, this detective named Wooten comes to my cell. He takes me to the judge for a hearing. On the way to the judge's office, Mr. Wooten stops and pulls a twenty dollar bill out of his pocket. He hands it to me and he says I can keep it if I swear that a man by the name of Bass took the stolen sugar. I tell him that wouldn't be right. His face just gets real red and he says, with an attitude like mine, I might just rot in the calaboose. I didn't like him saying that, Mr. Manly."

"Then what happened?"

"Well, then the whole thing comes up again. But this time it's a detective name of Conn. He comes to my cell 'bout midnight and rouses me up. He says he'll give me fifty dollars and get me out if I just swear Mr. Bass received the sugar, but I refused again. It was hard, though, Mr. Manly. I sure could have used that money."

"So at that point you were still in jail. How did you get out?"

"Well, I stay in jail a few more days and then they take me to the grand jury. The judge and the jury listens to my story and then the judge says, 'Go ahead and let him go.'"

"Did you tell the grand jury about the detectives—about how they offered you money?"

"I did, but they didn't want to hear it. They just said for me to go and I'd best stay out of trouble if I knew what was good for me. Mr. Camp was waiting for me when I left the station house. He says I got to make a statement. I didn't want to at first but he pushed me hard."

Manly sought out another black man, a drayman named Peter Williams. Williams said that, on the day the sugar was stolen, he was hauling for the Armour Packing Company. Harper had put the police on to Williams, saying he could attest to Harper's whereabouts that day. Williams had sworn under oath that Harper was helping him haul and could not have stolen the sugar. He told Manly the police then locked him up at the station house for thirty-six hours for no reason at all. As he was being taken to the station a detective accused him of knowing where the sugar was and if he didn't reveal its whereabouts they would work him over. Williams said the detective offered him twenty-five dollars to implicate Bass.

"So what happened while you were in jail?" Manly asked, already knowing Williams' story but wanting to hear it firsthand. Williams had shared it with an *Atlanta Journal* reporter as soon as he walked off the station house grounds and it had appeared that same evening on the front page of the newspaper.

"When I arrived at the station house, these detectives took me up these dark stairs—high up in the building. Goin' up the stairs I wondered where they were taking me. If I was ever goin' to leave that place. We went up into an attic or something. It smelled like mildew mixed with cigarette smoke mixed with old ashes. There was this room in the attic. They took me in there. Then they told me again, say the sugar was carried to Mr. Bass's store. I couldn't do that."

"I believe I know that room," Manly said, "but to my knowledge it's just used for storage."

"Well, Mr. Manly, I can tell you right now it ain't used for no storage. It was about empty. When we got in the room, the detectives sat me down in a rickety old chair," Williams continued. "It wobbled and the cane was starting to break in the seat. I was scared. I know I was shaking. They told me, look around. Then they left me by myself in that room."

"Williams, you're shaking now. I know it's not easy, but you need to tell me everything."

Williams breathed hard. "Well, there I was, sitting all alone. My eyes darted all around—quick like. There wasn't much in the room. But I saw a long wooden box in the corner, right across from where I was sitting. Standing on its end. The room was dark except one little light shined down on that box. Looked like a pine coffin. The wood wasn't painted and it looked old, like it was there a long time. Just when I laid my eyes on that box, I jumped a little in my chair. I thought I heard a noise coming from it. A scratching or a scraping. It got louder. It sounded like an animal clawing from the inside. Is it a rat or a possum, I thought? A squirrel? A cat? Maybe even a little dog?" And then all of a sudden, my eyes was fixed on that box, a ghost or a skeleton or something jumped out and lunged across the room at me. I fell backwards, just like this." Williams leaned back in his chair as if to fall. "The back of the chair crashed to the floor with me in it. Whatever it was it went away as fast as it came. I was picking myself up. The detectives came back in."

"'You scared boy?' one of them said. 'You should be. What happened in this room is just the start. You'd better do as we say. Do you understand me? Who knows what might happen if you don't. This time it was a ghost. Next time it might be a mad dog. And if you niggers hate anything it's dogs and ghosts.'"

"I just looked down at the floor. That's when one of them said, 'You look right up here at me, boy. Do you understand?' I said, 'Yes sir.' But I knew they done some kind of a prank, meant to scare me—to get me to lie. But I don't lie," Williams said. The corners of his mouth curled down. "So the men, they worked me over for another good half an hour before they gave up. 'We can't get nothing out of him,' one of them said. 'We'll have to let him go to trial.' Then they led me back downstairs and locked me up. The next day, they took me before a judge. The judge let me go. He knew they didn't have nothing on me."

"Do you know the names of the detectives—the ones that did that to you?" Manly asked.

"I'd know 'em if I saw 'em," he replied, "but I don't know their names."

Manly checked off the first two names on his list. He then set out to find the next man, Christopher Johnson—that old mudsill of a Negro that everybody knew—the one the police accused of stealing the tallow. Johnson repeated what he had sworn in the affidavit about the tallow stolen from the Branan Brothers store, which contradicted what Conn claimed Johnson had told the police when he was arrested, namely that he had sold the tallow to Bass.

"I took the tallow into the back of the store. I took the crate from around it and threw the crate out the back door," he said. "Then Mr. Bass came to the back of the store. I tried to sell it to him. He got mad and ordered me out. He refused to buy it, telling me that was not the kind of business he did and to take it away.

But there was a farmer in there from the country, and when I went out with the tallow he followed me outside. I sold it to him and put it on his wagon. And then I left."

Shortly after the incident in the rear of Bass's store, Johnson was arrested, hauled off to jail, and charged with stealing the tallow. He pleaded guilty and was sentenced to four months on the chain gang. Two weeks in, he was approached at the public works by two visitors with an offer.

"Mr. Conn and another detective, I think Mr. Bedford, came out to the works and told me that if I would swear I sold the tallow to Mr. Bass they would see the police commissioner and have me bonded out. But I try to be a man of honor. I can't say I always am but I try. I wouldn't be part of a lie and I ended up serving out with a clear conscience."

Johnson said he didn't know the farmer from the country and he couldn't recall his name. The only detail he could provide was that he had a greying doorknocker beard and bristly whiskers. Manly tracked the farmer down. His name was J. W. Miller. He said he was from the outskirts of Monk in Campbell County, the same town where W. J. Scarborough's store was located. Manly suspected Miller might refute Johnson's story. But, instead, Miller ended up filing his own affidavit supporting the black man's claim. He swore that in early May he was in the store on Peters Street when he saw Johnson try to sell a large container of tallow to Bass. He claimed to have heard Bass "curse the Negro and tell him 'damn him,' to get out of his store, that he wanted nothing to do with him or his tallow." Miller said he followed the black man out of the store and bought the tallow from him.

Another resident of Monk, a man named Wesley Scott, had come forward and filed an affidavit. Manly traveled to Monk and sought him out for questioning.

"Sometime in early June," Scott said, "I think it was around the seventh, Detective Conn arrested me at my work in East Point. He charged me with having an overcoat he claimed I'd bought from Mr. Scarborough. He also claimed Mr. Scarborough had bought it from Bass and that it was stolen. He hauled me to the police station for questioning. However, Chief Connolly ordered me released, saying there was not enough evidence to hold me."

"I was at the station house when you were brought in," Manly replied. "I remember that, but what happened then?"

"Well, when I left the station house," Scott continued, "I proceeded directly to the Union Depot and boarded the four twenty train for East Point. Detective Conn followed me from the station house to the depot and boarded the same train I was on. I had intended to get off in East Point and return to work, but before I could, Detective Conn backed me up against the wall in the train car and drew his pistol. He threatened to have me locked back up unless I stayed on the train. He cursed me. He accused me of trying to protect Mr. Bass. He said Mr. Bass was 'the damnedest thief in the country and, God damn him, I'd kill him if I had the opportunity.' That's what he said, Mr. Manly."

Charley Smith was familiar to the police, almost as well-known as Christopher Johnson. Manly didn't have any trouble finding him hunched over a fire half a block off of Butler Street, drinking stump liquor with his buddies. Manly took him to a doggery on the western edge of Darktown so he could hear his story away from prying eyes.

"Sometime in June I'm walking down the street when Detective Conn approaches me. 'Charley, you've been stealing a heap of things around town,' he says, 'and I always let you off when you was arrested, and now I want you to do something for me.' I say 'Mr. Conn, you hasn't ever let me off. I been cleared every time you hauled me in.' Then he says, 'Charley, don't you give me no sass. You know I've been good to you.' Mr. Manly, I guess when you think about it, he *has* been good to me..." Smith looked up and then went on, "...so I listen to what he wants me to do."

"What did he ask you to do, Charley?"

"Well, he points past the train station and says, 'You know that damn crook Bass on Peters Street. He's at the head of all these thieves in the city and I want you to find out who's hauling and selling him goods. If you do that I'll give you twenty-five dollars.' That's a lot of money, Mr. Manly, so I says I'll try. And I did. But I had to come back a few days later and tell him I didn't find nobody. That's when he puts me in a bad spot. He says, 'Charley, if you can't find out who's hauling for Bass, I'll give you the twenty-five dollars anyway if you swear you were the one that sold stolen goods to him and that he knew the goods were stolen, and I'll look after you. I'll see to it they don't lock you up.' I said 'Mr. Conn, I can't rightly do that.' That's when he got mad and told me to get my lazy nigger self out of his sight, which I did and that was the last of it."

As Smith was leaving, he turned around and looked back at Manly. "Mr. Manly, that man Conn used a word I never heard before. He said Mr. Bass was a damned larcener. What's a larcener?"

"It's a thief. A crook," Manly replied.

When news of Bass's death had broken, and when his family began seeking anyone who would swear as witnesses to police involvement, Smith knew he had to do the right thing. On the fourth of September, he appeared before George Barnard, the deputy of the United States District Court, to attest to what he knew. He carefully recounted to Barnard his recollection of events as they were transcribed in writing, below which he dutifully signed with a large bold X.

The final affidavit had been sworn by Herbert Jenkins, the only white man in the bunch. The tobacco salesman cited in the coroner's inquest. The man who claimed to know who had threatened Bass's life. The man who was never allowed to take the stand there. Jenkins' affidavit said he had learned that a man named Lem Mureau had been consigning and selling broken stocks of goods, including tobacco, to Baker Bass for some time. According to Ella's attorneys, Jenkins claimed Bass had bought the Wild Turkey tobacco from Lem Mureau. The attorneys said they had a bill of sale, somehow obtained and provided by Jenkins, to prove it.

Jenkins claimed he went to Bass and told him Mureau was a crook and should be avoided. He also said he knew Mureau had been going around town offering goods to merchants at rates cheaper than what they could be obtained for. According to Jenkins, upon learning this, Bass stopped buying goods from the man.

Jenkins swore he was present when the detectives claimed Bass had confessed to having bought stolen goods and that the detectives' claim was patently false. In fact, according to Jenkins, while Bass did tell the detectives he may have been indiscreet in not taking more care about the goods he purchased, he flatly denied any guilt.

Jenkins said he had been convinced more than a year ago that this Lem Mureau fellow was the head of a gang of thieves connected with the string of railroad car breakings. He said he told Mehaffey, who promised to find Mureau. And Mehaffey said that when he did find him he would run him and his gang of thieves in. But neither Mehaffey nor the other detectives ever located the man. No one they spoke with, except for Jenkins, seemed to know him.

"Mr. Jenkins," Manly stared into the tobacco merchant's flinty eyes, "do you think you know who killed Baker Bass?"

Jenkins sat ramrod straight in his chair. "I most certainly do, my dear fellow, but I shall not tell you just yet, not today anyway. If you or the powers that be in this city wish to subpoena me then I shall be forced under oath to reveal what I know on your terms. Otherwise you will find out soon enough. On my terms. You can be assured of that. Just be patient, my friend."

FIFTEEN

WILLIAM MANLY

A Brief Apprehension

SOMETIMES THINGS JUST HAPPEN. YOU'RE NOT QUITE sure why—or how. They just happen. That's how William Manly felt most of the time. *Why me? How can a poor farm boy—a sharecropper's son from Stirling Grove—lay claim to this butter-upon-bacon life?* At forty-four, he was the captain of the force and Connolly's hand-picked successor. If things unfolded as he anticipated, Connolly would retire at some point and Manly would become the chief of one of the fastest growing police forces in the south. *Why me?*

Until just a year ago, he had not been so fortunate in his personal life. At times he had worried that he'd never find a wife. After all, he was on the verge of becoming an old man, too old to plight his troth except with the homeliest of spinsters. But then Eunice McGilvary, sixteen years his junior, came along. He met her under the unlikeliest of circumstances. It happened on a sultry afternoon in the summer of 1894. He had ducked into the Markham House Hotel for a respite, albeit brief, from the stifling heat and humidity. It wasn't much cooler inside, but sitting under one of the massive ceiling fans in the lobby bar, drinking a bottled Coca-Cola, did the trick. He finished his drink, ascended the marble stairs from near the front door to the second floor, and walked out onto the hotel's balcony, the one that projected out over the sidewalk, catty-cornered across the street from the Union Depot. The balcony was normally taken up by visiting orators and various other guests who, for whatever reason, felt an urge to pontificate. But on that afternoon the balcony was empty. He looked down onto Lloyd Street. He surveyed the comings and goings of working wagons and carriages, of men in derbies and top hats scurrying to and fro, of porters pushing carts and lugging steamer trunks. His eyes were drawn to a woman exiting the station. She carried a parasol in one hand. A jacquard traveling bag in the other. When she reached the curb on the station side of the street, she sat the bag down beside her. She retrieved a handkerchief from her bosom and dabbed her upper lip. *Who is that comely young lady?* His first instinct was to bound down the stairs, cross the street, and assist her. Then he thought better of it. Surely she would not take to a stranger offering his hand. But she just stood there as if she didn't know what to do. And the carriages came perilously close to brushing her as they whizzed by. He noticed a puddle in the roadbed not far from where she stood. One carelessly steered wagon wheel into that puddle, he thought, and she would likely end up bespattered from head to toe. So he mustered the courage to exit the hotel and approach her.

"May I help you cross the street, Miss?"

At first, she was shy, standoffish, so much so that Manly took a notion to dispense with any hope of conversation and move on. But slowly, cautiously, she broke her silence. Perhaps it was his uniform.

"Oh, I'm not going to the hotel, if that's what you mean. I live here. I just need to hire a hackney to take me to my house on Gartrell Street. But there are none to be found. I suppose I'll just have to walk."

"But that's a long way, much too far—especially on a sweltering day like this—for a lady such as yourself to walk unaccompanied, lugging a traveling bag. The least I can do is assist you."

Manly carried her bag the fifteen blocks to the steps leading to her front door. It was a forty-five minute walk—enough time to engage in talk well beyond pleasantries.

Her name was Eunice, but her friends called her Nicie. (He never could bring himself to do so. It seemed too fatuous. Dewy-eyed.) Her father was from Nova Scotia but she was born in West Roxbury, on the outskirts of Boston. *A Yankee in my midst, and a foreigner no less.* Manly restrained a chuckle. She said her family had moved to Atlanta when she was ten so her father, a carpenter, could take advantage of the post-war building boom. She had a brother—two years her junior. Manly took care not to pry, but she volunteered that she was returning from an overnight trip to Tallahassee to visit her maiden aunt.

"Half my kin have moved from up north," she said. "It may be hot here in the summer, but the winters up there? Why, there are iceshoggles on the eaves all the way to Eastertime. Have you ever been up north, Mr. Manly?"

"I can't say that I have. Farthest I've been is Gaffney."

"Where's Gaffney?"

"Just up the road from where I come from in South Carolina. They call it the Upcountry."

William and Eunice agreed to see each other again. And then again. What started as a chance encounter on Lloyd Street developed into a whirlwind courtship. They married and settled into a house just two doors down from her parents—a house that Manly managed to buy free and clear with cash he'd saved up over twenty years.

It's downright humbling just to ponder it all, he thought.

Manly hadn't shared Connolly's childhood desire to wear a badge. Far from it. He never expected his life would amount to much. Hell, his father didn't even own the land they worked every day, from sunup to sundown. He had always assumed that, just like his seven brothers and sisters, he'd be tilling somebody else's soil until the day came when he was too feeble to handle the plow—and he'd surely die as poor as Job's cat. It wouldn't get any better. But it surely couldn't get any worse either.

At least that's what he thought. Then 1861 came. That was when his father enlisted in the South Carolina Second Infantry Regiment. Before that, Wim—that's what they called him back then—hadn't been sure which side his father would take up with—if that time ever came. He'd heard the grownups talk about all the Unionists around Greenville—there were almost as many of them as there were Secessionists—maybe more. And his parents didn't care a whit about whether the slaves were freed or not. They reckoned they didn't have anything to lose one way or the other. But one day a man named Ben Perry, an evangelist for the Southern cause, came around and did a mighty lot of convincing. That's when his father decided to go with the

Confederates. It would be a hard four years before his father mustered out, in 1865, at Appomattox.

His mother was thirty-three when her husband left for the war. His brother James was fifteen. Cynthia was thirteen. He, Wim, was ten. And John was nine. Then there were the little girls. Mary, Manda, Sarah Pauline, and Jennie. They weren't much good for anything—except maybe sweeping the yard and a few simple, childlike chores. Momma wouldn't let them help with the wash for fear the ash lye—she couldn't afford store bought soap— would put their eyes out.

Throughout Manly's father's absence, the family bounced around from farm to farm, landlord to landlord, year to year. One fall they might be in Anderson. The next they might end up in Travelers Rest. Or Spartanburg. For a time, Wim's mother took a part-time job, at the Markley Coach Factory on the Reedy River, to supplement their meager sharecropping income. The whole family turned out on Draw Days, the first Monday of each month, for free food rations—corn, potatoes, and an occasional cup or two of flour. They would leave the house marching single file, tallest to shortest—except for James, who was the appointed *caboose* of the family, following at the rear to keep the girls in line. When they got to the courthouse square, their self-imposed order tumbled into chaos amid the pushing and shoving, cursing and shouting, and generally unruly behavior of the hordes fighting each other for meager handouts.

The family thought things would surely get a little better when the war ended and Daddy came home. But they only got worse. There were no stores. There wasn't even any currency. Confederate notes were no good and, at least for the time being, nothing had yet replaced them. But that didn't matter much to the Manlys— they wouldn't have had any money to spend anyway. The post office was gone. And everybody was cut off from the rest of the world owing to the railroads having been destroyed. The whole area was terrorized by Confederate bushwhackers and Federal renegades. The South Carolina upcountry soil had never been very good for growing anything, but it would take years to restore the crop levels that had been there before the war. Able-bodied men were hiring out at fifty cents a day just to make ends meet. And they were still dependent on the kindness of strangers and the generosity of relief societies. "We are living in a strange way now," one of the relief workers said as she stood before the crowd of Draw Day supplicants.

William Manly became a police officer out of necessity. Gradually, as the area recovered, the railroads had been restored. Stores and post offices had reopened. If not for those changes, the opportunity to join the police force wouldn't have come his way. On a Monday afternoon in August eight years after the war had ended, he had wandered into the Spartanburg post office. He had gone there to seek work. He was convinced that if the family kept living day-to-day, tossed from one half-barren farm to another, it would send them all to early graves. Panic came over him like the frigid winds that swept across the Jocassee gorges in the dead of winter.

"I'm sorry," the postmaster said. "We got a letter carrier already. We don't need another one."

"No. No sir," Manly replied. "I didn't come here looking for a mail job. It's just that you know everybody in town. I thought you might know where they're wanting to hire. I don't have any skills to speak of, except I've worked farms since I was ten."

"Son, I wish I could help you. But half the men in town's looking for work just like you. And the coloreds got it even worse. Everybody's been suffering for years now. If you ask me, this dad-blamed town's plumb outta prayers."

Manly was about to leave when he saw a notice taped on the wall just to the right of the postmaster's desk. His eyes fell first on the picture of a policeman, decked out in a long coat with a double row of buttons down the front and a helmet sitting high on his head. The policeman held a truncheon in his right hand and cradled its striking end in his left. And he stared straight out of the picture—right at Manly. Just below the picture were the words: BRAVE MEN WANTED.

"What's that on the wall there?"

"What's what on the wall?"

"That notice."

The postmaster looked over his shoulder. "Came on the mail train two days ago. I put it on the wall. But it ain't no use to you. They're looking to hire policemen down in Georgia. Darned near two hundred miles away. What are you gonna do with an ad like that? Way up here in Spartanburg."

Manly's eyes shot to the bottom of the notice: APPLY IN PERSON. POLICE HEADQUARTERS. PRYOR STREET. ATLANTA. He couldn't leave the post office fast enough.

Back at the house, he didn't have a hard time convincing his mother and father to scrape together what little money they could—including fifty dollars they got for two cows, with a bedraggled mule thrown in—pack what few belongings they had, and head south. After all, what did they have to lose? James had left home and moved to Charleston. Cynthia and Mary were married off by then. And John, twenty-one years old, chose to stay behind and try to make do. Manda, Sarah Pauline, and Jennie, all in their teens, came along. *Hoping to find a beau in the big city, no doubt,* Manly thought.

When they reached Atlanta, Manly headed straight to Pryor Street. He didn't know the city at all. But the lady at the boardinghouse had drawn him a map. He walked south down Peachtree Street. At the corner of Peachtree and Cain Streets, he looked up at the most magnificent house he'd ever seen, a brick building, five stories high at the center, with a big porch and over twenty-five windows facing the street—he counted them. It was nothing like what they had back home. He would later learn that the building was the Governor's Mansion. Three blocks farther down the street, he passed the First Methodist Episcopal Church, with a center spire that reached all the way into the clouds. Just past the church, the street veered off to the right to become Pryor Street. He crossed the railroad tracks at the Union Depot. Just past Alabama Street he saw the station house. His heart raced. All he could think of was wearing that coat with the double row of buttons down the front, carrying a truncheon and sporting a sidearm. But being a policeman wasn't what thrilled him most. It was that, for the first time, he had an opportunity to make something of himself.

Whatever thrill he felt dissipated when he passed over the threshold into the station house and stood before the desk clerk.

"Where do you live?" the clerk asked.

"I'm staying at Miss Cordia Hull's boardinghouse on Spring Street."

"How long have you been there?"

"Just got into town today. Came down from Greenville."

It was then that Manly realized he should have read the fine print on the BRAVE MEN WANTED notice. The clerk informed him that he stood no chance of becoming a policeman if he hadn't lived in the city for at least a year. Manly questioned why, if that were the case, the notice had been taped to a post office wall two hundred miles away. The clerk shrugged. Manly pleaded his case, but to no avail.

Manly left the station house dejected but determined not to give up. He would find a job, any job, work at it for a year, and then decide whether he wanted to keep doing what he was doing or apply to become a policeman. He also needed to help his fifty-year-old father find work. It was one thing for a twenty-one year old with limited skills beyond farming to get a job in the city. But it was quite a different challenge for somebody his father's age. An old man with nothing but farming and soldiering to claim for himself? Those things didn't count as citified skills. And how could you train a fifty-year-old man to take on a new job? But Manly heard there was a shortage of night watchmen, and he convinced the supervisor down at the railroad to hire them both. When a year had passed, he applied and was accepted onto the police force. His father stayed on as a watchman for another ten years.

By 1895, William Manly had worked alongside Connolly for twenty years, first as a beat patrolman, then as captain of the force when Connolly took over as chief. Although becoming a policeman had not been his lifelong dream, he took his job seriously and served with pride. But he never gained the self-confidence that came naturally to his boss.

Why me? Sometimes things just happen.

By late evening on Saturday, the seventh of September, Manly called on Connolly at his home. He had interviewed all six affidavit filers as Connolly had ordered. None of what he had to tell Connolly came as a surprise, since the affidavits had already been published for the entire city to read. Both men agreed that the recent turn of events seemed damning of the detectives. They also agreed it was their duty to track down and arrest Bass's killer, regardless of who it turned out to be.

The detectives, on the other hand, had lashed out at their chief for not standing up for them, claiming outrage at the "infernal issue of lies" leveled against them.

"Manly, this is bigger than you and I can handle alone," Connolly said. "As much as I hate to do it, we'll have to get the commissioners involved."

Connolly vowed to discuss the matter with the commissioners right away.

At two o'clock on Monday, the ninth of September, the police commissioners called to order a special meeting. They agreed to let Connolly and Manly sit in as observers. Regardless of what the commissioners decided, it was important that they have the two men's support, even if it came grudgingly. The commissioners admitted that a complete investigation should be made. The public, urged on by Bass's family, friends, and attorneys, were demanding a full accounting.

But Mehaffey and Conn had hired their own attorney, who submitted a letter to the police and commissioners urging that they not jump to conclusions. The letter read in part:

In the *Journal* of Saturday afternoon and the *Constitution* of Sunday morning appear a number of alleged affidavits and a statement from the counsel of Mrs. B.A. Bass. They are intended to support the theory of the framing of Bass by one or more officers of the detective force of Atlanta. In order to make their theory more plausible, counsel gave their opinion that Bass was an innocent and persecuted man and that the detectives were forced to the methods set out in the alleged affidavits to obtain evidence against him, and failing in this, resorted to murder. Mrs. Bass's counsel further suggested that anything said in reference to the guilt of the dead man is an unkindness to a good wife and four innocent children. Were such an assertion gratuitously made, this would be true. But the men assailed and accused of this diabolical conspiracy and murder also have good wives and innocent children. Sentiment must not obscure the vision of justice and be used as a weapon to destroy.

One of the commissioners moved that, rather than begin an internal investigation, the commission should table the whole matter and take it up later. After an investigation had been done at some later date, the chairman would go before the grand jury and present all the facts. Another commissioner seconded the motion, saying that an investigation a week before the opening of the Cotton States and International Exposition would be a poor time to demoralize the police department by beginning an inquiry. Mayor Porter King was present and agreed. The motion passed. The matter would be taken before a grand jury at a later date.

Upon returning to the station house, Connolly let loose. "Those infernal blackguards have done it again, Manly. We need to find the killer. I don't care who he is. If it's one of our own, goddamn it, we need to know it. So here's what I'm asking you to do... No, I'm not asking. I'm directing you to dig around on your own, answering to me and to me alone. Follow any leads you get, but you have to do it under the cover of secrecy, sub-rosa as they say. Don't let anyone know what you're up to, especially the detectives. You got the grit for it, Manly?"

Manly nodded, turned to leave. As he passed through the doorway out of Connolly's office, the long hallway leading to the front of the building was absent the usual comings and goings of policemen and visitors. A brief apprehension came over him. He was on his own this time.

The task before him would not be easy. Prudence demanded that he do any digging with great care. Manly looked back over his interview notes from the six witnesses. One stood out—Herbert Jenkins. Did this man Jenkins really know who the killer was, as he claimed? Manly wanted to know more. But he risked the wrath of the commissioners if he were caught snooping around. So he devised a plan. He would engage a cooperative newspaperman to act as his proxy. It didn't take him long to find just the man, a reporter named Frank Keeler. Keeler consented, but only if Manly would agree that he could publish the recounting of his visit with Jenkins in the newspaper.

SIXTEEN

FRANK KEELER

That Must Be Jenkins

ON MONDAY MORNING, THE SIXTEENTH OF SEPTEMBER, two weeks and three days after Bass's death, the weather was cloudy but dry. The exposition would open the following Wednesday. Everyone involved, from organizers and pavilion workers to the majority of the city's policemen, who had been diverted from their usual beats to deal with the throngs of visitors, commented on the run of dry weather. The killer, assuming there was one, was still at large. Early that morning Frank Keeler walked the dozen blocks south of downtown to interview the man who claimed he could prove who killed Bass. He didn't know whether he would be able to find this man Jenkins. But he knew where he stayed when he was in town, a clapboard boardinghouse at 47 Crew Street. And he had a good idea as to what he looked like from Manly's description.

Keeler had been with the *Journal* for only four years, but he had been a newspaperman for twice that long. He had started out as a junior reporter for the *Raleigh News and Observer*. But he and the owner, Sam Ashe, didn't see eye to eye. For one thing, Mr. Ashe was an ardent Democrat. Keeler's family had been dyed-in-the-wool Republicans for upwards of two decades. At times, when Ashe was perturbed with Keeler about one thing or another, the old man would call him a scalawag under his breath. Keeler just ignored it. As long as that was the worst of it, he could put politics aside and just do his job. But then, in January of '89, Benjamin Harrison became President, having defeated Cleveland the prior November without even coming close to winning the popular vote. After that, Mr. Ashe became positively insufferable, storming through the newspaper office, flailing his arms and railing against "that nigger lover Harrison." It was more than Keeler could take. He said enough is enough and started looking around for another job.

Mr. Ashe kept, in the corner of his office, a stack of newspapers from other towns and cities. Keeler decided he would wait until the old man left for lunch, then he would go through the papers until he found one that struck his fancy. Fridays were good because, more often than not, Mr. Ashe would leave promptly at forty-five minutes after eleven and wouldn't return until well after two, stumbling through the front door with a brick in his hat. On those Friday afternoons Keeler knew the old man had had one too many pints. One such afternoon, shortly after Ashe had left, Keeler snuck into the old man's office. His heart pounded. His hands sweated as he rummaged through the stack of papers in the corner. He ran across a copy of the *Atlanta Journal*. Atlanta was a whole lot bigger than Raleigh—maybe three times as big—

maybe even bigger. *Surely,* he thought, *in the big city I won't have to deal with the small town attitudes of the likes of Ashe.*

Keeler wrote a letter to the newspaper office, addressed to no one in particular: THE ATLANTA JOURNAL, JOURNAL BUILDING, ATLANTA, GEORGIA. Five weeks later, he received a reply. It was from the owner of the paper himself, saying he would be delighted to give Keeler a try.

Leaving Old Man Ashe was one of the easiest things Keeler had ever done.

Captain Manly had given Keeler explicit instructions.

"Get everything you can out of that man Jenkins. Find out who did it. Find out how he knows they did it. Find out who else was involved. Hell, Keeler, you're a newspaperman. I don't need to tell you how to do your job."

"I'll do my best, Captain. I won't let you down."

Keeler remembered Manly staring at him as he wiped his hands on his pant legs. His palms had sweated just as they had that Friday in Ashe's office.

As Keeler neared the boardinghouse on Crew Street early Monday morning, he saw a man sitting on the porch. The man was dressed in a black single-breasted cutaway morning coat and grey striped trousers. He fit Manly's description of the tobacco salesman. *That must be Jenkins.* He approached, stopping just short of the first step leading up to the porch.

"Excuse me, sir. Is your name Jenkins?"

"Perhaps it is," the man replied without making eye contact. "Or perhaps not. If you're looking to buy tobacco, then I am most assuredly your man. But if you're from the tax office, then I've never heard of anyone by that name."

A ghost of a smile came to the man's face.

"Which is it, young man? Tobacco or taxes? Or are you a—what do they call them in the mother country? Oh yes—are you a constable in disguise?"

"My name is Keeler, sir. And I'm none of those things. I'm from the *Journal*. I'd like to speak with you about the Bass murder."

"Well you've come to the right place then. You have, indeed, found your man. My name is Herbert Jenkins. Herbert *Thomas* Jenkins to be exact. And it would be my pleasure to tell you what I know, if you would be so kind as to join me here on the porch."

Jenkins leaned back in his rocking chair, his hands behind his slightly balding head, his left foot on the porch floor and his right foot resting on the top of an overturned tobacco crate. A lamp by the stairs in the hallway leading to his room shone through the open door onto the porch, illuminating his face in the dim early morning.

"The mystery of the murder of Baker Bass is nearing a solution. The main points of evidence that will fasten the crime upon the assassin have been worked out. A few details remain to be looked into. Within a few days, the guilt of blood will be fixed beyond a doubt."

Jenkins flashed a sly grin. He was a handsome man of erudition and striking personal appearance, one who stood out among the residents of the boardinghouse and, for that matter, the city. He was tall, lithe and sinewy, with a Roman nose, a lean, angular jaw, and a Spaniard's swarthiness. And a light olive complexion. Keeler was intrigued by this strange man, who he guessed was around thirty-five, maybe forty at the most. Perhaps it was his physical appearance. Or the clothes he wore. Or his thinning black hair and bushy mustache, waxed at the tips.

"Young man, I do believe you're gazing admiringly at my hair and whiskers. Jet black, just like those of the Cavaliers, who rode with that merrie English monarch, Charles I, whose head dropped off his shoulders one day and was caught in a basket."

Or perhaps it was the strange way Jenkins talked. Keeler searched for the right word to describe him. *Hugger-mugger. That's it, there's a hugger-mugger about him.*

Jenkins waxed eloquent. "The pistol found in the alley beside the dying man has been identified. Its silent, unvarying, indisputable evidence will convict the murderer. The witness who can vouch for the truthfulness of its unspeaking testimony can be produced. He will prove that the tragedy was planned out. A reputable man can be brought forward who will swear that the assassin, running from the scene of the crime, almost brushed him in his flight."

Jenkins said that for the past five years he had been a salesman for William Bagby, a tobacco wholesaler. He and Bass were close friends and had done business together since shortly after Bass moved to Atlanta. He sold Bass tobacco and at times bought goods from him. In fact, he claimed to have carried an open account with Bass. He said that, the prior spring, when Bass had found himself in financial straits, Jenkins had loaned him money and that the current account was in his, Jenkins', favor.

"Mrs. Bass's attorneys dispute this claim, but I know it to be true," Jenkins said.

Jenkins claimed confidence that not only had Bass died at another's hand, but in fact he had been murdered by a policeman. He said that on the very day of Bass's death he, Jenkins, had revealed as much to others, including a friend named Joe Maddox.

"And will you tell me the name of the policeman—the one you say killed Bass?" Keeler asked.

Jenkins stared beyond the porch and across the front lawn. He took a deep breath and a pause. "I suppose I will. I have refrained from naming the man publicly until now. Mind you, that deputy chief, what's his name, Manly? He will be apoplectic when he learns I revealed it to a newspaperman rather than to him. But so be it, he'll find out soon enough." He fixed his gaze on Keeler. "But I will tell you only if you will commit to me that it—that *I*—will make the front page of the newspaper."

Keeler pointed out that he had no editorial control over the paper. But he assured Jenkins that a revelation the likes of which he was about to disclose would deserve front-page billing in the eyes of any clear thinking editor.

Jenkins leaned forward, his face no more than a foot from Keeler's, and continued. "It should come as no surprise to anyone who has followed the case to any degree that the assassin is none other than that dastardly Green Conn."

"Do you personally know Conn?" Keeler asked. According to Jenkins, he'd had several encounters with the detective. The first was in Bass's store when Conn and Mehaffey went there. Jenkins said he encountered Conn again when he went to the police station to post bond for Bass's release from jail. And Jenkins said he and Conn had a heated exchange on Peters Street regarding the provability of the fencing case against Bass.

"If I had had a weapon then, in the heat of our passage of words…" Jenkins stood, put his hands to his hips and in pantomime, as if to draw a pistol, pointed at Keeler's chest and said, "I would have killed him." Jenkins sat back down. A sly grin came over him. "Not really. I'm only joking with you. I did get a reaction from you, though. And your hands are percolating, young man. That tells me you're emotionally invested in this just like the entire damned town. A good reporter, you must know, never betrays his poker face. And he never, ever, perspires." Keeler rested his pencil and pad in his lap, wiped his hands on the sides of his pant legs.

"I decided a month before the poor man's death that he would likely perish at the hands of the detective," Jenkins said. "There's a woman mixed up in all of this as well. A friend of mine. And she was a friend of Bass's. But I will not reveal her identity. At least not yet."

Keeler motioned for Jenkins to continue.

"Well, on the Tuesday before Bass died, the woman paid him a visit. She told him to watch his back, especially after nightfall. Then, that Thursday afternoon, Bass asked me to come and stay with him because he was sure Conn was going to try to kill him. But I explained that I had an out-of-town obligation and couldn't do it. I left on the one thirty West Point train for an overnight business trip."

Jenkins and Keeler locked eyes.

"There's another thing you need to know about the woman," Jenkins went on, "and it has to do with the murder weapon."

As the two men sat on the porch on Crew Street, Jenkins elaborated on the story of the woman and the gun.

"First, let me tell you something. The detectives claimed a policeman, Thompson I believe, had taken the pistol from the site of the shooting and transferred it to the coroner's possession, where it remained. Well, that is simply not true. The pistol was taken to Grady Hospital sometime after the dying man was transferred there, how or by whom I do not know, but I suppose it was taken there so someone could check it out against the man's wound."

"And how do you know that, Mr. Jenkins? Were you there—at the hospital?"

"I was not. I was still away on my trip. I didn't return until Friday evening."

"So who told you the gun was taken to Grady Hospital?"

"The woman told me. Mind you, Bass was still alive at that point, hanging on by the most delicate of threads. There was no reason for the coroner, Paden, to be involved—at least not yet. The pistol didn't end up in Paden's hands until the man died. The same woman I am telling you about identified the gun while it was at the hospital. I ran into her four days ago. At first she was reluctant to talk. I urged her to reveal her secret. At last, she told me everything. The story I tell you now I heard from her own lips."

Jenkins leaned forward in his chair, he arched his eyebrows and wagged his right index finger in Keeler's face.

"And though her life has not been spotless, I am positive that she told the truth. I have verified her statement. I have seen the marks she made on the weapon. Several months ago she was in a house of assignation with Green Conn."

"I assume you mean a house of prostitution?"

"Sir, you can call it a house of prostitution. You can all it a brothel, a bagnio or a bawdy house. You can even call it a whorehouse if you wish. But I choose not to use such vulgar terms. I prefer to call it just what I did, a house of assignation. That dastardly Conn, on the other hand, would probably not hesitate to call it a whorehouse."

Jenkins continued. "Another couple was with them. Conn took his handcuffs and his pistol from his pockets and laid them on the table. The woman took up the pistol and, in a mood that may have been playful or may have been full of a deeper design, scratched the polished nickel surface with a pen knife. The scratch she made was deep and plain. She made it on the left hand side, directly beneath the hammer. It can never be obliterated."

"Who are the other two people—the ones you say were there with Conn and the woman?" Keeler asked.

"That's not important." Jenkins shook his head. "If you must know it was a harlot and her charge. I can assure you they don't want to get involved in any of this."

Keeler scribbled on his notepad: *Mysterious woman? Other couple? Name?*

"I see you writing every word down in your notebook, young man. It occurs to me that you can't escape thinking about the promotion you are sure to get at the newspaper now that I have revealed Bass's killer, and oh how the people of this city will swoon when they find out it is no less than one of the very men sworn to protect them," Jenkins crowed. "It would seem strange if it came about that the point of that woman's knife blade should indicate the murderer in a tragedy, the mystery of which has baffled the keenest intelligence. This woman was one of Bass's friends. When she heard of the shooting," he continued, "she jumped womanlike to a conclusion. As I have told you, she too had heard of Conn's threats to have the life of Bass. With her suspicion strong upon her, she hurried to Grady Hospital. She was taken to the bedside of the wounded man. She asked for the weapon that had been found beside him. Someone, I know not who, handed it to her."

Jenkins held his right hand out with his thumb and fingers splayed.

"And there by the deathbed, while Bass writhed and moaned in his agony, she found the deep scratch that her knife had made. Right here." He ran his left index finger in a vertical line along the palm of his right hand. "To her mind, if to no other, that man Conn stood forth a murderer."

"Have you seen the gun yourself? Have you held it in your hand?" Keeler asked Jenkins.

"I have indeed seen it up close, but I was not allowed to hold it. This past Wednesday, a mere twelve days after Bass's death, I paid a visit to the home of Coroner Paden on Houston Street. My intent was to see for myself if the scratch appeared on the pistol. His house is just past Jackson Street about three miles from the very spot where you now sit. I ascended the stairs onto Paden's porch and knocked on the door. At first no one answered. I knocked again, and again no one answered. Just as I was about to leave I noticed someone peering through the curtains at the front window. Soon the door opened. It was Paden's wife. I asked to speak with him. She said he was not in and asked what I wanted. I told an innocuous little lie and said I was an investigator. I explained that I had come to examine the pistol. She was suspicious from the start. She retrieved the pistol from inside the house and brought it to the porch. She would not let me enter the house, nor would she let me hold the pistol. She held it tightly in her hands as I examined it."

Jenkins recounted what he saw.

"The mark was plain. To me it was mute evidence of two things. It testified that the woman told the truth. And it identified the author of the tragedy."

Jenkins retrieved a piece of paper from the table beside his chair and drew an outline of the revolver. He pointed to the drawing.

"The scratch was here on the polished nickel, just underneath the hammer."

Jenkins further claimed that he had found a witness who had agreed to testify under oath that he had been standing by the wall of a building near Ellis and Ivy the morning Bass died. He heard a shot fired and soon thereafter saw Green Conn running from the scene.

"The gentleman recognized the detective. He could not have been mistaken. I will reveal his name in time but, with all due respect, not to you. Not now."

Jenkins stood. He retrieved his watch and opened the cover.

"Mr. Keeler, the noon hour is approaching. While I would be honored, on another day, to continue our little discourse, we must end it now. You see, a coachman is picking me up in fifteen minutes to take me to the station, as I am off on another overnight trip."

The two men shook hands. Keeler descended the porch steps and walked to the street's edge. As he stood at the curb, he penciled one last note: *Eyewitness? Who is he?*

SEVENTEEN

FRANK KEELER

The Gun Is Missing

KEELER HAD NO TIME TO SPARE. HE WOULD GO BACK TO the newspaper office and drop off his notes for a copy boy to type. Normally, he would never have relegated such a task to an underling, but he had to get to Manly as quickly as he could. Then he would go back to the newspaper office and review the typed story with his editor. All in time to get it to press before the three p.m. deadline.

"Jenkins says it was Green Conn," Keeler shouted, storming into Manly's office.

"Hold on a minute, Keeler. You're a good enough newspaperman to know you don't just run with the first allegation you hear. I've suspected Conn for a while now…or Mehaffey…or both of them. But I'm not jumping to conclusions. A man is dead. Buried six feet in the ground. He left behind a good woman and four progeny. We owe it to Bass to find his killer and bring whoever did it to justice. But the last thing we want to do is send the wrong man to the gallows."

"You're right. But I'll tell you one thing. This man Jenkins is convinced it was Conn. And he's laid out a good narrative."

Keeler briefed Manly on his visit with the tobacco salesman.

"I hope I didn't leave out anything. I left my notes with the copy boy."

"We'll bring Jenkins in and get his story firsthand. At the right time. And away from prying eyes. Keeler, you've done your job honorably. I gave you my word that you could print the story. I reckon you're going to."

"Yes, sir. It should be in this evening's paper…that's assuming I get it to the pressman in time."

"Well, getting Jenkin's accusation out in the open may be a good thing. You can learn a lot about people by the way they respond to news like that. If Conn is guilty…or whoever it is… we'll know soon enough. I hope."

Manly walked with Keeler to the office door.

"But Keeler, when you print the story, remember one thing. This is Jenkins' accusation. Not yours. Print his story as you heard it. But you don't go accusing a man of something he may or may not have done. Don't take liberties with another man's story. We've got enough of that already in the papers. I know you're better than that."

Keeler left Manly's office. He was halfway down the hall when the captain called out to him.

"And one other thing, Keeler. Don't go printing in your paper that I suspect anybody of anything. What I said is just between us for now."

The recounting of Jenkins' story was published in the newspaper that Monday evening, the sixteenth of September. Keeler, being the good journalist he was, made sure not to cross the line between Jenkins' narrative and his own hunches. His editor had no qualms about running the story at the top of page one.

"For something this big? How could I *not* put it on the front page?" the editor said.

Curious about the scratch on the gun and wanting to see it for himself, Keeler decided to call on Paden at his home the next morning. If he got there early enough, prior to sunup he thought, he might be able to see Paden before the coroner left for work. Paden lived halfway across town. It would take Keeler thirty-five minutes to get there on foot. Fifteen—twenty at most—on horseback. He mounted his horse and rode the sixteen blocks from the newspaper office to the house on Houston Street.

Keeler climbed the steps to Paden's front door. He remembered what Jenkins had told him about visiting the house six days earlier. Keeler stood on the porch. The house was dark except for a flickering yellow light through the curtains at the front window—the same curtains Jenkins said he had seen Paden's wife peering through. Keeler knocked—lightly at first. No one responded. He knocked again, but this time with a sharp rap of his knuckles on the door panel. He heard a rustling inside the house. The door opened. He stood face-to-face with a man he assumed was Paden.

"May I help you?"

"Sir, my name is Frank Keeler. I'm a newspaperman with the *Journal*. I've come to inquire as to whether I could perhaps look at the gun found in Mr. Bass's possession on the morning he died."

At first the man didn't respond—he just stood there staring at Keeler. The muscles in his face tensed, the skin bunched around his eyes. He looked to the ground.

"Please come in," the man said. He moved aside and swept the back of his hand in an arc across the open doorway.

The man walked over to the hearth. He placed a fresh log on the fire. Keeler took a seat with his back to the fireplace. The man sat facing him. A gambol of light and shadow danced on the man's face from the flickering fire.

Is this Paden or someone else? Keeler thought. *He hasn't even told me his name.*

The man buried his face in his open hands. "Three nights ago…"

He looked up. Bit his lower lip. "…someone broke into the house. The gun's gone."

"Have you told the police?"

"Yes, I summoned them when I discovered it missing. It must have happened sometime after ten o'clock Saturday night. I awoke early Sunday morning. I dressed and headed down the hallway toward the rear door. I was going to fetch an armful of firewood. But I never made it outside. As I neared the door, I noticed it was ajar. Someone had managed to pick the lock…that's the only thing I can think of. The hinges and lock were intact. So was the door itself. Come here. I'll show you."

The man led Keeler down the hall. Before they reached the rear door, he ushered Keeler into a side room. He pointed to an oak secretary set against the far wall.

"The gun was in that drawer…the one right there. The intruder, he made a mighty mess. Dumped the contents out of the drawers and scattered everything all over the floor. It's a wonder I didn't hear him. But I don't hear as well as I used to."

"Did he take anything else?"

"No. Just the gun. He knew exactly what he was looking for. I'm convinced of that."

"So what happened then?"

"Well, I was a bit flummoxed, if you want to know the truth. I've seen a lot of things in my career...unpleasant things¬... abhorrent...unlawful...tawdry even...but never within the walls of my own home. There's a colored man named Grover that helps me out on the weekends. As soon as he arrived Sunday morning, I sent him to the station house to get a detective. Grover said, 'Mr. Paden, I'll get there as quick as I can.'"

The man who Keeler now knew was Paden pointed down the hall to the rear door.

"Later on Sunday, a detective arrived. A man named Cason. I've always known him to be reliable. He looked at the door, studied the lock, then he examined the desk and all the things strewn all over the floor. He went out the back door. Said he was looking for footprints. He was in an all-fired hurry to leave after that. So he left."

"Tell me about the gun, Mr. Paden. Was it a Smith & Wesson?"

"No. It was a cheap imitation. I believe it was a Harrington & Richardson. It was a .38 caliber. Five-cylinder Model 2 Double Action. The barrel was about three inches long. That gun looks like a Smith & Wesson. And for good reason. Harrington & Richardson grew out of a company cofounded by the brother of Daniel Wesson, of Smith & Wesson fame. But hold it in your hand. Grip the handle. Pull back the hammer and pull the trigger. Examine the workmanship in the chambers. I bet you could tell the difference. There are probably as many men carrying Harrington & Richardsons in this town and claiming they're

Smith & Wessons as there are people carrying the real thing."

"Can you tell me how the revolver came into your possession?" Keeler asked.

"After the man died, Officer Thompson delivered it to me. I remember picking it up and holding it in the light. I peered into the end of the barrel. There was what appeared to be dirt in the muzzle. Some people have suggested the dirt could have gotten into the barrel when the gun was dropped on the ground, but if you ask me, that just defies reason. But there is more compelling evidence, irrefutable evidence in my opinion, that the gun had not been used to commit the crime. When a pistol is fired, the striking of the hammer on the brass shell makes a bright mark that remains for several days. And the inside of the shell will be blackened and there will be a lingering odor of burnt powder. The gun contained three empty shells, including one under the hammer. None of the spent shells exhibited a characteristic bright mark. I held the muzzle to my nose. The odor of burnt powder was absent. I took the spent shells out and held them up to my nose. No burnt powder smell. My conclusion was clear. The pistol had not been fired the morning of Bass's death. In fact, I don't believe it had been fired for some time before that."

"Mr. Paden, do you know who may have had custody of the pistol from the time Officer Thompson took it from the scene of the shooting until he delivered it to you?" Keeler asked.

"No, I don't. My assumption was that Thompson had it in his possession all along, but I don't know that."

"Mr. Paden, I have one more question. Do you remember any scratches or spurious markings on the gun? Maybe marks that could have been made with something like a pen knife?"

"I don't," Paden replied, "but that doesn't mean they weren't there. There could have been marks on the gun and I just didn't notice them. Especially if they were small. I was focused mainly on the muzzle and the spent cartridges."

"Do you remember anything strange, out of the ordinary, about the gun, other than what you've told me?"

Paden shook his head. "No, just what I've told you…"

Paden paused, pressed his index finger to his cheek. "…Wait a minute. There was one thing. I remember now. It was on the left side of the handle. The crisscrossed gutta percha had been worn away as if it had been abraded with sandpaper. You couldn't miss it."

Keeler raced back to the station house at a brisk gallop. He shot into Manly's office. Manly admitted he knew the gun was missing. But he and Connolly had decided to keep it quiet. To his knowledge, the only people who knew it had been stolen were he and Connolly, the detectives, Paden, the colored man Grover, and now Keeler. Oh and the desk clerk at the station house, but he was sworn to keep his mouth shut.

"Let's just leave it at that for now, Keeler. The last thing Connolly wants, at least for the time being, is for the commissioners to get word of it. And neither I nor Connolly want to raise the issue with the detectives. They obviously know all about it, but they're keeping it quiet too."

"Mr. Manly, do you think Conn could have been the one that broke into Paden's house?"

"I'm ruling out nothing at this point. It could have been anyone for all I know. My main concern right now is that it remain quiet so I can do the job the chief's entrusted me to do. Believe me, Keeler. The last thing Connolly wants is to pick up the evening paper and read a story about a missing gun."

EIGHTEEN

FRANK KEELER

A Good Scoop Man

FRANK KEELER HAD NO SOONER SET FOOT ON THE sidewalk outside the station house than the desk clerk came running out the door.

"Mr. Keeler, the captain would like to see you."

The newspaperman went back inside and to Manly's office. Manly pointed to the chair beside his desk.

"Have a seat, Keeler."

The captain walked across the room, returned to his desk, sat down, hesitated before speaking.

"Keeler, how would you like to do another task for me?" Manly asked.

"Sir, it depends on what it is? Do you want me to interview another witness?"

"No, Keeler. It's more complicated than that. Well…let me say it differently…it does involve interviewing at least one person, perhaps more. But not the way you interviewed Jenkins. It's bigger than just an interview. And you would have to promise me that whatever you did, you would not print your findings in the newspaper. Not one word."

"But sir, I'm a newspaperman. That's how I make a living."

"I understand. I wouldn't ask you to do this if there weren't so much at stake."

"I'll do what I can. But you haven't told me what you want me to do."

Manly got up from his desk, walked across the room again. He peered out the window onto Decatur Street. After a long pause, he spoke without looking away from the window.

"I looked out this same window once and saw a drayman struggling with a collapsed wheel. The contents of his wagon had spilled out all over the roadbed. I couldn't make out what it was. Crates of some kind. The man's draft horse was just standing there, waiting patiently. Passersby were ignoring the man. Carriages were speeding by. Dray wagons. Men on horseback. They were having to swerve to dodge the spillage into the street. Not one of them offered to help the poor soul. Finally, I went out and assisted him because no one else would."

Manly swung around.

"That's what I feel like right now, Keeler. The chief has given me a job to do. And I intend not to let him down. But I feel a bit like that drayman. At any time, with the simplest of missteps, things could fall apart. And everything could spill out. And it's likely that no one would back me up…except perhaps Connolly… and even he might not."

Manly walked back over to where Keeler was sitting. He leaned against the corner of his desk, arms folded, facing Keeler.

"You see, I am on a mission to find Bass's killer. But I must fulfill at least part of this mission, the investigation of one or more of my own men, in sworn secrecy. No one connected with the police force, except the chief of course, is to know of my efforts. Not the detectives. Not the commissioners. The commissioners made it clear there would be no internal investigation for now. Those were their orders. Essentially I'm going against them. And one thing you should know is that they'll just as soon hand out reprisals as favors. They can be ruthless when they take a notion to. And they're chosen by the city council, you know, so there is little recourse against them. That's why I enlisted you to interview Jenkins without my involvement. And you did an admirable job, Keeler."

"Thank you sir. I always try to do my best."

"And now I'm asking you for another favor. Not just for me, but for the chief. For the police. For Bass's family. For bringing a killer to justice. I understand your livelihood hinges on your job. And I don't want you to jeopardize that. But reporters, like detectives, have a way of snooping around, of digging and digging until, somewhere, they strike pay dirt. The average man on the street wouldn't have the foggiest notion how to do that."

"I appreciate that. And I appreciate your concern for me. I have bills to pay. Food to put on the table."

"I understand. That's why I'm prepared to pay you this time. A hundred dollars. Fifty more if you find that elusive pay dirt. That would be a nice little nest egg on top of what they pay you over at the paper, wouldn't it?"

"It would, but I'm still not sure just what you want me to do."

"Keeler, I'll get right to the point. I told you earlier, here in my office, that Conn is a prime suspect as far as I'm concerned. And the chief agrees with me. I want to know where Conn was the morning Bass was murdered."

Manly sat back down. He rubbed his palm across his face.

"And who broke into Paden's house and stole the gun. Is it mere coincidence or is it somehow connected to the murder? Where was Conn between ten o'clock Saturday night and early Sunday morning? Was he at home, sound asleep in his bed? Or might he have been out somewhere, up to no good? He has a wife. She won't be of any help. But he has neighbors. Maybe somebody saw something. Heard something. Maybe he's been talking around. No matter how much people try, they have a mighty hard time keeping their mouths shut."

"So you're asking me to speak with his neighbors?"

"I'm asking you to track down and speak with *anyone* who may know something about his whereabouts. About his actions the morning Bass was killed. Where he was when the gun was stolen. And another thing…who is this mysterious woman Jenkins told you about? And the supposed witness who says he saw Conn running from the scene? Find out who they are. Talk to them."

"I could go back to Jenkins, but I don't think he'll tell me anything that he hasn't told me already. And I don't want to have to tell him about the gun being stolen."

"No. Dig around, but *don't* go back to Jenkins, at least not yet. See what you can find without involving him. You may just turn up somebody who knows more than we know right now. Someone who can perhaps corroborate what Jenkins has said. That's the kind of pay dirt I'm talking about. Or maybe we'll find out Conn is an innocent man. I can assure you, I would like nothing more than that. I detest the thought of a member of the police force committing such an abominable act."

Keeler agreed to help out on the condition that his efforts to track down information on Conn not interfere with his job.

"And Keeler, you're not to tell a soul about my connection to this. As far as anyone is concerned, you're just snooping around like any good scoop man."

NINETEEN

JOHN BASS

The Fair

JOHN THREW OPEN THE LACE CURTAINS. "MAMA, YOU need to get out of here. It's downright unhealthful for you to stay cooped up in this dark, forlorn house. Get dressed. We're going to the fair."

"But, John, it's opening day. The crowds will be insufferable."

"The crowds will be bad every day. Come over here to the window. Look up at the sky. There's not a cloud to be seen. A bright and beautiful morning is dawning, and the summer heat is waning. We may not have another day like this. You know how much rain we've had lately."

"But what about the store? You should have left the house over two hours ago."

Ella's attorney had managed to wrest a two-week reprieve from the judge and C.B. Reynolds, the temporary estate administrator, to give the attorneys for all parties time to sort through the details of the alleged monies owed. The whole affair would likely get drawn out for months.

"There's bunting and banners and roisterers in holiday attire all over the city. Over half the stores in town are shut down for the grand opening. I figured I might as well do the same. People aren't thinking about buying groceries or tobacco or dry goods right now. Not today anyway."

"What about the children?"

"Of course. We'll all go. An opportunity like this won't come around again. My only regret is that Father isn't here to experience it with us." John knew the real reason for Ella's reluctance.

"Your father's been dead less than three weeks. It just doesn't seem right. What will people think, John? I just can't. Not yet." She winced. The cords stood out in her neck. The muscles in her face tensed. Her jaw clenched. "I'm under enough stress as it is. I couldn't sleep at night thinking I had dishonored your father by circulating like that. I can hear people now saying 'there goes that hottentot girl kicking up her heels.'"

John had a fleeting notion that perhaps he should drop it. But he persisted. "You know Father would want you to go. I remember him telling me how much you both enjoyed that fair in New Orleans, back when I was not much younger than Mary is now. He would delight in knowing you're doing the very thing he would have us all do together if he were here."

Ella ran her palms down the front panel and sides of her apron. Her jaw slackened and her lips parted. She looked at John with plaintive eyes. "I'd dare not go out of the house in anything but my mourning dress."

I'm making progress, John thought. *But am I pushing too hard?*

"I understand, Mama. You can wear your mourning dress. No one would expect anything less. It'll do you well to get out of the house. Why, it must make Father sad to look down and see you sitting for hours in your bedroom grieving in solitude."

John knew that getting his mother's mind off of his father's death and the ensuing challenges at the store, even for just a few hours, would do her a world of good. It would do him a world of good, too.

She looked up at John. "Isn't that what's expected of us? To grieve in solitude?"

Five minutes after the clock chimed eleven, they crammed into a hired hansom and headed to the exposition grounds. Fred managed to squeeze between John and Mama, she in her black dress and diaphanous weeping veil. Mary, a bit too old to be held but with no other option, teetered precariously on her mother's knee. At first the driver had balked at taking four passengers in a carriage built for two, but John slipped him a dime. Fred jabbed Mary in the side whenever the carriage took a turn and forced her into his meager space. Whereupon she would lean into him just for spite, and Mama would threaten to have the driver turn right around and take them both back home for a good old-fashioned visit with a hickory switch in the back yard.

Baker Jr. had to stay behind. Mr. Hughes had insisted he work all day preparing tarts and fancies for the visiting throngs.

They dismounted from the hansom and stood before the castle-like Administration Building, with its fake turrets, curtain walls, and battlements. John felt a twinge of unease as the turrets, arched entrance, and faux portcullis reminded him of pictures he'd seen and stories he'd read in Ainsworth's *The Tower of London*. Four hundred people were killed there, their blood issuing into the fetid River Thames in a seemingly unending stream.

"Wow," Mary said. "It's like something from a picture book."

Surely not like the pictures I've seen—the stories I've read, John thought.

"It sure is, Mary," he replied. "But unfortunately it isn't like a real castle. It's made from something called tinted staff."

"What's that?"

"It's a mixture of jute and plaster. It's a cheap imitation of stone and concrete. Most of the buildings you'll see today are made out of it. They'll all be gone in a couple of years."

Mary's eyes searched the ground and she let out a sigh. John knew at that moment that he had managed, without meaning to, to steal away with his sister's awe.

Mama had been right. The crowds were insufferable. It had taken twice as long as it usually would to get from Ellis Street to the exposition's Piedmont Avenue entrance. And when they got there, they had to endure a shoulder-to-shoulder crushing jostle just to buy tickets and get inside. John would later read that ten thousand people attended on opening day, and the crowds would grow to a one-day record of fifty-eight thousand on November twenty-eighth, Thanksgiving Day.

Upon passing through the turnstile at the main gate within the Administration Building, his unease dissipated. He was awestruck by the magnificence of the Grand Plaza and Lake Clara Meer in the distance. *What a stunning contrast—an imitation castle, built with plaster and jute—and the majesty of the plaza and lake beyond it.*

They had missed the opening ceremonies that morning—the downtown parade, the lighting of the electric fountain remotely by President Cleveland's hand, the firing of the cannon batteries, the military procession, the governor's horse guard, Booker T. Washington, Mayor King. (Governor Atkinson, originally slated to speak, was too ill to attend.) But they were sure to be entertained regardless—that is, as long as Mama could find the means to enjoy herself.

John noted the absence of the cheek-by-jowl throngs they had endured outside the main entrance. It must have been the bottleneck of the two available stile gates, surely a miscalculation on the part of the planners, given the expected attendance.

He had bought a daily program from a catalogue boy who was standing just past the turnstile. He opened it to the map in the front. Ella, Fred, and Mary gathered around as he pointed out the sites. "Here's the Transportation Building where I worked. We'll visit there later. But first, we'll go this way around the lake." He ran his finger around the map in a clockwise arc. "I could tell you most of the layout with a blindfold on—from all my break and lunchtime roamings."

The centerpiece, Lake Clara Meer, consisted of two manmade lagoons at more or less right angles to each other. A bridge crossed over at their junction. The upper lagoon ran roughly northeast to southwest, and the lower ran east to west. Together, they created a dogleg of sorts.

John pointed to a massive electric fountain on an island in the center of the lower lagoon. "That's called Atlantis. When the sun goes down, it'll release water sprays and mists. Colored lights will shine on it, creating magnificent opalescent images. I got to watch it at night when they were building it."

"What's that beacon over there—that tall thing in the water?" Fred asked.

"It's called the Floating Electric Tower of Lights. It's similar to Atlantis, but it doesn't have spraying water. It will light up at night with a thousand colored electric lights and will cast a shimmering glow over the lake's surface."

The Grand Plaza, second only to the lake in its splendor, ran roughly north to south and was flanked to its east by the upper dogleg of the lake and to its west by the main entrance. Most of the buildings on the grounds encircled the lake and the plaza. Midway Heights, where all the amusements could be found, ran parallel to Bleckley Avenue (also known as Tenth Street) along the southern edge of the grounds. To the east of Midway Heights could be found Buffalo Bill's Wild West Show.

John was sure Fred and Mary would be most enthralled with Midway Heights and Buffalo Bill. But those attractions, and the Mexican Village, near the southwest corner of the grounds, would be their last stops.

"Mama, if you look past the Grand Plaza, before the lake, do you see that building over there—the one with the columns and the dome? That's the Woman's Building. I'm sure you'll want to go there."

John's comment was met with a silent nod.

They walked to the left and ascended a slight incline past the Fire Building. Their first stop would be the Liberty Bell, which John had been told would be housed on a columned porch connected to the Pennsylvania Building.

"I haven't seen the bell yet. I rarely made it over to this part of the grounds when I was working here. Did you know they brought it all the way from Philadelphia on a special train? It stopped along the way for people to view it. I'm told there were cheering crowds at every station and points in between."

John looked at his mother. She lifted her veil and allowed the slightest smile. His sister seemed transfixed. Fred showed marginal interest.

John had read of the efforts by some Philadelphia officials to prevent the one-ton bell's being taken from its home. They feared the crack that ran from its waist past its sound bow would spread even more and break the whole thing apart. John decided to omit this little narrative.

They climbed the steps to the building and approached the columned porch. The bell was missing. A wooden scaffold structure had been constructed on the porch. But that was it. A guard stood nearby. *Guarding what? A missing bell?*

When they reached the top step, the guard approached them. "May I help you?"

"Where's the bell?" John asked.

"It's not here."

"What do you mean, it's not here?"

"Not yet anyhow."

"But what about the special train? The cheering crowds? I know I heard about that."

"Oh, you heard right. It'll happen. Just like when they took the bell to Chicago in ninety-three. That's probably what you heard about. It just hasn't happened here yet. The bell won't arrive for another three weeks. Come back then for the big celebration when they bring it in. There'll be pomp and pageantry. You won't regret it."

John knew his mother and Mary were disappointed. So was he. As for Fred, John wasn't so sure.

Ella, who had been quiet until now, asked to see the map. She pointed ahead, past where the Liberty Bell should have been. "John, is that the Fine Arts Building?"

"It is, Mama. Would you like to go inside?"

"I would. I read about it in the newspaper."

"So did I, Mother." *Did she detect a hint of sarcasm in my voice? Perhaps I shouldn't have been so brusque.*

"I hear it's filled with works from all over the world," she said. "New York. France. Italy. Holland. Wall hangings. Paintings. Sculptures."

John knew that Fred and Mary would end up as wearied of it all as he was, probably more so. But if Mama delighted in wall after wall of pictures and every square foot of floor crammed with naked and half-naked ancient statuettes—if another smile, however slight, could find its way to her brooding countenance— that was all that mattered.

They would spend what seemed like interminable hours in that sepulcher of a museum. But the elusive, sought-after smile did, indeed, reveal itself. And John was right—that was all that mattered.

As they descended the steps of the building, they heard the mellifluous voice of the carillon bells high atop the Chimes Tower across the walkway. They stopped to listen as the thirteen synchronized bells played "Nearer my God to Thee." Mama clutched her bodice.

They skipped the U.S. Government Building, although John had wanted to see the Weather Bureau and dead letters exhibits. As a worker taking breaks from claw hammer and jack plane and ratchet brace and saw, he had watched as men in blue work shirts and bib overalls carried various and sundry instruments—wind vanes and anemometers, rain gauges and huge thermometers—into the building. As for the dead letters exhibit, he wasn't quite sure why something so seemingly mundane would elicit such excitement, but it did. Perhaps he would return, by himself, on another day, and spend as many hours as he wished poring over all there was to see in that building. *Better than a fake edifice full of boring, fusty art.*

They continued around the Grand Plaza to the Manufactures and Liberal Arts Building, at the northwestern edge of the Lake Clara Meer dogleg. Dominating the eastern side of the Grand Plaza, it was, by all accounts, the largest and most commanding building at the fair. It was there that they witnessed telephone, phonograph, and typewriter demonstrations. And then there were the extensive collections of tobacco and firearms, two exhibits that were sure to elicit yet another pang of unease. John was careful to steer his family away from those displays.

Behind the building, flanked by its rear and the '49 Mining Camp, they found the alfresco barbecue dining pavilion, a massive wood-fired pit surrounded by rows of tables running parallel to each other and sufficient to feed not only the crowds of fairgoers, but also the hundreds of hungry military troops parading through the grounds each day. Lured by the aroma of fresh meat set over slow fires, they broke for a mid-afternoon lunch of barbecue pork and Brunswick stew, ably prepared by the exposition chef from the best squirrel, possum, and rabbit that could be hunted locally.

Atlanta is blessed with an abundance of birds—barn owls, mallards, mourning doves, Carolina chickadees, wrens, northern cardinals and, much to Mary's chagrin on this day, pigeons. Plain, old, run-of-the-mill domestic pigeons, hundreds if not thousands of them, had discovered and descended upon the fairgrounds. Their ultimate destination, not surprisingly, was the barbecue pavilion, with plenty of leftover pickings scattered about. Just as John and the family were leaving the table area, one of those pathetic excuses for a bird decided, mid-flight, to leave a little deposit with Mary. More specifically, with the top of Mary's head. This delighted Fred. He let out a loud guffaw, which was followed by a swift larrup in the stomach from a nine-year-old clenched fist. It was John, this time, who interceded and hauled Mary off to the nearest drinking fountain, leaving Fred drawn together in a hunch and Mama staring in bewilderment.

"Quite a punch you have there, young lady," John said as they headed for the drinking station.

Mary's hair took in the stream of running water as John stood watch. He dried her head with his handkerchief as best he could. "There, good as new," he said. Then they headed back to Mama and Fred.

"Women should never drink liquid with food or bathe after a full meal." Those words were spoken by a woman named Mrs. Minnie Thomas Antrim, from Philadelphia. Her Greek linen gown flowing as she moved dramatically about a raised platform in the Woman's Building's assembly hall, with its bright red walls, she spoke about something she termed women's physical culture. Another of Mrs. Antrim's maxims brought a brittle smile to Ella's face: "Woman—a paradox who puzzles when she pleases and pleases when she puzzles."

Thus had begun Ella, John, Fred, and Mary's visit to the Woman's Building. Their timing was such that they had happened upon the tail end of Mrs. Antrim's talk. Hundreds of eager women had packed into the hall. Ella had found the only free seat available. Mary sat on the floor at her feet. John and Fred, the only males in the room, stood along the back wall.

The only exhibit all four of them visited in the Woman's Building was Colonial Hall, a vast collection of eighteenth- and early nineteenth-century relics. The highlight of that exhibit, irrespective of George Washington's silver mug and the gun supposedly used to shoot Tecumseh in the chest when he turned to tomahawk his pursuer, was a shirt made of human scalps.

After Colonial Hall, John and Fred escaped to the Creole Kitchen, a food shack just outside, for bottled Coca-Colas to quench the spicy ghost of the Brunswick stew. They perched on a low stone wall, and there they waited for Ella and Mary to complete their tour of the women's exhibits.

John was eager to show Mama and the others the Transportation Building, where he had toiled for months prior to the opening. There were more exhibits crammed into that building than in any other at the fair—wagons, carriages, buggies, streetcars, trains, balloons, boats, steamships, and bicycles. Just walking through the building caused John's feet and muscles to ache. *There's no telling how many miles I walked, how many nails I hammered, putting the insides of this place together.*

The Train Shed, which housed the *General*, was down a few hundred yards from the Transportation Building. As John had told his mother and father that fateful Friday morning just three weeks past, the war's most famous iron horse was the fair's showpiece. Six Pullman luxury cars, sleeper cars, and numerous steam locomotives were also displayed in the Train Shed, but they all played second fiddle to the *General.*

As they left the Train Shed, Ella pointed across the street to the Negro Building.

"Mama, why in God's good name would you want to go there?"

"Because, John, it's part of our history and heritage just like everything else. You may not appreciate it, but those are the people I played with as a child. Why, if it hadn't been for the pickaninnies, I wouldn't have had anyone to play with—that is until I went off to school. They deserve at least a tad of our time."

Paris had the Eiffel Tower, Atlanta has the Negro Building. "Well I'm not interested."

John and his mother made a deal. She would spend as much time as she wished in that building—a tad or a ton as far as he was concerned. He and the others would ride the Phoenix Wheel. He could tell she didn't want to do that anyway. And he didn't encourage it. *I can't imagine a woman in black mourning dress and veil riding that big wheel. Better to let her bide her time in the colored building.* Mama agreed to meet John and the others at the base of the wheel when she was through. They would wait for her there.

"What's a Phoenix Wheel?" Mary asked.

"Do you see that big wheel reaching into the sky over there?" John pointed past the Train Shed to the eastern end of Midway Heights. "That's the Phoenix Wheel. See those twelve cages? We'll sit in one of them and ride all the way around."

"Why do they call it a Phoenix Wheel?" Fred asked.

"Well, it was made in a factory in Phoenixville, Pennsylvania. That's why it's called the Phoenix Wheel. They loaded its pieces into boxcars and shipped them here over the rail. I watched from afar as workmen put all the pieces together and erected it. It's one hundred twenty-five feet across and weighs two hundred fifty thousand pounds."

"I've never seen anything like that, even in books," Fred said. "Is it the only one?"

"No, there was a bigger one at the world's fair in Chicago two years ago. That was the first one. They called it a Ferris Wheel because it was designed and built by a man named Ferris."

The highlight of the ride on the wheel was the ascent to the top. "Because the wheel sits on a seventy-five foot hill, we're two hundred feet above most of the fairgrounds," John said when they reached the top. "You can see the whole fair and the surrounding countryside from up here. Look how tiny the people are."

Aside from Mary's momentary bout of qualmishness on the way down, for which John could provide little comfort, the ride was engaging. Not seeing Mama at the base, they decided to do it again. Only this time Mary would ignore the wambling by holding her breath and staring off into the distance, her mind far from what was churning down below.

By the time they disembarked from the riding cage the second time, Mama was waiting at the base of the wheel.

"Did you see us way up there, Mama?" Mary asked.

Ella nodded.

Midway Heights was like one big carnival, a spectacle and a sensory smorgasbord the likes of which none of them, save for Ella, had ever beheld.

"The best things are worth the wait," Mary said.

The four of them visited the Camera Obscura, an octagonal building in the shadow of the Phoenix Wheel. There, giant lenses atop the roof projected magnified moving images of the exposition's grounds and crowds.

The ostrich farm, its ponderous and flightless inhabitants having been secured from Mrs. S.C. Dooley's ranch in Los Angeles, was across from the wheel. Fred, failing to heed the warning sign's words, extended his hand a bit too close to the protective grate before yanking it away, barely managing to save his index finger from certain catastrophe.

Beyond the ostrich farm, on the same side of the Midway Heights' central east-west corridor called The Terrace, stood the Indian Village, Roltair's Illusions, and a quack finagler hawking yet another nostrum sure to cure all that ails, followed by the Phantoscope exhibit. There they watched, projected onto the wall, a moving picture of a lady named Annabelle dancing across the frame like a peacock butterfly to the music of a woman in the corner banging away on an upright piano.

Dusk was settling in. Much to John's discomfiture, they decided to forgo Buffalo Bill's Wild West Show. *When I return,* John thought. They lingered briefly at Hagenbeck's Animal Arena to see the trained elephants before moving on to their last stop, the Mexican Village. John was sure, based on stories he'd heard of the New Orleans fair, that bittersweet memories would beset his mother.

Pretty much everything Mexican had been stuffed into the village except bullfighting. The south-of-the-border organizers' plans had been thwarted by an outcry from Atlanta's citizenry, principally the ladies, who protested against sure cruelty to the bulls and the frightening of the horses. The exposition directors responded by banning the shedding of blood in the name of sport. Otherwise, there was plenty to see. Donkeys, carrying large woven baskets as big around as trundling hoops and led along by a sombrero-clad paisano donkey master. A working replica of a coffee plantation. Reproductions of famous ruins and missions. And, of course, a Mexican Norteño band surrounded by señoritas in flowing skirts.

John, standing beside his mother, placed his arm around her as he watched the tears well up. "Your father and I danced to that music. Oh, how he resisted. But I pulled him to me and led him step by step. Would that I could do it just once more."

As Ella, John, Fred, and Mary ambled toward the main gate, they stopped to watch the pyrotechnic show, which began at sundown. Even though the exploding rockets were fired from across the lake, that didn't stop Mary from plugging her ears with her fingers. Some projectiles shot straight up before exploding and tumbling down in a spiral of reds, oranges, and yellows. Some shattered mid-air in a violent burst of light and disappeared quickly into the night. Others sprayed an umbrella-like array of glittering wonder across the sky. A smoky haze and the acrid smell of sulfur filled the air.

John hailed a hansom driver, who this time wheedled not one dime, but two, for the inconvenience of an over-full load. They headed home. Even with all the jerking and bucketing of the carriage, Mary managed to fall asleep on her mother's knee. Ella wrapped her arm around her to ensure she didn't go tumbling into Fred's lap, a spill that would surely set off fireworks of another sort.

Baker Jr. missed a splendid day, John thought as the driver proceeded down Piedmont Road. *And Father, God rest him.*

At 74 Ellis Street, John removed the note, tacked to the door beneath the mourning arrangement. It was addressed to him. He unfolded it.

> Wednesday 18th
> John,
> Please call on me at the station house at your earliest convenience.
> Sincerely,
> Capt. William Manly

Part Three

THE TOBACCO MEN
AND
THE MUDSILL

TWENTY

ED CASON

A Cooked-up Plan

CONN THREW THE MONDAY EDITION OF THE JOURNAL to the floor with such force that its pages went flying every which way. The paper had come out the prior evening, and the whole city was in a dither.

"That bastard Jenkins is lying," Conn roared at the room full of detectives. He shook his fist in the air. His face was red. The veins in his temples pulsed. "He's cooked up a vendetta with one goal—to destroy the person and career of one of our own."

"It's not just *any one of our own, Conn.* It's *you*," Mehaffey replied.

"I know that—*obviously*—Mehaffey. I'm the one he's out to get. I'm the one whose survival is on the line because of a lying, no-account, goddamned son-of-a-bitch. We need to arrest him. Bring him in in leg irons and lock him up."

"I know that's what you'd like, Conn," Mehaffey said. "But we need some kind of proof. We can't just nab the man without evidence. The first thing we need to do is find that woman¬—the one Jenkins claims put the scratch on your gun."

"*Alleged* gun, Mehaffey."

"Yes, your alleged gun.

"You want to know what I think?" Conn said. "I think Jenkins bribed her. He's trying to frame *me* for Bass's death. *Me*—a sworn member of the police force."

Detective Ed Cason jumped in. "Conn, you're too caught up in all of this. You need to stay out of it for a while. You just hole up in the station house and let the rest of us do the work. We'll figure out how to catch him in his own game, whatever that is."

"Absolutely not," Conn shouted. "I'm not going to sit back while the rest of you go after that hornswoggler. It's *my* life at stake here, not yours."

"We'll discuss that later, Conn," Cason said. "But I will tell you this. Whatever plan we come up with, Connolly and Manly can't be allowed to know about it. At least not until we have solid evidence against Jenkins. But not a minute before. They'll mess things all up. Why, did you know Manly is nosing around on his own—not really on his own, but at Connolly's direction—to prove, or disprove, the allegations again *you*, Conn?"

"How do you know that?"

"I heard it through the grapevine," Cason replied.

"*What* grapevine?"

"Well, if you must know, the walls in this station house are thin. Things get said. And things get heard sometimes. Especially by someone—say a sergeant sitting in a room adjacent to the chief's office when the chief and his second-in-command are having a private conversation—someone who happens to overhear something that was not intended for his ears. That's the way grapevines start."

"Well I'll be damned. Even my own captain is out to get me."

"What did I say, Conn? Did I say he was out to get you? I said he was out to prove, *or disprove,* Jenkins' allegations against you."

"Well, say what you want, but it sure *sounds* like he's out to get me."

"Listen, Conn, put Connolly and Manly out of your mind for now. We have a job to do. Jenkins claimed this woman knows both you and Bass. And he said you met with her in a whorehouse. Surely that narrows things down a bit. Or perhaps it doesn't."

Conn glared at Cason. He then looked at Mehaffey, who was sitting across the room, then back at Cason.

"Listen," Conn said. "I'm a married man. The last thing I want is to get mixed up in a scandal over some woman in a whorehouse."

"I understand," Cason replied, "but you know as well as I that the *scandal,* as you call it, is already before the public. Read the newspaper. It's all right there."

"I've read the newspaper just like you, Cason. I know everything Jenkins has claimed."

"Well, are you denying you were mixed up with this mysterious woman in a whorehouse? The *Journal* has reported it. Are you saying Jenkins was lying about *that?*"

"No, I'm not saying that. But *mixed up* is a mischaracterization."

"So who is the woman?" Cason asked. "Does she have a name?"

"Listen, Cason. Her name is Delores Dampman. I met her casually. There's nothing more to it than that. We could probably bump into one another on the street and I wouldn't recognize her. And I can assure you—she's *not* a wagtail."

"Then why did you and she end up together at a brothel?"

"If you must know, I was there looking for a man on the run. It was all official business."

"What official business? What man on the run? And why was this woman friend of yours, Mrs. Dampman, there?"

"She's *not* a friend of mine. She was there because she was helping out the madam of the house, which she sometimes does. That's all. And it doesn't matter at this point who I was looking for."

"And where might we find this Doris Dampman?"

"Her name is Delores. Not Doris. She lives on Woodward Avenue. Number 201. With her husband George. He works for the Central of Georgia Railroad. She doesn't work—that is, except when she's helping out the madam."

"So, 201 Woodward Avenue. Mehaffey, bring me the city map," Cason said.

Mehaffey fetched a map from a shelf at the far end of the room and walked over to where Cason and Conn were standing. He unfolded it and laid it out on the table. The three men stood around the table and studied it together. Cason tracked the route to where the Dampmans lived. From Decatur Street down Piedmont. Across the tracks. A half-block offset at Hunter Street and on to Capitol Avenue. Past Fair Street. Then right on Woodward. He pointed to a spot on the map. He jabbed his finger into the paper. "Here, this would be the two hundred block. Right here. What's the next street over? Crew Street. Mrs. Dampman lives just a block away from where Jenkins stays."

Cason looked at his watch. It was 8:20 a.m.

"I'm going to find this woman, Delores Dampman, and meet with her."

"I insist on going with you," Conn said.

"That's not a good idea, Conn. We want this woman to tell us what she knows, don't we?"

Conn responded with a nod.

"Jenkins has said the woman and he are friends," Cason continued. "But you've claimed you barely know her. Nevertheless, you do know her, enough to know where she lives, her husband's name, what he does for a living. And she has supposedly implicated you in some way. Don't you think I'll get more out of her if you're not there?"

Conn relented. Cason set out to pay Mrs. Dampman a visit.

Cason left the station house on foot. He walked down Piedmont. He crossed over the iron bridge that spanned the east-west Central of Georgia Railroad line—nine sets of tracks— he counted them. Just past the bridge, he looked to his right. Railroad workers were maneuvering a steam locomotive into the massive roundhouse between the main tracks and Hunter Street. He wondered if one of the workers might be George Dampman.

He turned left at Hunter and walked the quarter block to Capitol Avenue. There were more people than usual crowding the grounds of the State Capitol. Throngs of men, women and children, black and white, gathered around the capitol steps. Halfway up the steps stood a distinguished looking Negro man. He was evangelizing about something. Then Cason remembered. *Of course, it's that colored man from Tuskegee. He's here to give a speech at the opening of the exposition in two days. Something about relations between the races.* He stopped briefly and looked on as Booker T. Washington regaled a mixed audience, most of whom, Cason supposed, had never seen a black man speak with such vigor and self-confidence.

Cason continued down Capitol Avenue. As he neared Fair Street, he rehearsed what he would say to Mrs. Dampman. That was assuming he would find her at home and not hanging out at some damned brothel at nine in the morning.

The house at 201 Woodward was a side-by-side, framed duplex. Like two shotgun houses jammed together, with a single porch across the front. There were two doors, one labeled 201 and the other labeled 201½. Cason approached the 201 door. He was reaching to knock when an older woman, perhaps sixty, sixty-five, opened the door.

"Are you Mrs. Dampman?"

"No, my name's Cheek. I own the house. Mrs. Dampman lives next door. The Dampmans rent from me—at least for now. I know she's home because I talked to her earlier. But she may or may not come to the door."

Cason went to the 201½ door and knocked. He heard footsteps approaching the door. Lumbering. Heavy. Like a man's. The door opened. A thick-set woman, middle-aged, stood in the doorway. She stared at him. Bulbous eyes through ponderous wire-rimmed lenses. He thought the woman had obviously been attractive in her younger years—and she had undoubtedly learned to take ample advantage of what God had bestowed upon her. But the thick layers of makeup covering her cheeks and under her eyes, and the stiflingly overdone scent of Florida Water, with its overtones of sweet orange and clove, suggested an attempt to hide her age and recapture an allure that had escaped her a decade or more earlier.

"Are you Mrs. Dampman?"

"Yes. What can I do for you?"

"Mrs. Dampman. I'm Officer Cason. I'm here to ask you some questions about a man named Herbert Jenkins and a colleague of mine, Green Conn."

"I don't have anything to say." She reached for the door handle.

"Please, Mrs. Dampman, if you could just give me a few minutes of your time. I'm not here to cause problems or to get you in any kind of trouble. But I'm given to believe you may know something about the events leading up to Baker Bass's death two weeks ago—and specifically a certain handgun that may have been used to kill him."

"I told Mr. Jenkins I didn't want him getting me involved in this. And as for that man Conn, did you say he was your friend?"

"Ma'am, we work together."

"Well I don't want to have anything to do with him."

"But Mr. Jenkins is your friend, isn't he?"

"He is."

"And if I told you there's talk around town that he may be guilty of trying to frame Conn, wouldn't you want to protect your friend from false accusations?"

"Well, I guess I would. But I told you, I don't want to get mixed up in all of this."

"But Mrs. Dampman, I'm afraid you already are. And think of it this way. Let's assume Conn *did* kill Bass. You could help us get to the bottom of your friend's claim and help us solve a murder. But suppose Conn *didn't* do it. The last thing anybody wants is for an innocent man to go to the gallows. I don't care whether you like the man or not. That's a heavy burden to bear. And Jenkins' attempts to pin the murder on Conn may be sincere—and not, as some people are alleging, a frame job. If that's the case, wouldn't you want to help clear Jenkins' good name as well?"

She looked off into the distance. Then back at Cason. "So what do you want me to do?"

"I'd like you to meet with Jenkins. At a time and place where the two of you can meet in private. Away from snoops and meddlers. From eavesdroppers and lurkers. Where he'll be comfortable opening up to you. Hopefully you can coax more out of him. I'm sure, Mrs. Dampman, with your persuasive powers, combined with a little libation, you can learn more. And you can report back to us what Jenkins told you. It's for his own good, you know."

"Well, I suppose I could do that. After all, he got me into this mess in the first place."

"Mrs. Dampman, is it okay if I come back tomorrow? We can spend a few minutes coming up with a plan for the two of you to meet."

She assented.

"And one more thing before I go, Mrs. Dampman. About that gun. Did you put a scratch on Green Conn's gun? And did you go to Grady Hospital, where Baker Bass was dying, and observe that same scratch on the gun there, in the hospital room?"

"That's what Mr. Jenkins claims."

"I understand, but I'm asking *you*. Is it true—what Jenkins has claimed?"

"I won't discuss the gun with you, standing here on my porch, Mr. Cason. Mr. Jenkins has made a statement to a reporter. And that statement ended up in the evening paper. We'd best leave it at that until I've met with him."

Cason raced back to the station house.

"Listen, men. I have a plan. And I've convinced Mrs. Dampman to go along with it—at least part of it. She's unaware of the *whole* plan."

"What is it?" Mehaffey asked.

"Here's what we'll do. I've convinced her to meet with Jenkins. To try to get more out of him. Some gentle persuasion—of the feminine variety, even from somebody like her—combined with a generous supply of knock-me-down bub and baldface corn, may just do the trick. I'll coach her beforehand. What she doesn't know is that we'll be there too, secretly listening in on every word. She thinks she's helping Jenkins out by doing this, but if things go as I hope they will, Jenkins will hang himself. And you, Conn, will get off Scot-free. As for Mrs. Dampman, she's gullible enough to play into our hands."

"And where will we do this?"

"I know of a house on the far edge of town. Tucked away in the woods. Sufficiently off the beaten path that we won't get caught. It's the perfect spot for our little ruse. But we need some support from higher up."

"Higher up? What do you mean?"

"If we try to pull this off without support at the top, it could backfire on us. There's one commissioner who will help us out and keep quiet—Commissioner Branan—he's on our side. None of the other commissioners need to know about this. And we certainly have to keep it from Connolly and Manly—that is, until we have enough on Jenkins to lock him up."

"Okay. I'm willing to go along with your plan," Mehaffey said. "But even if Jenkins incriminates himself, who's going to believe it, if we're the only ones there to hear it? Shouldn't we have somebody else there, listening in—a third party that can't be accused of having an ax to grind?"

"Do you have anybody in mind?" Cason asked.

"No, but I think we should try to find a man willing to do it. Even if Branan's there, listening in, I wouldn't call him a dispassionate third party."

Cason approached the door to leave the room. He swung around. Looked at Conn with a smirk.

"By the way, Conn. This Dampman woman. Why didn't you tell me she was a worn-out tart?"

TWENTY-ONE

FRANK KEELER

The Oddest Hours

ON TUESDAY AFTERNOON, THE SAME DAY CASON AND his fellow detectives were cooking up a plan to set Jenkins up in their elaborate confidence game, Frank Keeler left the station house and headed toward Decatur. He was on his way to Kirkwood, a quiet, tree-lined neighborhood east of the city. If he walked, it would take him an hour at a swift pace. He had considered riding on horseback but, once there, he would not have the freedom to navigate the streets and alleyways on foot with ease. He chose instead to take the South Decatur car line, which ran straight out Decatur Street from the station house and would drop him off close to Conn's residence.

He traveled light, with little more than a loose jacket—of the Norfolk variety—one that he preferred for its abundance of pockets. He ignored the likelihood that the jacket stood out and may have made him look more like a fox hunter than a reporter.

He was OK with that. It wasn't as if he was on a mission of espionage, like some secret agent. He could easily have fancied himself as one of those John Yates Beall types, but then he remembered that Beall had been arrested and executed for spying. And, after all, Keeler was just a newspaper reporter. He carried a pencil and notepad in his outer coat pocket, with extras of each in an inside pocket in case he needed them.

Howard Street, with its abundant water oaks, red oaks and maples, stood out among the streets, avenues, and alleyways in Kirkwood. The house where Green Conn stayed, at number 40 Howard Street, was a modest wood-frame dwelling, two rooms wide and two rooms deep, with weatherboard siding and a hip roof. The house sat close to the street, with a small, grassy yard. A pyracantha shrub covered much of the northwest corner of the house. Large clusters of bright reddish-orange berries provided a show of color across an otherwise nondescript yard, save for the trees lining the street. The neighborhood and the house struck Keeler as not the kind of place where he would have expected Conn to live, based on what he knew of the man. *Not a suitable backdrop for scoundrels and scamps, and it's so far outside the city. Downright idyllic.*

Keeler strolled down Howard Street past Conn's house, then down Hallman, one of several narrower, east-west cross streets that ran north of the trolley line. He wanted to get a feel for the neighborhood. One block north of Hallman, at the corner of Howard and Hardee Streets, stood the Kirkwood Baptist Church, a clapboard structure with a square bell tower on one front corner and a shorter, enclosed cupola on the other. Keeler stood before the church and gazed up at the bell tower. He could barely make out the faint sound of music coming from inside the church. He cupped his hand to his ear.

"He in the thickest darkness dwells,
Performs His Work, the cause conceals;
But tho' His methods are unknown,
Justice and truth supports his throne."

He climbed the seven steps leading to a set of large oak doors. He entered the church. The doors banged against the frame as they closed behind him. At the far end of the sanctuary, a dozen women, hymnals in hand, stood on a raised platform behind the pulpit. Aside from that, the church appeared empty. If not for the afternoon sunlight passing through the church's stained glass windows, the sanctuary would have been dark.

Keeler was about to turn and leave when a woman descended the raised platform and scurried toward him. As she approached, she placed her index finger to her lips.

"Quiet now," she whispered, "the ladies are practicing for the Sunday service."

"Ma'am, I meant no harm in the Lord's house. Could we speak briefly—outside?"

Keeler followed the woman out of the church and to the bottom of the steps.

"Ma'am, my name is Keeler. I'm a reporter for the *Journal*. I'm not familiar with the neighborhood. I'm looking for anyone who might know a man who lives on Howard Street. A man named Green Conn."

"I know *of* him, but I don't really *know* him. He and his wife—Stella's her name—live down the way there." She pointed down Howard Street. "In that house down there. The one with the big pyracantha bush. I can't tell you anything about him, really. They keep to themselves. That's all I know."

"Do you know of anyone in the neighborhood that I could speak with? Someone who might know more about him?"

"Mr. Keeler, did you say you were with the newspaper?"

"Yes, ma'am."

"Does this have anything to do with that man that was killed downtown last month? I read something in the paper about Mr. Conn being mixed up in it. Just last evening I read it. Was that your article?"

Keeler answered with a nod.

"Well, I hope they find the killer. I've prayed every night for his poor wife and children. I wish I could be of more help, Mr. Keeler, but I don't reckon I know of anybody you could talk to."

Keeler was halfway down the block when she called out to him.

"Wait, Mr. Keeler. I *do* know somebody. There's a man lives two doors up from the Conns. His name's Cooper. J.B. Cooper. He's the neighborhood busybody if you ask me. Pay him a visit."

"Thank you, ma'am. When you say two doors up, do you mean in this direction? On Howard Street."

"Yes, talk to Mr. Cooper. I just bet he can tell you what you need to know."

"May I help you?" The man, who looked to be in his late sixties, perhaps older, stood in the doorway.

"Are you J.B. Cooper?"

"Yes I am," the man replied.

Keeler explained who he was and that he was looking for information on Conn. "A lady at the church up the street— unfortunately I left without getting her name—suggested that I speak with you."

"Well, I suppose you've come to the right place. I'm here day and night. Ever since I retired. Taught school for forty-five years, except for a brief time in the middle when a little skirmish, you may have heard about it…" Cooper grinned. "…took me away for three of those years. Now I just sit here and read—and look out the window at all the comings and goings around here. Day and night. Please come in."

Keeler followed Cooper into the front room.

"Dalmanutha, bring this young man a cup of coffee," Cooper called out. He turned to Keeler. "How do you like your coffee? Oh never mind, she'll bring all the accompaniments."

A black woman entered the room with a tray. On it were two cups and saucers, a pot of coffee, and a creamer and sugar bowl. She set the tray on a low table between two chairs. The two men sat across the table from each other. As soon as the woman had left the room, Cooper leaned in.

"She doesn't need to hear me say this, but I don't know what I would do without her since my wife died. If you had told me five years ago that I would have felt for a Negress the way I feel for her, I would have said you were a mad lunatic. But here I am. And here she is."

Cooper filled both cups and pointed to the cream and sugar.

"Doctor it up as you please, Mr. Keeler. Now, what are you here for? Oh yes. Green Conn. You want to know all about Green Conn. Well, I can tell you this. The man keeps to himself. And he comes and goes at the oddest hours. Sometimes he leaves here at three or four in the morning. Where he goes I have no idea. I've assumed at times that it has something to do with his detective work. But it's still quite odd to me. And he comes home very late at night."

"Mr. Cooper, forgive me for asking, but as a retired man, why are you up at those ungodly hours?"

"Damnable insomnia, that's why. Ever since she—my wife, that is—passed. I've tried opium. Laudanum. Chloral hydrate. All they did was make me feel like a vacuous fool. Not worth it. So I toss and turn. And more often than not I end up right here in this chair in the middle of the night. Wide awake. Sometimes I think I should just go outside and howl at the moon."

"Mr. Cooper, think back if you can to Friday morning, two and a half weeks ago. The morning Baker Bass was killed. It was raining that morning. Do you remember seeing Conn leave the house?"

"I have trouble remembering that far back. He could have left early that morning. But I couldn't swear to it."

"Do you remember reading about Bass's murder in the *Journal* that same evening, the evening of the thirtieth?"

"Let me think." Cooper paused. "I do actually. I remember the headline on the front page, A MYSTERIOUS KILLING. I read the entire article. In fact, come to think of it, I happened to run into Conn later that day. He was returning home, I'm guessing around six o'clock in the evening. He was disheveled. Helter-skelter-like. Preoccupied. Distracted. I mentioned Bass's murder—or should I say suspected murder. He was evasive. It was clear to me he didn't want to discuss it. I assumed it was because they—the detectives that is—were investigating it and were sworn to keep their mouths shut."

"It's good you remember that. So think back to much earlier that day? Early that morning. The same day you encountered Conn. Do you recall seeing him when he left the house?"

"Well, let me think. I recall taking a nap that afternoon. I'd been up most of Thursday night and into the wee hours of Friday morning. I dozed off late that morning and slept well into the afternoon, until Dalmanutha awoke me with a cup of coffee and the newspaper. I remember her saying, 'Mr. Cooper. Look here. A man's been killed. On Ivy Street.' My eyes fell first on the picture of the man right there in the center of the front page—I didn't recognize him—and then I saw the headline."

"Do you remember a reference in the article to Mr. Bass being found sometime after four that morning?"

"I do. I remember that."

"So if you think back, I assume you were awake and probably sitting in that very chair. Right?"

"I was. As I recall, I'd been sitting here for upwards of two hours."

"Gazing out the window?"

"Yes. Gazing out the window. The rain was beating down hard against the glass. I remember that. And I remember something else. Around three fifteen, a common nighthawk flew into the window. They fly through these parts every year around this time. On their way to South America. They're nocturnal, you know, so I feel as if we have a lot in common. I've never seen one fly right into the glass like that. The high winds must have blown it off its course. I got up and walked over to the window. I looked out the window and down toward the ground in an effort to see if the bird had fallen into the grass. It was dark, but the light from inside the house partially illuminated the area below the window. I didn't see the bird, so I assumed it had flown away."

"How do you know what time it was, Mr. Cooper?"

"Because when I sat back down I looked up." Cooper pointed to a wall clock across the room.

"Did you seen anything else as you were peering out the window?"

Cooper sat in thought for several minutes. "I *did* actually. Now I remember. I saw a man leaving Green Conn's house. I likely would not have seen him in the dark had it not been for the lantern he was carrying. He was holding it close to his chest. I imagine he was trying to shield it from the rain and wind. I remember the man had on a raincoat and hat."

"Think hard, Mr. Cooper. The man you saw. Was it Green Conn?"

"I can't say with certainty. But I can tell you this. Have you ever seen Mr. Conn? He has a babyish face. Smooth as a cue ball. No mustache. No beard. From what I could tell, as the lantern shined on the man's kisser, it looked to be him." Cooper shook his head. "But I just can't say."

"This past weekend, between ten o'clock Saturday evening and early Sunday morning, did you happen to see Conn leaving or returning to his house?"

"Unfortunately, Mr. Keeler, I can't help you with that. That's one of the few nights lately when I've slept like a baby. All night."

"And I hope you didn't have to resort to becoming a vacuous fool, as you say, to do it."

"I'm glad to say I decidedly did not." Cooper locked eyes with Keeler. "Mr. Keeler, may I ask you a question? I read in yesterday's *Journal* that a man named Jenkins has accused Conn of killing Baker Bass. Is that why you're here? Do you think he did it?"

"Mr. Cooper, I'm a newspaperman. My job is to seek the facts, wherever they lead. I have no idea whether Conn was or wasn't involved in Bass's death. I'm just here to shed light on the situation. The only thing I have at stake here is my reputation as a journalist. Before I go, is there anything else you can tell me about Conn's comings and goings? Around the time of Bass's death, did he get any visits from people you didn't know?"

"He *is* visited regularly. By an older man. Distinguished looking. Heavy-set but well-dressed. And the most curious thing is the man's a spitting image of President Cleveland."

Grover Cleveland? In Kirkwood? Keeler laughed as he left Cooper's house.

He turned up the sidewalk toward number 40. Conn's house was quiet. It looked as if no one was home. He walked past the house. When he reached the far corner of the lot, he stopped. He looked back at the house. He wasn't sure what possessed him to turn back. But he did. He walked back past the house and into the yard. Beyond the pyracantha shrub. He looked around. He spotted a wooden crate leaning against the side of the house, near the back. He retrieved the crate and placed it upside-down under a window. He stepped onto the crate and peered through the window. Into a bedroom. *It must be Conn's room*, he thought. There was an unmade bed in the middle of the room. He looked around. He had to stretch to see a chest of drawers set against the outside wall, the wall nearest where he stood. He could see a pistol lying on the top of the chest. He couldn't tell what kind it was, let alone its caliber. Across the room was an armoire. The door to the armoire was ajar. A chamber pot sat on the floor on the side of the bed nearer to the window. A white shirt and a pair of black trousers were haphazardly thrown across the foot of the bed. A set of galluses lay atop the shirt as if they had been carelessly tossed there.

He stepped off the crate. He was about to move it to another window along the same side of the house when he heard a noise. It came from the other side of the pyracantha shrub. The abundance of berries prevented him from making out the noise's source or exactly where it was coming from, but it sounded like footsteps. He crouched behind the shrub. He tried to separate the bunches of berries—slowly, carefully—but to no avail. The thorns scratched his hands.

"What are you doing on my property?"

Still crouching, Keeler pivoted on the balls of his feet. And when he did, he lost his balance. His knees went to the ground. There he was, kneeling, with a man standing over him. It was Conn. No doubt about it. The barrel of a revolver pointed at the crown of Keeler's head. Keeler stood up with his hands in the air.

"I'm not here to make trouble. I promise. My name's Frank Keeler. I'm with the newspaper."

Surely my pencil and notepad will convince him. Keeler reached into his jacket pocket. When he did, he heard a *chkchk* sound. He looked up and saw Conn's thumb resting on the revolver's open hammer. Keeler slowly returned his hand to the air.

"What newspaper?"

"The *Journal.*"

"Are you the one that wrote that story about me?"

"If you mean the one in yesterday's paper, then yes, I was the one. But I was only relating what Herbert Jenkins told me. That's what a good reporter is supposed to do. It was Jenkins' story, not mine."

"Don't you think, before you go off writing a one-sided piece, you should get the other man's side of the story? Isn't that what a good journalist does?"

Conn continued to point the gun at Keeler, but this time at his forehead. The hammer was still open. Conn's finger rested on the trigger.

"That's why I'm here, Mr. Conn. I *want* to hear your side of the story."

"And you thought you were going to get it hiding behind by shrubbery?"

"No sir. I was just trying to see if you were home."

"I have this thing called a front door. All you had to do was knock. Now take everything out of your jacket pockets. Your trouser pockets. Throw it all on the ground in front of you. Pull all your pocket linings inside-out so I can see them."

Keeler hoped Conn wouldn't pick up the notepad, thumb through it, and read the notes he had made during his visit with Cooper.

"Keep your hands up and be still. One wrong move and you'll have a bloody hole between your eyes."

Conn held the pistol in his right hand. With his left, he felt along Keeler's right side and down his leg, all the way to the inside of his boot. Then the inseam of his left leg. Conn switched the pistol to his left hand and repeated the whole thing, searching Keeler's left side and the inseam of his right leg. He ran his hand across Keeler's chest. He put his hand on Keeler's shoulder and swung him around.

"Gather up all your things. Off we go, into the house."

Conn walked behind Keeler, the barrel of the gun pressed between the reporter's shoulder blades. When they got in the house, he directed Keeler to sit on a sofa at one end of the room. Conn sat in a chair across the room from him and placed the gun on a table beside his chair.

"Mr. Conn, all I want is to do my job. To be the best newspaperman I can be. I'm not here to judge any man. Or to assign guilt to any man."

"Who sent you here?"

"My editor sent me here." Keeler lied.

"Well, let me say this. For the record. I have no idea who killed Baker Bass. For all I know, the man put a gun to his head and killed himself. He was not an honorable man, you know. He was up to no good. It's true I'd been on his tail for a while. But I didn't kill him. And like I said, I don't know who did. But what I do know is this. That no-account Jenkins is out to frame me. And I'm not going to stand by and let him get away with it."

"Do you have a plan? To prove it I mean—that he's trying to frame you?"

"You interviewed the man. He cited two things that he claims prove I killed Bass. One involves a mark on a gun, supposedly my gun, that was found on Bass's person. The other is some man, as yet unnamed, who says he saw me fleeing the scene of the shooting."

"Do you know where the gun is now?" Keeler asked.

Conn faced Keeler across the room. His eyes shifted to his right and down toward the gun lying on the table beside him. Then back to Keeler.

"I have no idea. Maybe with the coroner. Maybe with the chief or his captain. Maybe resting on Bass's lifeless chest as we speak, buried with him in his funerary box, for all I know."

"But Jenkins told me he went to the coroner's house and saw the gun himself, well after Bass had been buried."

"That's what Jenkins told you. But is he to be believed? Maybe he made it all up."

Keeler knew the gun had been stolen from Paden's house. But he couldn't tell Conn that. And Conn probably knew full well that the gun wasn't buried with Bass. Keeler played dumb.

"And what about the witness? The one Jenkins claims saw you running down the street? Any idea who he is?"

"If you ask me, I think Jenkins just fabricated him out of thin air."

Keeler heard a rustling down the hall.

"Don't mind that. It's just Stella. Listen, Keeler, I think you're a good man. And I take you at your word that you want to be the best newspaperman you can be. If that's the case, I have a favor to ask. If you do it, you can walk away with what may prove to be the best story of your entire career, a far sight better than the horse manure Jenkins fed you."

"What do you have in mind?"

"We're planning to trap Jenkins in the passel of lies he's been peddling. Catch him in his game and lock him up. But we have to do it in secret. Only the detectives and a couple of other people can know about it until it's done. Every man involved has to be sworn to secrecy. And every woman, for that matter. But to be believed, we need an objective third party, somebody with nothing at stake except their career, as you said. Maybe a reporter who needs to redeem himself after being caught snooping around on another man's property. What do you think, Keeler?"

"But if it's all a secret, how can it be the best story of my career?"

"Because once it's done, once we have Jenkins behind bars, once the chief and the captain know about it, then you can print it all in your little paper. Hell, it may be the story of the century in these parts. Imagine every literate soul in the city picking up the afternoon paper and reading the headline, No-Good Thief Caught In His Game. Sent To The Work Farm. Detective Exonerated."

Keeler concluded his visit with Conn, caught the next inbound trolley, and returned to the station house. He found Manly sitting at his desk.

"Mr. Manly, I have some surprising news to share."

Manly stood up.

"Not here, Keeler. Let's walk down to the Markham House. We can talk there. It's safer."

Keeler related his visit with J.B. Cooper and his unplanned encounter with Conn himself. He told the captain of the scheme being cooked up by the detectives to catch Jenkins.

"Mr. Manly, it's a funny thing. As I was on my way to Kirkwood, for a minute or two I fancied myself on a mission like John Yates Beall. Then I realized that I'm just a reporter. But if I go through with this plan Conn has laid out for me, I'll be more like Timothy Webster."

"I don't know who Timothy Webster is, Keeler."

"Was. He was hanged in sixty-two. He was a double agent during the war. Pinkerton sent him down to Richmond. He posed as a courier for the Confederates. But what they didn't know is that he was passing information back to Pinkerton. When he was caught, the Confederates convicted him as a spy and sentenced him to death."

"I hope you're not worried about being *hanged*, Keeler."

"Of course not, but it does seem a bit odd, working for you and, at the same time, snooping for Conn and his cohorts."

"You just don't want to get caught. Whatever you do, don't let on that you're playing both sides. But in the end, this could prove to be a good thing, what you're doing. Especially if it sheds light on Conn's, or Jenkins', guilt or innocence."

The two men agreed that Keeler would participate in the detectives' ruse. They also agreed that every step each of them took was a step on a tightrope—with a flimsy net to protect them should they fall.

They returned to Manly's office.

"There's one more thing, Mr. Manly. This Cooper fellow told me Conn is visited regularly by a well-dressed, heavy-set man who looks just like President Cleveland. What do you make of that?"

"Hold on a minute, Keeler."

Manly walked to the back of his desk and opened a drawer. He took out a small booklet, a police department yearbook. He thumbed through the first few pages. He placed the booklet on the desk surface, opened to page five, facing Keeler. He slid the open booklet across the desk. He pointed to the picture of a man—a man who could have passed for Grover Cleveland's brother. Keeler's eyes fell on the caption below the picture, COMMISSIONER J.C.A. BRANAN.

TWENTY-TWO

WILLIAM MANLY

Circles on a Slate Board

"JOHN, HAVE A SEAT."

John Bass had come to Manly's office early Thursday morning, the nineteenth of September.

"I assume, Captain, you asked for a meeting because you have good news to share."

An awkward silence hung in the air.

"Unfortunately, we haven't found your father's killer. I called you here because I need your help. But first, how is your mother doing? And how are you—and the others."

"She's getting by. We're getting by. We went to the exposition yesterday. We were all tuckered out at the end, but as we headed home, I thought I detected the slightest bounce in Mother's step. The visit did her good. She needed to get out of the house. She spends too much time languishing in that dark bedroom. Baker—my brother, that is—couldn't go, but Fred and Mary had a grand time. They seem to have adjusted to Father's death. Of course they have their low times, but you know how children are. They're resilient in a way us older folk don't seem to be."

Older folk? Why, he's still wet behind the ears. "I wish I could have been there for the opening, but I'm too wrapped up in finding the killer. The chief was there. And much of the force. John, please tell your mother I'm thinking of her."

"I will. She's fretting something awful over not knowing anything. As am I."

"I understand. That's why I asked you here. You must hold what I tell you in the strictest confidence. You can tell your mother, but that's the extent of it. And we need to be discreet here in my office. I fear there are ears about us that are eager to hang on our every word." Manly pulled down the shades and locked his door. He walked across the room to a large slate blackboard. He took the longest piece of chalk he could find and drew four large circles. Within the circles he wrote Conn, Jenkins, Woman, Mureau—one name in each circle.

Beneath the Conn circle, he wrote:

> Jenkins accuses Conn
> Affidavits

Beside the Conn circle, he drew six smaller circles, within which he wrote Comm. Branan and the names of the five affidavit filers other than Jenkins—one name in each circle.

He drew arced lines connecting Jenkins, Woman, and Mureau.

Beneath the Jenkins circle, he wrote:

> Conn accuses Jenkins
> Set-up imminent

Beneath the Woman and Mureau circles, he placed large question marks, digging the chalk into the board as he drew the hooks and crooks and jabbing the tittles into the slate surface.

At the board's bottom left he wrote:

Gun
Bill of Sale
Enemies?

Manly stepped back from the board. "This is what we're dealing with as of…" He looked at his watch. "…eight fifteen this morning. As far as I'm concerned, every name up there, except perhaps the commissioner, is a suspect. But even he may be mixed up in all of this somehow."

"How could I possibly help you sort through it all?" John asked. "I don't know any of these people, except for a passing acquaintance with Herbert Jenkins."

Manly pointed to the last thing he had written. "John, I need to know—did your father have any enemies? I don't mean people he may have gotten a little crosswise with from time to time over picayune affairs. I mean real enemies. People who would have wanted to see harm done to him."

John was quiet for a moment. "The only ones I know of are Conn and that other detective."

"Mehaffey?"

"Yes, Mehaffey."

"I didn't put his name up there, but I should have." Manly chalked another circle, wrote Mehaffey inside it, and connected it with an arc to the Conn circle. "If he's involved, it's surely through Conn. Are you certain you can think of no one else who may have had it in for your father?"

"No, Mr. Manly, I can't. Everybody liked my father, except the ones I mentioned, and I don't know if those two really even knew him. Let me say this. The ones that really got to know him—they liked him."

"Did he owe anybody any large sums of money?"

"Well, some creditors have come forward, since my father died, claiming balances due. But they were all friends of his, and they aren't claiming large amounts, certainly not enough to warrant killing him. And anyway, as I said, they all got along well with him. Never a cross word, as far as I know. They wouldn't have harmed him."

"John, can you give me the creditors' names? You know what the man says about no stone unturned."

"I can, but I'm not convinced my father owed anybody anything. I've found no records of any outstanding debt." John took a tattered paper from his pocket and unfolded it. "J.J. Maddox—"

"Joe Maddox? The wholesale grocer?" Manly remembered Hal Harper, the Negro affidavit filer, saying he was hauling for Joe Maddox when he was nabbed in the sugar incident."

"Yes, that's him," John said.

"Did you know Maddox is a friend of Herbert Jenkins?"

"I didn't know that, but Maddox was a friend of my father as well. I can't imagine his being involved."

"Please go on. I interrupted you."

"Then there's a man named Cowan—Lewis Cowan—he sells work clothes—dungarees and shirts and things. And Mr. J.T. Lowry, the hardware man."

"Is that all, John?"

"To my knowledge, that's it."

Manly wrote the three men's names in the lower right corner of the blackboard. He drew a big asterisk beside their names as a reminder to follow up later.

"John, about the gun in your father's possession the morning he was shot. Are you—"

"It's not his gun."

"I'm aware that you have said that, but—"

"It's not just that I said it, Captain, as if it might or might not be true. I'm telling you, it's not his gun."

"I understand. But regardless, if it didn't belong to your father, someone had to have planted it on him that morning. Did you know the gun was taken from Coroner Paden's house in the still of darkness five nights ago?"

"I didn't know that."

"Well, we're being closemouthed about it. I suppose it will become common knowledge eventually, but for now it needs to be kept quiet. Had you ever seen that gun before?"

"Not before I held it in my hand the morning my father was shot. I knew then that it wasn't his, but I didn't say anything right away. The officer was waving it around, brandishing it and all—it just wasn't the right time to bring it up. There are a lot of cheap imitations around, you know."

"John, do you have your father's gun?"

"No sir. It's missing. I've looked all over for it. The house. The store. I'd be surprised if he hadn't had it with him that morning."

"Are there any markings on your father's gun? Anything that would help us identify it, should it turn up?"

"Yes. His initials, B.A.B., are engraved on the side plate just above the handle."

"John, there's something else I wanted to ask you about. Regarding that bill of sale, the one for the tobacco Conn and Mehaffey claim was stolen. Have you seen it?"

"I have. Mr. Jenkins turned it over to Mr. Camp, our attorney."

"Do you have any idea why Jenkins happened to have it?"

"I don't. All I know is he had it somehow and he turned it in as evidence. That's the extent of my knowledge of it."

"Do you know this man Mureau, the other party to the bill of sale?"

"No. I never met him. At first, I didn't even know his name. I thought it was Milroy or something, but Mr. Jenkins set me straight."

"And do you know of a woman who could be mixed up in all of this? We've heard about her from Jenkins but we don't know her name."

John shook his head.

Manly eased into a seat beside John. He leaned in. "John, we're doing everything we can to find the man, or men, who killed your father. But right now, we have one person fingering another. The second one fingering the first. Accusations flying back and forth. A missing gun—actually two missing guns. A man named Mureau, whom I have yet to meet. Some woman who hasn't been identified. And a bill of sale. That's all we have to go on." Manly looked up at the board. "Conn and a few of the other detectives are on the verge of some sort of effort to try to catch Jenkins in a confession—or at least to get him to allow something they can pin on him. I'm not supposed to know about it, but I've managed to contrive an opportunity for my own man—not a policeman, mind you—to be there when it all happens. It could happen as early as today."

Manly took a blackboard duster and erased all the circles and writing, careful to make sure no ghosts remained.

Later that day, Manly followed up with Maddox, Cowan, and Lowry, Bass's alleged creditors. He was careful not to get between them and John as to whether monies were actually owed. His sole mission was to feel out whether they were possible suspects. After spending several hours meeting with them individually, he decided John was right—they were friends with Baker Bass and had no reason to see harm done to him. In fact, to a man, they expressed shock that he had been felled, and only a couple of blocks from where he lived.

Joe Maddox shared additional information that appeared to corroborate something Jenkins had told Keeler. "There's one thing you need to know," Maddox had said as he and Manly stood outside the wholesale grocery warehouse on Lloyd Street. "I learned of Baker's death that Friday afternoon. Shortly thereafter, I ran into Herbert Jenkins downtown. I told him about it. He said he had been out of town and was unaware. He told me then that he was sure a detective had done it."

"Mr. Maddox, think back to that day. Did Jenkins tell you the detective's name?"

"No. I should have pressed, but I didn't."

TWENTY-THREE

FRANK KEELER

A Knock at the Door

CASON CAST A SIDEWAYS GLANCE AT HIS PARTNER. "Conn, you're not going."

"What do you mean I'm not—"

"I said you're not going. You've been bellyaching about this long enough. I cooked up this whole plan myself." Cason looked across the room at Keeler. "You found a reporter who's willing to tag along, and I thank you for that." Then to Mehaffey. "And I'm sure Mehaffey here thanks you too. But you're too close to this. I've told you that before. Besides, the closet in that little house is too small for more than three people. It'll be cramped enough as it is. We need Keeler as an impartial third party. And we need the commissioner to give us support. Otherwise, when we get Jenkins to step into the snare, and when we haul him to jail, we won't have Connolly and Manly to back us up. Only Commissioner Branan can do that."

It was eight thirty. Thursday morning. Cason, Conn, Mehaffey, and Keeler were meeting in the dimly lighted back room of a vacant building on Alabama Street, just east of Pryor. The owner of the building had agreed to let them sequester themselves there, away from eavesdroppers and meddlers. Cason looked at his watch. "Where's the commissioner? He's late."

Conn glared across the room at Cason. Tossed a half-smoked cigarette to the floor. Flattened it with his shoe. "Cason, when did you become the head of this affair? The last time I checked we were equals. But now you're acting like a bigwig."

"Because I contrived this whole thing, Conn. I'm doing this to get you out of the damned mess you're in. And the one that has the plan is the one that gets to call the tune. Get over it."

Around nine o'clock, the men heard footsteps approaching. Cason leapt from his chair. He eased the latch shut on the door separating the back room from the hallway that led to the front of the building. The footsteps grew louder. A knock on the door.

"Who's there?"

"It's Commissioner Branan." Said in a whisper.

Cason opened the door. The commissioner entered. For half an hour, the five men rehearsed the sequence of events they expected would unfold over the course of the morning and, presumably, into the afternoon.

At nine thirty, they left the building. They turned down Pryor Street. Conn and Mehaffey returned to the station house. Cason, Branan, and Keeler ran to the Kiser Building, at the corner of Pryor and Hunter, where a two-horse carriage and driver awaited them. They boarded the carriage. The driver sped down Pryor. Their destination was a little shy of three miles away. The driver estimated that, if he pushed as hard as he could, it would take about twenty minutes to get there. They had no time to spare.

The pavement turned to dry, rutted Georgia red clay. There they crossed the tracks near the East Tennessee, Virginia & Georgia railroad shops. The ruts were deep and the clay was hard. Keeler reached into his pocket and retrieved his watch. The carriage shook so violently that he struggled to make out the time. Ten minutes had passed since they had left the Kiser Building. Cason instructed the driver to maneuver the carriage as fast as he could through a series of furrows along a narrow strip of dirt road that cut through the woods. But the driver was going so fast, the carriage careening so severely that, at one point along the way, Branan urged him to slow down, lest they would all tumble out of the carriage, men and cargo alike.

They stopped at a ravine in the woods. Cason, Branan, and Keeler got out of the carriage. They removed several bottles of beer and whiskey from under the seats, where the driver had secreted them. Cason told the driver they no longer needed him. It would have been almost impossible for the carriage to make its way the remaining distance through the woods, and Cason said he was not keen on the driver knowing exactly where they were headed or what they were up do.

The men ran through the woods along a winding, briar-entangled path. Cason led the way. Branan and Keeler followed behind, lugging the beer and whiskey. At nine fifty-four, they reached the other side of the woods. They were at the end of McDaniel Street, well beyond the city limits. There they came upon a high wooden fence with a narrow gate. The gate was padlocked. The fence was so high the men had trouble seeing over it. Cason reached into his coat pocket and removed a large ring with a dozen or so keys on it. Even though the sun had risen three and a half hours earlier, he had trouble finding the right key. When he did, he unlocked the padlock. The men entered through the gate, which faced the rear of a small frame house. The house sat close to a picket fence in the front and faced a narrow country road that paralleled McDaniel Street. Cason instructed the other two men to hide behind a dilapidated outhouse in the backyard. He made his way to the rear door of the house. Soon he let out a low whip-poor-will whistle, the other men's cue to approach the house. They entered through the rear door. Inside, they encountered a young woman. Branan gave her a big hug. Cason explained that she was a friend of the commissioner. Branan had engaged her to help them in their mission to entrap Jenkins. She could not have been more than twenty-two or twenty-three years old. She was slight, with a tight-waisted dress that accentuated her figure. She looked to be about five feet tall.

"Is no one going to introduce us?" Keeler asked.

"Listen, Keeler," Cason whispered. "The last thing the commissioner wants to do is get the young lady mixed up in all of this, beyond her just being here to help out."

"Does she have a name?" Keeler protested.

"Of course she has a name. Everybody has a name."

"So what is it?"

"Let's just say her name is Alice. That's all you need to know. OK? And wipe the mud off your shoes before you come in."

The pine floorboards groaned as the men followed Alice down the hallway to a sitting room in the center of the house. In the sitting room, there was a small, empty closet. *There's no way we'll all fit in there,* Keeler thought.

The closet sat midway along a wall that separated the sitting room from a larger room in the front of the house. It looked to Keeler as if the closet had been added as an afterthought. Keeler noticed a small hole in the wall that separated the closet from the front room. The hole was about four feet up from the baseboard. He had to bend down to look through it. He assumed Cason, or someone following his instructions, had come to the house at some earlier time and had removed the wall plaster to create the hole. The men walked into the front room. A bed backed up to the wall shared with the closet. It stood out about eight inches from the wall. A wicker table and two matching chairs sat beside the bed.

"Commissioner, please sit there." Cason pointed to the chair adjacent to the bed. "And you, you sit there," Cason instructed Keeler, pointing to the edge of the bed close to the chair. "Now, I am going to go into the closet. I want the two of you to speak to each other in a low voice. I need to make sure I can make out what you're saying."

Cason left the front room. Branan and Keeler made idle conversation. Soon they heard a scraping sound coming from the shared wall. Keeler stood up from the bed. He saw the edge of a pen knife poking through, gouging into the plaster around the hole. Plaster powder fell to the floor behind the bed.

"Keep talking," Cason shouted from the closet. "I had to make the hole bigger. I could barely hear you."

"Should we speak louder?" Branan asked.

"No, speak just as you were. Let's try it again."

The men continued their conversation. Then Cason came back into the front room. "I can hear you fine now. But with all due respect, gentlemen, couldn't you two think of anything more interesting to talk about than the baseball pennant protests?" They all laughed.

Cason called for Alice to clean up the plaster powder from behind the bed. She entered the front room with a broom and dustpan in one hand, and what looked like a folded bedsheet, or something like that, draped over her other arm. She hastily swept the plaster into the dustpan. She then proceeded to tack a sheer linen wall hanging behind the headboard so as to hide the hole in the wall. The image on the wall hanging looked like pictures Keeler had seen of the East River suspension bridge in Brooklyn. He remembered reading about Robert Odlum, the first man to jump from the bridge. The poor man died shortly after hitting the cold waters of the East River. And just five months ago, an Irishman named Duffy climbed onto the railing and jumped, never to be seen again.

The three men returned to the middle room. They crammed into the closet. Cason shut the closet door. A narrow point of light passed through the hole from the front room, penetrating the dark. Pencil in hand, Keeler held his notepad up to the sliver of light. He would alternate between peering through the hole and writing under its faint illumination.

It was now ten thirty-five. The men heard a faint, almost indiscernible knock at the front door. Keeler leaned in and looked through the hole at an acute angle. The top of the headboard partially obscured his field of vision. The sheer linen cast a gauzy pall over the view before him. He could barely see across the front room and through the open door that led into the hallway. If he positioned his head just right and squinted, he could make out the front door. Alice opened the door. An older woman stood at the threshold. She said she was Delores Dampman. She was out of breath. She said she had made an appointment to meet Jenkins at ten thirty. She was late. Alice led her to the front room.

"Here, Mrs. Dampman, I'll take your hat and coat."

There was another knock. Again, Alice answered the door. This time it was Jenkins.

"I'm here to see the lady who just came in," Jenkins said. "Who are you?"

"Me?" She paused. "I'm an old friend of Mrs. Dampman's," she lied. "She's waiting for you." She led him into the front room, where Mrs. Dampman was standing.

Who is this Alice woman? Keeler thought. *She's handling the situation well, given her age. Branan must have done a lot of coaching. Or perhaps she's more worldly than her appearance suggests.*

Keeler strained to see Jenkins and Mrs. Dampman standing in the front room. He could make out, waist-up, that Jenkins embraced her, pressing her close to him.

"Where have you been, my dearest? You don't know how much I have wanted to see you. Oh, how I have suffered since we were last together."

"It's been less than two weeks, Herbert. Don't be so dramatic."

"But I wanted to have a long talk with you. Didn't you want to see me? I know you did."

Branan whispered to Cason. "I thought the plan was for *her* to seduce *him*."

Keeler watched as Jenkins wrapped his arms around Mrs. Dampman. He kissed her neck. Then he turned to face the young woman. He asked her if there was any beer in the house. She said there was. He asked her to bring two bottles, one for him and one for Delores.

"You see, my dear," Jenkins said as soon as they were alone in the room, "we need something to drink. I am the very lightest drinker you ever saw, but still I wish something refreshing this morning."

Jenkins again wrapped his arms around her. She pushed him away.

"Herbert, I have gotten my foot into it and all on your account. Now you must get me out of this scrape. Do you understand that?"

"Certainly I do, my dear. But why talk about such unpleasant topics now. There is plenty of time for that."

Alice returned with three beers. She opened them and handed one to Jenkins and one to Mrs. Dampman, keeping the third for herself.

"Let's drink and be merry," he said. "Should we not be merry?"

He addressed the young woman. "My dear girl, you can't imagine how jealous I have been. My sweetheart here has caused me more trouble and worry within the past ten days than I can tell. But why talk of that?"

He raised his bottle in the air.

"Here, drink. I'll propose a toast. In fact, we should all propose a toast." He laughed.

Mrs. Dampman had told Cason about Jenkins' inability to hold his alcohol, a detail Cason had passed along to Keeler and Branan. If only, in the course of the day and under the influence of an ample supply of beer and whiskey, Jenkins ended up shedding any light on the mystery of Bass's death, their hours spent crowded in a hot, dark closet would not be in vain. Keeler listened to Jenkins and the two women drinking, laughing, and joking in the front room. Either Jenkins was succumbing to the trap they had laid or he was a very good actor.

The joviality was broken, however, when Jenkins, in an apparent show of bravado, took a long sheathed knife from his coat pocket and laid it on the table. The blade itself looked to be at least eight inches long.

"What do you carry that for?" Alice asked.

"I carry it to protect my life. I don't know when I shall need it. I act squarely with my friends and expect them to do the same with me. But I have made some enemies of late. And if anybody ever attacks me, I'll do what's necessary to protect myself."

"Would a pistol not be more efficient?"

"Efficient? Perhaps. But, my dear, you must understand. I am not one to hide like a coward behind the barrel of a gun. If I'm going to protect myself I'll do it man-to-man, with my hands and a dirk—not with a mere trigger finger."

Alice excused herself. As soon as she closed the door behind her, Jenkins again wrapped his arms around Mrs. Dampman and pulled her close against him. He began kissing her. He appeared to caress her thighs, although Keeler had a hard time seeing below their waists. She tried to push him away. She tried again to engage in serious conversation, but he was unrelenting.

"There's plenty of time for questions and explanations. Why be in a hurry?"

"I told you before, Herbert. You got me to put my foot in it for you," she said, "and you must tell me how to get it out. That's all there is to it. You promised me you would save me if trouble came, and you must do it."

"I know that, my darling," he replied, continuing to press his body against hers as she tried to pull away. "But why can't you wait? We're in an awkward fix and I know it. But why worry over it? I promised to save you and I will keep my promise."

Jenkins opened the door. He stepped out of the front room and into the hallway. Cason placed his hand onto his holstered revolver. Jenkins called down the hallway for the woman to bring more beer. "And whiskey. Have you any whiskey?"

She returned with a tray. On the tray were three more bottles of beer, an opened bottle of Old Forester, and two shot glasses.

"Alas, this day will eventually come to an end. When shall we three meet again?" he asked.

"Perhaps tomorrow," Alice answered.

"Ah me! Tomorrow. Tomorrow. Alas, it never comes. But the time passes. See! The clock shows that the hours are gliding by. I'll stop the clock. Or should I turn the hands back to nine? That would be better. Tomorrow? Ah, it never comes. Let her go Gallagher!" He laughed.

Alice again left the room, closing the door behind her.

"Now, I want you to explain every detail of this whole Bass affair," Mrs. Dampman said. "I want a full explanation and I am going to have it if we're here all night. You promised to protect me and have failed to do it. I have been told within the past two days that if Green Conn had not been a policeman, he would have already been tried, convicted and possibly hanged for the murder of Bass—and on my testimony alone."

"Perhaps, my dear," Jenkins replied, "but we will talk about that later."

"No we won't. We'll talk about it right here and right now. I want you to understand that I would never have gone so far as to have seen Conn hanged because of me. Now I'm going to go over this affair in all its details and you have got to talk to me about it."

"All right, sweetheart, but there's no hurry."

"Yes, there *is* a hurry. Time's passing. Now I want to know, didn't you promise me five hundred dollars for my testimony about that pistol?"

"Yes, dearest. I had heard there was a thousand-dollar reward for anyone who found Bass's killer—three hundred from the mayor and seven hundred from Mrs. Bass herself—and I was to give you half."

"But didn't you promise me five hundred dollars outright?"

"Yes, that's correct. But you see the detectives don't believe our story. We must settle on a plan of action and stick to it. If necessary, I will send you out of town where no one can reach you."

"Why did you get me involved in this mess in the first place? Why did you tell them about me and the scratch on the gun?"

"My dearest, when one is so convinced, as I am now, of the perpetrator of a cold-blooded murder, then it sometime becomes necessary to engage in some well-intentioned trickery to catch the man who did it. That contemptible, lying Green Conn. And I have no compunction at all about my actions if they result in retribution for *his* actions. Can you really compare the two? A little chicanery versus the killing of a man? Trust me, the authorities will thank me when they discover I was right all along."

Mrs. Dampman looked over at the wall hanging, right where the hole was. For a moment, Keeler wondered if she somehow knew they were hiding in the closet. *Did someone tip her off, or is it a mere coincidence?*

"Herbert, the first time I ever heard of that pistol being marked was from you. You told me about the marks. You said you had seen them, and I agreed to go along with it."

"Delores, how can you say that? We obviously have a fundamental disagreement as to the facts. But of one thing I am certain. You've made a mighty mistake, sweetheart, by talking too much. And now something must be done. But I do forgive you."

"*You* forgive *me?* And another thing. I want you to tell me who that little black-eyed man is. The one that calls himself Moore. I know you sent him to me in the dead of night."

"No I didn't."

"I believe you did, Herbert. He came to my door late at night. I was preparing for bed. He knocked on the door. I cracked it open just enough to hear what he was saying. He told me to send a note to Baker Bass at his store the Tuesday before he died. To tell Bass his life was in danger. The man's voice was very soft, almost a whisper. He had what sounded like a French accent. Like those nasty foreigners from the exposition that visit the brothel. Then the man disappeared into the darkness as quickly as he had arrived."

"No, my love, you are mistaken. I never sent anyone to you. I don't even know who he is. I don't know a man by that name." Jenkins paused. "Did you get a good look at him? Perhaps if you describe him I might know who you're talking about."

"No. It was too dark. All I could see were his black eyes. It was almost as if he had rubbed lampblack on his face, around his eyes."

"So what happened then—after he left?" Jenkins asked.

"I went to Bass's store that Tuesday morning. I decided to tell him in person. It was raining hard. He asked me what in the world I was doing out in the rain. I told him I came to warn him his life was in danger."

"Did you tell Bass who was out to get him?"

"I told him exactly what that man Moore had instructed me to tell him. That it was Green Conn."

Jenkins changed the subject. "Didn't you tell me Conn's pistol was an imitation of a Smith & Wesson?"

"No, sir. I did not. It looked like a Smith & Wesson to me."

"So you *did* see Conn's gun after all."

"Yes, once," she replied. "I only saw it once."

"Before you and I first talked about it?"

"I remember when you asked me if I had ever seen Conn's pistol and I told you I had. But I never said anything about it being marked."

"You don't remember describing the mark on the pistol."

She glanced again at the hole behind the wall hanging. "No, I don't. You described it and I went along with you."

"And did you visit Bass in the hospital, when he was in his final hours? And did you not see the gun there?"

"Herbert, I *did* visit him. I admit that. And I saw a gun there that resembled Conn's gun. It was lying on a table in the room. There were a lot of people in the room. Doctors. A nurse. The ambulance driver. Bass's wife and son. And there was a policeman. I assumed he had brought the gun with him, perhaps so the doctors could compare it to the bullet lodged in Bass's skull, although I didn't know that. But I'll tell you one thing, I never said anything about seeing a scratch on the gun, let alone having put the scratch there myself."

"So you saw the gun *twice,* not once!"

"I told you, Herbert, I saw a gun in the hospital that could have been Green Conn's gun, but I don't know that."

For several hours, there in the front room of the house, the two of them argued.

"Listen, Herbert. You're lying about that scratch. And I think you're not telling the truth about that man Moore."

Jenkins gazed out the front window. He remained silent for several minutes.

"Sweetheart, I am feeling unusually light-headed." He walked over to the edge of the bed. "I suspect it's the whiskey. Please indulge me while I lie down for a spell."

After a few minutes he stood up. He swung around to face Mrs. Dampman. "OK my dear. I'll tell you the truth about this man you call Moore. But you must understand the motive behind my denying knowing him."

"So you *do* know him after all!"

"Yes, I do. But you are mistaken about his name. It's not Moore. It's Mureau. Lem Mureau."

"And so you sent him to me?"

"No, I did not. But your description fits the man."

"But I didn't even describe him to you. I said I couldn't make out anything but his black eyes in the dark."

"Yes, my dear. It was your description of his eyes. And his accent. He's a Huguenot. Came from France by way of South Carolina. And he, too, used to sell tobacco to Bass—far inferior to my own, I might add."

"But why did you lie to me when you denied knowing him?"

"Because he's a crook my dear. And I don't want to have anything to do with him. I don't even want to hear his name. He's the one who sold the Wild Turkey tobacco to Bass—probably the only decent product he ever sold him. And I told the police and Mrs. Bass's attorneys as much. I even gave them a bill of sale to prove it. And I'm sure he's behind those railcar break-ins. And another thing. It wouldn't surprise me to find out that he and his gang have been in cahoots with Conn from the very beginning."

"And how did you happen to have the bill of sale?"

"I got it from Bass himself. I went to him before he died and told him this man Mureau was a crook and that he shouldn't buy goods from him. As we were speaking, in the middle of his store on Peters Street, I saw it lying on the counter. When he turned his back, I took it."

"So you *stole* it from him. He didn't give it to you. Why would you do something like that?"

"Because I needed proof that this man Mureau sold the tobacco to Bass. Now I just need to connect Mureau to that contemptible Green Conn. Mureau may have been the thief, but Conn pulled the trigger that killed Bass. Of that I am convinced."

"Herbert, I don't know why I should believe anything you say."

"Because, my dear, we're in this together. You have to trust me."

By two o'clock that afternoon, after much alcohol-infused bantering, the conversation was going nowhere. Jenkins urged Mrs. Dampman to agree that they should summon a detective, in his words to help them figure out how to keep her name out of the papers. To protect her. She acquiesced. Jenkins called for the young woman.

"Dearest, could you please get us a detective?" he asked.

"I can, but why do you need a detective?"

"Because, my dear, Mrs. Dampman and I are embroiled in a dispute that we cannot seem to resolve."

Alice departed through the front door. Cason slinked out of the closet.

Ten minutes later, Cason returned.

"What's going on?" Keeler whispered.

"Well, I snuck out through the rear door. Those infernal floorboards. I hope Jenkins didn't hear them squeak. I circled around to the front of the house. Agnes was lingering there."

"Agnes? Who's Agnes?" Keeler asked.

"I mean Alice. I told her to wait about thirty minutes then return through the front door. To tell Jenkins she'd gone to the nearest call box to summon a detective. To say they refused to come but agreed to meet him early this evening at Weinmeister's Hotel. To hear him out. Weinmeister's will provide the perfect backdrop for the crescendo to this little trap we've set."

"Is there a call box nearby?" Keeler asked.

"There's one about a mile from here. But she's not really going to it. She'll just tell Jenkins she did. He won't know the difference. The truth is he probably couldn't tell a call box from a mailbox."

Alice—or Agnes—or whatever her name really was—returned around two forty-five. She told Jenkins what Cason had prompted her to say. Mrs. Dampman faced her. "My dear, I need a sympathetic ear. You need to know what this dispute between Mr. Jenkins and me is all about."

"Delores, stop. You don't need to drag her into this. Can't you just—"

"No, Herbert. I need to tell her my side of the story. Women have a special way about them that you just wouldn't understand. I need to tell her, woman-to-woman."

Mrs. Dampman laid out the sequence of events. She denied any involvement in marking Conn's pistol. She expected Jenkins to back her up. Instead, he contradicted her, saying she had first described the pistol to him and told him about the scratch, not the other way around.

"Well, you both can't be telling the truth. You'll likely be locked up by the authorities, unless you can explain this pistol business."

"That's what I've been telling her all day. We're in this together and we must get out of it somehow."

"Just to make sure I understand." Alice (Agnes) addressed Mrs. Dampman. "You're maintaining you never had access to Detective

Conn's pistol, so there's no way you could have marked it. Is that right?"

"She marked it with a hairpin," Jenkins said.

"I did nothing of the kind. First you had me marking it with a hat pin, then with a pen knife, and now with a hairpin, when the truth is I never marked it at all."

"There's nothing I can do. You two need to hash this out with the police." Alice (Agnes) looked at Jenkins. "Six o'clock at Weinmeister's. They said they'd meet you there." She turned and left.

Jenkins headed toward the door. He turned to Mrs. Dampman. "My dear, I thought we were the closest of friends. But I now fear that, having been faced with indisputable facts and forced to protect yourself, you have chosen to betray me."

Jenkins left the house through the front door. She left five minutes later.

After sufficient time had passed to ensure both Jenkins and Mrs. Dampman were gone, the three men in the closet exited through the rear door and hurried on foot back to the city.

"Keeler, I'm going to go by the station house and get Mehaffey," Cason said. "Meet us in the lobby of Weinmeister's Hotel. No later than five thirty."

Keeler went to the newspaper office to pass time before making his way to the hotel. He would have preferred to go straight to Manly to fill him in, but he knew not to go near the station house.

Cason and Mehaffey were already at Weinmeister's when Keeler arrived. They were sitting at a table in the bar past the lobby. Cason was nursing a half-full glass of beer. Mehaffey was casually chomping on what looked like a backstrap steak.

At five forty-five, Keeler took a seat at a table in the far, dark corner of the bar where, hopefully, Jenkins wouldn't see him. The last thing he needed was for Jenkins to get wind of his involvement in the entrapment business that had taken place earlier that day.

Cason and Mehaffey positioned themselves on each side of the door leading from the lobby, just inside the bar. There they waited.

TWENTY-FOUR

ED CASON

They Seized Him

WEINMEISTER'S WAS AN UNASSUMING HOTEL ON Forsyth between Marietta and Walton Streets. It was owned and operated by Carl Weinmeister. He lived there with his son, Carl Jr., a timekeeper with the Atlanta Gas Light company. Cason had intentionally not told either father or son about his plans to confront Jenkins in the hotel.

A little after six o'clock on Thursday, the nineteenth of September, Jenkins walked through the front door and into the hotel lobby. Mrs. Dampman followed close behind. Just as Jenkins passed the door into the bar, the two detectives seized him. Cason ran his hand into Jenkins' right coat pocket. He retrieved a long knife, presumably the same knife Jenkins had brandished in the entrapment house.

"What are you doing with this?" Cason asked.

"I have it in the event I should need it to protect my life. Especially from the likes of you."

"Jenkins, you must go with us, and you may as well do it without making a scene. Mrs. Dampman, it's getting late. You need to get on home."

"Can I see Chief Connolly?" Jenkins asked.

"I suppose you can," Cason said, "but only at the station house."

"What are you arresting me for? What have I done?"

"We're not *arresting* you. We're taking you in for questioning."

Jenkins agreed to go with the men on the premise that he would be able to meet with the police chief. He left the hotel, flanked by Cason and Mehaffey.

When the three men arrived at the station house, the detectives entered through the rear door. They slipped Jenkins upstairs and placed him the same small room on the top floor where the drayman, Peter Williams, had been sequestered. Only this time the casket-like box had been removed and a thin, single mattress had been placed along one wall.

"I thought I was going to see Chief Connolly," Jenkins said.

"He's gone home for the day," Cason replied. "You can see him in the morning."

"So you *are* arresting me."

"No. We're detaining you for questioning."

"What's the difference? You're locking me in this room. You're holding me against my will. You're arresting me."

Cason and Mehaffey locked the door behind them and left.

They returned the following morning. They peppered Jenkins with questions, centering mainly on the allegations that he had conspired to frame Conn for Baker Bass's murder. But after several hours, it was apparent they were getting nowhere. Things basically boiled down to Jenkins' word against Mrs. Dampman's. Without the gun, and absent corroborating witnesses, the detectives were stymied.

"Get Connolly. I demand to see him," Jenkins said.

"You'll see him in due time," Cason replied. "But let's talk about something else now. Let's talk about your whereabouts the day of Bass's death."

"What does that have to do with anything? Surely you're not claiming that *I'm* a suspect in Bass's murder. You and your gang are determined to do anything you can to deflect attention from one of your own. You're the crookedest bunch of dastards I've ever seen."

"We're not claiming anything, Jenkins." Cason glanced over at Mehaffey. "What do you think, detective? Here we are, way up here in this little room, tucked away in the top of the building where no one can hear us. In fact, nobody even knows we're up here." He looked back at Jenkins. "It's just you—and us. You can choose to cooperate. But if you don't, maybe we'll just entertain ourselves up here, all alone in this room." Cason struck his nightstick against the palm of his hand. "I have a lot of pent-up energy I need to get rid of somehow."

"I *want* to cooperate," Jenkins said. "And you can put your truncheon away. It doesn't intimidate me in the least. I just don't know what you want me to do. I've complied with your every demand for the past two hours."

"Well, you actually haven't, Jenkins. We've wasted the last two hours with you. But let's move on. Why don't we start with three more questions."

"And those are?"

"Where did you go when you left, as you have claimed, on the West Point train at one thirty on the afternoon just before Bass's death?"

"I will not answer," Jenkins replied.

"When did you return to the city?"

Jenkins again refused to answer.

"Mr. Jenkins, are there witness who can attest to your whereabouts on the morning of Bass's death?"

"Of course there are, but I'll not reveal them to you. Not until you have granted me the benefit of speaking with my attorney."

Cason walked over to the corner of the room and reached down to the floor. He retrieved a pair of Tower double-locking handcuffs. "Well, Jenkins. You've given us no choice."

Cason and Mehaffey arrested him for conspiracy. They moved him to a cell on the ground floor. Cason knew the evidence against Jenkins was scant. There were no other witnesses to corroborate Mrs. Dampman's story. The gun, with a supposed scratch on the polished nickel just under the hammer, was missing. And there was this mysterious man Lem Mureau, but the detectives had not yet been able to locate him.

Later that morning, Cason summoned Mrs. Dampman to the station house. She sat in a chair facing Cason and Mehaffey. She spent a little over an hour with the two detectives. Cason asked her if she had ever been under the same roof with Conn.

"Just one time. At the brothel on Ira Street. And I can assure you, it was less than friendly."

"Mrs. Dampman, what happened that day—at the brothel?" Cason asked.

"Well, I was helping Madam Brumbelow, the keeper of the house, while she was away. I do that sometimes. I heard a knock. The madam always keeps the door locked. To keep out the riffraff and to protect the ladies. There's a peep hole. I looked through it and saw Conn. I opened the door and told him that he couldn't—"

Cason stopped her. "Mrs. Dampman, how did you know it was Detective Conn—when you first saw him through the peep hole—if you had never seen him before?"

"Oh, I knew it was him all right." She rubbed her eyes behind her eyeglasses. "There was no doubting that. He had a reputation at the house. And the madam had given me explicit instructions not to let him in."

"And why would she do that?" Cason asked.

"Because Madam Brumbelow told me he wasn't nice to the ladies."

"OK. Mrs. Dampman. I'll accept that for now, but be careful what you say. You don't want to be hit with a libel charge, do you? Continue."

"Where was I? Oh yes, I opened the door and told him he couldn't come in. I told him why."

"And how did he react?"

"He was angry. Indignant. He got louder and more aggressive. But I just stood there in the doorway, my legs wide apart, with my hands on my hips. I refused to let him in. As you can see, my girth is considerable. I blocked the entire opening."

"I see, Mrs. Dampman."

"Then he said something like I'm not here for entertainment today. I'm looking for a man on the run, and I have reason to think he's hiding out here. I said, 'Detective Conn, do you expect me to believe a story like that?' He got huffier and asked for the madam of the house. I told him she wasn't in. I said he would have to deal with me and me alone. He threatened to arrest me if I didn't let him in."

"And then what happened, Mrs. Dampman?"

"Well, that's when things got a lot worse. He shoved me, just a little at first. That angered me and made me steel my resolve. I squared my shoulders and dug in. But then he pushed me harder, so hard I almost fell down. I was struggling to regain my balance. He pushed past me and barged into the house. I followed him through the front parlor but by then it was obvious that I could not drag him out of the house. If George had been there, he could have wrestled him to the ground and gotten him outside."

"George?"

"George Dampman, my husband."

"Please go on, Mrs. Dampman."

"He went all through the house. He said he was looking for a fugitive, but I wondered at the time if he was looking for one of the ladies, a girl named Sally. The madam told me Conn had taken a liking to her. Sally was the one responsible for him being banned from the house in the first place. She's a good girl, that Sally."

"And how long did Conn remain there?"

"Maybe thirty minutes. Maybe longer. I don't remember."

"And what did he do during that time? And what did you do?"

"As I said, he went from room to room. Some of the rooms were even occupied, but he just barged in. I followed him around until he gave up and left."

"Mrs. Dampman, what I'm about to ask you is very important. And you must tell me the truth. Did you ever have access to Detective Conn's gun?"

Mrs. Dampman knitted her eyebrows and touched her lower lip. She looked up at the clock on the wall, to Cason's left.

"No, I saw his gun when he was at the brothel. He set it on a table there. But I never had access to it. And I most certainly didn't put a scratch on it."

"When did this encounter at the brothel occur, Mrs. Dampman?"

"I can't remember. Maybe three months ago."

"And did you ever see Green Conn again?"

"Never."

"Are you certain of that?"

She leaned forward. "Mr. Cason, of that I am certain, as sure as I am sitting here today."

"But Mrs. Dampman, if, as you have claimed, Detective Conn had a reputation at the house, he must have been a regular visitor. And you have said you helped out the madam—what's her name? Brumbelow?—from time to time. If both of those things are true, don't you think you would have run into Conn more than once?"

"I suppose, but I didn't," she replied.

"Mrs. Dampman, I need to ask you about your visit with Herbert Jenkins, at the house at the end of McDaniel Street."

"What do you want to know? You were there. You know everything that was said?"

"What do you mean I was there?"

"You know—and I know. You were there."

"Mrs. Dampman. I have no idea what you're talking about."

She stared straight through him. "Mr. Cason, I'm no fool. Look at me. Do I look like somebody that just walked in the door? I know what's o'clock, as the man says. I knew right off that you, or somebody, was there listening in."

"Well, I'm not going to lie to you. But how did you know?"

"For one thing, did I think for one minute you'd send me off to get Herbert to talk without somebody being there to hear what he said? And another thing, I thought that was a mighty odd place for a silk wall hanging, half behind the bed and half not. And then I happened to look down at the floor, behind the bed post, and there—right there plain as day, was this little line of plaster right up against the wall—like somebody had tried to sweep it away but hadn't gotten it all. Like I said, I'm no fool."

A slight grin formed. "And then I heard a noise coming from the other room. Sounded like whispers. And I put two and two together. Mr. Cason, I may not be able to see worth a darn without my glasses, but with them I could see that plaster just fine—and my hearing is corking good."

"So Mrs. Dampman, do you stand behind what you said there in the house, and what you're telling me now, about the gun."

"Of course I do. I have no reason to lie."

Was Mrs. Dampman's story plausible? Cason was skeptical. Of the three people who had been in the front room of the entrapment house, he now knew that at least two of them—Alice (Agnes) and Mrs. Dampman—had been well aware their every word was being listened in on. That was her opportunity, if she were so inclined, to shape the conversation to her favor.

The detectives allowed her to leave the station house without further questioning, but with the understanding that she might be called back in.

TWENTY-FIVE

FRANK KEELER

The Notebook was Missing

"THEY'RE OUT OF CONTROL." CONNOLLY SLAMMED THE palm of his hand on his desk with such force that the sepia of the detectives toppled over. "The whole rotten bunch. They'll do whatever it takes to protect their own. Even so far as to trap a man and lock him up on a flimflam. And to think—Branan was even in on it. You can't trust the lot of them."

He leveled a long glare at the captain. "Manly, how did you let this happen?"

It was the morning of the twentieth of September. Keeler had called on Manly. He planned to fill the captain in on the little escapade at the entrapment house—and on Jenkin's subsequently being hauled off to jail in the arms of Cason and Mehaffey. But almost as soon as Keeler opened his mouth, Manly had stopped him. He had led Keeler into Connolly's office. "The chief needs to hear this first-hand."

"Where in the Sam Hill is the damned gun, Manly?"

"Sir, we haven't fou—"

"Well, find it. It's our best link to Conn's innocence or guilt."

Manly and Keeler got up to leave. But before they made it to the door, Connolly called out.

"Keeler, do you shoot street craps? Like them niggers in Darktown?"

"I can't say as I have, sir," Keeler replied.

Connolly looked at Manly. "Well, the captain here thinks it's an abomination. Isn't that right, Manly?"

Manly responded with a half-nod.

"Do you know what boxcars is, Keeler? In craps I mean."

"No sir, I don't."

Connolly leaned back in his chair. "Boxcars is when you roll six pips on both dice. It's a rarity. There's a one in thirty-six probability you'll get boxcars when those dice go flying out of your hand and come to a stop. But the niggers don't know that. They think there's some kind of black magic in those ivory cubes. Some kind of mumbo jumbo voodoo."

Keeler looked askance at Manly. Then at Connolly.

"You're both wondering why I'm talking about craps. Well, I'm not a betting man, just like Manly here. But if I were, I'd put the odds of a scratch not being on that gun about the same as rolling boxcars."

Connolly spit a wad of tobacco. "Manly, keep a close eye on Conn. I don't trust him as far as I can spit. In fact, keep a close eye on the whole lot of them."

Jenkins had been arrested and charged earlier that morning. That evening, Keeler called on him at his jail cell. Jenkins agreed to a second interview to "set the record straight," as he said. His intent was to tell Keeler what he had refused to tell the detectives the night before—to lay out in explicit detail his whereabouts in the hours leading up to Bass's murder.

"Yesterday evening, those miscreants, Cason and Mehaffey, locked me in a dirty upstairs room without arresting me. There I stayed all night. Without food or drink. Nothing but a mattress and a dirty chamber pot. Unable to contact friends. Unable to reach my attorney. I can only assume neither Connolly nor Manly had any idea I was there."

"When did they find out? Connolly and Manly, that is."

"I have no idea. They must have discovered my being here sometime today, but I've seen neither hide nor hair of them."

"So from the time you were booked and moved to the ground floor until now, has anyone visited you? Has anyone made an effort to secure your release?"

"Earlier today Colonel Austin called on me here at my cell. Do you know him?"

"I know of him, but I've never had the pleasure of meeting him."

"He's with the law firm Austin and Parks. I retained him to get me out of this godawful hellhole of a penitentiary. I have a clear-cut defense. The colonel agreed with me. He tried to have me released earlier today on a writ of habeas corpus."

Jenkins rubbed his chin with his thumb and forefinger.

"That's Latin, young man." Jenkins drew his words out. "It's short for *habeas corpus ad subjiciendum.* I know. I know. It all sounds like a bunch of hocus-pocus. That's because some lawyer came up with it. What did Mr. Bumble say? The law is a ass — a idiot. In plain, unadulterated English, it means the bastards must prove they've imprisoned me in this pigsty of a calaboose lawfully."

"Mr. Bumble?"

"Dickens, young man. *Oliver Twist*. Read it sometime."

Jenkins continued.

"Colonel Austin took out the writ. But he was unable to get a judge to hear it before Monday." Jenkins locked eyes with Keeler. "Any statements I made in that house—the one out at the end of McDaniel Street—were coerced. I made them under the influence of beer, whiskey, and whatever else. I became intoxicated and, under those circumstances, whatever I said cannot be used against me."

"What do you mean, whatever else?"

"I'll tell you exactly what I mean. I believe I was drugged. I drank something that caused me to quickly lose my senses. I ended up dazed and confused and lying on the bed. As a result, I didn't know what I was saying or doing. In fact, I didn't even know who I was for a moment."

"Who would have drugged you?"

"Why, it had to have been that young woman who was there, or Delores. Delores Dampman."

"Why was Mrs. Dampman there?" Keeler played dumb.

"She's the one who lured me there. I had arranged to meet her that morning with the intention of securing a statement in writing that she had put the scratch on Conn's gun. We met in front of the Aragon Hotel. Unbeknownst to me at the time, she had made plans to lure me into a trap. From the Aragon, I followed her to the Traction Company car line, and then to that house, where she asked me to stay behind for several minutes before joining her. And it was there that she got me drunk with the intent of trapping me."

"Mr. Jenkins, tell me again about the gun—and the scratch."

Keeler detected a hint of a frown.

"Well, prior to our meeting in that house, she had admitted to marking his pistol. Then, when we were there, she turned on me. Do you want to know what I think?"

"Of course," Keeler replied. "You're closer to Mrs. Dampman and her motives than anyone."

"I think she changed her story under duress. To protect herself. That's my assertion. And when I see her next, I'll tell her that to her face."

Jenkins went on to tell Keeler about his comings and goings on the day leading up to Bass's death.

"I left the city on the Atlanta & West Point train at one thirty in the afternoon the day before Bass was killed. I got off in Newnan and took another train to Turin, a few miles east. At the Turin station I hired a horse and buggy. I asked the driver to take me to Sharpsburg, which he did. There I happened to run into a salesman for the Lorillard Tobacco Company."

"And then what did you do?" Keeler asked.

"Well, we rode together back to Turin and then about five miles to Senoia. By the time we got to Senoia all the stores were closed except the drug store, so we decided to spend the night in town. We had supper and afterwards several men, including myself, the Lorillard man and another salesman played whist."

"Do you remember the name of the Lorillard salesman or the other man?"

"The Lorillard man's first name was John. I remember that. I don't remember the other man's name. But if I had my notebook and papers, I could tell you their first and last names. I wrote them down. But the detectives confiscated them when they arrested me. And they still refuse to give them back to me." Jenkins continued. "We played whist until around eleven o'clock and then went to bed."

"Where did you stay?"

"We stayed at a roadside inn. I don't recall its name. The Lorillard man and I slept in the same room. Early the next morning he hunted down another tobacco salesman, who was having breakfast at a hotel nearby."

"Do you remember the name of that man—the other tobacco salesman?"

"No I don't. Again, I wrote it in my notebook, but as I told you, it is no longer in my custody. Then, around nine o'clock, I took a buggy to Starr's Mill, then to Brook's Station. I then took the Atlanta & Florida Railroad to Griffin, arriving there around noon on the day of Bass's murder. I returned to Atlanta that afternoon, where I heard from a friend, Joe Maddox, that Bass had been murdered. I told Maddox then and there that a detective had done it."

The case against Jenkins could have gone in any of several directions. He could have been arraigned before a justice of the peace on a formal conspiracy warrant. The case could have been referred to the grand jury. Or the charges could have been dropped altogether. But one point was incontrovertible. You can't convict one person alone for conspiracy, and no other arrests had been made.

Keeler was at the courthouse the following Monday, September twenty-third. A little after one thirty in the afternoon, Judge Van Epps ordered Jenkins released after ninety-seven hours of confinement. He left in the company of attorneys and friends and made no public statement. The conspiracy charge was withdrawn and he was released on the consent of the attorneys for both sides. The attempted entrapment had by most accounts been an abject failure and had set back law enforcement's efforts to solve the murder. The prosecuting attorneys had agreed to withdraw the conspiracy accusation against Jenkins for the present. They would set the charge aside but reserved the right to reinstate it at some point in the future if they chose to do so.

Regardless of Jenkins' release on the conspiracy charge, murder was quite a different matter. Why had the detectives gone down that path in the first place? Did they know something they weren't sharing with the public? Or were they grasping at straws, intent on finding Bass's murderer and, if possible, pinning it on Conn's accuser?

Keeler sought out Cason in an effort to find Jenkins' notebook. Cason denied any knowledge of ever having seen it. Keeler sought out Conn. Then Mehaffey. Same response.

Jenkins' notebook was missing.

TWENTY-SIX

WILLIAM MANLY

Not One Ray of Light

CHIEF IN NAME ONLY.

Manly's eyes fell on the headline. A disquiet came over him. He knew, before he read another word, that facing Connolly the following morning would not be agreeable. He read on. Just below the headline:

Our Police Chief Has a Title, but Little Official Power.

Then, in column three of the article, a quote from an anonymous source:

There are more gamblers in the city than we have had in years. There are more thugs and cutthroats. There is more burglarizing of houses. This is largely due to the great influx of people to attend the exposition. It is a notable fact that no mysterious crimes are ever cleared up by our police and detective departments. From the conduct of things, it would seem that no cases requiring the exercise of detective skill are ever worked out. The detective and police forces are poorly organized.

Followed by the newspaperman's assessment:

Unfortunately this sort of criticism is all too common.

At least it's on page seventeen, right next to PROF. DEXTER'S SIX GREAT MAGNETIZED REMEDIES, *and not on the front page.*

It was Sunday, the twenty-ninth of September. A month after Bass's death. As hard as it was for him to admit, Manly knew the paper got it right. The police were fending off attacks from all directions—from the press, from the citizens of Atlanta, from the mayor, from the city council. The criticisms were harsh and more frequent than Manly had ever seen. Critics claimed the detectives had botched cases, most noteworthy the failure to identify and capture Bass's murderer. They said the police had not shed one ray of light on any of the important crimes committed over the past several months. They also said the entire force was demoralized. And the commissioners' heavy hand in day-to-day management was largely to blame.

The anonymous source, Manly read, was "a gentleman who has been connected with the police department." *From inside the station house? Perhaps. Or maybe it's somebody in the mayor's office. What if it's the mayor himself?*

In a sense, it didn't matter who the source was. Anybody who paid the least attention to what was going on in the city knew the truth. The whole gang of detectives were in the commissioners' pockets. *Who doesn't know that?* And the chief himself couldn't take one step without the commissioners second-guessing him and telling him what to do. But Manly knew something else too. He knew Connolly well, better than anybody else on the force. And he knew the chief would whip his weight in wildcats before he let them get the better of him.

Early the following morning, Manly stood in Connolly's office doorway. He shot an anxious look across the room at the chief. He knew, before he approached Connolly's desk, that he was in for a drubbing. Connolly waved his copy of the newspaper in the air. His jaw set. His face a vivid crimson.

"Did you read this, Manly? Did you see what they're saying about us?"

Before Manly could answer—Connolly went on.

"It's been a month. Nothing. Jenkins accuses Conn. Conn accuses Jenkins. Cason locks Jenkins up on a dupe—and Branan goes along with it. The judge lets him go. Of course he let him go. And here we are. We have nothing—absolutely nothing. Bass's slayer walks the streets. We have no solid evidence. Nothing but hearsay. The killer may work right here in this building for all we know. Brushing by us as we pass in the hallway. Laughing at us under his breath. Or he may not. Did Bass know the man who confronted him that morning and shot him in the head? Or didn't he? The whole dratted affair makes us look like incompetent rubes." Connolly threw the paper onto his desk. "Which we *are*, Manly."

"Sir, the exposition hasn't helped the situation. It's taken up almost the entire force. It's drawn their attention away from other matters. I wonder if the Bass case would have been solved by now were it not for that."

"Don't blame it on the fair, Manly. I gave you a job to do, but as far as I can tell you've turned up nothing. And you haven't even been near the exposition grounds since it opened, have you? So don't blame it on that."

"I'm working on it, Chief." Manly felt his knees wobble. "But do you know how difficult it is to—"

"Don't tell me how hard it is. You've worn that badge for a long time. Nobody said it would be easy."

"I realize that, sir. But— "

"Manly, listen to me. We've got witnesses contradicting each other. Who's telling the truth? Who's not? Who can we trust? Who'll stab the next guy in the back on a barefaced lie? We've got a worn-out trollop that hangs around a whorehouse saying one thing. And we have Jenkins saying another. And we have this man Lem Mureau that I keep hearing about. Who is he? *Where* is he? How is he mixed up in all of this? And the gun. The gun Bass held in his hand the morning they found him. The gun with the supposed scratch on it. It's still missing. And Jenkins' notebook. It's missing."

"Sir, the detectives deny ever having seen Jenkins' notebook. And the gun's nowhere to be found. This is a big city, you know."

Connolly threw up his hands. "Yes, it's a big city alright. With a hapless police force ridden roughshod over by the commissioners." He stared at Manly with half-lidded eyes. The lines between his brows drew together. "Manly, whether you like it or not, the burden falls on you. Don't count on the detectives to solve this case. It'll never happen."

Manly walked out of Connolly's office. His heart raced.

TWENTY-SEVEN

WILLIAM MANLY

Search for Mureau

WHO IS THIS MUREAU FELLOW? BEFORE MANLY WOULD go to Jenkins, he wanted to see if he could locate the man on his own. Did he have the spelling right? He referred back to the newspaper article from early September—the one that reprinted the affidavit Jenkins had filed. He scanned the article. There it was. First name L-E-M. Could be short for Lemuel. Last name M-U-R-E-A-U.

His first stop was the records room, one floor up from his office. Ten yards down the hall. There he found the Atlanta city directory, sitting on a shelf across the room. At waist level. He retrieved the directory. Plopped it down with a thud on the table in the center of the room. All 1405 pages.

He thumbed to the alphabetical listing, then to the M's, almost three-quarters of the way through. He ran his finger down the left-hand margin of page 986. Munnerlynn, Wilson.

Munns, Henry. Murden, Alfred. No Mureau. *Perhaps Jenkins got the spelling wrong. Or the person who transcribed the affidavit. It wouldn't be the first time.* Moreau? Morrow? Murro? Murrow? Thumbed back eight pages. No Moreau. Forward five pages. Fifteen Morrows but no Lem. No Lemuel. Nothing close. No Murro. A James Murrow but no Lem. In each year's city directory, there is a section of changes, corrections, and new names received too late for regular insertion. Nothing there either. He returned the directory to the shelf and retrieved the prior year. Nothing. Nothing in 1893 either. Nor 1892.

It occurred to Manly that he could be barking up the wrong tree. Might Mureau be from another town, in which case Manly would never find him in the Atlanta directory? Unless, of course, he had placed an ad on one of the two dozen or so commercial pages in the front. That was doubtful, but Manly took the directories back down from the shelf and looked anyway. Nothing there either.

An examination of police records going back several years revealed no reference to a Lem Mureau.

Manly's best chance of locating Mureau lay with Jenkins. He would take a ride over to Crew Street. Hopefully he would find Jenkins there.

Manly's horse was unusually ornery that evening. Perhaps it was the bright red-orange glow cast over the sky as the sun set on the horizon past the Union Depot. The firmament lit up in flames—the likes of which the residents of the city surely hadn't seen since Sherman passed through. Or perhaps the old courser had a premonition that was lost on its rider—an animal sense that something unexpected might unfold. Manly held the reins in one hand. Placed the other on the exposed area of the horse's withers, just in front of the saddle's gullet. He felt the horse's muscles tighten between its shoulder blades. *Forget it, Manly,* the captain thought. *It's just a horse.*

Manly made his way down Calhoun Street from Decatur Street. Crossed over the railroad tracks. At the corner of Calhoun and Mitchell Streets, right where Crew joined the other two at its north end, he touched the left rein to the horse's neck, shifted in his saddle, and squeezed gently with his legs. The horse proceeded down Crew Street in a light jog.

By the time Manly reached the boardinghouse at number 47, dismounted, and tied his horse to a tree at the curb, the flame in the sky had dissipated. Manly approached the house on foot. A single, faint patch of light showed through the porch window. Manly ascended the steps onto the porch. He peered through the veil curtain. No movement inside. *That's odd,* he thought. *It's a boardinghouse. It's the dinner hour. Why is it so eerily lorn?* He rattled the doorknob. It was locked. He knocked lightly.

"What took you so long, Captain Manly?" Jenkins stood in the doorway. "I wondered how long it would be before you graced me with your presence." He motioned Manly inside. "We can seat ourselves in the parlor. I'm glad you came. Dusk is my favored time of day. When the sun is low behind the horizon and a Delphic shroud descends upon us."

Jenkins wore a dark waistcoat, crisp dress shirt with a Patricide collar, and a Windsor tie. He held a lit billiard pipe.

"Mr. Jenkins, did I come at a bad time? It looks as if you're about to go ou—"

"Why no, my dear Manly. You came at a perfect time. Ah, my sartorial taste must have thrown you. A gentleman must always have his wits about him. And be on guard. He never knows when an esquire might show up unexpectedly."

Manly looked around. The place looked deserted. Unnervingly quiet. "Where is everyone?"

"They all decided to go to the exposition. I refused. I abhor crowds. Don't you?" Jenkins took a draw from his pipe. "It's not that I haven't been. I've covered every square foot of the grounds. From the Chinese Village to the Parapet. From Lake Clara Meer to the Mining Camp. They're expecting over a million wandering souls after all is said and done. I choose not to subject myself, yet again, to the insufferable humanity of it all. Have you been?"

"Not since before it opened."

"Well, visit once more. But only once. You will likely not be disappointed. You may actually be astonished…" Jenkins looked past Manly to a sideboard positioned along the wall behind where both men sat. "Please forgive my churlishness. I'm disrespecting my guest. May I offer you coffee? Tea? What do you say to a cup of oolong?"

Jenkins left the room momentarily.

He returned with a pot of steeped tea. He filled two emerald green porcelain teacups, placed the pot on the sideboard, and sat back down.

"Now, where was I? The exposition's opening was a garish affair. I expected nothing less, given the contortions and contrivances the organizers went through to outdo Chicago. The electric company—I suppose it was the electric company—perhaps it was Western Union—had run lines from Gray Gables…have you heard of Gray Gables? Well of course you have. President Cleveland's summer home. In Massachusetts. They ran the electrical wires along the main Western Union telegraph line, all the way to Atlanta and on to the exposition grounds…but I may be telling you what you already know."

"I read it in the newspaper, but please continue."

"Well, shortly after three o'clock in the afternoon, the president, sitting at his desk, placed his finger on a black rubber button and pressed it. An electric current pulsed across a one thousand mile span. Suddenly the flash of light from a bright, incandescent lamp illuminated the Machinery Building on the exposition grounds. The current activated two electric valves on a massive, four million-gallon Frick steam engine in the Machinery Building. The valves opened, steam poured into the cylinders of the engine and the wheels began turning, announcing the grand opening. Standing on the banks of the Clara Meer, a crowd of twenty-five thousand spectators witnessed an ostentatious display—quite gaudy actually—of fountains of light, fireworks, and a salute of over one hundred bombs." Jenkins looked deep into Manly's eyes. "I know firsthand. I was one of those spectators. I was standing way behind the throng. As I said, I abhor crowds."

"How do you know so much about the opening? The steam engine. The valves. The cylinders and wheels."

Jenkins tilted his head back. A ghost of a grin formed. "Because I read the newspaper too, Mr. Manly. And I have a God-given propensity for remembering detail."

"It must have been a spectacle. I remember the paper said the deed of magic has been done, or something to that effect."

"A spectacle? Yes. Magic? Perhaps. There are things at that fair that defy logic. Things you could read about in a Mary Shelley book. Science and the supernatural. If you haven't read her work, do so. She will intimidate you if nothing else. She'll probably scare the devil out of you. But back to the fair. If you should find yourself there, go to the Living Pictures exhibit, a few hundred feet from the southern shore of the Clara Meer. They have a device there called a Phantoscope. A loop of film passing in front of a rapid-shutter light source. It gives the impression of movement. A horse running across a field. A dancing man with top hat and cane. A fair maiden saved by her rescuer from a villainous demon. You'll think you're right there with them all. But enough of that. Mr. Manly, I imagine you're here to talk about Green Conn."

"Actually I'm not. I'm here to talk about Lem Mureau."

The color drained from Jenkins' face. He shifted in his chair.

"Mureau! You came here to discuss Mureau?"

"I did. I need to loca—"

"A filthy Huguenot! That's what he is. No better than a Jew or a Freemason. Captain Manly, you need to stay away from him if you know what's best for you. He'll steal you blind at the first opportunity."

"But didn't he sell the Wild Turkey tobacco to Bass? I need to know what involvement he had with the man. Do you not have a bill of sale?"

"I *had* a bill of sale, but I turned it over to Mrs. Bass's attorney, Charles Camp."

"Do you know where Mureau gets his tobacco, Mr. Jenkins?"

"Do you mean the tobacco he *buys*—fair and square—or the tobacco he *purloins?*" Jenkins shook his head. "I have no idea. Perhaps somewhere in Virginia."

"Is it possible that Mureau could be mixed up some way in Bass's murder?"

"Listen, Mureau is a crook. It's as simple as that. So is that damned Conn. And it wouldn't surprise me at all to find out the two of them were in together on the whole thing. Stole the tobacco—or maybe Mureau stole it while Conn made sure the detectives were looking the other way. Sold it to Bass, and then, when Bass got caught, saw to it that Bass would never expose them. Conn and Mureau. Birds of a feather. Isn't that what they say?"

"That's my point. If there's any chance at all that this man Mureau is involved in Bass's murder, I have to find him."

"He never lived here, you know. He's a traveling tobacco drummer. Doesn't stay in one place more than a night or two. And, honestly, I think he does most of his business elsewhere. Not even around here. I've wondered how he got mixed up selling tobacco to Bass in the first place. But your guess is as good as mine."

Jenkins laid his pipe down. The color was returning to his face. He set his eyes on Manly. "Word is that he returned to South Carolina—where I suppose he lives. Or perhaps North Carolina. I don't remember."

A God-given propensity for remembering detail? Manly thought.

Jenkins continued. "You may want to start in Charleston. There are a damned lot of French Calvinists along the Cooper River."

WUX ATL GA OCT 2 95 905AM 21PD
CHARLESTON SC POLICE DEPT
SEARCHING FOR A LEM OR LEMUEL MUREAU
(STOP) PLS ADVISE WHEREABOUTS (STOP)
MAY BE INVOLVED IN CRIME (STOP)
WA MANLY ATLANTA POLICE DEPT

Manly left the Western Union office hopeful he would hear back from the Charleston police. He waited three days. Then came the reply:

WUX CHARLESTON SC OCT 5 95 1103AM 17PD
WA MANLY ATLANTA GA POLICE DEPT
NO RECORD OF LEM OR LEMUEL MUREAU
(STOP)
CJ STEVENS CHARLESTON POLICE

Manly sent a telegram to the Charleston postmaster. The same response—no record of a Lem Mureau.

He sent messages to police departments and postmasters in other cities—Greenville, Columbia, Charlotte, Greensboro, Raleigh, Chattanooga, Augusta, Macon. No one knew of a man by that name.

He had posters printed up. He sent them by rail to post offices throughout Georgia and the Carolinas. Nothing.

The man was nowhere to be found. Was he on the run? Hiding out in some off-the-beaten-track farmhouse in a remote town somewhere—waiting for the Bass affair to pass? Perhaps even as far away as Louisiana—a lot of Frenchmen down there. Or maybe he'd just moved on—unaware of anything that was happening in his wake—a traveling drummer looking for his next sale.

On Thursday, the tenth of October, Manly paid a visit to Charles Camp, Ella Bass's attorney. He asked to see the bill of sale Jenkins had turned over to him. Camp retrieved the document from a file on his desk and handed it to Manly.

It listed a single line item—a large quantity of Wild Turkey tobacco. The place where the seller's address normally would have been filled in was blank. The signature, in florid script, read Lemuel P. Mureau.

"When did Jenkins give this to you?"

"He delivered it to me shortly after Bass's death. I don't remember the exact day. He told me he had taken it from Bass's store. I don't have any details beyond that. I wish I could be more helpful."

"Of course I remember that black-eyed Frenchman."

Manly had come to visit Mrs. Dampman at the Woodward Avenue side-by-side.

"I thought his name was Moore," Mrs. Dampman said. "But Herbert told me it was Mureau. The man showed up at my door one night. I had already dressed for bed when I heard the knock. I was careful not to open the door more than the slightest crack. George—that's my husband—was away. A girl has to protect herself, you know."

"What did he say to you, Mrs. Dampman? Mureau, I mean."

"He told me to tell Baker Bass to watch his back. He said something about a detective being involved. Then he left."

"Did he name the detective?"

"He did. He said it was Green Conn."

"And you never saw him again?"

"No. I never saw him after that. I went to Bass's store and conveyed the message. Then, three days later, I found out Bass was dead. Even with the warning, I still couldn't believe it."

"Mrs. Dampman, about that scratch on the gun—"

She removed her glasses. Manly noticed a bright red line coursing its way across the bridge of her nose. She wiped the lenses with the hem of her dress. "Mr. Manly, I've said everything I'm going to say about that gun. I suggest you go back to your own detectives and talk to them. I have nothing more to add. Throw me in jail. Keep me there without food and water—like your men did to Herbert. Arrest me if that's what you want to do. But unless you get a court order and haul me before the judge—unless you make me testify under oath—I'm not saying any more about it. Now if you'll leave me be, I have work to do."

Might other merchants in town know of Mureau? Manly spent two days visiting tobacco retailers and general provisioners. Some had heard of the man but had never met him. Some said they had received letters from him in recent weeks, offering to sell them tobacco at a reduced price. One merchant had returned on a recent afternoon from a grocery delivery to find a note from Mureau.

"He tacked it to my front door. The note said he stopped by to introduce himself and that he would come by at another time. It was signed Lem Mureau, Wholesale Purveyor of Fine Tobaccos. But he never returned."

How do you find a man who has no address, little to no footprint, and a dearth of past leads? Manly was undaunted. He vowed to continue to search for the man who might—just might—provide a connection to Bass's murder.

TWENTY-EIGHT

GREEN CONN

A Nigger in the Woodpile

I BOUND OUT THE DOOR. LIGHT AS A FEATHER. *Barefoot, wearing nothing but my nightshirt. A full moon approaches the western horizon. A curious yellowish red cloaks the sky to my right. A coon dog howls in the distance. I place my right foot onto the cool grass. Then my left. I round the northwest corner of the house. Flames leap from the pyracantha bush. I need water. Fast. I run toward the well at the back of the house. A large pile of fresh hewn hickory, neatly stacked, lies before me at the northeast corner of the house. It looks to be a cord, perhaps a cord-and-a-half. Where did it come from? I didn't put it there. As I approach, I hear a noise. From the far side of the pile. I slowly inch my way around to the side of the pile I cannot see. There, a black man lies spread-eagle on the ground. He holds in one hand a Y-shaped slingshot. It looks to be fashioned from a buckthorn bush. In the other, a stone half the size of my fist. "Good morning, Massa Conn," he says with a broad smile. "You'd best put shoes on before you catch your death of a cold."*

Conn bolted from a deep sleep.
A nigger in the woodpile. That's it.

Conn had blamed Cason for botching the scheme to snare
Jenkins. What had Cason said? *I cooked this up myself.* Or
something like that. He sure cooked it up all right. So much
so that Jenkins went Scot-free. And that Delores Dampman.
Wasn't she supposed to help Cason and his co-conspirators trap
their prey? And what did she do? She just made things worse.
When she got backed into a corner, she wouldn't even give a
straightforward answer about the gun.

I need a nigger in the woodpile—a real nigger in the woodpile.

Five black men had filed affidavits in the wake of Bass's death.
Surely one of them could be wangled into helping Conn do
Jenkins in. It might take a little money on the side—and not just
twenty-five dollars. It might take intimidation and threat. But
surely...

He ran through the men's names. One stood out—Christopher
Johnson. *Johnson knew Bass. Hung around Bass's store. Had sketchy
dealings with him. Sold him the stolen tallow. Probably knows Jenkins
too. In and out of trouble. Spends half his time at the labor camp. If I
can't make him squeal, who can I?*

Back at the station house, Conn shared his plan with Cason
and Mehaffey.

"Do you remember that nigger Johnson? We tried our best to
get him to nail Bass—but he wouldn't take the bait. He ended up
filing an affidavit. Made us look bad. Real bad. Now Bass is dead.

And it's retribution time for the way he raked us over the coals. He owes us, and we can bring him around."

"I'd like nothing more than to pin Bass's murder on Jenkins, and I know you would, Conn. More than anybody. After all, he's accused you from the start," Cason said. "But we have nothing to go on. Not a thing. And what makes you think Johnson does?"

"I have no idea whether he does or he doesn't," Conn replied. "But I guarantee he'll sell Jenkins down the river if that's what it takes to get *himself* off."

"So you're going to threaten to sell *Johnson* down the river to get him to turn on *Jenkins?* Listen, Conn. It just doesn't feel right to me."

"Cason, what did you say to me just before you went and botched the deal at the McDaniel Street house? I think you told me it was your plan and I just needed to get the hell out of the way. Well, this is *my* plan." Conn looked over at Mehaffey. "Mehaffey, are you with me on this?"

"Niggers'll say whatever you want them to, as long as you scare the dickens out of them, engage in some good old-fashioned coercion, and promise them a few dollars," Conn said to Mehaffey. "I guarantee you, if we get to the right people that know Johnson, and get them to talk, we can see him hanged—or should I say *threaten* to see him hanged. That's all it'll take for him to turn on Jenkins."

Conn and Mehaffey spent two weeks tracking down a handful of Johnson's friends and acquaintances. They turned up two possible confederates. An elevator boy named Jesse Jones. And an old souse named Sarah Scott. They met with both of them. Cooperative? Likely. Reliable? Time would tell.

Both the elevator boy and the old souse obliged.

At four thirty in the afternoon on the twenty-ninth of October, Conn and Mehaffey found Johnson at the Peachtree Inn hotel on Fourteenth Street, where he worked off and on as a janitor. They arrested him and charged him with Bass's murder. They took him to the Fulton County stockade and had him locked up there so as not to arouse suspicion—at least not yet—on the part of Connolly and Manly.

The next morning, Conn visited Johnson at his cell. The black man stood inside and peered out through the iron bars. At first, he refused to talk, saying he would say what he had to say only with an attorney present.

"Do you realize the people in this town have been energized by your arrest? They wanted us to catch Bass's killer, but they had almost given up. And then this. The ones I've talked to are eager to see you hanging from the gallows, just like that nigger Ford. The one that killed that man Keller earlier this year. They would just as soon see you suffer the same fate as give you a fair trial. You know, don't you, that you can get yourself out of this mess, but only if you'll work with me? "

Johnson sat his slight frame on the foot of the cot. Looked up at Conn. "I am an innocent man. You're trying to bamboozle me again."

"To *bamboozle* you? I'm doing nothing of the kind. You got yourself in the mess you're in. I can tell you right now, the walk from the county stockade to the scaffolds is a long and lonely one." Conn leaned in to the bars, lowered his forehead and stared into Johnson's eyes. "Now you don't want to take that walk, do you?"

"But I'm telling you, I'm innocent."

"You know Jesse Jones, don't you? He claims he saw you running from the scene of the shooting."

Johnson sprang from the cot. "Jones is lying. I know him and his kind. He doesn't like me. He'd do anything to see me destroyed. Mr. Conn, I'm telling you. Don't trust anything he says."

"Can you prove you're innocent?"

"Yes. I can. I have a woman friend. Her name is Rachel Stowers. The day Mr. Bass was killed, she was staying down on Whitley's Alley off Auburn Avenue. I'd gotten out of the stockade, right here where you're standing, the Thursday before the murder. I stayed with her that night and all Friday morning."

"Will I find her on Whitley's Alley? Will she support what you're saying?"

"She's living somewhere on the south side of town now. I don't know the street. But if you find her, she'll back me up."

This was the first Conn had heard of a Rachel Stowers. "I'll locate her, but tell me something. We found another witness—one that'll say you bragged about killing Bass. She'll say Bass owed you money and had promised to see you through any trouble. But then when you were sent to the stockade, Bass not only failed to help you, but he denied owing you the money. And you vowed to do him in. Which you did."

"Bass didn't owe me a red cent when he died," Johnson shot back. "You've found false witnesses against me."

"Well, let's just say for now that you're telling the truth and you didn't kill Bass. Do you know who did?"

"I do not."

"Do you know a man named Herbert Jenkins? Did he do it? C'mon Johnson, you can tell me. Think back on that morning. It was Jenkins that did it, wasn't it? You want to walk out of this godawful place a free man, don't you?"

"Anything I say would be a guess. But I'll tell you this. Mr. Bass and I were friends. I wouldn't have done anything to harm him. As for Jenkins, I have no idea." Johnson went on, "You and your partner, Mehaffey, have been out to get me from the start. I don't know why you've picked me. Maybe because you think I'm an easy dupe. Maybe because you've decided I'm a disreputable drunk. You tried your best to pin those stolen goods on Bass and then you tried to pull me into it. And now you're trying to claim I killed him."

Conn bristled. "You'd better watch what you say, boy. You've got a lot of nerve accusing me of anything. I'm not trying to do you or anybody else in. But with your attitude, nobody would say a word if you left here in a pine box."

"Pine box or no pine box—you know I'm right. That incident with the tallow—that was just one big set-up." Johnson glared at Conn. "I never once saw Mr. Bass knowingly accept or sell any stolen goods. He wasn't that kind of man. And now you're trying to set me up again—for something a lot worse."

It was all Conn could do to keep from reaching through the bars and strangling the uppity bounder right then and there. But he thought better of it.

"Johnson, I heard somebody call you an old mudsill once. But I'm thinking maybe you're not a mudsill. Do you consider yourself an educated Negro? Smarter than most? Smart enough to know what's good for you?"

"I guess I do. But I don't consider myself better than the next man."

"Well, I'll leave you here to think about your future, sitting in your cell all alone." Conn began to walk away. Swung around. "I have one more question. Somebody claimed you planted the pistol in Bass's hand that morning—after you shot him. One of your so-called friends will come forward and testify that it belonged to her and you took it from her."

"That's a confounded lie," Johnson bellowed. "Now you get out of here. I have nothing more to say."

TWENTY-NINE

CHRISTOPHER JOHNSON

Smarter Than Most

WHAT DID GREEN CONN SAY? I'M AN EDUCATED NEGRO, *smarter than most.*

Christopher Johnson was born in Appling County at the dawning of the war. His mother, a house slave named Milly, was chattel of Elijah Johnson, a wealthy plantation owner. In adulthood, Christopher would learn he was the issue from a fateful evening when Elijah presented himself at the door of Milly's room in the basement of the main house. As a house bondwoman, Milly had considered herself fortunate not to have to live in one of the broken-down slave shacks out back. But proximity may have been a factor when Elijah forced himself on her that evening.

Christopher supposed his father and grandfather were one and the same, Elijah having allegedly also spawned his mother sixteen years before his own birth. When he looked in the mirror—at his sharp features, narrow nose and mulatto complexion, his high forehead and prominent cheekbones—it made sense.

He was not born Christopher. The name given to him at birth was Millard Fillmore. His mother hadn't named him. She likely had no idea who Millard Fillmore was. It was Elijah who bestowed upon him that name. Years later, when Christopher, née Millard, attended the Summerhill Public School for Negroes in Atlanta, he would learn about the thirteenth president. His blood boiled when he thought about being named for the man who fought for the Compromise of 1850 and the Fugitive Slave Act. He hated that name more than anything. He added Christopher Columbus as an adult, having heard stories of the explorer as a child while sitting at his mother's feet. He was grateful that Milly, having taught herself to read and write, had instilled in him a desire to learn.

At the end of the war, many slaves throughout the South, finding themselves freed but with nowhere to go and no opportunities beyond the only place they'd ever known, chose, or were forced, to stay on their former masters' farms. But not Milly. She was determined to strike out on her own, to do whatever it took to provide for herself and her only child, freed from Elijah Johnson's heavy hand. They moved from Appling County to Macon and later to the edge of Atlanta. She worked as a maid, doubling up as a seamstress to make ends meet. Being a single Negro mother was hard, but she made sure her son received a good education, enrolling him in the Summerhill School as soon as he was old enough to attend.

Upon leaving Summerhill, Johnson embellished his given name and, as Christopher Columbus Millard Fillmore Johnson, married a young woman who had grown up on Martin Street, just a few blocks from the school. He got a job at the Fulton Bag and Cotton Mill. He dropped Millard Fillmore from his name. For several years thereafter, things went well. Each morning he would walk to work, carrying his metal lunch pail in one hand. In his other, he carried a slingshot, his only means of defense against big-city troublemakers. He would put in an honest day's labor, stopping only for a brief midday lunch—an oval of corn pone, a slice of salt pork, a piece of cheese, perhaps a sliver of yam pie on a good day. At the close of the week he would take his place in line at the paymaster's window. While he never considered himself smarter than most, fortune had bestowed upon him a job, a wife, three meals a day, and a place to rest his head at sundown.

But in the fall of 1884, three things happened that would change his life. Milly died of dysentery at the age of thirty-nine. Then, almost three months to the day later, his wife lost her life to pneumonia. He was disconsolate, wondering if he had the strength to carry on. He was overcome with grief. He had trouble sleeping. Eating. Even getting up in the morning. He found it harder and harder to concentrate. And it was this mental state that played a role when, on an early January morning in 1885, a flying shuttle at the mill took out his left eye. He lost his job. Any one of these events would have been a challenge, but their combination over a short time set him on a self-described path of destruction. It didn't take long before the bottle got the best of him. He began drinking to the point of stagger almost every night. Eking out a living by day wherever he could. Stealing when necessary.

A week after Johnson's arrest for Bass's murder, he was still in the county stockade. A grand jury had indicted him, based on the urging of Conn and the testimony of Jesse Jones and Sarah Scott. His case was added to the court docket for the first of November. But there were too many cases before his, including indictments for bigamy, embezzlement, arson, and assault with intent to murder. The first of November came and went.

Two weeks later, Johnson was still behind bars. His date to appear before the superior criminal court was rescheduled for the second of December, but Judge Candler postponed the trial another twenty-four hours to give the attorneys for both sides more time to gather additional evidence and round up witnesses.

The evening before the rescheduled trial was to begin, Conn paid another visit to the stockade.

"I told you before, Johnson. You can walk out of here a free man. All you have to do is name Bass's killer. Otherwise, if this goes on much longer, there's nothing I can do. It'll be out of my hands. Your fate will lie with the judge—and a jury of twelve lily-white men. Imagine that, thirteen God-fearing citizens holding the fate of one wretched nigger in their hands."

"Mr. Conn, I don't know who killed Mr. Bass. I'm scared to death. But I'm not going to lie for you."

"Listen to me. You're going to go to the gallows for what somebody else did. Do you understand? Is that what you want? To hang for another man's deed? You can get yourself out of this mess, but you have to do it now. When you get in that courtroom, nobody, not even God Almighty himself, can help you."

Johnson looked down at his feet.

"Say Jenkins did it and you walk. Who's paying you off, Johnson? Who's paying your lawyer fees? Why, you can't even afford a pot to piss in or a window to throw it out of. Somebody's gotten to you."

Johnson remained silent.

"You're a dead man, Johnson," Conn said as he walked away.

At eight o'clock on the third of December, the bailiff ushered Christopher Johnson, shackled and handcuffed, into the courtroom. Johnson had never participated in, nor witnessed for that matter, a trial of such import. He was filled with angst. He scanned the room. Conn. Sarah Scott. Jesse Jones. They were all there. He beamed when he saw Rachel Stowers sitting in the back row.

The twelve jurymen shuffled to their seats, notepads and pencils in hand.

The state opened its testimony at eight thirty sharp. Paden was the first to take the stand. He led the jury through a recounting of the coroner's inquest, its findings and conclusions. He reiterated that Bass's death had been caused by a gunshot wound to the back of the head just below the right ear, and that the coroner's jury had ruled against suicide. Paden then unwrapped a large bundle containing the clothes Bass had been wearing on the morning of his murder. The bailiff showed Bass's coat, pants, shirt, and underwear to the jury. The prosecution submitted them as evidence.

Doctors Westmoreland and Shaw, each testifying individually, followed Paden on the stand. Then Thompson and Moncrief. To help the officers with their testimony, the prosecution provided a poster-sized diagram showing the precise location of the shooting, the embankment, the alleyways, and the surrounding streets.

Sarah Scott, the black woman Conn and Mehaffey had met with, was the next witness. She said she and Johnson had been intimate for several months before Bass's death. She swore that, just before the murder, Johnson asked her to visit him at the stockade, where he was being held on a larceny charge. He asked her to find Bass and secure bail money for his release. She sought Bass out, but he refused to come up with the money.

"When I went back to the stockade, I told him…" She pointed across the room to where Johnson sat. "…I told him Mr. Bass wasn't goin' to give him no money. That's when he said he'd get even with Mr. Bass. Why, he said he'd kill him the first chance he got." She shook her head in reproach. Looked up at the judge. "And you know what else, your honor? He was back at my house the night after Mr. Bass was killed. He waved a pistol around. Never pointed it at me, mind you. But he waved it around alright. He claimed he used it to shoot Mr. Bass. He begged me to leave the city with him, but I wouldn't do it."

Under cross-examination, Scott admitted she had been arrested on numerous occasions for public drunkenness and had been turned out of her church for frequent and blatant lying.

Jesse Jones took the stand next. He said he was an elevator boy at the Norcross Building, on Marietta Street near Five Points. He said he was on his way to work around four o'clock in the morning on the day Bass was shot. He walked up Courtland Street to the corner at Ellis Street. He turned on to Ellis. As he neared Ellis and Ivy Streets, he saw a black man running from the corner. When the man ran under a street light, Jones recognized him. When asked on the stand if he could identify the man, Jones pointed across the courtroom at Johnson. "That's him. That's the man I saw. Christopher Johnson." Jones further testified that, several days after the shooting, he ran into Johnson in a saloon on Decatur Street. When he asked Johnson why he had been running that Friday morning, Johnson replied that he had had some trouble up on Ivy Street and was trying to get away.

Under cross-examination by the defense, Jones initially stuck to the story he had given a few minutes earlier under direct questioning. But when grilled by Johnson's attorney, he relented. Jones' story quickly fell apart. He admitted he had not seen Baker Bass's body the morning of the shooting. When he heard the gunshot, he thought someone had fired at either a burglar or a chicken thief. It wasn't until later that day that he found out Bass had been murdered. He conceded that it was dark, even with the illumination from the street light, and he could perhaps have been mistaken about the identity of the man running down the street. When pressed further, he also admitted that he, in fact, had not talked to Johnson in the saloon. Rather, he had overheard Johnson speaking with another Negro across a crowded and noisy room. He thought he made out what Johnson had said—that Johnson had had trouble with Bass, and because Bass had refused to get him out of the chain gang a few days earlier, he had fixed him—or something to that effect.

The prosecution called Paden back to the stand. He said the missing pistol, when taken from Bass's hand, had three empty shells and two unfired ones, but that the gun did not appear to have been fired recently. He recounted a peculiar mark on the gutta percha handle of the gun. But he did not recall whether or not there was a scratch on the polished nickel beneath the hammer. He admitted that a scratch could have been there and he didn't notice it.

The state rested, but not before asking for the privilege of possibly introducing one or two additional witnesses later.

The defense opened. Rachel Stowers approached the stand. She faltered as she stepped into the witness box. The bailiff jumped up to help her. Her hand gripped the edge of the witness chair so hard that it wobbled as she seated herself.

"When Mr. Bass was killed, I'd been keeping a colored boardinghouse." She pointed toward the south wall of the room. "Down on Whitley's Alley. Mr. Johnson showed up late Thursday evening, the day before the shooting. I reckon it was close to nine o'clock when all of a sudden there he was, knocking at my door. He said he'd been staying at the house across the street, but when he got off the chain gang there wasn't any room for him there. My boardinghouse was full. The only spare bed was in my own room. But he looked tired and worn out. So I agreed to take him in for the night."

Stowers said Johnson went to bed shortly after arriving. She said she was a very light sleeper and would have been awakened if he had left the house during the night. She woke him around five o'clock the next morning. She had to shake him and call his name several times before he stirred. He left her house around six o'clock that morning and did not return until late that evening. When he returned, she asked him if he had heard Bass had been shot. He said he had. He seemed distraught over it.

When questioned by the prosecution, Stowers said she knew Sarah Scott, that the woman could not be trusted, and that her character was of the worst kind. The attorneys for the state pressed Stowers about how well she knew Johnson.

"Now do you really expect us to believe you took a complete stranger into your bedroom and let him spend the night there? Surely you know we're smarter than to fall for a story like that."

"Well it's true."

"Tell me this. Are you accustomed to sleeping with people you've never met?"

Johnson's attorney rose to object. "Your honor, the question is argumentative and immaterial to my client's guilt or innocence. The witness has stated twice now that she took my client in for the night. That should be enough to satisfy the prosecution that she's telling the truth."

"I agree the line of questioning is argumentative, but it touches on the witness's, and the defendant's, character. And besides, I'd like to hear the answer." Judge Candler looked over at the prosecutor. "You may proceed."

"I will repeat the question. Are you accustomed to sleeping with people you don't know?"

"I most certainly am not." The indignance in her voice resonated. "I took him in because I felt sorry for him. And I didn't sleep with him. At least not that night."

Restrained snickers could be heard throughout the courtroom.

"At least not *that* night?"

"Mr. Johnson and I got to know each other after that, and I've seen him frequently ever since."

The prosecutor asked her to repeat what she had told the defense attorney about Johnson's whereabouts the morning Bass was killed. She said she was positive he had spent the entire night at her house, that he was sound asleep all morning, and that he didn't leave her room until past sunrise, two hours after the fatal shot had been fired.

The defense then called a Negro woman named Mary Stark. She said she knew all the black witnesses who had testified before her. She also impugned Sarah Scott's reputation and credibility, saying Scott had had it out for Johnson for a long time. In short, Scott was not to be believed.

On cross examination, Stark said Sarah Scott was a sot who became violent under the influence of the bottle, going so far on one occasion as to threaten to burn down the house where Johnson stayed prior to his most recent stockade stint. She said Scott had wanted Johnson to take her to Chattanooga and, when he refused, Scott threatened to get even with him.

When asked if she knew Herbert Jenkins, Mary Stark said she did. When questioned further, she admitted that Jenkins had approached her in the hall just before she was called into the courtroom to testify. The prosecution began to question her about her conversation with Jenkins, but Johnson's attorney objected, saying it was irrelevant. Judge Candler ruled in Johnson's favor. Mary Stark's testimony ended.

The defense then called a Negro night watchman named Jacob Stanley. He testified that he lived with Jesse Jones. He contradicted Jones, saying that upon returning home around four thirty on the morning of the shooting, he entered the house and found Jones sound asleep. There was no way Jones could have been near the scene of the shooting when it occurred.

Judge Candler then announced a short recess for dinner.

When the trial resumed, the defense called Jenkins to the stand. Jenkins evidently intended to talk about Mrs. Dampman and the McDaniel Street incident in an effort to call into question the reliability of Conn and his cohorts. But he managed to get only a few words out before the prosecution objected, cited immateriality. Judge Candler agreed and his testimony was not admitted.

Christopher Johnson then took the stand. He backed up Rachel Stowers' testimony. He denied having anything to do with Bass's murder. He further stated that he was never in the Decatur Street saloon and Jesse Jones was either lying or had mistaken him for someone else. He swore that both Jesse Jones and Sarah Scott were out to get him and would stop short of nothing.

Sitting there on the witness stand that afternoon, with his fate in the balance, Johnson considered accusing Conn of bribing Jones and Scott, but he thought better of it. It would likely have gotten him in more trouble than he was already in.

Upon cross-examination, Johnson admitted to having stolen the tallow and taking it to Bass's store. But he said Bass refused to buy it. He further testified that the detectives had tried their best to get him to claim Bass was guilty of receiving stolen goods, but he stopped short of accusing Conn or Mehaffey of bribery.

The defense rested.

Johnson found it odd that neither side ever called Conn or Mehaffey to testify.

After closing arguments from both sides, Judge Candler charged the jury, instructing them to work into the evening to reach a verdict and to report back to him at eight thirty the following morning.

"Gentlemen," the judge roared, "I bring to your attention something called Blackstone's formulation. The English jurist William Blackstone stated it most eloquently when he said, over a century ago, 'It is better that ten guilty persons escape than that one innocent suffer.' I remind you that you can find the defendant guilty only if you are convinced beyond a reasonable doubt of his guilt."

The bailiff took Johnson, still handcuffed and shackled, to a holding cell in the basement of the station house. There he would stay until the jury reached a verdict. Eight thirty the following morning passed. Almost two days went by with no word. Johnson was nervous. Restless. He couldn't eat, in part because of his condition and in part because the muck they served him barely passed as food. He tossed and turned all night. Then, on the fifth of December, shortly before five o'clock on the afternoon, the bailiff appeared at Johnson's cell. He handcuffed and shackled Johnson and escorted him back to the courthouse.

The jurors filed into the room. They were haggard and worn. Their eyes were red from lack of sleep. Johnson could relate. The foreman stood beside the eleven other men who had spent the last two days deliberating Johnson's fate. The foreman held a sheet of paper in his hand. The crowded room fell silent.

"We, the jury, find the defendant not guilty."

As the words fell from the foreman's lips, several Negroes in the courtroom let out a prolonged cheer. Johnson sprang to his feet and raised his cuffed wrists to his heart. The judge called for order.

Johnson turned around and searched the courtroom for Conn. He saw the detective sitting in the back row. Conn's face was drained of color.

The bailiff removed the handcuffs from Johnson's wrists. The shackles from his ankles.

At six fifteen, Christopher Columbus Johnson walked out of the courtroom a free man, having been acquitted by a jury of twelve white men.

Christopher Johnson could breathe a brief sigh of relief. But things just never seemed to work out for him anymore. Upon leaving the station house, he headed straight for a Negro saloon on Decatur Street, not far from the courthouse. He ended up drinking too much whiskey. The police arrested him and locked him up, this time to give him a few hours to let the spirits depart. He was released around noon the following day, but by four in the afternoon he was sozzled again.

THIRTY

WILLIAM MANLY

Two Strikes

MANLY HAD KEPT HIS DISTANCE FROM THE DETECTIVES ever since the commissioners ruled against any notion of an internal investigation. But after Christopher Johnson's trial, he could no longer hold back. The morning after the verdict was read, he strode down the station house's center hallway to the room where the detectives sat. He stood just outside the door. The detectives were engaged in muted conversation. He strained to make out what they were saying, but he couldn't. They went quiet as he walked through the door. He scanned the room. Green Conn was leaning back in an armchair against the far wall, the two front chair legs hovering three inches off the floor. Without hesitating, Manly walked over to Conn. The detective looked up without the slightest change in deportment or position.

"Do you like baseball, Conn?"

"Of course I do. Doesn't everybody?"

"Do you ever go to the Athletic Grounds? To watch the Crackers? That Jimmy Knowles. Best manager in the Southern League. Don't you think? All dash-fire and grit."

Conn cocked his head. A quizzical frown came over him.

"You're probably wondering why I just sauntered in here and started talking baseball."

"The thought crossed my mind."

"Have you watched Billy Calihan pitch? I mean *really* watched him pitch? The crazy way he winds up. Knee high in the air. Arm cocked. Releases the ball. It flies to the plate like a rocket. A crack hurler if you ask me. Strikes 'em out more than most. One right over the plate. Two. Three. Batter's out." Manly glared at Conn with a twisted scowl. Then he turned and faced the other detectives. "Herbert Jenkins. Now Christopher Johnson. You men just got thrown your second strike. Why don't you go back to honest detective work instead of trying to frame people?"

Conn's chair legs slammed to the floor. He leveled an icy stare at Manly. "Captain, what's come over you? You're not yourself this morning. If you ask me, you're in a downright pucker."

"Thomas Greenberry Conn. Why, I remember the day you first walked through the door of the old Pryor Street station. Callow and cocksure. Was it eighty-one? Eighty-two? I thought at the time, this kid'll make a good cop one day—once he loses his swelled head. And here we are almost fifteen years later. And what do you have to show for it?" Manly looked around the room. "For that matter, what do any of you have to show for it?"

Mehaffey spoke up. "I think we do a good job, considering everything. And the commissioners think so, even if you and the chief don't."

"Considering what, Mehaffey? Considering that you men walk around all day with a cloud hanging over you? Considering that you're sitting around here talking about—whatever you were talking about—instead of doing your jobs? Considering that you spend more time trying to frame Jenkins for Bass's murder, with little to go on except what sure looks like a vendetta? And meanwhile, Bass's killer is somewhere out there walking around in broad daylight. Or maybe even right here in …" Manly stopped short. Changed the subject. "And if I were you, I wouldn't bring the commissioners into this."

"Trust me. We know exactly what we're doing." The muscles in Conn's face tensed. "That man Jenkins may think he got off Scot-free. But he has no idea what's coming to him. I wouldn't want to be in his shoes right now."

Manly walked back to his office. He sat down at his desk. An angst came over him when he thought back to the day Connolly had given him an ultimatum—find Bass's killer—but do it on the sly. His knees had wobbled when he left the chief's office. A couple of months ago, he probably wouldn't have found the dash to amble into a room full of detectives and confront Conn the way he just had.

He reached into his desk drawer and retrieved the newspaper from a week earlier. Still folded to page seventeen. The words circled in bold black pencil stung.

No crimes are ever cleared up by our police.

Three months and a week had passed since a single shot rang out in downtown Atlanta, felling Baker Bass. The police were no closer to arresting the killer than they had been on that Friday morning. The detectives—*a feckless lot if there ever was one*—had botched two attempts to frame suspected offenders—and no doubt shift attention from Conn and his cronies. What else did the newspaper say?

No cases requiring the exercise of detective skill are ever worked out.

Manly feared Conn and his cohorts would redouble their efforts in the wake of the McDaniel Street incident and the Johnson trial—going after Jenkins, Johnson, perhaps even Delores Dampman.

He opened his memorandum book, thumbed to the first blank page, and penciled in *Delores Dampman, Herbert Jenkins, Christopher Johnson, Green Conn, William Mehaffey.*

After Mehaffey's name he wrote *Ed Cason? Other detectives?*

He looked over the names and added one more. *Lem Mureau.* Next to Mureau's name, in parentheses, he wrote *(Nowhere to be found).*

Manly read through the list. Every one of them was a suspect to one degree or another. Then again, it was possible the killer was not even on his list. An unnamed assassin could be lurking out there in the shadows, eluding the police and enjoying his perverse cat-and-mouse game.

THIRTY-ONE

WILLIAM MANLY

Grief and Fear

WILLIAM MANLY APPROACHED THE CORNER OF IVY AND Ellis Streets with a mix of sympathy and trepidation. *Will she greet my offer of condolence with open arms? Or will I encounter hostility? Forgivable, I'd say. How would I feel if Eunice had been gunned down and three and a half months had gone by with no solid leads?*

He turned right onto Ellis. He saw a silhouette approaching from down the street. Although the sun was barely dawning on the winter horizon, the house at 74 Ellis Street was pitch dark inside. The curtains were drawn tight. The yard was unkempt. The brown scrap of grass was understandable. It was December, after all. But the scraggly, two-foot-high weeds along the verge of the walkway leading to the porch were out of character for the neighborhood—and for Ella.

A mourning arrangement—black crepe and white ribbon—was affixed to the door. He hesitated briefly before climbing the steps, summoning the pluck to continue. He stood on the porch, his eyes fixed on the door.

"She isn't accepting visitors now."

Manly swung to face a woman on the sidewalk at the edge of the yard. She was no more than thirty years old. An empty wicker market basket dangled from her right forearm.

"She isn't taking visitors. Hasn't in weeks. The poor woman's still grieving miserably. Knock if you wish, but she won't come to the door."

"Is John home? Her son?"

"John? Why he hasn't been here for coming up on a week."

"Do you know where he is?"

"May I ask who you are?"

It dawned on Manly that he wouldn't expect to be recognized out of uniform. He had chosen to don street clothes and a grey fly-front overcoat in place of his standard issue navy blue Prince Albert coat and badge. He had reckoned it would make his visit more personal. Then, too, a part of him wondered if he had avoided wearing a uniform so as not to remind Ella of the feeble job his men had done.

"My apology, ma'am. I'm Captain Manly. From the police department. I'm here to pay my respects and to see how the family's doing. And you are?"

"Mrs. T.G. Black. I live two blocks down." She pointed to her left.

"Has John moved away, ma'am?"

"He took the morning train to Thomasville. Last weekend, I believe. With the other children. To visit kinfolk. As I said, knock if you wish. But I doubt she'll come to the door." Mrs. Black proceeded down the street toward the center of town, her empty market basket swaying to and fro.

A sliver of brass peeked from behind the mourning arrangement. The crepe and ribbon covered the knocker. *The dreaded reaper has come and gone, spiriting away the soul of a man. Knock softly.* He gently tapped his knuckles on the right-side door stile, just above the knob.

He rapped again, this time slightly harder, but not so hard as to offend the mourning spirits. Still no response. *Surely she heard me,* he thought. *If I wait here long enough, perhaps she'll come.*

Manly walked to the edge of the porch, leaned over the bannister and peered down the side of the house. A faint light shown through a far side window, washing the ground beneath it with a pale yellow. *She must be awake.*

He knocked a third time. A light appeared in the front room. Two squinting eyes peered through the slightest break in the curtain. The eyes disappeared. There was a rustling inside. The door opened just a crack.

"Mrs. Bass, I'm Captain Manly. You may remember me. From when you visited the station house? I know it's been a long time, but I've come to pay my respects."

The door edged open. Manly stood face-to-face with the likes of an old woman, much older than her years, haggard and pale. *What must she be? Thirty-seven? Thirty-eight?* She wiped her tear-salted eyes with the hem of her apron and beckoned him inside. He followed her across the front room. Her back was hunched. Her head was down. Her gait was unsteady. She lifted her arm midway from her side. Pointed to the sofa. He sat resting his arm on a dingy tatted antimacassar. She eased into a straight back chair facing him. He saw two flat top steamer trunks in the corner. The lids were closed. The draw bolts were open, as were the center hinges.

Manly looked down at his hands.

"I don't know what came over me. I know better, but I've come empty-handed."

"It's OK Mr. Manly. I'd offer you coffee. Tea. But there is none." She searched him with languid eyes. "Do you have news to share?"

"Unfortunately, Mrs. Bass, we've had no break in the case." He paused. "But I'm here today not as an officer. My call is personal. I've intended to make this visit for weeks now. And you may find this strange, coming from a police captain, but for reasons I may never understand, all confidence deserted me. I'm here to ask how you're getting along and if there is anything I can do for you."

"Mr. Manly. I don't have to tell you. It's been hard. John has been a Godsend, but he can't take Baker's place. No one ever will. The day John and I and the children returned on the train from Thomasville after the funeral…when I walked into this cold, dark house…I wondered how I possibly could go on without the man who had been my life, my rock, for twenty years."

Manly reached out. Took her veined hand in his. "Mrs. Bass, I can only imagine what you're going through. I've seen death come to those close to me. Family. Friends. Even people I never got to know well but who came into my life through my work. But no one so close as Baker was to you."

She lowered her eyes to her hand still resting in his. "Mr. Manly, I know you're not here officially. But I need to know something." She looked back up at him. "Why would one of your own men try so hard to take a good man down?"

Manly shook his head. "I wish I knew. I've pondered that since it all began back in May. Or was it June? But it's not just one man, Mrs. Bass. Yes, Green Conn may have been the one that started it all. But Mehaffey was right there with him. And perhaps others. Either they were convinced your husband was mixed up in a string of questionable business dealings…or they knew better but decided, for whatever reason, to go after him anyway."

Ella Bass pulled her hand away. "Mr. Manly, my husband was an honest man. An honorable man. A God-fearing Christian man. He never would have done the likes of what those men accused him of. And if they had not gone after him the way they did, he might be alive today."

"I understand." Manly looked at the trunks. "Mrs. Bass, where do you go from here?"

She stood. Walked across the room and fetched a Bible. Sat back down. She opened the Bible. He fully expected her to read a passage. But instead, she pulled out a folded paper. It looked as if it had been folded and unfolded so many times that the crease was about to come apart. "I have kept this poem, written by a woman named Lucy Knox, near to me at all times. I read it daily. There's a line in it. 'I have a leaden grief, and with it fears.'" She looked at Manly. "That's my life today. I am consumed with a leaden grief. And I fear what will happen to me. I know John will get by. He's a strapping young man with mettle and ambition. And Baker Jr. But the others. They're so young." She hesitated. "Mr. Manly, surely you know about the lawsuits."

He nodded.

She continued. "No fewer than three men have come forward and filed suits against Baker's business. Creditors, they allege. Staking claim to monies they say he owed them for merchandise. John has searched the company's books and finds records of business dealings with all of them. But nothing of balances due. Mr. Manly, we're barely getting by as it is. John's done yeoman's work to try to keep the store open—and I'm so proud of him—but it's just not working out. And now, with these lawsuits hanging over our heads, the good Lord would have to bestow a miracle upon us to get us out of the mess we're in."

"Have they produced any evidence—the creditors, that is?"

"I haven't seen the lawsuits. But my lawyer, Charles Camp, says they have it in writing. Mr. Manly, we just don't have the money to pay them. And even if we decided to go to court, Mr. Camp's bills would eat up what little nest egg we have."

"I understand." Manly changed the subject. "Your neighbor—Mrs. Black. She said John had gone to Thomasville with the children."

"Yes. He's there." She looked over at the trunks. "And I plan to join him. As soon as I can get my affairs in order here. I'll need to sell the house. Baker's dear friend, Young Gresham, has agreed to handle that for me. He'll also help us shut down the store. We'll sell whatever we can of the inventory." The skin bunched between her eyes. "Mr. Manly. The only family I know, they're all in Thomasville. I have no brothers or sisters, but my mother is still there—in the house I grew up in. And I have cousins. They'll take care of us. And the town is growing. People are moving there from all over. John can find good work there. And the town is smaller. Safer."

"Mrs. Bass, please let me know if there is anything I can do for you."

"The only thing you can do for me, Mr. Manly, is find my husband's killer."

"I will do everything in my power, Mrs. Bass, if it's the last thing I do."

Manly walked back down Ellis Street, then left on Ivy. He couldn't shake two things out of his mind. The look of anguish on Ella's face as she had stood on the porch and bid him farewell. And the words from the poem. *I have a leaden grief, and with it fears.*

He walked the Ivy Street block between Ellis and Houston to where Bass had been shot. The eight-foot embankment was still covered with overgrowth, albeit browner than a few months earlier. The alleyways, cutting through the embankment to the hotel and the opera house, were well-trodden. A reddish-brown vestige lingered on the sidewalk at the very spot where Bass's head had lain.

Manly looked back down the street toward Ellis. He squinted. For a moment, he thought he saw Baker Bass walking up Ivy Street. Just as Bass passed by, a tall, indistinct figure slid down the embankment. A scuffle ensued. A single shot rang out. Bass fell. The figure vanished.

Manly shook his head, rubbed his eyes, and continued down Ivy Street. A cold shiver came over him. *Was she right? Would Baker Bass be alive today had it not been for the efforts of my own men to bring him down?*

Part Four

THE CAPTAIN

THIRTY-TWO

WILLIAM MANLY

Witness Tampering

FOUR DAYS HAD PASSED SINCE MANLY LAST STRODE into the detectives' office and confronted Green Conn. This time, he hadn't gotten more than two feet into the room when Conn jumped up from his chair and confronted him.

"That no-good Jenkins. We caught him red-handed," Conn said.

Manly pursed his lips. Shook his head. "Red-handed? What is it *this* time, Greenberry?"

"Proper today are we, Captain?"

"That *is* your name, isn't it? So what did Jenkins supposedly do this time?"

Conn placed his hands on his hips. Thrust his chin forward. "Witness tampering."

"Witness tampering? *What* witness tampering?"

"Two women. Jenkins threatened them. Coerced them to agree to testify on Christopher Johnson's behalf."

"And who are these witnesses that he supposedly threatened?"

"Well, Mary Stark for one. Do you remember—on the stand—what she said about Jenkins?"

"Conn, if you recall, I wasn't there. I was back at the station house doing my job."

"Well, she said Jenkins came up to her in the hallway outside the courtroom, just before she went in to testify."

"OK. So Jenkins came up to her in the hallway. What is your point?"

"My point is what do you think they were talking about? Surely not *baseball*, Captain."

"Conn, your sarcasm doesn't impress me."

"Well, regardless, when that woman was there on the stand and the prosecutors tried to question her about Jenkins, what did the judge do? He shut her down. Said it wasn't relevant. Wouldn't let her say a damned thing."

"Conn, that proves nothing."

"Well, I have it on good authority she's planning to submit a statement to the judge. Let's see what happens then."

"*What* good authority?"

"Would you believe the good authority of the old woman herself?"

"Conn, with you I never know what to believe."

"Well, I heard it with my own ears. Straight out of her mouth. Standing right there at the door to her little Darktown seven-by-nine."

"So you visited Mary Stark." It was all Manly could do to contain his pique. "Sounds like just more Green Conn chicanery to me."

"No shecoonery here, Captain. Just good old sleuth work. Why, you should be proud of me."

Manly looked askance at Conn.

"Why Captain, if I didn't know better I'd swear you just cutty-eyed me."

Manly let Conn's comment pass. "And the other witness?"

"Another colored woman—named Carrie Barnes. She says Jenkins threatened to do bad things to her if she testified against Christopher Johnson."

"What bad things?"

"You'll find out in due time. She's going before the judge, too."

"So since I wasn't there, tell me this. Did she also testify that Jenkins approached her outside the courtroom?"

"They never called her to the stand. But she'll say Jenkins came to her house in the Third Ward and threatened her. She'll probably visit the judge today."

"One more thing, Conn. How did you come to even know about this second woman if she didn't testify?"

"Mary Stark told me."

"And did you also visit this Barnes woman at her—what did you call it—her seven-by-nine?"

"Captain, you ask a lot of questions that, frankly, don't matter."

"Conn, I'm willing to give anybody the benefit of the doubt. Maybe these women are telling the truth. If Jenkins threatened them, then he needs to be held accountable." Manly tilted his head down. Stared at Conn beneath lowered brows. "But promise me one thing. Promise me this isn't just one more scheme you've cooked up to try to frame Herbert Jenkins."

Manly waited a couple of days before showing up at Judge Candler's chambers, allowing enough time for both women to meet with the judge, assuming they actually were to do so.

The judge was sitting at his large mahogany desk flanked by four leather-upholstered armchairs, two at the sides and two facing the desk front. Manly had never been in the judge's chambers. He looked down at a plaque at the desktop's edge. It read JOHN SLAUGHTER CANDLER ESQ. With a quotation under it, "YOUR FRIEND AND PROTECTOR." The judge stood, walked around to the front of the desk, and motioned for Manly to sit in one of the two front-facing armchairs. Candler seated himself in the other. Manly had spent countless hours in Candler's courtroom, but he had never been face-to-face with the judge, up close. The first thing that struck him was the judge's baby face. *Maybe it's the lack of facial hair...and no glasses,* Manly thought. *He looks a little like Green Conn. Surely the comparison ends there.* The second thing that struck him was the judge looked more full at the belt without his flowing black robe.

"What can I do for you, Captain?"

"Your Honor, forgive me for imposing this morning, but it came to my attention that two colored women planned to visit you about Herbert Jenkins. To claim witness intimidation in Christopher Johnson's trial." Manly pulled his memorandum book out of his pocket. "A woman named Mary Stark. She was a witness for the defense. And another one—let's see—I want to get her name right—here it is. Carrie Barnes."

"Both women did, indeed, visit me. The one, Barnes, two days ago. And the other just yesterday morning. They both signed affidavits claiming Jenkins browbeat them. They say he threatened to do them bodily harm if they didn't testify on Johnson's behalf. If what the women have claimed is true—and as far as I'm concerned, Jenkins is innocent at this point—but if what they say can be proven, then Jenkins is in serious trouble." Candler sighed. "And there's another thing you should know. Carrie Barnes claimed she was so distraught over this, and so fearful for her safety, that she needed some form of personal protection. God only knows what she expected me to do."

Manly looked around the room. "Your Honor, I know that, in the eyes of the law, Jenkins is innocent until proven otherwise. But tell me something. Personally. Here in the privacy of your chambers. Do you believe the women?"

"Captain, I became a skeptic early in my adult life. I was a schoolteacher for a short while before I became a lawyer, and now a judge. Schoolteachers and judges learn quickly not to take what just anybody says at face value, whether it's a nine-year-old mischief maker or a witness in the courtroom. Or in my chambers. I have no idea whether these women are telling the truth. I need to hear Jenkins' side of the story. At this point, it's just *he said, she said,* and I haven't even heard the *he said* part yet. On the one hand, I have the word of two Negresses, both of whom, I am told, are known to congregate with questionable characters. These two women have impugned the reputation of a respected businessman, perhaps unjustly. But on the other hand, Jenkins may very well be guilty as charged. And if he is...well, we'll just see."

"Assuming the women *are* telling the truth, why do you think Jenkins would care about what happened to Christopher Johnson?" Manly asked.

"Mr. Manly, I'm not normally one to speculate, but since you asked, and since we're sitting here, just the two of us, let me ask *you* a question. Who accused Johnson in the first place? Who saw to it that he ended up being tried for Bass's murder?"

"Green Conn did."

"Precisely. And why do you think Conn did that? Does he *really* believe Johnson is the murderer, or was he hoping the Negro, when facing the prospect of a guilty verdict, would turn on Jenkins?"

"Knowing Conn, I wouldn't put anything past him," Manly said.

"So let's go back to your question. Why would Jenkins care about the fate of an old Negro drunkard? Well, perhaps it's as simple as one man trying to help out another man he believes is innocent. Listen Manly, if you were convinced Conn killed Bass, like Jenkins claims, and now Conn is trying to frame an innocent man, would you try to help get that man off?"

"Of course I would, but I would stop short of witness tam—"

"Of course you would. Now that's *one* explanation. But there's another. Let's assume Jenkins was somehow mixed up in Bass's murder. Or maybe somebody else was—somebody Jenkins wants to protect. And let's assume Johnson knows something about the whole affair—something Jenkins wants kept quiet." Candler looked over his shoulder at the door. Leaned in. Lowered his voice. "Listen, Manly. You've been around a long time. Have you ever known a nigger not to squeal if his back's against the wall? Johnson would say *anything* to avoid the gallows. 'I be tellin' you whatever you wanna heah, massa.' What would Jenkins do to keep Johnson from ever getting to that point?"

"Of his back being against the wall?"

"Yes. Of his back being against the wall. Why, he'd find witnesses who would help get Johnson off." Candler sat up straight. "But this is all speculation. I need to hear Jenkins' side of it."

"Are you planning to bring him in?" Manly asked.

"Well, he's absquatulated, as they say. We can't find hide nor hair of him. I sent the bailiff to get him. The bailiff looked all over the city. Spent most of the day yesterday looking. And into the evening."

"Jenkins is a traveling tobacco drummer. He never stays in one place for long. Maybe he's moved on."

"Perhaps. But we'll keep looking."

Manly left the courthouse, changed at the police station into the same street clothes he had worn when he visited Ella Bass, and headed straight to Crew Street—to the boardinghouse where Jenkins stayed when he was in town.

The proprietress met him on the porch. He asked for Jenkins.

"Are you a friend?"

"Of sorts, ma'am. It's important that I speak with him soon, for his own good." A twinge came over Manly. It was unlike him to stretch the truth so boldly. So blatantly.

"He's not here. He left in a mighty big hurry. Must've been four days ago." She looked across the yard toward the street. "Yes, I remember now. It was four days ago. I know because that's the day a new boarder came in. Earlier in the day. He moved into the room right next door to Mr. Jenkins."

She took her handkerchief from her dress pocket and wiped her forehead.

"Anyway, it was late when I heard a rustling. I had already retired for the night. I put on my robe and went to see what it was all about. There was Mr. Jenkins at the bottom of the stairs. He had three small trunks and a valise. He was having a mighty hard time lugging them to the door. He usually travels a lot lighter. He keeps a room here, you know, with all his things. Anyway, I said, 'Mr. Jenkins, where are you going?' That's when he told me he'd gotten a telegram and had to leave town." She grimaced. "He never received a telegram. Nobody came that day—or the day before—delivering a message. I never left the house either day. I would have known."

"Is it possible that Mr. Jenkins may have gone to the Western Union office earlier in the day and picked up a wire?"

"He could've. But why was he sneaking out in such an all-fired hurry—and so late in the evening? If he got a telegram earlier in the day, wouldn't he have said something? Instead of just trying to slip out like that after I'd gone to bed?" She shook her head. "It's just not in his nature to act that way. To tell you the truth, I'm worried about him."

"Did he let on where he was going?"

"No. Just that he'd probably be gone three weeks, maybe four."

"Did he give you any indication that he may have been in some kind of trouble?"

"With Mr. Jenkins it's always hard to say. He's a right peculiar fellow, with his dashing and noble airs and all. And the highfalutin words that come out of his mouth. He's a tad offish too, you know." She paused. "But he must have been in some kind of fix. You're the second one that's come looking for him. Yesterday a bailiff showed up. Said something about taking Mr. Jenkins in for questioning."

"Did you ask the bailiff what it was about?"

"I did, but he got huffy all of a sudden. He wouldn't let on anything."

"So what did you tell him?"

"The same thing I told you. Mr. Jenkins left in a mighty big hurry and I have no idea where he went."

"Did you tell the bailiff what you told me about the telegram and the trunks?"

"No, I didn't. I protect my boarders, you can be sure of that. And when the law comes looking for one of them, I'm not one to say much, especially when the one doing the asking gets all huffy. I was mad at Mr. Jenkins alright, but I'll still look out for him. Now, I've probably told *you* more than I should, but you seem like a nice enough fellow."

"I appreciate that. I have just one more question. How did Mr. Jenkins manage to leave with all that luggage?"

"An open-back carriage was waiting for him. It took him two trips to tote everything to the carriage. There was a driver, but I didn't get a good look at him. Or it may have been a woman. I couldn't tell. Except the driver was heavy set. I know that. And Mr. Jenkins' trunks were teetering on the back of the carriage when the driver took off. They looked like they might fall off any minute."

"Well, I'd best be on my way, ma'am. Much obliged for your time." The captain turned, descended the porch steps, and headed for the sidewalk.

She called out to him.

"Why, I don't think you ever told me your name."

"I'm Captain Manly, ma'am, with the police force."

THIRTY-THREE

WILLIAM MANLY

Ask the Old Bawd

FRIDAY MORNING, THE THIRTEENTH OF DECEMBER, THE day had dawned bleak and cold, and the clouds hung low. Manly set out to pay a visit to Delores Dampman. *She, of all people, may know where Jenkins has gone.*

At the Woodward Avenue side-by-side, he knocked on the door on the right side. No answer.

The other door opened. "Who are you looking for, Delores or George?"

"Delores, ma'am."

"She isn't here."

"Do you know if George is in?"

"He's not here either."

"Do you know when they'll be back?"

"As for her, I have no idea. She left about a week ago. We haven't seen her since."

"And her husband?"

"He's at work. He'll be back tonight, but he won't be good for nothing by the time he staggers home. And anyway, he doesn't know where she's run off to."

"Is there anybody who might know her whereabouts?"

"Ask the old bawd. She may know."

"The old bawd, ma'am?"

"Brumbelow. For the life of me, I don't understand why Delores Dampman hangs around with that dreadful tramp of a woman."

Manly's next visit was to Madam Brumbelow's brothel. He was about to knock when he caught sight of an eye staring at him through the peep hole.

"The companions aren't presentable yet." A woman's voice—the madam?—from beyond the closed door.

"I'm not seeking a companion, ma'am. I'm looking for a Mrs. Dampman. Delores Dampman. Is she here?"

"You just wait right there. I'll be back."

He looked at his watch. It was nine forty-five when the voice returned.

"Hold on." The door bolt disengaged. A young woman eased the door open and ushered him into the parlor. *Surely that's not the madam,* he thought.

"Make yourself at home. The lady of the house will be in to see you soon." She smiled coyly, tilting her head down but never losing eye contact. "And if you should decide to stay awhile, I'm sure you won't regret it. The ladies are just now fancying up."

He made himself at home as best he could. He sat in a wingback chair covered with vermilion velvet and adorned with decorative buttons of the same fabric. On the table next to the chair was a bronze filigree lamp. Its brocade shade, trimmed with fringe and glass bead strands, screamed frippery. Lying beside the lamp, printed on heavy card stock:

GENTLEMEN'S RULES
Treat the ladies with respect.
No profanity.
No sleeping.
Cuspidors are for tobacco only.
No discharging of firearms.
Payment for services in adva—.

An attractive woman of perhaps fifty entered the room. She wore a blue satin dress, tight at the waist, with leg of mutton sleeves. Her dark brown hair was pulled into a tight bun. A touch of carmine adorned her cheeks—not too overdone. Given his expectations after having met Delores Dampman, Manly was pleasantly surprised. And contrary to what the neighbor had said, she sure didn't look like an old bawd to him. He stood up to greet her.

She extended her hand. "Miss Frances Brumbelow. But please, call me Frannie. Everyone else does. And you?"

"Miss Brumbel—"

"Frannie, please."

"Miss Frannie…" Manly had difficulty uttering the word. His upbringing had taught him not to address a lady, even one of Miss Brumbelow's persuasion, by her first name. "…I'm William Manly, from the police department." He had debated whether to be so forthright from the start, but he decided, after the guilt pang from his little ruse on Crew Street, that honesty was in order. "I'm looking for Mrs. Dampman. I went to her house. She wasn't there, but her neighbor said you might know where she is."

"You must be talking about Mrs. Cheek. That's her landlady. I'll be honest. Even if I knew where Delores was—and I'm not saying I do—I don't reckon she'd talk to you. She's skittish about police, you know."

"I understand. It's just that she accepted me into her home two months ago. I was working on a murder case and she helped me out."

"Was it about that man Bass?"

"Yes, ma'am. I just need to ask her a few more questions. She was so accommodating before—"

"May I interest you in a cup of chamomile? Coffee? Or perhaps you'd like a little bub?"

"I'm fine, ma'am."

"Mr. Manly, will you be so kind as to wait here while I attend to a pressing matter? I won't be long."

Frances Brumbelow crossed the parlor and ascended the stairway at the far end of the room. Manly sat back down.

At ten fifty, he looked up to see a figure standing at the top landing. It was Mrs. Dampman. She was in a plain cotton house dress. He rose to greet her as she descended the stairs and crossed the room. She was barefoot. Her barely-brushed hair fell limply to her shoulders. As she neared, he noticed the slightest stain on her dress, midway down the front and slightly to her right. She sat in the chair nearest his. The lamp's glow illuminated her face, which was covered with heavy makeup, barely concealing the black and blue mottle on her left cheek. Her eye on the same side was puffy and crimson. Her wire-rimmed glasses sat heavy on the bridge of her nose, their massive lenses accentuating the pooling of blood below her iris. Both upper and lower lids were badly bruised.

"Mrs. Dampman, thank you for seeing me again. How are you doing?" He tried not to stare. Avoided bringing up the obvious.

"I've been better."

"Is there anything I can do for you?"

"You can lock up that tosspot of a man I'm married to. That's what you can do." She held out her arm with her palm facing up. Blue bruises and red scratch marks ran the length of her forearm. "See what he did to me? And my face. Look at my face. Can't you arrest the man on this?"

"When did it happen?"

"A week ago. He came home from work blundering and besotted. He accused me of having a dalliance with Herbert Jenkins. I stood my ground and said I'd done nothing of the kind. That's when he went into a rage. That's when he hit me. And that's when I left." She looked at her lap. "Mr. Manly, I blame your detectives for George thinking that. If I hadn't agreed to spend the day at that house on McDaniel Street, I don't think that idea would've ever entered his mind."

"Mrs. Dampman, I'm sorry you had to go through this, and I apologize if my men were somehow responsible for it. There's nothing I can do, after the fact, about what happened in that house, but as for your husband, I'll see what I can do about that." At first, given her condition and state of mind, Manly hesitated to mention her relationship with Jenkins. But her denial of a 'dalliance,' as she called it, couldn't go unchallenged. "Mrs. Dampman, I don't mean to pry, but I thought you and Mr. Jenkins were quite close."

"We are. But not that close. I've been known to have my little flirts and do the bear with him from time to time, but I would never go beyond that. Now Herbert, on the other hand. He'd jump in my bloomers in a second if I gave him the opportunity."

"Mrs. Dampman, are you aware Mr. Jenkins has gone missing?"

"Mr. Manly, I have no idea what you mean by gone missing. He's always on the road, running from one town to the next. That's how he makes his living."

"His landlady told me he left in a mad rush five days ago. She said it was unlike him to leave in such a hurry. Have you by any chance spoken with him since then?"

"Mr. Manly, did you come here to talk about Herbert? Because if you did, I don't want to get involved in his affairs any more than I already am. Now, are you going to do something about George for me?"

"I'll follow up. I promise. But Mrs. Dampman, I need to know when you last spoke with Mr. Jenk—"

"Listen, whatever you do, don't tell George I'm here. The madam took me in yesterday, battered and disheveled as I am. She didn't have to, you know. The last thing I want is for George to show up and cause trouble."

"I understand. I won't say a word. Now, about Mr. Jenkins."

"I saw him briefly before he left town, but I have no idea where he is or when he's coming back."

"Do you know why he might have left in such haste?"

"I don't know what you're talking about. He left town. There's nothing strange about that. I can't say why he may have left in a hurry—assuming he did."

Manly looked up to see Frances Brumbelow across the room. *How long has she been standing there?*

"If you would like to stay and visit with one of the ladies you're always welcome," the madam said. "You won't leave disappointed. But otherwise, I'll kindly ask you to leave. Mrs. Dampman has had a rough few days. She arrived quite late last night and has gotten little sleep. She needs her rest."

"I understand, Miss Brum… Miss Frannie." He turned to Delores Dampman. "As soon as I leave here, I'll go straight to your house and have a word with Mr. Dampman."

"I'd wait awhile. He won't leave work 'til five or six. And he won't go straight home anyway. He'll stop along the way and get tanked up first."

"Mrs. Dampman, please take care of yourself. And regarding that other issue, if you hear anything, let me know. It's important that I locate our man Jenkins."

Manly waited until well after nightfall before returning to Woodward Avenue. As he approached the side-by-side, a man who he guessed was Mrs. Dampman's husband was sitting in a straight back armchair on the porch, silhouetted by light from the window behind him. He held a lighted cigar in one hand and a bottle in the other.

"Are you George Dampman?"

The man looked up and squinted across the darkened yard. The moon was in the last stage of a waning crescent and the sky was clouded over. Other than the light from inside the house, only the nearby streetlamp provided any relief from the darkness.

"Who are you?"

"I'm Captain Manly, from the police department."

"What do you want?"

"Are you George Dampman?"

"So what if I am?"

"Mr. Dampman—I assume that's who you are—I met with your wife."

The man sprang to his feet, grabbing hold of the chair arm. He staggered to the front edge of the porch. "Where is she?"

"I'm not at liberty to say. But I *will* tell you this. I've seen the bruises about her. She's mighty roughed up. And she says you came home drunk. Hit her something awful."

"I did nothing of the kind. I may be known to down a pint or two. And I never claimed to lead a spotless life. But I can assure you, I didn't touch that woman." A slight smirk formed. "Hell, have you taken a good look at her? The woman's as big as me. I'd be scared to lay a hand on her."

"So you're telling me you *didn't* hit her?"

"*Of course* I didn't hit her. If that's what she told you, then she's downright batty. Listen, what did you say your name was again?"

"Manly."

"Listen, Mr. Manly. I may be under the sway of the bottle, but I know what I'm talking about." He sat back down. "Come up here and have a seat. I don't care what that church bell said, I'll tell you the *real* truth."

Manly climbed the steps and sat beside him.

"Want a swig, Mr. Manly?" Dampman extended the bottle.

"No, but thank you for the offer. Now Mr. Dampman, tell me, in *your* words, what happened."

"Well, last Saturday, she just up and leaves without saying a word. It's late in the afternoon. I'm out back chopping wood. She's inside doing something—God only knows what—I don't know what she does half the time. Anyway, I come in with an armful of firewood. I call out to her. She doesn't answer. I look all through the house. She's nowhere to be found."

"Did you go looking for her."

"Well, I waited a while. Finally, I went next door. Mrs. Cheek hadn't seen her. I went all up and down the neighborhood. Nobody knew anything. I thought somebody might have noticed her leaving—either alone or in the company of somebody else—

but that didn't turn up anything. I rode over to Miss Brumbelow's. She said she hadn't seen her in two or three days."

"Am I to assume she went away on foot?"

"Unless she left with somebody, she had to have left on foot."

"Did you consider going to the police?"

"I thought about it." He finished the last of the bottle and set it on the window ledge behind him. "Mr. Manly, let me tell you something. This isn't the first time she's done this—just run off without a word. If it's like the other times, she'll come back. I'm not traipsing all over town looking for her."

"Mr. Dampman, as a police officer, I'm in something of a dilemma. She says you hit her. And you say you didn't. Should I believe you over her? Could anyone, perhaps Mrs. Cheek, vouch for you?"

"I don't need anybody to vouch for me. I said I didn't touch that woman and that's that."

"Mr. Dampman, do you know a man named Herbert Jenkins?"

"I know who he is. That's about it. He's Delores's friend, not mine."

"Mrs. Dampman said you hit her in a fit of rage over Mr. Jenkins."

"I told you I didn't hit her, and that's all I'm going to say about that."

"OK, but about Mr. Jenkins. Do you have any reason to question her relationship with him?"

"I don't know what their relationship is, and to tell you the truth, I don't really care. She goes about her business and I go about mine. I can't tell her what to do. She wouldn't listen to me anyhow." He hesitated. "But if you see her again, tell her she needs to get back here and put some damned food on the table—not that what I say will make any difference."

Manly left not knowing which one to believe. Mrs. Dampman's bruises and scratches were right there, plain as day. But that didn't mean her husband did it. Manly couldn't just lock the man up on nothing more than a woman's accusation. And even if he did do it, was it provoked? He considered returning to the bordello that night but decided against it. His immediate interests lay elsewhere.

Manly returned home knowing he would have to deal with the Delores and George situation later. For now, he had a job to do. *Find Herbert Jenkins.*

THIRTY-FOUR

WILLIAM MANLY

Your Quarry is Missing

THE LETTER ARRIVED BEFORE DAYBREAK ON MONDAY, the sixteenth of December.

The message boy had come on a bicycle, scurried through the door, handed the envelope to the desk clerk, and left without saying a word.

"What is it?" Manly asked.

"It's a letter or something. It's addressed to Detective Conn."

"Give it to me." Manly grabbed the envelope. "And don't say a word about this to Conn—or to anybody for that matter. As far as you're concerned, you never saw it."

Manly returned to his office and shut the door.

Here he was, sitting at his desk, envelope in hand. He wasn't sure what had possessed him to yank it from the clerk like that. The only outside marking read:

Det. Thomas Greenberry Conn, City Police, Decatur Street

He picked up the faint scent of Florida Water. He held the letter opener in one hand, the envelope in the other. He hesitated momentarily. Then he carefully slit through the top crease, his hands unsteady. The rasp of metal against paper pierced the silence of the room. Inside was a single five-by-eight sheet, folded in half. He unfolded it.

16th December

My dear Green,

The truth may be stretched thin, but it never breaks, and it always surfaces above lies, as oil floats on water. The search for truth is a tortuous road, long and circuitous. Are you the watchman of the truth or the lie? I am not here to decide which, nor shall I judge. Those are things best left for the day of reckoning, when that day comes.

No, I am not here to judge you. I am here to goad you. Your mission to defeat your quarry is failing. And now your quarry is missing. I know a man who can help get you out of the fix you're in. But you must seek him out. You will find him at the exposition in nine days, at sunset. He will be standing under the Phoenix Wheel. He will wear a coat, green with black stripes, and a jet black Basque beret pulled low and tight. Let him know you in the dark from afar by the cadent call of the whip-poor-will. Follow him, but not too close. He will lead you to the far reaches of the grounds. Approach him then. He will know you by a single watchword, Eidgenossen. The sun will set. The sky will erupt.

Forever,
Your humble servant.

The note was written in simple, childlike script. Manly scratched his head.

Was it coincidental or providential, he wondered, that he had happened to be standing just inside the station house when the bicycle messenger arrived? What in his gut compelled him to grab the envelope, slice it open, read the letter? He walked back to where the clerk sat.

"I assume you told no one about this?"

"That's correct, sir. And I'll not tell a soul without your say-so. In fact, as you instructed, as far as I'm concerned I never saw it."

"And you won't even tell the chief?"

"Not even the chief."

"You're a good man."

"Is there a problem, sir?"

"It needn't concern you. It's just an internal matter."

Manly decided to wait a day or two to try to make sense of it all before saying anything to Connolly.

The following morning, the same clerk appeared at Manly's door. He handed the captain a second envelope and promptly left. Manly detected the same mild redolence of citrus and clove. Inside was another message in the same childlike script. This time with an odd cross-out.

17th December

My dear Green,

Jean ~~Valerie~~ Vallière. An unfortunate soul. Died at a pig market. They tied him to a thatch. The executioner held the torch. Lit the thatch. The odor of flesh was smelt for miles. It was August. Almost four centuries past. There was rain, but not enough to foil the immolation.

A rainy day in August and a man died.

Yours truly,

Your humble servant.

Manly laid the two notes side by side and studied them. He folded them, unfolded them, folded them again, returned them to their envelopes and carried them to Connolly's office.

"Manly, whoever wrote these letters, what do you think he means by your quarry is missing?"

"Look at the second letter. What does it say? A rainy day in August and a man died. I could be wrong, but I think that's a reference to Bass's murder. And who is Conn's quarry? Do you think it could be Jenkins? After all, Conn's been out to get him from the beginning. And now he's missing."

"But Jenkins has been out to get Conn."

"I know. That's the perplexing thing about all of this. Each man has accused the other. Frankly, I don't know what to believe. Maybe they were in on it together. Or maybe they're both innocent."

"Do you know that word toward the end of the first letter, Manly?"

"I don't, Chief."

Connolly shook his head. "Died at a pig market? Lit the thatch? Watchman of the truth or the lie? If you ask me, these letters were written by a lunatic. I can't make head nor tail of them. But stay on it. I'm sure you'll figure it out." The chief went back to his business.

Manly returned to his office. He found it a bit strange that Connolly never questioned why he had two letters in his possession that had been intended for Conn. But then again, the chief didn't trust the detective any more than Manly did. And after all, the envelopes had been addressed to Detective Conn, and they had not been marked Personal.

Two cryptic letters that made no sense. Assorted pieces of a jigsaw puzzle. *But I'm not sure they're even from the same puzzle.* Manly was particularly perplexed by the historical references and foreign words. The only person he could think of who might be able to help him understand it all, the only one in his circle who could claim any degree of erudition, was Judge Candler. He paid the judge a visit that afternoon.

"Vallière. That's French. And that other word looks German. Beyond that, I'm afraid I can't help you, but here's what I'll do."

Candler penned a short note and handed it to Manly.

"Here, take this introduction to my elder brother Warren. He's at Emory College. He's the man of letters in the family. Not I. I might've been a grammar school teacher once, and I damned well know the law, but that's pretty much the extent of my refinement."

Wednesday morning, the eighteenth, Manly boarded the seven fifteen local bound for Augusta.

He disembarked in Covington and entered the station. A man in a dark blue three-piece uniform and a leather-brimmed conductor's hat stood at the ticket window, on the public side, his arm resting nonchalantly on the counter. Manly asked him for directions to the campus. "It's a thirty-minute walk that way." The man pointed north across the tracks and past the water station. "Just keep straight. You'll come to the town of Oxford. The college will be to your left. You'll see a sign. You can't miss it."

The first person Manly met upon setting foot on the college grounds directed him to Seney Hall, a five-story brick Victorian Gothic building at the center of campus

"That's where the president is," the boy had told him.

The president? Judge Candler had failed to tell Manly that his brother Warren was the head of the college.

Manly walked into an imposing office filled floor to ceiling with books. Warren Candler greeted him just inside the door. *If a person saw the brothers together, he could easily mistake one for the other.* But as Manly soon realized, that was where the comparison ended. Candler the president was more refined, deliberative, choosing his words with care. And when he spoke, the words fell trippingly from his lips with a slight British timbre.

Manly handed Candler the letters, but only after gaining assurance that whatever the two men discussed would be held in the strictest confidence. Candler studied the second letter. He walked across the room, stepped onto a dark wood footstool, and pulled a massive tome from an upper shelf.

"Jean Vallière was a Frenchman. A Norman hermit, actually. They burned him at the stake at a Paris pig market in the early sixteenth century. Whoever wrote that letter knows a little history. I would venture that there are not a dozen people in the entire state who have ever heard of Vallière."

"Why was he killed?"

"They labeled him a heretic. He was a disciple of Martin Luther. The Catholics did him in."

"And what about that word at the end of the other letter, eegendosen?"

"It's *Eidgenossen*. It has a long *I* sound. And the emphasis is on the third syllable. It is an obscure German word. It refers to a group of confederates bound together by a common oath. While it is usually associated with Swiss cantons during the Middle Ages, I suppose it could also apply to the oath Vallière and his Protestant compatriots took."

Or perhaps a modern-day pact between coconspirators, Manly thought. *Could there be hidden references in the letters that only the intended recipient and his fellow oath-takers would understand? Is this whole thing bigger than just one man?*

"It's an odd word to put in a letter," Candler said. "And the mention of a watchword is curious. Are we to assume the word Eidgenossen is a code or password of some sort, a sign of recognition between two people who are meeting for the first time?"

"That thought crossed my mind."

"Mr. Manly, this person Green—is he someone you know well?"

"Better than most people, I'd say."

"Is *he* a heretic?"

"If by heretic you mean is he a nonconformist, I would say so. But if there's a religious connotation to your question, I have no idea. Beyond that, I'd rather not go into detail about him."

"The salutation and the close suggest your letter writer here is a friend of this man Green. Is that the way you interpret it?"

"Perhaps, but it could also be nothing more than a ruse."

"And the crossed-out word. As I said before, the letter writer knows more history than most people. I find it odd that he would have misspelled Vallière's name and had to correct it. The handwriting, too, seems out of character for someone of his literacy."

"Unless the intent was to throw the reader off—to ensure the writing wouldn't be recognizable."

Candler traced his jawline with his hand. "One other thing comes to mind, but I doubt it has any relevance to what you're dealing with here. I bring it up only because of Vallière's alleged heresy, and the fact that the word Eidgenossen is believed by some to be the root of the name of another group of branded heretics."

"What group is that?"

"They were a sect of French Calvinists who were influenced by Martin Luther. They originated in France, but they scattered throughout Europe. In the French Wars of Religion, in the latter half of the sixteenth century, members of the Basque region were the ones who led them to battle. There may be a connection to the Basque beret reference. They came to America beginning in the mid-sixteenth century and continuing through the seventeenth. It was all part of a great diaspora. Their descendants can still be found in America. They settled primarily in five states. They were called Huguenots."

THIRTY-FIVE

WILLIAM MANLY

Lit the Thatch

MANLY AWOKE AFTER A FIVE-HOUR NIGHT OF UNNERVING fits and starts. He rolled over to face Eunice. She was dead to the world. It always impressed him how she could will herself to a deep, nightlong slumber under any conditions and no matter what cares might have possessed her during the day. *I should be so fortunate.* He fumbled for his watch, which he had placed within reach on the nightstand. It was twenty 'til four.

He lay awake, plumbing the depths of his memory in search of a clue, anything to help him make sense of the letters. But nothing came. He knew from experience that, when he needed to remember something important, he was most successful if he got his mind off of it.

He stumbled to the kitchen. He stoked the fire in the stove and put on a pot of coffee. When it was piping hot, he poured himself a cup—strong, syrupy thick and unadorned—just the way he liked it. He would go through a third of the cup before the early morning fog of *awake but not fully awake* lifted. Yesterday's newspaper lay on the kitchen table across from where he sat. It seemed not to have been touched since Eunice had placed it there. He picked it up and struggled to focus on the front page. *The eyes always seem to trail the head on mornings like this,* he thought. Dominating the news were a plea for enforcement of the Monroe Doctrine in Venezuela—with calls for war with England if that's what it took—and violent labor riots in Philadelphia. *Our little troubles pale in comparison.* Further in the paper, the story of a young lady accidentally shooting and killing her lover in Fort Valley. *Accidentally? What a shock that must have been—for the lady and her lover!* On page six, in the ETCHED AND SKETCHED column, an article about French plans for a world exposition four years out, an effort to outdo the Columbian exposition in Chicago just two years past and the Atlanta exposition currently underway, and an apparent response to rumors of Germany's plans for a world's fair. A Chicago fair commissioner was quoted, "France appears to be in the position of a man who has bitten off more than he can chew." *Perhaps I have more in common with the French than I realized.* Manly let out a hushed chuckle.

He otherwise would have said the revelation came to him out of thin air, but it must have been the article's reference to the French and the expositions.

The words straight from Jenkins' mouth, as the two men had sat on the boardinghouse porch almost three months ago, sprang to mind. *A filthy Huguenot. That's what he is. No better than a Jew or a Freemason.* At the time, Manly hadn't paid enough attention to what Jenkins had said. Over the past few months, he had grown accustomed to the tobacco salesman's inflated and dramatic tongue. Even so, the words must have lingered somewhere in Manly's subconscious, waiting for the right time to come alive.

Manly had heard about Huguenots before, but he knew nothing about them—that is, until he met with Warren Candler. Jenkins' comment about Jews didn't surprise him in the least. But come to think of it, Jenkins' reference to Freemasons did strike him as odd. After all, the city was crawling with them. And some of the most upstanding members of the community were probably of their persuasion. He suspected Judge Candler was one. And Mayor King. Maybe even the chief. Or Commissioner Branan. They kept to themselves, with their secret handshakes and passwords and all. And their clandestine rites. But he knew they were all around.

Manly remembered what else Jenkins had said about Mureau that day. Called him a crook. Said he and Conn were *birds of a feather. Stay away from him if you know what's best for you.* Manly had certainly done a good job of staying away from him, but not for lack of trying to find the man.

Manly had kept the letters with him wherever he went. He padded silently into the bedroom, retrieved them from the coat pocket of his uniform, and returned to the kitchen. He took the letters out of their envelopes, unfolded and reread them. *Eidgenossen. A black Basque beret pulled low and tight. You'll find him at the exposition.* Could the pieces of the puzzle be coming together after all? Had a secret meeting between Lem Mureau and Green Conn been arranged? And why? And by whom? *My dear Green.* A close friend of Conn's? A coconspirator? Were Mureau and Conn perhaps mixed up in the same tangled thicket, one whose creeping tendrils extended all the way to Baker Bass's death?

Manly knew of only two people who had had personal contact with Mureau—Herbert Jenkins and Delores Dampman. Jenkins was missing. And the woman was marginally cooperative.

He would pay her another visit. But before he did, he had to decide how to deal with her accusations against her husband. *Ma'am, I can't just take your word against his. Ma'am, you've suffered something awful, but he says he didn't do it. Ma'am, do you know of anybody who can back you up?* If he didn't have a good explanation for why he hadn't hauled George off to jail, an explanation she would accept, then she would never open up to him—not about Jenkins—and not about Mureau. And to meet with her again, he'd have to get past *Frannie the Gatekeeper.*

Manly had six days, before the sunset tryst at the exposition, to meet with Delores Dampman, find Herbert Jenkins and Lem Mureau, and make sense of whatever was to happen on Christmas evening—yes, Christmas evening, of all nights.

Do I tell the chief what I know? Do I tell Green Conn? Do I turn the letters over to Conn with a mea culpa—'yes, Green, I opened your mail?' Or do I keep quiet?

He waited until sunup before dressing and going to the station house.

"Have you seen any more letters for Detective Conn?" he asked the clerk.

"No sir. Just the two."

"Anything else? Messages? Telegrams?"

"No sir."

"Is it possible more arrived when you weren't around?"

"I told the other clerks to give me anything that came in by messenger or mail. And to keep quiet about the whole thing. I told them I had instructions straight from you. Don't worry, you can trust them. They won't say anything."

On the afternoon of the nineteenth, Manly summoned the mettle to return to the brothel, this time in uniform. If Delores Dampman gave him any trouble about her husband not being arrested, he was prepared to tell her the same thing he had told George—that, as a police officer, he faced a dilemma. He had two people, each accusing the other, with no identifiable way to determine who was telling the truth. The courts wouldn't let him lock either of them up without more evidence than that. In other words, he opted for the my-hands-are-tied defense.

He climbed the steps onto the porch. He didn't have to wait for the voice through the closed door. Instead, the door opened to Madam Brumbelow standing at the threshold.

"Come in Mr. Manly." She ushered him into the parlor and to a chair at a far corner of the room. She eased into the chair beside him. Unlike before, the parlor was populated with several patrons, attended to by the madam's coterie of charmers. He recognized a few of the men in the room, but they kept to themselves, never making eye contact. Perhaps it was his uniform.

In the opposite corner of the room slumped a man he swore was Officer Moncrief, the night shift policeman. The man's face was buried in a newspaper, obscuring all but the top third of his head. Manly sensed the man was trying to hide from him. But those bushy eyebrows and unkempt hair. And that slump. A dead giveaway. The ladies were ignoring him.

"I assume you're here for Mrs. Dampman."

"That's right. Is she available?"

"Mr. Manly. She isn't here. She left three days ago. Late in the afternoon. I have no idea where she went, or with whom."

"Did you have any inkling she would be leaving? Or did she just up and go?"

"She just up and left."

"Did she go back to George?"

"I seriously doubt it." The madam hesitated. "Let me say this. She told me there was no way she would go back to him. But then again, with Delores you never can tell."

"Does she have the wherewithal to get by on her own?"

"She isn't on her own. I promise you that. She's with somebody."

"Do you have any idea who?"

"Well, any other time I would have suspected that man Jenkins. But she claimed she hadn't seen him in over a week and had no idea where he was."

"I'd like to better understand Mrs. Dampman's comings and goings from the time she left the Woodward Avenue house—let's see, I believe George said that was on Saturday, the seventh—and when she showed up here five days later. You have no idea where she disappeared to, is that right?"

"Mr. Manly, there's something I need to tell you. Mrs. Dampman showed up twice asking me to take her in. The first time was late on the afternoon of the seventh. I let her stay here. George came around looking for her. I told him I hadn't seen her. She stayed until late in the afternoon the following day. She left and I didn't see her after that."

"Until she showed up on the twelfth, battered and bruised?"

"That's correct."

"I have one more question. Have you ever heard of a man named Mureau—Lem Mureau?"

"I can't say I have. Is he a friend of hers?"

"Let's just say their paths have crossed."

That evening, Manly went back to the Woodward Avenue side-by-side. Neither George nor Mrs. Cheek had seen Delores Dampman since she left on the seventh. George said he'd just as soon give up on her as make an effort to run around after her—wherever she was.

The following morning, the twentieth, Manly returned to the Crew Street boardinghouse.

"So you show your face here again, Mr. Policeman," the proprietress said with a jeer.

"Yes, ma'am. When I was here before I should have told you right away who I was. I apologize for not doing that."

"Like I told you then, when the law comes looking for one of my boarders, I keep my mouth shut."

"I understand. And I know your boarders are grateful for that," Manly said. "I'm not looking to cause any trouble—for Mr. Jenkins or for you. I'm actually here to help him. It's for his own good that I speak with him as soon as possible." The same twinge as before came over him.

"So he's not in trouble?"

"No ma'am. In fact, I think he can help us find a missing person who may be tangled up in some way in a murder case. That would be good for him and for us. Just think, one of your boarders could come out a hero in all of this. Wouldn't you want that? Wouldn't he?"

"And you swear that if I help you it'll be good for Mr. Jenkins?"

"Yes ma'am." *I hope the good Lord doesn't strike me down and send me straight to Hell.*

She was closemouthed.

But with a heavy dose of cajoling, she opened up. "How well do you know him?" she said. "He's a touch fluky, you know."

"I know that. That's what makes him so interesting."

She wiped her brow just like the last time. "He turned back up, but not for long," she said. "Came in here last Saturday, sashayin' right bodaciously like he does. All he had was his own self and his valise. Stayed 'til Monday night and he was gone again." She put her hands on her hips and shook her head. "That man beats all. But you can't help but like him, with his charm and everything."

"What did he do when he was here?"

"He seemed out of sorts. A little on edge. Came and went a lot. I gave him the Christmas postcard that came in the mail while he was away."

"The postcard?"

"Yes. It was from a man with a French-sounding name."

"Was the name by any chance Mureau, ma'am?"

"That's it. Mureau. I don't make a habit of reading other people's mail, but it was a postcard, after all. It was hard not to read it. It had a right pretty snowy holiday scene on the front and a note on the back."

"What did it say?"

"It said—let me think—it said, 'Wishing you well. I hope your Christmas will be as eventful as mine.'"

"What did Jenkins do when you gave it to him?"

"He just stuffed it in his pocket...oh, and he asked me if I had seen who it was from. And if I had read it. I didn't lie to him."

"Do you remember—did it have a return address?"

"It didn't."

"Did you happen to notice the postmark?"

She shook her head.

"Is there anything else you can tell me about what Jenkins did while he was here? Did he say anything about where he'd been?"

"Nothing that I recall."

"Did you tell him I had come looking for him last Thursday?"

"Of course I did. Like I told you before, I look after my boarders."

"And how did he react when you told him?"

"He didn't react at all. Just thanked me and went about his business."

"You said he left Monday night. How did he leave?"

"Well, it was late. Just like the last time. But this time it was a new moon, so there wasn't much light in the sky. As far as I could tell, though, it looked like the same carriage and driver as before. They took off and that was that."

I hope your Christmas will be as eventful as mine.

Manly decided not to tell Conn about the letters and the planned encounter at the exposition. He would go there instead. Unless Manly was headed down a dead-end trail, he would finally meet this Lem Mureau fellow. If his suspicions were right, Mureau knew something and was prepared, on his own, to share it with Conn. Either that, or whoever wrote the letters had contrived a meeting between the two men. Whatever was to happen Christmas night, it could be a turning point.

Manly left Crew Street and went to the station house.

The desk clerk ran up to him as he passed through the door. "Sir, you need to see Chief Connolly right away."

"About what?"

"He's plenty upset."

"Do you know why?"

"Sir, I have no idea."

"Still not a word to anyone about the letters, right?"

"That's right, sir. Not a word."

"And nothing new?"

"No sir. Nothing new."

Manly went to Connolly's office at a normal pace. *I'll take my own sweet time. No need to overreact.* Connolly sat at his desk. Cap Joyner, the chief fire engineer, sat across from him. Connolly was visibly shaken. Every drop of blood had drained from his face. Beads of perspiration collected on his forehead.

"Have a seat Manly. Are you aware of a fire at the exposition shortly after sundown this past Monday?"

"No sir." Manly had been preoccupied all week with the letters and the search for Jenkins and Mureau.

"I didn't think so." He looked over at Joyner. "Cap, why don't you tell Manly here what you told me?"

"Well, as the chief said, there was an incident at the exposition. A thatch hut in the Mexican Village caught on fire. It's a miracle we managed to put it out before it burned to the ground, but we had a brigade nearby." Joyner looked at Connolly. "I told the chief here how proud I am of your men. They descended on the village from all over the exposition grounds as soon as they got word of it. We didn't think much about the fire—they happen, you know— until we discovered, just yesterday morning, an empty kerosene can in a nearby trash barrel. The guards and the police say they saw nothing suspicious in the area, but my men are convinced it was arson. The village butts right up against Piedmont Avenue. It would have been easy for somebody to start the fire and then slip away through the fence. In fact, the police pointed out a large hole in the fence not far from where my men found the can."

"Over the past twenty-four hours, this whole thing has gotten out of hand," Connolly said. "Manly, do you remember when that Mexican army man, General Gutierrez, spoke at the exposition back in October?"

"Vaguely, sir, but I wasn't there."

"I didn't *think* you were." Connolly looked back at Joyner. "The captain here seems to have been out of touch these past few months." He continued. "Well *I was* there. And I remember what he said. He said, 'I had never dreamed that so close to our border we had such a friendly nation.' Well, do you know what, Manly? As soon as the word *arson* got out yesterday morning, the news traveled all the way to Washington. Ambassador Romero sent a telegram to the governor. And now the mayor's gotten involved. It seems the Mexican government is claiming it was an outright act of provocation. It doesn't help that lynchings of greasers in this country, especially here in the South and down around the border, are second only to those of Negroes. The ambassador demanded an apology—and an investigation. The governor apologized by telegram. The mayor apologized. But do you realize how bad this looks for us? And it couldn't come at a worse time. You know I'm already on the outs with the commissioners and, by all accounts, the press and half the city."

" I do, sir."

"Well, get your men on it. I want answers."

Manly walked to his office.

The executioner held the torch. Lit the thatch.

THIRTY-SIX

WILLIAM MANLY

Cold as a Wagon Tire

A MILLION DROPS OF RAIN POUNDED THE TIN ROOFTOP. The water outside pressed against the windows, aching to come in. Tap-tap-tapping on the glass. The glooming, the incessant clamor, the closing in made William Manly's little house even smaller than it was. The sky was stygian and somber. *How could something so clear, so pure as water make the clouds so dark and foreboding,* Manly thought.

It was Friday the twentieth. Farmers' Day at the exposition. Grangers and plowmen and harvesters would be descending on Atlanta from all over the state and beyond. Most days, they would have welcomed the opening up of the heavens, but not today. His brother John, the only one who had stayed behind in Anderson, or Travelers Rest, or wherever he found himself, might come for the occasion, but only if he had elevated himself to tilling his own well-worked soil. Manly regretted that, with the passing of time, he and John had not kept in closer touch. He hoped his little brother had left behind the sharecropper days of their youth.

His attention returned to the deluge outside and to the challenges that lay before him. He had five days to make sense of everything. Two cryptic dispatches. A secret rendezvous at the fair, one he was not even supposed to be party to. A meeting intended, so it seemed, for Green Conn and someone he, Manly, had never met. And now, an arsonist to contend with. He was sure they were all related somehow. And they hearkened to Baker Bass's death. *A rainy day in August and a man died.*

Maybe, just maybe, if he could find the one who lit the thatch, he would begin figuring out how to make those pieces of the puzzle fit instead of jamming them together and ending up with a blasted mess. But time was running out.

Today he would brook the elements and set off to the exposition grounds. Talk to people working at the Mexican Village. Ask around. *Did you see anything strange Monday night? Anything untoward? Anybody who seemed out of place? Loitering? Lurking?* He would leave the detectives and the rank-and-file police out of it. At least for now. Too many unknowns, fingers pointing every which way, including to Conn and the bureau.

Manly wasn't sure how easy it would be to find an hombre willing to talk—or who could even speak enough English to be understood. He knew from the newspaper that they had brought most of the Mexican Village workers up here from beyond the Rio Grande, bedecked them in their costumes and sombreros, hitched them up with burros and ropes and accordions and castanets, taught them just enough words to get by, and told them to entertain the fairgoers with their smiles and theatrics. And as for Manly, he didn't know a lick of Spanish. But usually if you search hard enough you can find the boss, the tall one with the half-smoked cheroot and the Stetson. And he will likely speak suitable English, albeit with a south-of-the-border cant.

He found the man alright. Leaning against a reconstructed three-quarter-size coffee bean drying barn at the edge of the miniature coffee plantation. Just under the overhang so as to avoid the torrent. And sure enough, he held the fag end of a cheroot in his stubby hand, his face lost in a cloud of blue-grey smoke, a rain-soaked Stetson with an exceptionally wide brim sitting low and cocked forward. Manly, in an India rubber raincoat but drenched to the gills, introduced himself to the man, who said his name was Alejandro.

Alejandro had not been on the grounds when the fire broke out, but he knew all about it. As for anything strange that may have happened that night, aside from the fire itself, he knew nothing.

"Come with me," he said, and they entered the barn. Inside, the room smelled of sweet hay and grass. A worker was spreading green coffee beans onto large metal pans. Alejandro approached the man and spoke to him. Manly heard the words but understood nothing.

"Señor, ¿puedo hablar contigo por un momento?"

The man looked up. Nodded.

"¿Viste algo extraño aquí el lunes por la noche, cuando estalló el incendio?"

"No. Estuve trabajando en el granero toda la noche."

Alejandro interpreted. "I asked him if he had seen anything strange on the night of the fire. He said he had seen nothing. He had been working in the drying barn all evening."

"Pero ve a ver a Pedro, el maestro de los burros. Él puede saber algo," the man said.

"He says we should see the man with the donkeys."

Manly followed Alejandro through the rain to find Pedro, the ersatz donkey master. Maybe he had seen something. Heard something. They found him hunched with his asses under the eave of an outbuilding at the edge of the Mexican Village.

At first the man was reluctant to talk. "He doesn't want to get involved," Alejandro said. "I think he knows something. Let me see if I can get him to open up."

Manly listened as Alejandro spoke in a near whisper. At one point a scowl came over the man. He stood up and spit in the dirt. Jerked the donkeys' ropes as if to leave.

Then Alejandro raised his voice to a bark.

"¿Quieres que te envíe de vuelta a Monterrey con nada más que la camisa que llevas puesta? Lo haré si no hablas."

"What did you say to him?" Manly asked.

"I told him if he didn't talk I'd send him back home with nothing but the shirt on his back."

The man relented. He said he had seen someone throw something in a barrel soon after the fire broke out—the same barrel where a fireman later found the empty kerosene can. Everyone had been in a frenzy. People were running around agog. The donkeys had been jittery from the fire, so he led them to the edge of the village. That's when he saw the out-of-place stranger. He couldn't make out much in the dark, but he saw them run over to the barrel and then to the big hole in the fence. They disappeared through the fence and that was that.

"Could you ask him if he could tell what they were wearing?" Manly said.

"¿Podrías decir lo que llevaba la persona?"

"Apenas podía decirlo, pero parecía un poncho encapuchado. O tal vez un rebozo y una capucha," the man said. "Fue algo ondulante."

"Do you know what a poncho is?" Alejandro asked.

Manly nodded.

"How about a rebozo?"

"I don't know what that is," Manly replied.

"It's like a cross between a large scarf and a shawl. They're common in Mexico. As far as the man could tell in the dark, the person was wearing something like a hooded poncho—or perhaps a rebozo and a hood. But he said it was billowy."

"Ask him if the person was white or colored?"

"¿Era blanco o negro?"

"Estoy bastante seguro de que no eran negros, pero no soy positivo. Aunque estaba oscuro," the man replied.

"Not a Negro. At least he doesn't think so, but it was dark," Alejandro said.

The rain had abated somewhat. Manly and Alejandro roamed the village looking for others who may have seen something. But no one had—or perhaps they demurred.

Manly inspected the hole in the fence. It was large, about three feet across and almost two feet high. It looked as if someone had cut through the flimsy metal mesh to form an L-shaped slit and then pulled the mesh back. It surprised Manly that none of the exposition officials had noticed it or, if they had, they hadn't bothered to repair it.

At least the poor peasant won't be sent home with just his shirt, Manly thought as he left the village.

Manly ascended the hill past the main gate to the Fire Building, just up the way from the Mexican Village. Three arched entryways set off the front of the building. The one on the left was closed. The center one led to the exhibits of fire paraphernalia, hoses and such. He entered through the one on the right side, which was reserved for the working firefighters assigned to protect the exposition. He spoke with the man who had discovered the kerosene can. He met with several others who had rushed to the village when the fire broke out. None of them claimed to have seen anything out of the ordinary. No one coming or going who seemed out of place. No one leaving through the fence. But they were busy putting out a fire, not looking for a suspect.

Manly asked to see the can. It was a dull red. With KEROSENE OIL emblazoned in block, shaded letters on two arced lines that created an oval—with a small horseshoe printed in the center. He held the spout to his nose. The pungent petroleum odor was unmistakable. He shook the can. Swish. There was still a small amount of liquid in the bottom.

Outside the grounds, Manly inspected the area around the fence hole. There were no footprints or any grazing of the grass and dirt to indicate someone had scrambled through. Not that surprising, since Monday had been a clear, dry day. He looked up and down Piedmont Avenue. The trees and shrubs lining the street would have made it easy for someone to get away unnoticed. And it would have been dark. A perpetrator leaving on foot would likely have headed south toward Tenth Street so as to avoid the main gate. If on horseback or in a wagon, they could have taken off either way and been far gone within minutes.

Manly reentered through the main gate and walked toward the police outpost, inside the Auditorium along the western edge of the Grand Plaza. The police assigned to the exposition had been relegated twelve-hour, eight-to-eight shifts due to recent force reductions. Manly looked at his watch. It was six minutes after ten.

Whoever is around this morning, he thought, *should have been on the grounds when the fire broke out.*

He entered the police outpost through the small, unmarked side door that he reckoned had been designed and situated so as not to attract attention. Four officers were playing cards at a square folding table across the room. *Whist? Poker? And two hours into their shift?*

One of the men looked up with a start. He thumped the table with his fingers. The other three looked up. All four stood and faced the captain as he crossed the room.

Manly decided to let the card playing pass. He could address that later. He had bigger issues to deal with.

"Were you officers here when the fire started Monday night?"

"We were, all four of us," one of the men responded, "plus a dozen or so others."

"Were you there when the fireman found the kerosene can—the one in the barrel?"

"No, sir. But they showed it to us later. We didn't have anything to do with finding it."

"Did you see anything out of the ordinary, either before, during, or after the fire?" *Or did you just go back to playing your little card game and forget about it?* Manly thought.

The four shook their heads.

Another one of the men spoke. "It was just like any other day. Oscar here…" He motioned to the man across the table. "…and I had been close by, on The Terrace working over a plug-ugly, when we saw flames shooting up at the other end of the midway. Lucky for the thug. We let him go and took off in the direction of the blaze. Oscar here can't run too good 'cause of an ornery bunion, so it took us a little while to get there. By the time we did, the hose men was doing a good job of putting it out." He paused. "You know, as we were heading that way, I had a notion it might have been that thatch hut. Who builds a grass shack like that anyway, knowing any little spark could set it off? One of them no'count foreigners, I guess. But back to what you asked me, we didn't see anything queerish. As far as I know, none of us did. If anybody had, I'd know it."

"What about the hole in the fence?"

The first man spoke. "I'm the one that saw it and pointed it out. But that was later. After they found the can."

"Did it look like someone may have crawled through it? Did you see anything that would have suggested that?"

"I couldn't rightly tell. But they could've."

"Did anybody call a detective? About the hole in the fence?"

"Not as I know. I sure didn't. The fire was out by the time I saw the hole. I just went back to doin' what I'd been doin'—lookin' for trouble on the midway."

Before leaving the exposition, Manly hailed a Herdic buggy, one of several one-horse, two-wheeled cabs provided by the organizers to carry people around the fairgrounds. He instructed the driver to take him to the Phoenix Wheel. The buggy wove in and out as the man swerved to avoid the crowds, careened around the Grand Plaza to Lake Clara Meer and across the bridge separating the two lagoons, past the Negro Building, around the Train Shed, and to the base of the wheel.

"Wait here," Manly said. He walked around the base of the wheel. *This is where he'll be,* he thought. *I'm to follow him, but I have to make out like I'm Conn.* He looked westward down the midway. *I'll approach from that direction, from down near the animal arena. I'll keep my distance.* He hopped back on the Herdic. "Head that way…" He pointed toward the animal arena. "…and then back to the main gate."

Manly decided to visit several stores that afternoon. Perhaps someone could shed light on the kerosene can. Where might it have been purchased? If Manly could find that out, he might be able to determine who bought it.

Some merchants recollected having sold cans fitting the description. Some didn't. Some had kept records of the buyers, while most hadn't. He headed for home that evening with a list of about a dozen names. None of them stood out. He would go to the office tomorrow morning and search for them in the city directory.

He arrived home well after dinner time to a table set for two and a pot roast warming on the stove. Eunice—*bless her*—had waited all evening for him, having no idea when he'd show up.

He went to the office mid-morning Saturday and headed straight to the records room. He pulled the city directory from the shelf and began thumbing through it. He thought back to two months earlier when he'd done the same thing—only that time he had been looking for Lem Mureau.

He pulled the list of names from his coat pocket.

Frank B. Lippitt, 20 Morrison Av

Captain Marshall, 8 Walker's Alley

Caleb Dye, 145½ Auburn Av

Emmet R Edwards, 28 Tatn—

"Captain Manly." It was Moncrief. Standing in the doorway. Shifting his weight from foot to foot. Shaking like a leaf. "Captain Manly."

"What is it Moncrief? And what are you doing here at this time on a Saturday?"

"Captain Manly. A call just came through—from a call box. I took it."

"Why did *you* take it? There should be a clerk at th—"

"He'd stepped away. He must have had to take care of a privy need. There's a body, Mr. Manly. A body. Just like before."

"Settle down and stop quivering for a minute, Moncrief. What are you talking about? What body? And what do you mean 'just like before?'"

"They found a body. Fourteenth and Juniper. Shot in the head the same way. Just like that man Bass. The one whose killer's still runnin' around loose." Moncrief grimaced. "But Mr. Manly. This one was already dead when they found him."

"Moncrief, is the officer still at the call box?"

"Yes sir. He's waiting for somebody to call him back."

"Call him back. Tell him, whatever he does, not to let an ambulance or a hearse take the body away until I get there." Manly returned the directory to the shelf and placed the list of names in his pocket. "And Moncrief, you never told me what you're doing here."

Moncrief hung his head. "Captain, if you want to know the truth, I came by here at eight, right after I got off my night shift—

just for a few minutes, I thought. I went to the locker room to change into my street clothes and do you know what happened? I sat down in the chair and was taking off my boots—when I fell asleep—slumped right there in the chair. I woke up, finished changing my clothes, and was walking out the door when I heard the call come in."

"Maybe you're not getting enough sleep, Thaddeus. Could it be you're spending too much free time at Madam Brumbelow's?" Manly said as he walked out the door, not lingering long enough to register Moncrief's reaction.

Manly mounted his horse and set off at a brisk lope. Decatur Street to Courtland. Right on Courtland. North fifteen blocks to the half-block offset at North Avenue, where Courtland became Juniper. North another thirteen blocks to Fourteenth Street. By the time he arrived, crowds had gathered. Two officers stood nearby. But there was no body. Manly dismounted and approached the officers.

"Where is the body?"

"They took it away. To the county morgue. He was cold as a wagon tire. Probably been that way for a few hours by the time we found him. He was over in the bushes there where no one would have seen him unless they were looking hard. My partner and I walked by and just happened to see a hand sticking out—all bluish-whitish like."

"But I asked that he not be disturbed until I could get here. Did you not get those instructions?"

"No sir. I waited at the call box but nobody called back, so I went ahead and summoned the coroner."

"What can you tell me about the man?"

"Well, he didn't have much in his possession when we found him. No watch. No money. No identification. Not even an empty wallet. It looked like a robbery gone bad to me."

"Did he have any identifying characteristics? What did he look like? What was he wearing?"

"He was a right distinguished looking fellow, with dark hair and a little goatee-like beard. He had a mole right here." The policeman pointed to his neck, on his right side just below his jawbone. "And he had acquired a new hole in his head, right between the eyes."

"And what was he wearing?"

"He was in a three-piece suit. Looked expensive. We searched all around for anything that might help identify him. All we found was a beret. About three feet from where he was. Between him and the curb."

"A beret?"

"Yes, a beret. Charcoal grey. With a label inside. All I remember is the word Paris. There may have been the name of a shop or something, but I can't recall."

Manly remounted his horse and retraced his path, this time not at a lope, but at a lively gallop.

Could it be Mureau? he thought as he sped down Juniper toward the Pryor Street morgue. *Will I show up for a little duet Tuesday night only to find it's become a solo…because the other invitee is dead with a newly-acquired hole between his eyes?*

THIRTY-SEVEN

WILLIAM MANLY

Desires of Ruttish Men

THE COUNTY MORGUE WAS TUCKED AWAY IN THE basement of the courthouse building at Hunter and Pryor, three floors below Coroner Paden's office. While it was not uncommon, as with Baker Bass, for bodies never to make it there, especially if their identity and proximate cause of death were known, it was an almost certain destination otherwise. Such was the case with the body found earlier that morning at Fourteenth and Juniper Streets.

Manly approached the Pryor Street morgue entrance. He descended the four steps leading from sidewalk level to the exterior door. The tiny sign on the door read JACKSON PADEN - COUNTY CORONER, and below that, PRIVATE. He turned the knob. The door was locked. He knocked lightly. An older man, gaunt, ill-shaven, and in a full-length leather bib smock, opened the door no more than three inches. Apparently recognizing Manly, he ushered him into the room.

The morgue was cold, damp, and dim, save for the incandescent light hanging over a pine table at the far end of the room. The rough granite walls imparted a dungeonlike feel. A body, covered with a white cotton sheet, lay on the table. Three men, one of them the coroner, gathered around the body. Manly watched a lone cockroach meander down the nearest wall and engage in a random crawl across the floor toward them. The body lay in a shallow metal pan. Two bluish-grey feet extended beyond the sheet.

Manly approached the table. He saw another man standing in the shadows about ten feet away, holding a dark belly western fedora. Manly recognized the man—and the hat—immediately.

"Conn, for mercy's sake! What are you doing here?"

"What am I doing here? I'm doing my job. What are you doing here, Captain? Aren't you supposed to be out there ordering us grubs around like you usually do instead of gawking over a dead man?"

Manly ignored Conn's taunt. "It's Saturday. How did you even find out about this?"

"From Thaddeus Moncrief—when I stopped by the station house. I came right over as soon as he told me. I figured they'd bring the body here."

"And what do you think you can do—beyond getting in the way? Do you think you know this man—or who shot him? Or are you just nosing around again—looking for some new scheme to cook up?"

"I'm a detective, sir. That's what I do. Nose around. That's what you pay me to do, in case you've forgotten." He stared at Manly. "A paltry sum, I might add," he said under his breath.

"Detective Conn, unless you're here on official business, which you most assuredly are not, I'm ordering you to leave—now," Manly roared.

Conn stood his ground, hands on his hips and chin jutted forward. Manly and Paden both converged on Conn, at which point the detective stormed to the door. He turned to face Manly across the room. "You can go to hell or wherever you please." He threw open the door and exited without closing it behind him.

Manly had tolerated Conn's insolence, his belligerence, his conniving. But he could not abide outright insubordination. On top of everything else, he would have to deal with that—but later.

Paden, visibly taken aback by Conn's behavior, turned to Manly. He extended his hand. "Good morning, Captain. Some detective you have there. The baddest of bad eggs if you ask me."

"What did he say when he came in? Did he let on why he was here?"

"The assistant cracked the door," Paden replied. "Conn said he was here to investigate the man's death and walked right in like he owned the place. I just assumed he'd been assigned to the case."

"He hadn't been assigned to the case. They just discovered the body two or three hours ago. We don't move that fast, especially on a Saturday. And Conn isn't even supposed to be working today."

Paden looked back at the man lying on the table.

"Do you have any idea who it is?" Manly asked.

"Not a clue. The man was carted in here with no identification, no wallet, no watch, no jewelry. Just the clothes he was wearing. And a hat."

"Can I see the hat?"

"Of course." Paden took the hat from a wooden box on an adjacent table and handed it to Manly.

It's a beret alright. But dark grey, not black. He looked inside. *Lock & Co. Paris.*

"Could I see him? His face, I mean."

Paden led Manly to the head of the morgue table. He carefully lifted the sheet, pulling it down past the man's shoulders.

The bullet hole was jagged and torn around the edges, suggesting a very close-range shot. Blood spatter covered the man's face, which was puffy and tumid. He had jet black hair and a small, equally black goatee—Manly thought they called these petite goatees. No mustache. And the prominent brown mole—Manly estimated it was three eighths of an inch in diameter—just below the man's cheekbone. His eyes were closed. His mouth was partially open. His lips were violaceous and swollen. Manly paced off the distance from the top of the man's head to his feet. He reckoned the man was about 5'9" tall. Slim. He looked to be no more than thirty or thirty-five. Forty would be pushing it.

Manly was about to turn away when he noticed something curious—the top of a smallish tattoo on the man's right upper arm, about three inches below his shoulder. He asked Paden to pull the sheet down a little more. The tattoo was of a coat of arms. A shield with a crenellated tower in its center. And the letters F and L below.

Before heading off to the station house, Manly instructed Paden to notify him if any leads came in as to the man's identity.

When Manly arrived at the police station, Conn had departed, as had Moncrief. *I'll deal with Conn on Monday. And Moncrief— why didn't he call the officer back? Did the little sleep-deprived scoundrel nod off again?*

Manly prepared two identical handwritten notices:

> Please print prominently in the next edition of your newspaper.
> Capt. William Manly, City Police:
>
> UNIDENTIFIED BODY FOUND
> Deceased white male discovered Saturday morning, the 21st, in the vicinity of Fourteenth and Juniper Streets. Approximately five-feet-nine-inches tall and thirty-five years old. Slim. Black hair. No mustache. Small goatee. Prominent mole below right cheekbone. Tattoo on upper right arm with escutcheon, castle tower, and the initials F.L. Anyone having information regarding his identity or the circumstances behind his death, please contact City Police or the Fulton County Coroner immediately.

"Here, get a message boy. Have him deliver these right away," Manly instructed the desk clerk. "One to the *Journal* for tonight, and one to the *Constitution* for tomorrow morning. Have him take them straight to the city desks." Manly looked at his watch. *If the boy hurries he should be able to get it to the* Journal *well in advance of press deadline.*

Manly walked back to his office. He plopped into his chair, buried his face in his palms, and shook his head.

Manly returned home that afternoon resolved to spend what precious little time he could with Eunice. For the first time in a week, she wouldn't have to await his late arrival for dinner. He would try to get his mind off of everything swirling around him as he stood by for possible word of the dead man's identity. *If it's Mureau, could Bass's killer have struck again?*

It wasn't until almost ten that evening that he heard a knock. It was Paden. Manly walked onto the porch, shutting the front door behind him.

"We've identified the man," Paden said.

"Who is it?" Manly's heart pounded like a pile driver.

"His name is François Latour. A French delegate to the exposition."

Manly felt a mix of relief and bewilderment. For almost twelve hours, he had conjured up visions of Lem Mureau having finally been found, albeit in the thrall of the grim reaper. And now, in a split second, those conjurings evaporated into the night air.

"How did you find out?" Manly asked.

"I left the morgue and went home shortly after you departed," Paden said. "Around seven o'clock this evening, two men from the French delegation showed up. They were accompanied by Horace Bradley, the Fine Arts department chief. If it hadn't been for Horace, the Frenchmen probably never would have known who I was or how to find me. They had seen the notice in this evening's paper and right away knew it was Latour. All of us went directly to the morgue. And there, under the incandescent light in that mausoleum of a room, the Frenchmen provided a positive, incontrovertible identification."

"Had he been missing long?"

"They hadn't seen him in about twenty-four hours. They said they returned to their hotel early yesterday evening but he stayed behind."

"What hotel?"

"The Kimball House. Latour remained at the exposition. He said he would be back at the hotel later that night and would meet with them the next morning—this morning—for breakfast."

"And I take it he didn't join them for breakfast."

"Correct. He never showed up. They knocked on his door several times. Finally, they tracked down a chambermaid, who opened the door for them. Everything was in order. His bed was made. It looked as if he had not slept there last night. They went on to the exposition and looked for him there."

"He had a room of his own?"

Paden grinned. "He's a Frenchman, Manly. They must not cotton to room sharing like we do."

"Did his colleagues notify the police?"

"No, and this is where it gets a little thorny. Apparently, Latour's been known to carouse around a bit. Hang out at whorehouses and such. Especially when he's traveling. They just assumed he'd found a stray bed somewhere and spent the night there. That is, they thought that until they saw the notice in the paper."

"Do you have any leads on the killer?"

"We don't. That's for your men, Manly. I'm just a lowly coroner. You're the sleuth master."

"How did you leave things with the Frenchmen?"

"As we were wrapping up at the morgue, the senior one said they would handle Latour's arrangements after mass tomorrow, but I made it clear we could not release his body until we'd done a thorough examination. I'm assuming by mass he was talking about the Catholic Church on Hunter Street, six blocks across the tracks from the hotel."

"Does he have relatives? Latour, I mean."

"They mentioned a wife. They said they would go to the Western Union office and send a telegram. What a terrible way to learn something like this—a messenger showing up at your door with news your husband is dead—four thousand miles and a week away by steamship."

Early Sunday morning, Manly mounted his horse and rode downtown to the Kimball House. By the time he got there, the Frenchmen had already left for mass. At least that's what the hotel manager said.

The manager remembered having seen Latour leave early Friday morning. But he never saw him return. "He walked out the door an hour before sunrise and boarded a hackney. Said he was headed to the exposition. Dressed in that fancy get-up and with all the gold about him?"

"Gold?"

"Why, he wore two big gold rings. One on his right middle finger. And another on his pinkie, right here." The manager held up his left hand, raising his little finger and clenching the others in a fist. "The middle finger one had a little diamond in the center. And he had a long braided gold chain, bigger than most, that ran from his vest button to his watch fob. Captain, if you ask me, somebody robbed and killed him. Probably some good-for-nothing…well, let's just say I'll bet somebody shot him for his riches. He was a walking target for an ambush. He may have had a passel of money on him, too. Wouldn't surprise me, him being one of them flashy foreigners. They beat all. I've been seeing 'em throw their cash around like it was worthless Greybacks."

Manly waited around at the hotel until almost noon, but the Frenchmen never showed up. He concluded they probably left the church and went straight to the exposition, or possibly to the Western Union office in the train depot, catty-cornered from the hotel. He went there. The Western Union man said that yes, two Frenchmen had stopped in earlier that morning and had laid out $46.80 for a ten-word telegram. But they had left close to an hour ago.

On his way from the Western Union office to the exposition grounds, Manly couldn't get something off his mind. *How do you tell a woman, in ten words, that she's a widow?*

Manly conjectured he would likely locate the Frenchmen in the Fine Arts Building, where their country's art exhibits were housed. When he first saw the men in the upper gallery, he had little doubt that they were the ones he was looking for. They were standing in front of a painting of a nude woman. Manly remembered Adrien-Louis Demont's *A Seated Nude,* perhaps the most salacious of the exposition's offerings. Its presence created chatter among the nicer class. The painting they stood before may have been Demont's. But as far as Manly could tell, the men weren't admiring the art. Rather, they both seemed in deep conversation, the one—the older of the two—looking away and stroking his beard as they conversed.

Manly approached them. He introduced himself and asked if they would accompany him to a park bench along the edge of the Grand Plaza, just across the walkway from the building's entrance.

"François liked to walk," the older of the two said. "And he liked to flaunt."

"He liked to flaunt?"

"Let's just say he had a penchant for les belles choses de la vie—how do you say in English?—the finer things in the life. And he liked showing them off. It wouldn't surprise me to learn that he decided to walk home late Friday evening and was robbed and killed. It would take about an hour to walk from here to the hotel—that's assuming he made it all the way. I know because we've done that walk before. He likely would have walked up Fourteenth Street to Juniper and then headed south to downtown. The walk down Juniper Street is a pretty one, even in winter, as I'm sure you know better than I."

The younger man remained silent. Manly surmised his English was limited.

"I have to ask you something," Manly said. "Is there any way your friend Latour could have been mixed up in anything going on in the city outside of the exposition?"

"What do you mean?"

"Well, this is a long shot, but I'm in the throes of investigating a murder that happened not long before the exposition opened. A man of French descent may be mixed up in it all. And there's a woman who helps out at a brothel on Ira Street—she's involved somehow as well. I have heard that Monsieur Latour liked—"

The older Frenchman held up his hand. "I know where you're going with this, so I'll help you out. Françoise had a penchant for les prostituées, or, as I believe you call them, mesdames du soir. When he didn't show up for breakfast yesterday morning, our first inclination was that he had found a companion Friday evening and had decided to—how do you say?—bed with her for the night. But then when the police discovered his body, and all of his possessions were missing, we concluded it must have been a robbery."

"I suspect you're right," Manly said. "But I have two more questions. I'm curious about something. Have you ever heard of a Frenchman named Mureau?"

"Oh, but of course—"

Manly sat up. "So you *have* heard of him?"

"But of course. Gilles Mureau. He was one of the most famous of French Renaissance composers. Everyone in our country, at least every man and woman of a certain age, knows of Gilles Mureau."

"No. No. I mean living today. And his name is Lemuel, not Sheila."

The older man looked at the other and said something in French. The younger one shook his head. "No, neither of us has heard of a man named Lemuel Mureau. Lemuel is not a common given name in our country. Sheila isn't either, by the way. It's Gilles. Not Shelia. And your other question?"

"Do you have any reason to believe your friend Latour would have visited the house of prostitution on Ira Street? I've heard tell that some French exposition visitors may have gone there."

"Where is Ira Street?"

"On the southwest side of town. Probably a mile-and-a-half from your hotel."

"Near the railroad tracks?"

"Yes, it's near the railroad tracks. It's run by a Madam Brumbelow. Very attractive. Elegant. Nice figure. Dark brown hair, which she often wears in a bun." Manly described the parlor. "Do you know it?"

The older Frenchman looked past Manly and shook his head vigorously. Wagged his finger like a metronome. "No. No. I don't know of a madam or a house like that. No." He consulted his watch. "Mr. Manly, at the risk of being rude, I must cut our little talk short. My associate and I need to get back to our delegate duties."

Both men rose to leave. As they walked away, Manly had the nagging feeling that not only had Latour visited the madam, but his associates may have as well. Not that it would necessarily have any bearing beyond the pent-up desires of ruttish men alone in a foreign country.

Manly returned to his house Sunday afternoon. He would spend the evening trying to make sense of the events of the past thirty-six hours and whether they might have any connection to Bass's murder.

He had a job to do. And he was running out of hours. He couldn't afford to spend time and effort on something that might have nothing to do with the mission he had set upon. *Priorities, Manly. Priorities.*

At the same time, the Latour killing demanded attention on someone's part. While a little voice inside said *be careful with your plainclothesmen,* he decided to turn the case of Latour and his killer, or killers, over to the detectives. It sure looked like a robbery gone bad. And since the victim wasn't Mureau after all, and the Frenchmen claimed not to know of a man named Lemuel Mureau, the chances of Latour's murder being connected in some way to Baker Bass seemed a long shot at best.

Manly had three days before the planned encounter under the Phoenix Wheel. And the thatch fire—*the infernal thatch fire*—still hung over his head.

There was another potential benefit to turning the Latour affair over to the detectives, one that did not occur to Manly at first. Green Conn was a scoundrel and a churl. Everybody—well, almost everybody—knew it. And Manly detested the idea of getting him involved on any new case right now, especially one he, Manly, had just, a mere twenty-four hours earlier, ordered Conn to keep his nose out of. But he needed to divert the bureau's—especially Conn's—attention away from the Bass investigation for the next three-and-a-half days, at least until after Christmas evening.

But before he turned the Latour case over, he would fill Connolly in.

By the time Manly approached Connolly's office on Monday morning, the twenty-third, news of the Frenchman's death had made the rounds through the station house. Manly knew the chief would be apoplectic. He braced himself before he passed through Connolly's doorway.

"First Mexico. Now France. Manly, I'm a dead man. I guarantee you, before the day's over, the mayor's going to pay me a visit to tell me the French ambassador has filed a formal complaint. I'll be lucky if I have a job tomorrow."

"I understand, Chief. That's why I'm putting the detectives on Latour. I need to focus all my effort on the Bass affair and the thatch fire and, frankly, I need to keep the detectives as far away from those things as possible."

"Because they may be mixed up in it."

"Precisely."

"Are you putting Conn on the case, Manly?"

"I may as well. He's already stuck his nose in it part of the way. Why not let him stick it all the way in?"

Manly paid the detectives a visit. It was all he could do to maintain his composure and keep from lashing out at Conn. But Manly was a professional, and he had a job to do. He briefed them on the Latour case. He told them about his visits to the morgue and with the hotel manager and the Frenchmen, and he charged them with finding the killer. He could literally feel Conn gloating as the detective leaned back in his chair at the far end of the room, his arms folded across his chest, his upper lip curled.

"From what I can tell, it looks like a robbery gone bad," Manly said. "Follow that trail, but if you find it veering off in another direction, I want to know about it right away."

The city was flourishing with holiday adornments, so much so that many older residents decried the blatant commercialization of Christmas, one man going so far as to claim the whole damned town had gone holiday crazy. The big downtown department stores, M. Rich & Co., Davison & Douglas, Chamberlin-Johnson-DuBose, were busy selling readymade goods for the season. The newspapers were pushing Christmas like a godsend fix to an opium urge.

But Manly had little immediate regard for such frivolities. He spent Tuesday paying final visits before Christmas day—to the Crew Street boarding house, the Woodward Avenue side-by-side, and Madam Brumbelow's comfort house—looking for Jenkins and Mrs. Dampman. And if, miraculously, the elusive

Lem Mureau happened to turn up, that would delight him. But his chances of finding any of them were slim.

His efforts bore no fruit. In half a day of traipsing all over the city, he had not managed to cast one glimmer of light on their whereabouts.

He returned to the exposition that afternoon to see if any new information about the thatch fire might have turned up. Again, nothing.

Time was running out. A shroud of resignation hung over him as the sun slowly found the horizon. He would spend the better part of Wednesday preparing himself for the evening tryst.

THIRTY-EIGHT

WILLIAM MANLY

Whip-poor-will

HE BEGAN WITH THE SCISSORS. HE WINCED WITH EACH coming together of the blades. *Snip. Snip. Snip.* Eighth-inch clippings of coarse brown hair fell about the porcelain wash basin. He wouldn't cut it off all at once. He would take his time. *After all, how many years has it been?* He recalled, twenty years ago, the eighteen-year-old hobbledehoy who sauntered into the Spartanburg post office one day and happened upon the police advertisement, a fortuitous encounter that would change his life. *Brave men wanted.* By that time, the adolescent patch of fuzz on his upper lip had matured into an early prototype of the Imperial he had sported until now.

Boiling water from the kettle on the kitchen stove. A generous lather of shaving soap, warm from the scuttle. Followed by the application of a stiff boar bristle brush and a well-stropped straight razor. The metal's keen edge rasped across his upper lip, his chin, his cheeks and jowls, his neck. He wiped his face dry and ran his palm across his freshly-shaven skin. Smooth as a baby's backside.

He stood before the mirror. Who is that hoaxer? This was the first step in preparing to pass himself off as someone he wasn't.

It was Wednesday, Christmas Day. The sun had not yet graced the morning. In a matter of an hour or two, the city would be abuzz with revelers and merrymakers. Women all over town, Eunice included, would be toiling in their kitchens, in final preparation for holiday meals—wild turkey and venison, perhaps a roast goose with sage stuffing, turnips and greens, sweet potato croquettes, cranberry sauce and mince pie.

Manly rehearsed the day's unfolding.

Around noon—nearer to one, actually—he and Eunice would sit down to Christmas dinner with her parents, her brother and sister-in-law, and her maiden aunt from Tallahassee. He would no doubt spend more time than he would like explaining his newly-shorn mug.

A leisurely postprandial interlude, before the evening's festivities, would follow. The men would assemble in the parlor—playing cards, smoking claros (*Thank God Speaker Reed kept the president from cutting off the Cuban supply*), and sipping brandy and crème de menthe Judges. The women would gather around the kitchen table mooting the latest society gossip (*Did you hear about the fluffy-banged woman at the exposition, in a most ill-fitting gown of that dreadful shade of grey?*) and discussing the familial affairs of the day.

Shortly before four o'clock, he would excuse himself. He had prepared Eunice for his planned absence that evening, although he had shared little detail with her. They had been married long enough that she understood not to ask questions.

But the others?

I must attend a holiday party at the station house.

At the station house? On Christmas evening?—they would surely ask. *When you should be at home celebrating with your family?*

I am seeing after a dear friend who has fallen gravely ill.

What friend? How ill? Has a doctor been summoned?

I've been called away on an urgent police matter.

Will we read about it in the morning paper?

Knowing his father-in-law's prying ways, Manly imagined the old man's suspicions would run wild. But what was the captain to do?

Upon leaving the gathering of family, under whatever pretense he deemed most plausible and least likely to raise the old man's dubitation, Manly would retire to the bedroom. He would lightly coat his face with Eunice's powder in an effort to mimic Conn's youthful, whey-faced visage. He would don clothing appropriate for the rendezvous—it was the detective's wont to dress more casually than Manly when not on duty. He needed a hat to match Conn's dark belly western fedora. He had a buckskin—close enough. He would position the fedora low on his forehead, folding the front brim down in order to hide as much of his face as possible.

At four thirty, sufficiently made up in the guise, Manly slung his grey fly-front overcoat over his shoulders. In the lower right pocket was his police issue .41 caliber revolver, out of sight but close enough for easy retrieval. He slipped out the rear door, rehearsing the detective's audacious swagger. He eased his arms into his coat. He felt a bulge in his left pocket. He reached in and retrieved the core of a half-eaten apple—a White Pearmain. The remaining flesh had become brown and dried. He gave the desiccated remnant to Bessie, gently stroked her withers—*it'll be OK, girl*—and hoisted himself into the saddle.

Manly passed through the turnstile thirty minutes before sundown. The throngs of holiday merrymakers were greater than he had anticipated. He headed straight to the animal arena at the western end of Midway Heights. There he would wait.

At five thirty-five, the sky behind him was awash with brilliant orange and red as the sun began its descent below the treetops. Across the midway to the East, the day's cerulean blue had begun to fade to grey. Manly pulled his fedora down and nipped toward the Phoenix Wheel. When he reached the Phantoscope exhibit, he stopped. He saw, just ahead, a solitary figure standing at the base of the wheel. Aside from the man's hatchet-chinned profile, silhouetted by the wheel's lighted backdrop, Manly could not make out his features. The man wore a coat, but in the twilight's murk, Manly couldn't tell what color it was. The outline of a beret atop the man's head, however, was unmistakable.

Manly let out a loudish *whip-poor-will*, as the letter had instructed its intended recipient. The man turned away and walked at a swift pace in the direction of the Train Shed. Manly followed, narrowing the man's lead but careful not to get too close. At the far edge of the shed, the man turned a hard left and walked north past the Negro Building on his right. Just past the building, the man stopped and looked at his watch. Manly gained a few more feet before the man continued northward past the Georgia Manufacturing Building.

Manly was close enough now that he could make out the man's green jacket with black stripes. The man quickened his pace. Just past the Electricity Building, he dropped something to the ground. It was a piece of paper. Manly approached it and picked it up. It was in a Regency letter fold without a seal, which struck Manly as oddly quaint. He unfolded it. Inside, it read:

Savor the evening. Who knows what tomorrow brings.

Unlike the prior two cryptic letters, this note was written with a clean, crisp, elegant hand.

Manly looked ahead. The man had stopped, presumably to give his pursuer time to read the note, then resumed his pace, not looking back.

As they neared the Transportation Building, Manly sensed something going on behind him. A small gathering of people along the eastern edge of the lake, near the bridge, let out a collective gasp. Over his left shoulder, Manly saw flames leaping hundreds of feet into the air. The flames came from the direction of the Mexican Village. He paused briefly before he realized the man had not stopped walking. Manly had a decision to make. *Do I carry on? Or do I change course and head toward the fire?* He knew there were numerous police and firemen on the grounds. He scuttled in the man's direction.

By the time Manly rounded the northwest corner of the Manufactures and Liberal Arts Building and neared the barbecue pavilion, the crowds had thinned to a scattering of no more than a few people. He followed the man past the '49 Mining Camp. Even though the camp was closed for the evening, both it and the pavilion were still illuminated by the strings of overhead incandescent lights, powered by the massive generators in the Machinery Building.

A few hundred yards past the mining camp and just this side of a dense stand of denuded white oaks, the man paused, his back to the captain, then trampled through the leafless trees to the top of a steep embankment. The weeds around his feet were overgrown. The dead oak leaves surrendered to his every stepping. He never looked back. Manly followed, further narrowing the man's lead to no more than a few yards. Manly recognized the spot at the top of the hill. Down the embankment, beyond where the man stood, was Clear Creek, at a crook where it veered westward away from the Southern Railway tracks. The man just stood there with his back to Manly, appearing to gaze into the distance beyond the creek, beyond the tracks.

Manly waited and watched. The man lit a cigarette. Smoked it. Flicked the lighted butt over the embankment. Shifted his weight from one foot to the other.

Approach him then. He will know you by a single watchword, Eidgenossen.

"Eidgenossen," Manly called out in a near whisper. No response. He called out again, this time louder.

The man took two steps forward. His shoulder twitched. He took something from his jacket. He swung around, pistol in hand, pointed squarely at Manly's chest.

Manly found himself face-to-face with Herbert Jenkins—a glint of madness in the tobacco drummer's eyes.

The captain held out his left hand, fingers splayed, palm facing Jenkins. He thrust his right hand into his coat pocket and drew his gun. He moved slowly in Jenkins' direction, careful with every footfall.

The two men stood face-to-face, pistols drawn on each other.

"You're not Conn. Where's Conn. I summoned the detective, not you."

"So it was *you*. You wrote the letters."

A smirk came over Jenkins. "An astute conclusion. But you're mistaken on one minor point. I composed the letters. But my dear Delores scribed them for me. She's a sweetheart. Such a doll. Or should I say moll?" He tittered. "She will do just about anything I ask, such is her thrall in my presence."

"I thought, from the letters, that I was coming here to meet Mureau. The Huguenot. You're not Mureau."

Jenkins lowered his gun. Let out a frightening horselaugh. Fixed it again at Manly's chest. "Of course I'm not Mureau. The poor Frenchman. Oh, that he could breathe the evening air. Could feel the hairs stand military straight on his skin, as yours undoubtedly are underneath that coat of yours, Captain. Could know fear. Joy. Pain. Hurt. The poor Frenchman. He's a mere figment of your imagination. The man does not exist—that is, except in the hearts and minds of hopeless ninnyhammers like you."

"What do you mean, he doesn't exist?"

"You heard what I said. He is my own contrivance." Jenkins pointed to his bereted head with the index finger of his free hand. "The spawn of a brilliant mind, I'll have you know. And you fell for it. You, of all people, were foolish enough to succumb to my little ruse. Oh, and that sham reporter of yours. I had him playing along too."

"But why make up a fiction?"

"Because, you see, it was I who sold the Wild Turkey to Bass. That infamous Wild Turkey that started an unfortunate cascade of events that brings us here tonight. I'll admit it now. What have I to lose? And yes, it was stolen. I needed someone I could pin the sale on. To deflect attention away from me. Who better than another tobacco drummer, a man no one knew, from out of town, elusive, untraceable? And a crafted bill of sale to prove he was the purveyor. Brilliant. A perfect deflection, if you ask me. But just because I happened to peddle some goods of, shall we say, doubtful provenance, that doesn't mean I leveled the gun to Baker Bass's head and killed him."

"And why should I believe you?"

"Because, my good Captain, a goodly supply of Wild Turkey notwithstanding, I'm an honorable man."

"An honorable man—with a gun trained at my chest."

"Coming from a man who has his sidearm leveled at me, that seems a might hypocritical, don't you think, Captain?"

"What did you expect?...So if you didn't kill Bass, who did?

"Captain, surely you jest in asking such a foolish question. I've made that clear more than once, to your sweaty-handed newspaperman, to you, and to the entire city."

"So Conn did it—killed Bass. That's still your contention."

"Of course. And I lured Conn here tonight, or so I thought, to settle things once and for all. The man's no good. He's part of a cabal bigger than any you've ever known. And he has confederates in high places. He's been trying to do me in ever since Bass died. And I'll have none of it." Jenkins took aim squarely at Manly's forehead. "But now, Captain, you've made a grave miscalculation by coming here tonight in Green Conn's stead."

Manly held his disquiet in check. "Regardless of the Wild Turkey, if you're innocent of Bass's murder, as you claim, then work *with* me, not against me. Help me bring justice to the man that did it. Don't do something you'll regret."

"It's too late for that."

Manly cocked his pistol.

Jenkins threw off his beret and lunged at Manly, sending his fedora catapulting through the air. He grabbed Manly's wrist and wrenched his arm behind his back. Manly's pistol flew from his hand and cascaded down the embankment toward Clear Creek.

Manly pulled back and shifted to the side. He pushed Jenkins' arm down and away.

Jenkins leveled his revolver again at Manly. His finger was inside the trigger guard but not on the trigger. He thumbed back the hammer.

This is my only chance, Manly thought. *Either I seize Jenkins' gun or I don't leave here alive.*

Manly charged, grabbed Jenkins by the nape. He tried to wrest Jenkins' revolver, clenching the barrel with his free hand, while he kept his other hand around Jenkins' neck, pressing his thumb into the man's jugular.

Jenkins thrust a stiff left hook into Manly's stomach.

Manly felt a hot surge rising from his belly to his throat. He reeled but never lost his grip on the barrel. He let go of Jenkins' neck and planted a hard fist into his face, bloodying his nose. Jenkins faltered but quickly regained his footing. Manly popped him again, this time in the jaw.

Jenkins drove Manly's arm over and back. He twisted the revolver in an effort to wrench the barrel from the captain's grip.

Manly pulled his free hand away and grabbed Jenkins' wrist, pulling it down and toward him, while he kept his other hand firmly on the barrel of the gun.

Explosions thundered in the distance. The fireworks over Clara Meer had begun. *The sun will set. The sky will erupt.* For a split second he lost concentration. *Focus, Manly.*

Holding Jenkins' wrist with one hand and the barrel with the other, Manly tried to pivot the pistol around and out of Jenkins' hand. He saw that Jenkins' finger was no longer inside the trigger guard. He felt Jenkins' wrist tense.

Jenkins drove his free hand into the captain's shoulder, almost knocking him to the ground.

Manly regained his footing. He let go of Jenkins' wrist, grabbed the chamber, and twisted the gun down and toward Jenkins' feet. He grasped the chamber with his left hand.

Jenkins held onto the handle. With his free hand, he tried to release Manly's grip on the barrel, grabbing the captain's wrist and jerking hard.

Manly tightened his grip, his finger now inside the trigger guard. *Twist the barrel away,* he thought. He pivoted the gun away and toward Jenkins, wrenching Jenkins' wrist at a ninety-degree angle. He released his hand from the chamber and wrapped it around Jenkins' right hand, pulling hard on Jenkins' hand and fingers. He felt Jenkins' grip on the handle loosen slightly.

This is my chance.

Manly almost seized the gun. Jenkins rammed his head into the captain's shoulder. A sharp pang radiated down Manly's arm. A numbness came over him. He staggered. His heart pounded. A surge of electric energy pulsed through his body. He had to think quickly. He couldn't buckle. His survival depended on it.

He tightened his clutch on the barrel with his right hand, enveloping Jenkins' fingers on the handle with his left. With the gun twisted around, he repositioned his grip on the barrel so the pistol faced away.

He and Jenkins continued to fight for control of the gun, both of them nearly crashing to the ground. The gun twisted and turned in all directions as they scuffled.

Manly's mind raced at lightning speed. Every sensation was intensified—the throbbing of his heart, his labored breathing, the feel of his fingers wrapped around the gun barrel, the sight of Jenkins' teeth bared in a demonic grin with furious eyes and flared nostrils lunging toward him.

But in the heat of the moment, Manly had the odd feeling of everything unfolding before him in slow motion. Of time standing still.

The fireworks continued, the distant light show intense and chaotic. The detonations were ear-piercing, even from across the midway. But they did little to mask the single violent report, the sulfuric flash of light, the sudden and irrevocable discharge from the fought-over revolver.

The fireworks came to an end. A stillness set in. The pungent odor of gunpowder lingered in the air.

And a man lay stone still on the hard, winter ground. A single projectile, fired at point-blank range, had pierced his chest, slightly off center and just clearing his sternum.

When a gun is fired no more than a few inches from a man's torso, the projectile spins like a flying drill bit, piercing the body with such speed and ferocity that it rips a ragged entry wound, lacerating the skin, flesh, and muscle in a savage fury and shattering any bones it may encounter on its path.

An abrasion ring of stretched and grazed skin, and charring from the hot gases that exit the barrel, will encircle the wound. Soot and powder will embed into the skin, causing a tattooing or speckled pattern around the wound. That is, if the victim is shirtless. Otherwise, the man's clothing will collect the soot and heat, the charring and tattooing. And blood.

The sound is deafening, the brunt jolting, but only momentarily. Then it's over, save for a lingering ringing in the ears that may seem as if it will never pass.

The unfortunate casualty may cling to precarious life, if he should be so lucky. But the projectile, which likely will have penetrated several organs on its journey to a final resting place somewhere between chest and back (assuming it doesn't consummate its travel by exiting the body altogether), is unforgiving and uncaring.

The distant fairground lights began to dim as the revelers headed home. Closer by, the overhead lights at the mining camp remained illuminated, most likely awaiting the arrival of a worker to shut them off.

An eerie quiet descended over the grounds. The winter's chill clung to the deathly still night air. The bare limbs of the white oaks reached to the sky like so many gaunt and emaciated outstretched arms beckoning the heavens.

Manly's eyes fixed on the revolver resting in his tremulous hand. His grip was precarious, but his index finger was still inside the trigger guard. He released his finger and rested it against the barrel. For a moment, the gun's handle felt too comfortable in his palm. Then a numbing emptiness came over him. *Is this what shock feels like?*

The faint sound of scurrying—crinkling leaves at his back—broke his trance. He swung around, expecting to find himself face to face with a man come running at the sound of the report. But there was no man. A grey Virginia possum, the size of a housecat, planted its beady eyes on his—*an accusatory stare?*—then scurried away and over the embankment.

Jenkins' eyes were closed. He lay motionless. The front panel of his shirt, on the left side, was bright crimson, speckled with charring and soot from the powder that followed the bullet out of the muzzle.

Manly fell to his knees. Still holding the gun in his right hand, he searched for Jenkin's pulse with the other. He placed his ear against Jenkins' chest opposite where the bullet had entered. He listened for the shallowest of breathing. He lifted Jenkins' lid to find a glassy, lifeless stare.

Jenkins was dead.

Manly wondered why the tobacco drummer hadn't gone ahead and shot him when he had the chance. Perhaps it was because he had his own gun leveled at Jenkins. The two men likely would have suffered a mutual end at each other's hands. Or perhaps Jenkins' bluster was just so much cockalorum, and he never intended to do Manly harm.

Manly turned his attention to the revolver. It was a Smith and Wesson, .38 caliber. Not one of those fake ones from *god-knows-where*. He tightened his hold on the grip. He cupped the body of the gun with his free hand and disengaged the cylinder latch with his right thumb. He pushed the cylinder open and slid his two middle fingers through the frame to fully expose the chambers. He held the gun up so the light from the mining camp shown on the cylinder end. Not one, but two of the cartridges displayed telltale firing marks. Were it not for the faintest glint of reflection off the indentations in the centerfire casings, he may not have even noticed. He closed the cylinder and reengaged the cylinder lock.

For what seemed an hour but was no more than a minute or two, he remained on his knees, staring at the gun. In the semidarkness, he noticed something engraved in small letters on the left side plate. He tried to make it out. He brought the gun closer. Angled the gun so the nearby light reflected off the side plate. Squinted. Forced a focus.

And there, just above the handle, the initials *B.A.B.*

THIRTY-NINE

WILLIAM MANLY

How Do You Kill a Man and Brush it Aside?

MANLY HAD TO ACT QUICKLY. HE PLACED THE SMITH
and Wesson in the lower right pocket of his overcoat where his
own gun had been. He rolled Jenkins' body over and removed the
man's green jacket. He was about to cover Jenkins with the jacket
when he felt something heavy in an inside pocket. He reached
in and removed another revolver. A five-cylinder Harrington
& Richardson. He briefly examined the gun. The gutta percha
handle had been abraded. A faint glint reflected off a scratch on
the polished nickel beneath the hammer.

He covered Jenkins with the jacket, stuffed the Harrington
& Richardson into the left pocket of his own coat, and took
off. He found a policeman patrolling on the north end of the
Manufactures and Liberal Arts Building. It was Oscar, the officer
with the ornery bunion.

"Why, Captain Manly. I almost didn't make out who you were, what with your whiskers gone. What's a big bug like you doin' out here on a night like this?"

"There's a dead man at the top of the embankment." He pointed in the direction of Jenkins' body. "Just past that stand of trees beyond the '49 Mining Camp. Get somebody over here. Have them take the body to the morgue. Don't ask any questions. I'll follow up with the chief and the detectives."

Oscar hobbled away, leaving Manly standing alone trying to make sense of all that had happened. In his decades of service to the city, he had never killed a man.

Manly hovered in the saddle as Bessie hurled down Piedmont Avenue toward the center of town. Her leg muscles tensed and released against his inner calves like powerful hydraulic pistons. Her breathing was heavy and tempestuous with each stride. *It'll be OK, girl.*

He drew the reins in and brought the horse to a halt in front of Chief Connolly's house on East Hunter Street, six blocks and across the tracks from the police station.

The curtains were fully open. A group of six or seven people were gathered inside the parlor. Manly could see the chief standing near the window with what appeared to be a champagne glass in one hand, raised before the holiday partyers. A bottle in the other. His wife, Agnes, stood at his side.

Manly regretted having to break up the revel. But he had no choice. He knocked, but they didn't hear. He turned the knob and eased open the door.

Connolly swung around. "Manly, what are you doing here?"

"Chief, I need to speak with you. Alone."

"You're white as Dickens' ghost. What is it? And where did your whiskers run off to?"

Manly didn't think it was the right time to explain that Eunice's face powder was the likely source of his pallor. Or was it? And the smooth upper lip? He would explain that later.

"And what happened to your hand. It's all black and blue," Connolly continued.

"There's been a terrible accident," Manly whispered, hopefully out of earshot of the others. "At the exposition."

Connolly stepped onto the porch and shut the door.

"If you don't mind, Chief, it would be better if we moved away from the window."

The two men went down the porch steps and into the yard. They stood near the curb.

"What is it, Manly?"

Manly recounted the events of the past few hours. The scissors and the razor. The face powder. The appointment at the exposition––"I went there in Conn's place. I thought I was meeting Lem Mureau, but it turned out to be Jenkins." The shadowing to the far edges of the fair. The confrontation. The struggle for the gun. His injured hand—"Let's just say it had a little run-in with Jenkins' jaw." The fireworks. The single report from the Smith & Wesson. Jenkins lying stone cold on the ground. The initials above the gun's handle. The second pistol, a Harrington & Richardson with a scratch beneath the hammer.

"Manly, look me in the eye and tell me it was an accident."

"Of course it was an accident. I never would have killed the man."

"Where is the body now?"

"I hailed an officer walking the exposition grounds. He's taking care of it."

"Did you tell him what happened?"

"No, just that there was a dead man."

"Have you said anything to anybody else?"

"Just you."

"Did anyone see you and Jenkins together?"

"No. I followed far behind Jenkins until we got near the stand of trees on the hill past the '49 Mining Camp." Manly paused. "I did pass a group of people, but they were preoccupied with a fire at the far end of the exposition."

"Another fire?"

"Yes, another fire. I have no idea what it was. I obviously had my mind on other things."

Connolly walked across the yard. He kicked the dirt around the gnarly roots of an elm tree. Put his hands in his pockets. Walked back to where Manly was standing.

"You weren't there, Manly."

"What do you mean, I wasn't there?"

"You may have been at the exposition. And you may have happened upon Jenkins' body. But you weren't on that hill when he died. For all you know, he shot himself. After all he's been through, the poor wretch."

"But Chief, I pulled the trigger. I have the gun that killed him."

"Of course you have the gun. You took it from Jenkins' possession when you stumbled upon him. It's evidence, you know. As the number two man on the force, you had every right to take it. Do you understand?"

"But Chief, why would I have just stumbled upon a body at a far stretch of the fair, on a hill beyond a stand of barren oaks?"

"You had to relieve yourself, right? And the nearest comfort station was occupied. You did what any red-blooded man would do. And as you were standing there, pissing down the embankment, trying your best to pepper the bottom of the hill, something to the right caught your eye. And there, a mere yard or so from where you stood, you saw a body. And what did you do? You found the nearest policeman. Who was it, by the way? The policeman—I mean."

"It was Oscar."

"Oscar?" Connolly let loose with a cackle. "The one that won't stop talking about his bunion?"

This is not the time for jollity, Manly thought. "And another thing, Chief. When Oscar got to Jenkins, he would have found Jenkins covered with his own jacket. And no gun anywhere. How could that be if, as you suggested, Jenkins shot himself?"

"Manly, think about it. You came upon the body while relieving yourself. You covered the dead man with his own jacket—what any decent man would do. And you took the gun—guns—as evidence. It's as simple as that. You'll be fine. Just do as I say. Now, I need to get back inside. You just go on home and lay low for a day or two. It's the holidays. No one will think anything of your taking a couple of days off. You deserve it, what with the hours you've been putting in. And the shock of stumbling upon a corpse—the corpse of a cold-blooded murderer."

"But Jenkins vehemently denied killing Bass."

"Of course he did. Why wouldn't he? But he had Bass's gun, didn't he? To me, that's a pretty solid indictment."

Manly began to plod back to his horse. Connolly called out to him. "Manly."

"Yes?"

"You're a good man. Go home. Be with your family. It's Christmas, for Christ's sake."

A horse's slowest gait, short of walking, is a languid, lumbering trot. On the ten-block trip home, Manly just didn't have it in him to push any harder than that. Bessie was sapped of energy. And so was he.

How can you kill a man and brush it aside as if it didn't happen?

By the time Manly reached the house on Gartrell Street, the lights inside were dimmed. Eunice's parents, brother, and sister-in-law had gone home. And her maiden aunt had no doubt retired for the evening. No need to slip in through the rear door, the same door he had slipped out of a few hours earlier. He unlocked the front door and entered quietly. Eunice was waiting in the darkened parlor. Her anxious countenance betrayed her words.

"William, the others waited for a while, but I told them you would likely be late returning." She looked at the clock on the mantel. "They left no more than thirty minutes ago. They asked me to give you their regards."

Manly searched her dolesome eyes. They darted across the room but did not engage with his own. He saw her tight-lipped smile. The deep lines running from the bridge of her nose halfway up her forehead. Her shrinking carriage. She let out a little nervous laugh when she spoke.

"Eunice, come sit with me." He eased onto the chesterfield. She joined him. He took her hands in his. "Eunice, I know it's been hard lately. My erratic comings and goings. Your not knowing whether I'll make it home for dinner—or make it home at all, for that matter. And then on Christmas night, of all nights, I'm not here with you and your—our—family."

She looked at him but didn't speak. She didn't have to.

"Wherever I am, whatever I do, you are always in my thoughts," he continued. "I can't share everything with you. In due time, likely soon, that moment will come. But not now. Certainly not tonight. I imagine things will slowly, steadily, get back to the way they used to be. But it may take a few days—perhaps even weeks—for that to happen. Please trust me as you have never trusted me before."

She rested her head on his shoulder. "William, I've been worried sick over you."

Alone in the parlor late that night, long after Eunice had retired, Manly searched for the right words to settle his own unsettled soul. Two things would keep him going. His character. And courage in the face of fear.

He remembered what a man much wiser than he once said about character—that you couldn't dream yourself into it—you had to hammer and forge one for yourself. The person Manly saw when he looked in the mirror each morning was the product of a lifetime of hammering and forging.

How can you kill a man and brush it aside as if it didn't happen?

His eyes fell on the copy of *Master Thoughts of Master Minds* in the bookcase across the room. He thumbed to the index. Courage. Page ninety-six.

Courage consists not in hazarding without fear, but being resolutely minded in a just cause. The brave man is not he who feels no fear...but he whose noble soul subdues its fears, and bravely dares the danger nature shrinks from.

He would muster the strength of character, and the courage, to wait out an unsure befalling. He would trust the chief to do the right thing. But at the moment, he wasn't certain what the right thing was.

Manly lay low as instructed.

FORTY

ARTHUR CONNOLLY

Wakin' Snakes

ARTHUR CONNOLLY REMEMBERED HIS LAST WORDS TO Manly on Wednesday evening. "You're a good man. Go home. Be with your family. It's Christmas..." He also recalled the plaintive look on Manly's face as the captain turned and walked away. *Hopefully, two days of rest will have done him a world of good and dispelled any foolish notion of bloodguilt.*

Early Saturday morning, the twenty-eighth, he sent a messenger to Manly's house. "Come to my office."

"Come in, Captain. Have a seat."

Manly sat in one of the two chairs at the front of the chief's desk. Connolly walked across the room, shut and locked the door, and took the seat beside him. He leaned in. "I am more convinced than ever that spies are about us. Caution is the watchword. Even on a Saturday."

Manly nodded.

"We have a new prisoner as of last night," Connolly continued. "Caged among the ragtags and bobtails. And not the least bit happy about it, I might add."

"Who is it?"

"Delores Dampman."

"Delores Dampman? What did you nab *her* for?"

"Well, we thought we were just bringing her in for questioning yesterday morning. She was too mixed up with Jenkins for us not to. We found her holed up at Madam Brumbelow's—again. By the time we got to her, she had already heard about Jenkins' untimely death at the hands of an unknown assailant."

Manly looked away.

"We sat her down right here. Right where you're sitting."

"Who is we?"

"Thaddeus Moncrief and me."

"Thaddeus Moncrief? That feckless little man?"

"Let me explain. I couldn't get the detectives involved. And I wanted to keep this as low key as I could. But I needed somebody here with me when I questioned the woman. Who's the one man on the entire force, aside perhaps from the bunioned Oscar, that's enough of a gull—well, perhaps gull isn't the right word—let's just say enough of a simpleton to help me out without asking a lot of questions and without spreading it all over god-only-knows-where? That's assuming I ordered him not to talk. Which I did."

"When you put it that way, Chief, Moncrief's your man."

"So, early yesterday morning, Thaddeus and I went to the bordello together. We knocked on the door. And would you believe that when the madam opened it, she greeted Thaddeus like they were old friends, and he just sauntered right in—well, not really sauntered, more like shuffled—like he was a regular there?"

"Doesn't surprise me, Chief."

"So we hauled Mrs. Dampman in, expecting to have to pry information from her, but as soon as she sat down she just spilled her considerable guts all over the floor. If you look around your feet, Manly, you might see some of them."

The captain looked at his shoes, then back at Connolly.

"I'm not quite sure where to begin, so I'll just start where she started." Connolly consulted several handwritten papers stacked on the corner of his desk. "It seems that Jenkins did, indeed, kill Baker Bass—at least that's what the woman says. But you probably figured that out already, seeing as he had Bass's gun.

"As best we can tell, on that Friday morning in August, he waited at the top of the Ivy Street embankment. He slid down just as Bass passed. They engaged in a fight. At some point, Bass was felled by a single shot from his own gun. Jenkins, perhaps in a panic, or perhaps because Bass's gun was a far sight better than his own, planted the Harrington & Richardson in Bass's hand and took off with the Smith & Wesson."

"Did Jenkins intend to kill Bass?"

"We'll never know…but what we do know is that Jenkins was actively fencing tobacco in the city. Bass was one of Jenkins' biggest customers, although we have no reason to believe he knew he was buying stolen goods. When the detectives started snooping around and it was clear to Jenkins they were getting too close to home, he knew he had to do something. He was worried Bass would finger him. That's when he confronted Bass. To plead with him? To scare him? To kill him? We just don't know."

"And Delores Dampman told you all this?"

"Yes, but there's a lot more. She sat right here for the better part of the day before we locked her up. She drinks a mighty lot of water, by the way. And she perspires a lot for the dead of winter. Must be her ample girth."

Manly grimaced.

I'll be damned, Connolly thought. *The man's so wound up he doesn't even have a sense of humor about him.* Connolly stood, walked around his desk, and took a tobacco tin and a pack of rolling papers from his drawer. He sat back down, rolled two cigarettes, and offered one to the captain. "Here, have one. It's Wild Turkey, the best around. The only thing I don't know is whether it was stolen from a railcar somewhere."

"Thank you, but I'd prefer not."

"Jenkins went to great lengths to set Conn up as Bass's killer, before the fact," Connolly said, "which suggests to me that Jenkins intended to kill Bass all along...but I guess we'll never know." Connolly reminded Manly of what C.T. Hughes had testified at the coroner's inquest—that the day before the killing, Bass had been warned by someone to watch his back, that a policeman had threatened to kill him. "I believe Jenkins was the one who warned Bass," Connolly continued. "It was all a big setup. Jenkins hoped Bass would tell somebody about the warning...and apparently it worked. Bass told several people."

"Why Conn?" Manly asked. "Why would Jenkins go to such lengths to try to pin the murder on him?"

"I'll tell you why, and this is the reason the detectives have to stay out of this, even with Jenkins dead. Mrs. Dampman told me something that didn't come as a great surprise, but part of what she had to say gave me pause. I've known something was up with Conn for a long time." Connolly leveled his eyes at Manly. "And so have you, Captain."

Manly nodded. "It's seemed that way. Going back long before Bass was killed."

"Well, Mrs. Dampman provided third-party confirmation that Conn has been involved in a secret fencing ring for some time now, totally unrelated to whatever Jenkins was up to. Mehaffey may be wrapped up in it as well. That's why, when the order came to the detectives, straight from my office I might add, to track down the culprit in the railcar break-in, Conn and Mehaffey zeroed in on a merchant that Jenkins, not Conn, was selling to. That's when it started getting too close to home for Jenkins."

"Knowing Conn, that all makes sense," Manly said.

"Yes, but here's the twist. Commissioner Branan is in cahoots with the detective."

"Chief, do you remember what Conn's neighbor told Keeler?"

"Keeler?"

"The reporter."

"Ah, yes. The reporter."

"Do you remember what the neighbor said? Conn came and went at all hours, and a man who looked like Grover Cleveland hung around there a lot?"

"I remember that now."

"Well, sitting in my office right after that, I showed Keeler a picture of Branan. We both agreed he could have passed for the president's brother. And another thing. Keeler commented at the time that it was odd for Conn to live so far outside the city. Maybe that's a convenient way for Conn to stay out from under our noses."

"Perhaps. In any case, it seems we have a crooked detective on our hands—and an equally crooked commissioner. I'll tell you, Manly, I've said it before but I'll say it again. I may be out of a job come tomorrow."

Connolly waited for some sign of commiseration. It never came.

"Chief, there's something I've been puzzling over. Something you haven't said a word about. What about Lem Mureau? Jenkins said he made him up. But I thought Mrs. Dampman met the man."

"Delores Dampman confirmed he doesn't exist. It wasn't until recently that she found that out, when Jenkins owned up to it. Remember how she said Mureau had visited her late one night at her house?"

"Yes. That's my point," Manly replied. "She said she had seen him."

"She is now convinced that it was actually Jenkins in disguise."

"But how did she not recognize Jenkins, of all people?"

"Well, for one thing, the woman is blind as a bat without her spectacles. She had already dressed for bed when there was a knock at the door. She went to the door without putting her glasses on. Cracked it just a bit but never really opened it. The man spoke in a near whisper, in what she now believes was a made-up French accent. And remember how she said the man had dark eyes, like he had lampblack or something on his face? She thinks Jenkins did that so she couldn't make out who he was."

"But to go to such extremes to fabricate a man from whole cloth?"

"Jenkins needed a tobacco alibi. Mureau was his way of pointing the finger at somebody else for having sold the stolen tobacco to Bass. A person he knew we could never track down. And the bill of sale? Jenkins forged it outright. Jenkins accomplished two things by posing as Mureau at Mrs. Dampman's door. It gave him another person who could attest to Mureau's authenticity, if it should ever come to that. Not knowing any better, she would surely affirm he was real. And remember, he instructed her to convey another warning to Bass, further bolstering the deception. By using a proxy to have her pass along the warning, Jenkins laid additional groundwork for accusing Conn of Bass's murder, should death happen to befall the merchant."

"So there I was, in a cat-and-mouse game with a man I thought was Mureau," Manly said. "And it was really Jenkins. And Jenkins thought he was luring Conn to the exposition. To kill him?"

"Perhaps. Or to confront him. I don't know. Delores Dampman claims not to know. What is obvious, though, is that Jenkins wanted to do Conn in one way or the other to protect his own hide. That's why he used the letters to lure Conn—or he thought he was luring Conn—to the exposition. And he had Delores Dampman scribe them so as not to link them back to him in any way."

"But why would she go along with it?"

"I'll get to that in a minute. But first, about the Harrington & Richardson. As far as we can tell, Jenkins made up the story about the scratch under the hammer. Mrs. Dampman knew nothing about it until he convinced her to go along with his deception. When Jenkins realized he was getting deep into his own lie about the gun and needed to get out of it somehow, he broke into Paden's house, stole it, and put the scratch on it after the fact. At least that's what she says. And it makes sense to me. Whether Jenkins planned for the gun to resurface at some point with a scratch, we'll never know."

"Any idea why the gutta percha was abraded?"

"I'm at a loss to say. Maybe there was something on there that Jenkins didn't want anyone to see. Perhaps his own name or initials. Or maybe it's nothing but a coincidence. At this point, it probably doesn't really matter, given that we have Bass's gun, and his killer is presumed dead."

Connolly told Manly he was convinced the story about the notebook Jenkins claimed was confiscated by the police—the one that would prove he was out of the city when Bass was killed—was another of Jenkins' lies. There never was a notebook—or, if Jenkins had one, it never ended up in the hands of the police. Perhaps it would turn up one day. Or perhaps not. But Connolly was sure that, if it ever did, there would be nothing in it about a made-up trip.

"Oh, and one other thing—about Sam Green's testimony at the coroner's inquest. He said he saw a man running from the scene of the Ivy Street shooting wearing a green jacket with black stripes. What was Jenkins wearing when you—I mean when someone—shot him Christmas night?"

"A green jacket with black stripes."

"Precisely. Now, as for Mrs. Dampman. Do you know why she's behind bars?"

"I have no idea. Surely not accessory to murder. Based on everything you've told me so far, she hasn't implicated herself for anything other than transcribing a couple of letters—and not coming forward with information Jenkins shared with her along the way."

Connolly struck a match, lit the cigarette, and held the lighted match in the air before waving it out. "Arson."

"Arson?"

"Yes, Arson. Delores Dampman lit the thatch fire at the exposition—and the bigger fire Christmas night. She confessed to both. Claims Jenkins put her up to it. The first one was a trial run. To see how much attention it would draw. The second one—that was to attract the police away from whatever Jenkins had planned for Conn. And it was a big blaze. It was also in the Mexican Village, but this time a wood frame building, the one that housed the workers, burned to the ground. One poor Mexican couldn't escape the fire. It wouldn't surprise me to see Delores Dampman sent up for manslaughter."

"Do you know who died?"

"A donkey keeper named Pedro."

"I knew Pedro. I met with him. He's the one that said he saw somebody throw the kerosene can in the barrel and run away through the hole in the fence—the first time. God rest his soul. The person he saw must have been Delores Dampman."

Connolly grinned. "No wonder the hole was so big."

Manly shook his head. He glared at the chief. "So why did she go along with it?"

"Carrot-and-stick, as best I can tell. There's no question, at least in my mind, that she was in Jenkins' thrall. The timing was perfect, with her being fed up and ready to leave her husband. But Jenkins needed more than that to sway her. That's where the threats and intimidation came in. It was Jenkins, not George Dampman, who beat the daylights out of her. Threatened to kill her if she didn't play along. At least that's what she says now."

"She was so insistent that her husband had beaten her. She wanted me to put him in the lockup—where she now finds her own self."

"Now she says that was all a cover-up, to protect Jenkins."

"And she would have had her husband go to jail for something he didn't even do?"

"Apparently." Connolly fixed his gaze across the room. "Let's just say there doesn't appear to be any love lost between those two—George and Delores. It wouldn't be the first time."

Connolly finished his cigarette and stubbed the fag end in the ashtray. He reached into his trouser pocket. "Here, give this to Ella Bass if you ever see her again."

"What is it?"

"It's a souvenir token. From the New Orleans World's Fair. Didn't she say Bass carried it with him everywhere he went? And that it was missing? Paden's assistant, at the morgue, found it in Jenkins' own trouser pocket."

Manly took the token. He held it in his hand. Lowered his head. "Chief, my heart goes out to Mrs. Bass and her family. Her husband's presumed killer is dead. And that's retribution—in some small way—for the death of an innocent man." Manly looked up. "But I killed a man, too. And whether he was guilty or not. Whether it was an accident or not. He never had his day in court. He never will."

"Manly, Jenkins is dead. You need to put it behind you. It doesn't matter how he died. He was guilty—it's as simple as that—and now he's dead." Connolly walked across the room. Stared out the window in silence. Swung around. "You discovered him, remember? When you were standing there, irrigating the hillside. I doubt we'll find the guilty party."

"What about Conn. Don't you think people will suspect he did it?"

"I'm certain Conn has an alibi. Surely he was home all evening with his family."

"But I wasn't home with *my* family. And my gun—it's somewhere down there along the creek bank. Surely someone will find it."

"I'll send Moncrief to look for it. He won't breathe a word about it to anybody. He'll bring it back and give it to me. I'll get it cleaned up and return it to you, as good as new."

Manly stood. He put the token in his pocket and headed for the door.

"Manly, I said don't worry about it. Put it behind you. You're my right-hand man. I need you more than ever. Go home. Enjoy the weekend. I expect you here bright and early Monday morning. We have a corrupt detective and a complicit commissioner to deal with. Eighteen and ninety-six is going be a year for wakin' snakes."

FORTY-ONE

WILLIAM MANLY

What Tomorrow Brings

EARLY SATURDAY MORNING, THE 4TH OF JANUARY, william Manly sat at one end of the mahogany bench that ran almost a quarter of the width of the waiting room. At the other end sat a mother with an infant in her arms and two young girls playing cat's cradle at her feet. An elderly couple, hand in hand—she in a hunch, he struggling with a portmanteau with his free hand—hobbled across the room to the ticket window. A young man, probably no more than twenty-one and in a foppish and frilled dress shirt and a silk cravat, whisked past them on the balls of his feet like one of those Flying Dutchmen straight from DeGive's Opera House. A colored porter entered the room with a pushcart brimming with steamer trunks. Behind him followed three gentlemen whose dress and demeanor suggested distant strains. Manly wondered whether perhaps they had been delegates to the exposition just ended and were headed to the port of Savannah for the long trip home.

Who are these people? What are their stories? Where are they off to so early in the morning? Manly marveled. Everyone going about their daily lives, caught up in their own worlds, with their own cares and concerns. Their own tics and peculiarities. A mélange of humanity arrested in the moment. Unaware of what tomorrow may bring. Manly looked out the station window and into the distance. *Unaware of what tomorrow may bring.*

At seven forty-five, his small overnight bag in hand, he boarded the eight o'clock Georgia Central bound for Albany. He took a window seat in the frontmost 2+2 open coach.

"All aboard," the conductor called out.

The steam wailed. The whistle let out a piercing three-chime howl. *Whoo-whoo-whoo.* The train jerked and pulled out of the station.

Manly wore his full uniform, with Prince Albert coat and kepi headgear. This visit was more than personal. It was a canonical endgame. A fitting paean to a closing act.

Telegrams had preceded the trip. He had requested a visit with Ella. She had accepted.

How can you kill a man and brush it aside as if it didn't happen? No matter how hard he tried, he couldn't shake the thought.

The locomotive coursed a southeasterly path toward Macon. Manly peered wistfully out the window. The winter landscape did little to ease his mind. Barren cottonfields waiting patiently for a spring awakening. Herefords huddled in groups of ten or more. Farmers turning the hard dormant soil, their mules struggling against the cold morning wind that whipped across the fields. The occasional ramshackle hovel emblematic of rural economic blight, a legacy of the war three decades past and a striking testament to the inevitable demise of King Cotton.

The train pulled up to the Griffin station. Manly was reminded of what Herbert Jenkins had told Frank Keeler. *I took the train to Griffin, arriving at noon on the day of Bass's murder. I wrote it in my notebook.* But there was no notebook. At least that's what Connolly contended. But what if there *was* a notebook? What if one of Manly's own men had destroyed it? What if some entry, somewhere in that book—the name of a witness, the Lorillard salesman, the roadside innkeeper—would have exonerated Jenkins. *What if I killed an innocent man?*

Manly knew the prospect of Jenkins' innocence was slim. After all, Jenkins was carrying the dead man's gun. And the souvenir was found in his pocket. And Delores Dampman attested to Jenkins' admission of guilt. But innocence or guilt notwithstanding, Manly still couldn't get shed of the thought of killing a man. And now, Connolly wanted to brush it aside and move on as if it never happened. *Put it behind you,* he had said. *It doesn't matter how he died.* But it *did* matter. And Manly wondered if he would ever be able to put it behind him. To go a full night without bolting from a deep sleep, beset by the haunting image of Jenkins lying on the ground.

The train took a hard right at Macon and proceeded southerly toward Albany. The turn in the track was so severe that Manly had visions of a derailed train, with coaches, passengers, and luggage spilling over the roadbed.

Five hours after leaving Atlanta, the train rolled into the Albany station. A carriage awaited Manly for the final, sixty-mile leg.

McKinnon's Grove was somber, funereal. Not at all what he expected.

Broadleaf magnolias, bereft of blooms, lined the long drive leading to the house. Their leathery leaves clung hopelessly to the limbs. Dismal, dark, dull green under the cloudy sky. Their brown spotted forebears, casualties of the spring leaf fall, still littered the ground beneath. A stand of Stuart pecans, leafless and forlorn, fought back the winter cold.

The house itself was no more inviting. The eight ionic columns across the front imparted a sense of bucolic privilege. But the white paint curling from their surfaces, manifest as the carriage neared, the unkempt azaleas flanking the steps, and the sagging shutters skirting the windows, belied whatever glory may have graced the homestead's presence in years past.

Manly imagined an earlier time. A young girl, perhaps five or six, tripping across the porch, scampering down the steps and doing somersaults in the yard, without a care in the world, oblivious to the conflagration soon to come, one that would strip much of the region to the immediate north of its vitality. And now, thirty-five years later, that little girl surely found herself trapped in a demon's snare. What had she called it? *A leaden grief. And fear.*

"Come, Mama. The policeman's here," Mary called out. Ella eased open the door and walked onto the porch. John—*the spitting image of his father, he's become*—joined his mother at her side. He held Mary's hand. Baker, Jr. and Fred took their places to the flank and slightly behind their mother.

"We've heard the news." Ella spoke first. "It was in the *Times Enterprise* yesterday morning."

She ushered the captain into the outer parlor. Manly, his kepi in his lap, sat across from Ella. Just as he was about to speak, an elderly Negro woman entered the room carrying a silver tray. On the tray were an array of teacakes and two china cups and saucers. She approached Ella, who waved her off. "Thank you, Lula. Not for me. But I'm sure Mr. Manly here would like something after his long journey." The woman left the room, returning shortly with a pot of tea, bypassing Mrs. Bass for the captain.

"News travels fast, Mrs. Bass."

"I'm sure it had something to do with Baker's long history here in Thomasville."

"What did the article say?"

"That Herbert Jenkins was killed by an unknown assailant. That Baker's gun was recovered some time thereafter and traced back to Jenkins, but the details were not made clear in the paper. That a woman came forward and confessed to being Jenkins' accomplice and to his having killed my husband."

Manly chose not to tell her the full story behind Jenkins' death. He reached into his coat pocket. He felt something oddly shaped and slightly moist to the touch. He removed his hand to reveal a peach pit with a smattering of flesh remaining. The remnant of a snack from the all-day train ride. His immediate thought was of Bessie and the White Pearmain. He quickly returned the pit and wiped his hand with a napkin. From his other pocket, he retrieved the fair souvenir and handed it to Ella. "They found this in Jenkins' possession. I believe it was your husband's."

She held the token in her hand without speaking. Her eyes welled.

"Mrs. Bass, your husband's gun is secured at the station house as evidence. I had hoped to bring it. Unfortunately, it has to remain in custody for a little longer. I hope to visit again soon to give it to you."

"Please do come back. You're always welcome here."

Ella had implored Manly to spend the night at McKinnon's Grove, but he had respectfully declined. She and the others needed their privacy. And so did he.

John maneuvered the carriage down Broad Street. As they approached the Masury Hotel, at the corner of Broad and Jefferson, Manly was struck by the hotel's majesty. Balustrades running the full length of the building. The onion-domed tower commanding attention at the corner. The illuminated rooftop escutcheon bearing the hotel's name in bold letters. But his room was dull and drab, an unexpected surprise, given that the hotel had opened a mere six years earlier. Manly had hoped for something a bit cheerier to ease his unsettled spirit. *The Misery Hotel*, he thought.

Early Sunday morning, he hired a carriage back to Albany.

There he boarded the next available train to Atlanta. Diverse thoughts preoccupied him on the five-hour trip back. The death of two men in the space of a mere four months—the one killed in an ambush, the other felled by Manly's own hand. Ella standing on her porch, handkerchief in one hand and token in the other, her look of quiet desperation as he and John pulled away from the house on their way to The Misery Hotel. The sundry strangers in the Union Depot the prior morning, going about their business, in their own world, unaware of what tomorrow would bring.

What will tomorrow bring?

Time heals wounds, to a degree. William Manly managed to make some semblance of peace with his unease over the killing of Herbert Jenkins. He couldn't put it behind him. But he could learn to live with it.

He and Arthur Connolly made it their mission to bring an end to the alleged fencing ring, even if it meant destroying the reputation and standing of a police commissioner—and the career of a detective. As for Conn's reputation and standing, from everything Manly could tell, there wasn't much there to begin with.

But the wheels of justice sometimes turn roughly. They can wobble. They can shake and shudder. And sometimes a wheel falls right off the axle, stopping the seeming juggernaut flat in its tracks. Especially when the mayor, the city council, and the commissioners—to a man—vow to do whatever it takes to waylay it.

Neither Commissioner Branan nor Green Conn ever saw justice dealt for whatever illicit and nefarious activities they may have been involved in, at least insofar as the fencing of stolen goods was concerned.

However, Conn would go on to find himself in trouble several years later over accusations of witness intimidation and suborning perjury. He would resign from the police force on the 11th of October, 1899 under a cloud of disgrace. A fitting comeuppance.

No suspect was ever officially identified, no arrest ever made, no retribution ever delivered in the killing of Herbert Jenkins. The case went cold and faded from public interest. Perhaps it was because people knew in their hearts that Baker Bass's killer had finally been brought to justice, albeit in an unexpected way.

After two days of traipsing through the weeds along the Clear Creek bank, Thaddeus Moncrief found Manly's gun. He returned it to the chief, no questions asked, no mention made of it. Connolly had it cleaned up and returned, like new, to the captain. Manly would carry it through the duration of his career. But whenever he placed his palm on the grip, he would remember Christmas night, 1895, when it went flying out of his hand and down the embankment to Clear Creek.

With the death of Herbert Jenkins, the case of Baker Bass's murder had finally been put to rest. In the spring of 1896, Manly returned to Thomasville and gave Ella her husband's gun. This time, the magnolias and azaleas were in bloom. The Stuarts were bearing fruit. But the paint still curled from the ionic columns. The shutters still sagged. And Ella still bore the scars of a leaden grief and fear.

Two short years later, Arthur Connolly met his untimely death when, in the summer of 1897, he made the mistake of traveling through the humid lowlands of Savannah. He contracted malaria—swamp fever—and died that August.

William Manly rose to take Connolly's place.

It was much sooner than he had ever expected.

But he was ready now.

Acknowledgments

I WOULD NOT BE THE WRITER THAT I AM, AND THIS WORK likely would not have been completed, were it not for my fellow writers, Glen Heefner, Julia Sennette, Dru Sumner, John Ripma, and the late John Edwards, may he rest in peace. They guided me through every chapter, every page, and every word of *Dead Beckoning*, and they continue to inspire me every day. For that I am grateful.

I am indebted to my daughters, Mandy Rahiya and Laura Sadri, who edited the book in its entirety and provided valuable feedback. In addition, Mandy Rahiya designed and formatted the book, including the front and back covers and everything in between.

Caren, my wife of forty-three years, stood by my side and provided encouragement every step of the way. She continues to give me the support I need to pursue my passion for writing. She is my soulmate in every sense.

A special thanks goes out to the wonderful researchers at the Atlanta History Center. They undoubtedly grew tired of the countless hours I spent at the Kenan Research Center, poring through archived documents, microfilm, and electronic records.

In short, I had a lot of help writing this book. I could not have done it alone.

Landmarks Then and Now

COTTON STATES AND INTERNATIONAL EXPOSITION

The exposition took place at what is now Piedmont Park. Most of the structures from the exposition itself are long gone, but a few remain. Without the exposition, it is doubtful that Atlantans would benefit today from one of the most popular parks in the city.

ELLIS STREET HOME

A multilevel parking garage now sits at 74 Ellis Street.

UNION STATION AND MARKHAM HOUSE HOTEL

Union Station was located at what is now Wall Street between Pryor Street and Central Avenue. The Markham House Hotel sat across the street from the train station. The Georgia State University complex now occupies much of the area.

PETERS STREET STORE

The area where Bass's store sat is still heavily industrial/commercial. The Peters Street viaduct now passes over the nearby railroad tracks.

ARAGON HOTEL

The Aragon Hotel was located on Peachtree Street at the southeast corner of Ellis Street, across the street from what is now the Ritz Carlton and near the Peachtree Center MARTA station. Its location is now part of the Georgia Pacific Center.

DARKTOWN

Eleven years after Bass's death, Darktown would become the crucible of the Atlanta Race Riots of 1906. Today, much of the area is replaced by a maze of expressways and urban renewal development.

IVY STREET

Ivy Street is now Peachtree Center Avenue. The shooting occurred along the sidewalk where the Georgia Pacific Center now sits.

GRADY HOSPITAL

The original Grady Hospital building, now designated a Landmark Building Exterior by the Atlanta Urban Design Commission, still sits at 36 Butler Street, SE. It is now called Georgia Hall.

FULTON COUNTY COURTHOUSE

The old courthouse, at the corner of Pryor Street and Hunter Street (now MLK Jr. Drive) was demolished in 1911 to make way for a new courthouse at the same location. The Fulton County court complex still occupies the space.

ATLANTA POLICE HEADQUARTERS

The police headquarters remained at its Decatur Street location until 2009, although the building that existed in 1895 had been demolished and replaced by a more modern facility. The area is now part of the Georgia State University complex.

ATLANTA *CONSTITUTION* BUILDING
The newspaper was located at the corner of Alabama and Forsyth Streets, not far from the Zero Mile Post, which marked both the Southeastern terminus of the Western and Atlantic Railroad and the city's earliest settlement. A newer facility, which was built at the opposite corner of the intersection, remained vacant for decades.

CREW STREET BOARDING HOUSE
The boarding house where Herbert Jenkins stayed was razed, along with dozens of blocks surrounding it, to accommodate a labyrinth of cloverleafs and overpasses at the confluence of I75/85 and I20 just south of downtown

MCDANIEL STREET STING HOUSE
While the sting house off of McDaniel Street was well outside the city in 1895, it is now within the city limits south of downtown. The area has been economically depressed for many years

WEINMEISTER'S HOTEL
The Forsyth-Walton building, at the corner of Forsyth and Walton Streets in Atlanta's Fairlie-Poplar District, was built in 1900. It is one of the oldest commercial buildings in the area and sits roughly where Weinmeister's Hotel was located.

IRA STREET BROTHEL
Madam Brumbelow's brothel was located in a neighborhood not far from the McDaniel Street sting house. The area has been economically depressed for many years.

KIMBALL HOUSE HOTEL

The Kimball House Hotel was the second hotel by that name to occupy an entire city block at the south-southeastern corner of Five Points. It remained a cherished Atlanta landmark until its demolition in 1959. The space is now occupied by a parking garage.

About The Author

MIKE COBB'S body of literary work includes both fiction and nonfiction, short-form and long-form, as well as articles and blogs. While he is comfortable playing across a broad range of topics, much of his focus is on true crime, fictionalized true crime and historical fiction. Rigorous research is foundational to his writing. He gets that honestly, having spent much of his professional career as a scientist. He vehemently refuses to box his work into a specific genre.

Mike splits his time between Atlanta and
Blue Ridge, Georgia.

MGCOBB.COM

MGCobbWriter

@mgcobb

cobbmg

About The Type

This book is set in Adobe Caslon, a typeface designed by Carol Twombly and based on William Caslon I's original design dating to the mid 1700s. Caslon, a trained London engraver and typefounder, is widely credited for creating the first original typeface of English origin and establishing a national typographic style. Caslon's self-titled typeface is know for its enduring style and legibility.

In the late 19th century the Caslon typeface was adapted for hot metal typesetting with the gaining popularity of mass-market printing.

CPSIA information can be obtained
at www.ICGtesting.com
Printed in the USA
LVHW020423170322
713568LV00008B/976

9 780578 339887